Dancing in The Duke's Arms

Copyright

"May I Have This Duke" Copyright © 2015 by Grace Burrowes
All rights reserved. No part of this book may be reproduced in any form or by any electronic or mechanical means including information storage and retrieval systems—except in the case of brief quotations or excerpts for the purpose of critical reviews or articles—without permission in writing from Grace Burrowes, author and publisher of the work.

"Duchess of Scandal" © Copyright 2015 by Miranda Neville
All rights reserved. No part of this book may be reproduced in any form or by any electronic or mechanical means including information storage and retrieval systems—except in the case of brief quotations or excerpts for the purpose of critical reviews or articles—without permission in writing from Miranda Neville, author and publisher of the work.

"Waiting for a Duke Like You" Copyright © 2015 by Shana Galen
All rights reserved. No part of this book may be reproduced in any form or by any electronic or mechanical means including information storage and retrieval systems—except in the case of brief quotations or excerpts for the purpose of critical reviews or articles—without permission in writing from Shana Galen, author and publisher of the work.

"An Unsuitable Duchess" © Copyright 2015 by Carolyn Jewel
All rights reserved. No part of this book may be reproduced in any form or by any electronic or mechanical means including information storage and retrieval systems—except in the case of brief quotations or excerpts for the purpose of critical reviews or articles—without permission in writing from Carolyn Jewel, author and publisher of the work.

Published in the four-novella compilation, Dancing in the Duke's Arms, by cJewel Books, PO Box 750431, Petaluma, CA 94975-0431.

ISBN: 978-1-937823-41-2

Cover design by Seductive Designs.

Cover images:
Dancing Couple: Jenn LeBlanc / Illustrated Romance
Other images: Liliana Fichter/Depositphotos.com, Claudio Giovanni Colombo/Depositphotos.com
Mariusz Patrzyk/Depositphotos.com, Luibov Kondratenko/Depositphotos.com

Table of Contents

May I Have This Duke?
Grace Burrowes 1

Waiting for a Duke Like You
Shana Galen 71

Duchess of Scandal
Miranda Neville 139

An Unsuitable Duchess
Carolyn Jewel 221

Books by Shana Galen

If you enjoyed this story, read more from Shana, Carolyn, Grace, and Miranda in their upcoming anthology, Christmas in Duke Street.

Pre-order Shana's upcoming release, The Rogue You Know.

Covent Garden Cubs series begins with Earls Just Want to Have Fun.

The Lord and Lady Spy series begins with Lord and Lady Spy.

The Jewels of the Ton series begins with When You Give a Duke a Diamond.

The Sons of the Revolution series begins with The Making of a Duchess.

The Misadventures in Matrimony series begins with No Man's Bride.

The Regency Spies Series begins with While You Were Spying.

Books by Miranda

The Wild Quartet

The Second Seduction of a Lady (novella)
The Importance of Being Wicked
The Ruin of a Rogue
Lady Windermere's Lover
The Duke of Dark Desires

The Burgundy Club

The Wild Marquis
The Dangerous Viscount
The Amorous Education of Celia Seaton
Confessions From an Arranged Marriage

Also

Never Resist Temptation
Christmas in the Duke's Arms
At the Duke's Wedding
At the Billionaire's Wedding

Books by Carolyn Jewel

HISTORICAL ROMANCE SERIES

The Sinclair Sisters Series
Lord Ruin, Book 1
A Notorious Ruin, Book 2

Reforming the Scoundrels Series
Not Wicked Enough, Book 1
Not Proper Enough, Book 2

Other Historical Romance
Anthology *Dancing In The Duke's Arms* (Carolyn Jewel, Grace Burrowes, Miranda Neville, Shana Galen)
An Unsuitable Duchess, novella from anthology *Dancing In The Duke's Arms*
Anthology *Christmas In The Duke's Arms* (Carolyn Jewel, Grace Burrowes, Miranda Neville, Shana Galen)
In The Duke's Arms from Anthology *Christmas In The Duke's Arms* (Carolyn Jewel, Grace Burrowes, Miranda Neville, Shana Galen)
One Starlit Night, novella From the Midnight Scandals Anthology
Midnight Scandals, Anthology
Scandal, RITA finalist, Best Regency Historical
Indiscreet, Winner, Bookseller's Best, Best Short Historical
Moonlight A short story
The Spare
Stolen Love
Passion's Song

PARANORMAL ROMANCE

My Immortals Series

My Wicked Enemy, Book 1

My Forbidden Desire, RITA finalist, Paranormal Romance, Book 2

My Immortal Assassin, Book 3

My Dangerous Pleasure, Book 4

Free Fall, Novella 4.5

My Darkest Passion, Book 5

Dead Drop, Book 6

My Demon Warlord, Book 7

Other Paranormal Romance

Alphas Unleashed, Anthology Dead Drop

A Darker Crimson, Book 4 of the Crimson City series

DX (A Crimson City Novella)

FANTASY ROMANCE

The King's Dragon, a short story

EROTIC ROMANCE

Whispers, Collection No. 1

May I Have This Duke?

By
Grace Burrowes

Dedication

To the care givers

Chapter One

"YOU WISHED TO see me, Your Grace?"

Gerard Juvenal René Beaumarchand Hammersley, Eighth Duke of Hardcastle, pretended for one more moment to study his list of tenants, because he emphatically did not wish to *see* Miss Ellen MacHugh. The woman destroyed his focus simply by entering a room, and when she spoke, whatever remained of Hardcastle's mental processes came to an indecorous, gaping halt.

An indecorous, gaping, *sniffing* halt, because Miss MacHugh had the great temerity to carry about her person the scents of lavender and lilacs.

The duke rose, for Miss MacHugh was a lady, albeit a lady in his employ. "Please have a seat, Miss MacHugh. I trust you're well?"

They'd perfected a system, such that they could dwell in the same house for much of the year, but go for days without speaking. Weeks even. Hardcastle's record was thirty-three days straight, though admittedly, he'd been ill for part of that time.

She, by contrast, had the constitution of a plough horse. She never lost her poise either, while he fumbled for words in her presence or prosed on about the weather.

Or some other inanity.

"I am well, Your Grace. Thank you for inquiring. Christopher is well too."

"If he were unwell, and you had failed to notify me, you'd be without a post, madam."

She dipped her chin, a rather stubborn little chin. Her hair was dark russet, and her height was sadly wanting, but that chin could be very expressive.

Miss MacHugh was not willowy, she was not blond, she was not subservient, she was not—oh, her faults were endless. She wasn't even entirely English, her mother hailing from the Scottish region of Peeblesshire.

"Did you summon me for a reason, sir?"

Hardcastle clasped his hands behind his back, marched to the library window, and attempted to recall what lapse of sense had prompted him to summon—ah, yes.

"I'm to attend to a house party up in Nottinghamshire," he said. "Christopher will accompany me, and you will accompany the boy."

"When do we leave, Your Grace?"

"We leave Tuesday. Please ensure Christopher has everything he might require for a two-week stay in the country. You and he will share the traveling coach, and I will go on horseback. Thank you, that will be all."

She rose to her inconsequential height, and yet, such was Ellen MacHugh's presence that Hardcastle remained by the window, yielding the rest of the library to her.

"Has Your Grace considered tutors to take over Christopher's education?" she asked.

What queer start was this? "He's barely six years old, Miss MacHugh. Unless I mistake the matter, the boy is learning what he needs to learn from you. I hadn't any tutors until I was eight."

She flicked a gaze over him that nearly shouted: *And look how well that turned out.* "Christopher is exceedingly bright, Your Grace, and eager to learn."

"As was I. Unless you believe a six-year-old boy's education to be beyond you, this conversation has reached its conclusion."

More and more often, when Hardcastle spoke, his grandfather's voice emerged, condescending, gruff, and arrogant. Had Robin lived, he'd have laughed himself silly at his older brother's metamorphosis into a curmudgeon-in-training.

"I'll take my leave of you then, sir. I'd like to call one other item to Your Grace's attention, though."

Hardcastle knew that tone and knew what it portended. Miss MacHugh was preparing to scold her employer.

The woman excelled at scolding her employer. She'd been in the nursery for nearly three months before Hardcastle had realized what her gentle, polite, well-reasoned discourses were. He'd been slow to catch on, because a duke of mature years had little to no experience being scolded.

By anyone.

"Unburden yourself, Miss MacHugh. What item remains for us to discuss?"

She had the most beautiful complexion. All roses and cream, with a few faint, delicate freckles across her cheeks. Hardcastle knew better than to stand within freckle-counting range, because when he got that close to her, his thumbs ached to brush over her features.

Aching thumbs on a duke were the outside of absurd.

"I'm giving notice, Your Grace, of my intention to quit my post. I thought you might like some warning. If we leave on Tuesday, and the house party lasts two weeks, you should expect my departure from your household at the end of the house party. I leave it to you to explain the situation to Christopher at the time and place of your choosing. Good day, sir."

She offered him a graceful curtsey and bustled off toward the door.

Hardcastle strode to the door as well, and because his legs were significantly longer, and his resolve every bit a match for Miss MacHugh's, he was first to reach their destination.

"Miss MacHugh, after living under my roof for three years, caring for my heir, and otherwise functioning as a member of this household day in and day out, you simply announce an intention to leave?"

Of course she'd want to leave *him*. He was a demanding, ill-tempered, patently unfriendly employer. Hardcastle could not fathom how she'd leave the boy, though.

"This is how it's done, Your Grace. The employee gives notice, the employer writes a glowing character. You wish me well, and I thank you for all you've done for me."

She peered at him encouragingly, as if willing him to repeat that sequence of disasters back to her.

"All I have done is pay the modest wages you tirelessly earn, madam, but this giving of notice will not answer. In Nottinghamshire, I'll be expected to socialize morning, noon, and night. The entire region is infested with dukes, thus its unfortunate style, the Dukeries. Because I myself am a duke—lest you forget that detail—I am obligated to exchange courtesy visits with half the shire."

He kept his hand on the door latch, in case she took a notion to flee before he'd made his point. "How can I find a replacement for you if I'm dodging the hopeful young ladies?" Hardcastle went on. "Shall I interview your successor when I'm playing cards until all hours with the fellows? When I'm rising at dawn to ruin good boots tramping about in the fog, shooting at pheasants, drunken viscounts, or other low-flying game?"

Miss MacHugh turned her smile on Hardcastle, proving once again that she had no conscience. Her smile would make small boys confess to felonies and large boys long for privacy, preferably with her, a freshly made bed, and a few bottles of excellent spirits.

"Your Grace is an eminently resourceful fellow," she said. "If you turn your mind to locating a successor for me, then I'm sure a parade of candidates will materialize in the servants' parlor in an instant."

Ellen MacHugh was a temple to mendacity, pretending to compliment him, while instead mocking his consequence.

"My agenda for this house party, Miss MacHugh, is to locate a candidate for the position of Duchess of Hardcastle. Her Grace, my grandmother, claims I have forgotten to tend to this task and must address the oversight before I'm a pathetic, graying embarrassment, falling asleep over the port and importuning the housemaids. I'm to parade myself before the debutantes and matchmakers, sacrifice myself once again on the altar of duty, and for good measure, be a good sport about surrendering my bachelorhood."

And in the depths of the ducal heart, Hardcastle suppressed a plea as honest as it was dismaying: *Don't let them take me.* Ellen MacHugh wouldn't deride him for that sentiment either, for she was a woman who treasured her independence fiercely.

The corners of her serene smile faltered. "Her Grace is a formidable woman. I can understand why you'd make her request a priority. But tell me, sir, how does one *forget* to get married?"

One became a ducal heir at age seven, a duke at thirteen, and arrived to the age of three-and-thirty with one freedom, and one freedom only, still intact.

"I expect, Miss MacHugh, I neglected to marry the same way you did. I occupied myself with other, less disagreeable matters. Doubtless, you will now admit that your departure from the household would be most inconsiderate, particularly at this juncture. I will regard the topic as closed until further notice."

Russet brows twitched, a gratifying hint of consternation from a woman who was the soul of self-possession.

"You have my leave to return to the nursery, madam." They stood near the door, within freckle-counting range. The fragrance of lilacs and lavender, like a brisk, sunny morning, provoked Hardcastle into opening the door for his nephew's governess, as if he were a common footman.

"Your Grace, I do apologize for the timing of my decision, but this once, I cannot change my plans for your convenience. I have reason to believe another situation awaits me. You have just shy of a month to replace me, sir. If you do find a lady willing to be your duchess, she will certainly take an interest in choosing Christopher's next governess."

Then Miss MacHigh-and-Mighty was gone, gently pulling the door closed behind her.

The voice of the previous duke nattered on in Hardcastle's head, about good riddance to a woman who'd never known her place, and governesses being thick on the ground, and small boys of excellent station needing to learn early not to grow attached to their inferiors.

The seventh duke had been an arrogant old windbag. With a couple of bottles of port in him, he'd had the verbal stamina of a Presbyterian preacher amid a flock of adulterers.

The eighth duke didn't care for port. He liked Ellen MacHugh's self-possession, her good opinion of herself, her boldness before her betters, and her infernally alluring freckles.

Hardcastle had never admired *or desired* a woman more than he did Miss Ellen MacHugh. She had no use for him, though, so perhaps he'd best find a replacement for her after all.

"HE'S GROWING WORSE," Ellen said, hems whipping about her boots in the confines of the housekeeper's sitting room. Two days after her interview with the duke, she was still upset with him. "I didn't think Hardcastle could grow worse. He informed me that accepting a post in the north would not suit his convenience. 'Doubtless,'

sayeth the duke, 'you will now admit that your departure from the household would be most inconsiderate.' God help the poor woman who must conceive children with him. She'll suffer frostbite in a delicate location."

"Ellen, that is unkind and unladylike."

Dorcas Snelling had been housekeeper to the Duke of Hardcastle since the present titleholder had been in dresses. She was the closest thing Ellen had to a friend, but when it came to ducal infallibility, Dorcas might as well have been a papist discussing an especially virtuous pope. Dorcas was at that moment embroidering golden flowers on the hem of a curtain that would hang in the ducal dressing closet, for pity's sake.

"I barely exaggerate Hardcastle's sangfroid," Ellen rejoined. "He can't even bring himself to look down his nose at me, and he has a deal of nose to look down."

On the coal man such a nose might have been unfortunate; on Hardcastle, it was splendidly ducal. Shoulders broad enough to do a Yorkshire ploughman proud were also ducal on Hardcastle. Dark eyebrows that put Ellen in mind of a pirate prince were—on Hardcastle—ducal.

His stern mouth was ducal, and his silences were nearly regal. The only feature that defied the title was Hardcastle's hair, which was as curly and unruly as Christopher's, albeit much darker.

"You're determined to leave?" Mrs. Snelling asked, knotting off a gold thread.

"I never meant to stay this long, but Christopher has wrapped his grubby paws around my heart. Now His Grace is determined to marry, and Christopher will have an aunt to look after his welfare."

To be fair, Hardcastle was a conscientious guardian. Christopher's material needs were met in every particular, and when the head footman had raised his voice to the boy for sliding down the front banister, His Grace had sent the man to a lesser estate in East Anglia.

Christopher had been denied any outings on his pony for a week. Only a duke would fail to see that the governess was the one punished by such a scheme. Christopher's abuse of the banister had happened on Ellen's half day, but she'd made sure his unruly behavior hadn't reoccurred.

"Miss MacHugh!" The boy himself came charging into the housekeeper's sitting room. "I've found you. Nurse says I mightn't have to come in if you're willing to walk with me in the garden, but I had to come in to ask you. I found a grasshopper, and eleven ants, and four butterflies. That's a lot."

"It's a pretty day," Ellen said, extending a hand to Christopher. "A walk in the garden will help us settle to our French when we come in. How many insects did you see in all, Christopher?'

"A lot?"

"Let's count, shall we?"

While Ellen walked the child through a basic exercise in addition, she also tried to memorize the garden where she'd spent many peaceful hours over the past three years. The roses were beyond their glory, but the perennials—daisies, hollyhocks, foxglove, salvia, verbena, lavender—were still in good form.

Come Tuesday, Ellen would leave this place, despite His Grace's fuming and pouting.

She'd miss Hardway Hall, miss the routine and orderliness of it, miss the child she'd come to love ferociously, and even miss the duke. He was predictable in his severe demeanor, he paid punctually, and he didn't intrude into the nursery. Without intending it, Hardcastle had provided Ellen a place to heal her wounds and mourn her dreams.

Many women hadn't even those luxuries.

"Why do roses have thorns?" Christopher asked, sniffing a rose without touching it anywhere. He was a careful boy, but not a worried boy. Ellen would miss him until her dying day.

"Thorns protect the roses from being grabbed carelessly," Ellen said, "from being eaten by passing bears, from being handled without respect."

Would to God young ladies were given a few thorns before the young men came sniffing about.

"I like daisies better," Christopher said. "They aren't the color of blood, and they don't make you bleed if you touch them. Daisies are happy."

Christopher was happy, curious, and full of energy. He ran down the length of the rose border, made a turn past the end of the laburnum alley, and was pelting back in Ellen's direction when he came to an abrupt stop.

Where an exuberant little boy had stood, a ducal heir appeared, suggesting His Grace was approaching from the stables. Christopher drew his shoulders back, swiped a hand over his hair, and drained all animation from his features in the time it took for a breeze to set the laburnum leaves dancing.

In other words, Christopher was trying to be good.

"Christopher, greetings," said the duke, striding along the crushed-shell walk. "Shouldn't you be at your studies?"

Christopher shot Ellen a look, a plea for intervention. Soon enough, she would be unable to intercede for the boy. Perhaps the new duchess would be kind, though. Ellen could hope for that.

"We are at our lessons, Your Grace," Ellen said. "What better place to learn botany than in a garden?"

The duke treated her to one of those reserved, slightly annoyed perusals, as if from one day to the next, he forgot who Ellen was and how she'd come to be in his household.

"Miss MacHugh, good day."

"We're taking a walk," Christopher said, making a grab for the duke's glove, but stopping short and tucking his own little hand behind his back, much as his uncle often did. "I'm counting bugs, and Miss MacHugh was explaining about thorns."

"Who better to discourse on the topic of thorns? Perhaps I'll walk with you."

Christopher was so enthralled with this prospect, he spun in a circle. "Please, sir! I know lots of flowers, and birds, and how each bird sings differently so his friends and family will hear him. I know I must never, ever, ever touch the laburnum, anywhere, and don't let anybody or anything eat any part of it."

"My garden is apparently full of hazards," Hardcastle remarked.

Was the duke waiting for Ellen to invite him to join them? And why was he going on about thorns and hazards?

"Your garden is beautiful, sir," Ellen said. "Please share it with us."

He stared at the laburnum as if it too, were some sort of interloper he didn't recall hiring. "I knew the laburnum was poisonous. I got the same lectures as a boy Christopher did, but I'd forgotten."

The duke winged his arm, a courtesy he'd rarely shown Ellen before. She took it, because that was what a lady did when a gentleman was on his manners.

"Many other plants are equally dangerous," she said, "but we admire them, carefully, for their beauty or other properties. Then there's foxglove, which can help at the proper dose and kill at an improper one."

"You are not a governess," Hardcastle said. "You are a professor in disguise. How am I to replace you?"

"Please don't wheedle, Your Grace. My nerves couldn't bear it."

"Nor mine, alas," he said, in perfect seriousness.

Christopher had galloped off toward the heartsease, which enjoyed a shady bed near the fountain. Even in high summer, they were doing well, for temperatures in recent weeks had remained moderate.

"I have a rehearsed apology," the duke said, leading Ellen to a wooden bench. "I can't seem to recall it now that the moment to recite has presented itself. I planned to summon you to the library so I could express my remorse for our last conversation."

"No such expression is needed, Your Grace." Though even for him, he'd been high-handed—or nervous? "I will leave my post at the end of this house party, nonetheless. I suggest you explain the situation to Christopher so he'll have time to adjust."

"He won't adjust," Hardcastle said, taking off his gloves and using them to bat imaginary dust from the bench. "Will you sit with me, Miss MacHugh?"

Ellen wanted to refuse Hardcastle, for the simple, contrary novelty of thwarting him, but also because a duke in an apologetic mood upset the balance between them. She was not, however, a recalcitrant schoolgirl overdue for an outing, so she took a seat.

"I was seven when my parents died," Hardcastle said, coming down beside Ellen, and stuffing his gloves in a pocket. "My grandfather had been traveling on the Continent, and it took him some months to return to England. He came swooping into our lives like the wrath of King George, and nothing was ever the same."

"Losing our loved ones is hard." Losing just this pretty, peaceful garden would break Ellen's heart.

"I was managing," Hardcastle said, "as was Lord Robin, mostly because we had a fine governess. Miss Henckel maintained order and routine for us, let us have our tantrums and sulks as we adjusted to the loss of our parents. She knew when to discipline and when to look the other way. Miss Henckel alone took on the burden of explaining to us what was afoot when Papa's coach overturned. I was... attached to her."

Ellen suspected the duke's disclosure was a revelation even to him, but she couldn't afford to waver.

"Not fair, Your Grace. Christopher's parents died three years ago, and he's a happy little boy. He has the staff wrapped around his finger, he has every comfort, and you will not make me responsible for his happiness and well-being. He has *you* for that."

"I hardly know the boy."

His Grace regretted this state of affairs, apparently, but for the first time, Ellen realized why the duke had kept his distance from Christopher, another orphan thrust into the role of ducal heir at a tender age.

"What happened to Miss Henckel?" Ellen asked.

"She was replaced with tutors, of course, and then public school and university. Grandfather and the trustees he chose for me did not believe in coddling a ducal heir."

"I'm sorry," Ellen said, though offering condolences to Hardcastle was an odd turn in their dealings. "The one adult you loved should not have been taken from you when the rest of your life was in chaos. Christopher's life is not in chaos."

At the other end of the fountain, Christopher experimented with passing a stick through the spray and momentarily re-directing the flow of the water. A green maple leaf came drifting down to land on the duke's muscular thigh, a bright contrast to his fawn riding breeches.

He took the leaf in his fingers, twirling it by the stem. "I was fond of Miss Henckel. In any case, I acknowledge that you have the right to abandon your post with proper notice. I do not like it, but I could have turned you off without a character at any point, and you would not have liked that."

"Your Grace is a scrupulously fair man," Ellen said. "You would not have treated me thus." He wouldn't treat anybody with such disregard for common decency, though his version of the civilities and fair play was frosty, at best.

"I want to treat you badly," he said, tossing the leaf into the fountain. "I'm quite wroth with you, madam." He didn't sound angry. He sounded rueful, like a small boy who must abandon the garden for his French lessons.

In the quiet end of the fountain's pool, the leaf spun slowly this way and that as the breezes and currents shifted.

"We have, from time to time, been out of charity with each other," Ellen said. "I'm sure we'll muddle through this as well. I'll help look for a replacement." She could not say more, not with the boy at the other end of the fountain.

She patted the duke's hand—his bare hand—and abruptly was hit with a faint, cool mist across her cheek.

"Sorry!" Christopher bellowed, chortling merrily. "I'm trying to water the flowers!"

"Trying to get a birching," the duke muttered, rising and extending a hand to Ellen. "He's nearly as bad as I was at his age. Have I apologized for my brusque demeanor adequately, Miss MacHugh?"

He'd explained more than apologized, but the explanation was the greater gift. Ellen put her hand in his.

"Your apology is accepted, sir."

He stood for a moment peering down at her, their hands joined. They hadn't touched like this before, bare-handed, casually. Or rather, Ellen hadn't touched His Grace. Had he been waiting for that overture before presuming himself?

"My objective is accomplished then. Find a way to accidentally knock the boy into the fountain. He'll love you for it." The duke bowed and marched off through the laburnum alley, while Christopher shrieked something about having found a great, brown warty toad.

PRIDE, EVEN DUCAL pride, could carry a man only so far.

Hardcastle's pride had carried him three miles beyond the coaching inn, three miles of wet verge, muddy road, and relentless rain. Three miles of cold trickling down the back of his neck no matter the angle of his sodden top hat and no matter how many times he adjusted the collar of his great coat.

Ajax bore it all stoically—he was the personal mount of a duke, after all—but when thunder rumbled to the north, and lightning joined the affray, Ajax's equine dignity threatened to desert him.

Hardcastle signaled John Coachman to pull up, tied Ajax to the back of the coach, and climbed inside.

"Uncle! We're playing the color game. You're very wet!"

"Miss MacHugh, your charge is a prodigy." Where did one sit when one was a large, sodden duke who reeked of wet horse, muddy boots, and disgust with this entire outing? Hardcastle shrugged out of his great coat and hung it on a peg on the back of the coach door.

"Christopher is a bright boy, Your Grace," her governess-ship replied. "I tell him that frequently."

Miss MacHugh sat on the forward-facing seat beside Christopher, both of them dry and cozy, the boy having the audacity to smile.

Nothing for it then.

A gentleman did not drip indiscriminately on a lady or on a child. Hardcastle took the backward-facing seat and silently cursed all house parties.

"My grandmother will answer for this," he muttered, taking off his hat and getting a brimful of frigid rain water across his *lap* for his efforts. "If it's not the blazing heat, the flies and the dust, it's the mud, the rain, and the cold."

"I'm not cold," Christopher said. "Would you like to play our game with us, sir?"

Hardcastle would rather have throttled his dear grandmama. "A duke, as a rule, hasn't time for games."

The child's face fell, which was durance vile for the uncle sitting across from him. Christopher wasn't to blame for the weather, or for the queasiness that had already begun to plague Hardcastle. Worse, Miss MacHugh's expression had gone carefully blank, as if once again, Mr. Higginbotham had arrived at Sunday services tipsy.

Farmer Higginbotham was probably still tipsy on a Wednesday afternoon, also warm and dry by his own hearth.

"I find," Hardcastle said, "that the luxury of time has been afforded me by the foul weather, the execrable roads, and the boon of present company. What is this color game?'

"Does that mean he'll play?" the boy asked his governess.

"Not everybody has the skill to play the color game, Christopher," Miss MacHugh said, brushing her hand over the child's golden curls. "We've had plenty of practice, while His Grace will be a complete beginner."

"You are no great respecter of dukes, are you, Miss MacHugh?" Hardcastle asked.

"I respect you greatly, sir, but the color game requires imagination and quickness, and Christopher is very good at it."

"Alas, then I am doomed to defeat, being a slow, dull fellow. How does one play this game?"

The coach swayed and jostled along, Hardcastle's belly rebelled strenuously against traveling on a backward-facing bench, and across from him, governess and prodigy exchanged a smile that was diabolically sweet. For a moment, they were a single entity of impish glee, delighted with each other and their circumstances.

For that same moment, Hardcastle forgot he was cold, wet, and queasy, and nearly forgot he was a duke.

"It's simple, sir," Christopher said. "One person picks out an object, then we take turns naming as many colors as we can that describe the object. The person with the most colors wins. I'll give you an example," the boy went on, his manner as patient and thorough as any duke's. "Your breeches are brown, gray near your boots, and buckskin. Also... sort of umbrage where the mud has splashed on them."

"Umber," Miss MacHugh corrected gently—smirkingly. "Umbrage refers to indignation. Umber is a rusty, sienna, orange-y dark brown."

"The game seems simple enough," Hardcastle said. Also tedious and pointless, but not entirely without possibilities. "Let's describe the colors in Miss MacHugh's hair."

"Keen!" Christopher chortled. "Miss MacHugh's hair is ever so pretty, but she's wearing her bonnet."

"She might be willing to part with her bonnet," the duke replied, stretching out his legs and taking care not to let his boots come near her pristine hems. "For the sake of my education regarding the pressing topic of colors, of course."

Sitting backward did not agree with Hardcastle, being damp and cold did not agree with him. Ruffling Miss MacHugh's feathers was unworthy of him, but agreed with him rather well.

"The difficulty," Miss MacHugh said, "is that I cannot assess my own hair as thoroughly as the other players in the game. I will oblige by removing my bonnet, but cannot participate in this round."

She managed to get her bonnet off without disturbing a single tidy hair on her head, then looked about for a place to stash her millinery. Hardcastle took the hat from her and put it on the seat beside him. A hopelessly plain, straw bonnet, but also a prize surrendered into his keeping.

"I'll go first," Christopher offered, turning a serious expression to his governess. "This is a good opening round, sir."

Miss MacHugh smoothed a hand over her skirts. No rings, not even a touch of lace at her cuffs, and yet she did have very pretty hair. Casual observation would call it red, and thick, and plagued by an unladylike tendency to wave and shine.

Hardcastle put a hand over his belly, for the horses were managing a good pace, despite the ruts, and his digestion was suffering accordingly.

"I'd say Miss MacHugh's hair is auburn," Christopher announced, "but I don't know the words for the colors the coach lamps put in it. Fire-colored and the color of laughter."

"Thank you, Christopher," Miss MacHugh said, beaming at the boy. "You pay me such compliments, my bonnet will never fit on my head again."

They shared another moment of complete accord, while the ale and cheese Hardcastle had partaken of miles ago intruded on his awareness most disagreeably.

"Miss MacHugh's hair is auburn," he said, "also red, russet, gold, blond, and *sienna* and the color of having the right answers even when not asked for them."

Christopher's brows twitched down. "You've won, sir. I'd forgot sienna even when Miss reminded me of it. We must play again, or it's not sporting of you."

What did a six-year-old know of sporting behavior? Miss MacHugh's arched eyebrow—Titian, with a hint of amused chastisement—suggested Christopher knew a good deal.

"Very well," Hardcastle said. "My turn to choose, and in the spirit of the opening round, I choose Miss MacHugh's lips."

"You must go first because you won the description of her hair," Christopher said, as earnestly as if the rules of fair play had been devised by Wellington and Napoleon on the eve of Waterloo. The child was very dear in his good sportsmanship. Hardcastle peeled off his damp gloves and tousled Christopher's hair.

"I have set myself up for failure," the duke said. "For I gaze upon the challenge before me, and all I can think is Miss MacHugh's lips are... pinkish."

"They are pinkish," Christopher allowed, "but if they're pinkish, they're also reddish, and maybe with a hint of... well, pinkish and reddish. Do I win?"

Hardcastle made a production of studying Miss MacHugh, who bore his scrutiny with patient indifference. By the light of the coach lamps, he could not quite count her freckles, thank heavens, but he could admire the clean line of her jaw, follow the swoop of dark brows, and mentally trace the shape of a mouth more full than ought to grace a governess's physiognomy.

"I concede, Christopher," Hardcastle said. "My descriptions are apparently in want of color. Shall you play the next round, Miss MacHugh?"

Fourteen thousand rounds later—Hardcastle's muddy boots, Christopher's storybook, Miss MacHugh's beaded reticule—Christopher was yawning hugely and the duke was ready to cast up his accounts. The prospect of riding Ajax in the continuing downpour guaranteed an ague, but that was preferable to a loss of dignity.

"Perhaps I'll ride a few more miles," Hardcastle said, peering out the window at a sopping, green expanse of central England. "Or perhaps we should put up at the next coaching inn, rather than risk the horses in this mud."

His teams were prime cattle, and they'd negotiate any footing handily. His bellyache had been joined by a throbbing head, though.

"Christopher, time to rest your eyes," Miss MacHugh said. "We must ask His Grace to switch seats with you, so you can stretch out on the cushions."

"The boy can sleep in the coach?"

"So I arrive fresh and on my manners," Christopher explained, extricating himself from Miss MacHugh's side. "Miss sometimes rests her eyes too."

The child pulled off his boots as if napping in the coach was simply part of his routine.

Hardcastle shifted to the forward-facing seat, and immediately his head thanked him and his belly quit threatening outright rebellion.

Miss MacHugh folded the opposite bench out, so the boy had the width of a trundle bed to sleep on—they were in a ducal traveling coach, after all—but this left not as much room for Hardcastle's legs.

"I don't bite, Your Grace," Miss MacHugh said, when she'd tucked a wool blanket around Christopher and settled back on the forward-facing seat. "Conditions in even your coach will be crowded when three of us are in here."

"Quite."

Hardcastle abruptly had nowhere to put his arms, his legs, his muddy boots, his anything. He wasn't facing backward, but tumult of another variety assaulted him. He smelled of wet horse, even miles later, while Miss MacHugh smelled of... governess. Lilacs and lavender, sunny gardens, and... happy memories.

They rocked along for another mile, the child falling into a relaxed slumber. The movement of the coach swayed him gently amid the blankets, while Hardcastle felt his own eyes growing heavy.

"You were very kind to let Christopher win half the rounds," Miss MacHugh said, nudging her bonnet way from the boy's feet. "He's sensitive and wants badly to have your approval, though he also has an excellent appreciation for sportsmanship."

"Which he must have acquired from you," Hardcastle concluded. "I certainly haven't spent enough time around the boy to be much of an influence."

Not something to be proud of. He and Christopher were the last surviving Hardcastle males, after all.

"Christopher will recall today fondly," Miss MacHugh said, patting Hardcastle's hand. She'd done that once before, in the garden by the fountain. Very few people presumed to touch a duke, and yet, when Miss MacHugh took liberties, she was relaxed and confident about it.

"You will recall today less than fondly," Hardcastle observed. "I had no idea how tedious traveling with a small child could be."

Miss MacHugh twitched the blanket up over Christopher's shoulders. The boy had to be exhausted to be sleeping so soundly, but then, children did sleep soundly, while dukes rarely did.

"You will recall today miserably," she said, settling back. "If I'd been asked to describe your complexion, sir, I would have started with green, followed up with bilious, and concluded with shroudly pale."

Shroudly wasn't a word, suggesting the governess was teasing the duke.

"Why thank you, Miss MacHugh." Had she suggested Christopher's nap out of consideration for her employer? "If I had to describe the color of your lips, I'd say they were the vermilion glory of sunset at the end of a beautiful summer day spent in the company of good friends whom one has longed to see for ages. They bear the rosy tint of the tender mallow flowers at the height of their bloom, the fresh hue of ripe strawberries glistening with morning dew, and the tantalizing delicacy of raspberries nestled in their thorny, green hedges."

Those vermilion, rosy, strawberry, raspberry lips curved up. "Very good, Your Grace. I know where Christopher gets his aptitude for the game. Very good indeed."

She didn't pat his hand again.

Well.

Hardcastle put an arm around the lady's shoulders to steady her against the jostle and sway of the coach.

"Rest your eyes, Miss MacHugh. We've miles to go before we reach an inn up to my standards of accommodation, and the boy will waken all too soon."

She startled minutely at Hardcastle's forwardness, a reaction he detected only because they were in close proximity. An instant later, she eased against his side, tentatively, then more heavily as sleep claimed her. Hardcastle's belly had quieted entirely, and his headache had departed, but his mind went at a dead gallop down a muddy road indeed.

He did not want to go duchess hunting amid the great houses of the Dukeries, neither did he want to allow Ellen MacHugh to leave his household. He was a duke, however, and those wretches were doomed to a lifetime of marching out smartly, intent on accomplishing tasks they truly did not care to complete.

Hardcastle was damned sick and tired of being a good duke. Perhaps the naughty boy in him should be allowed some long overdue attention.

Only as sleep stole over his mind did Hardcastle admit to himself that he would always strive to be a good duke, and Ellen MacHugh would have little interest in a naughty boy—but perhaps she'd spare a lonely man a bit of company, under the right circumstances.

Chapter Two

"UNCLE LIKES YOU," Christopher said, passing his pencil to Ellen for a sharper one.

"I respect His Grace greatly," Ellen replied, accepting the dull pencil and passing over a fresh one. Something in Christopher's observation was not entirely innocent. He was six, and children at his age matured rapidly and in unexpected directions.

"No, I mean Uncle *likes* you," Christopher said again.

They'd settled in at Sedgemere House late the previous night, among the last of the guests to arrive.

After being confined in the coach for three eternities—one of them with His Grace—Ellen was happy to be out of doors, sketching on a blanket in the Duke of Sedgemere's sunken garden. The morning was spectacularly beautiful, and the governess responsible for Sedgemere's three boys had suggested this quiet retreat.

"I like His Grace as well," Ellen said, fishing a penknife from the sketching box and getting to work on the pencil.

She did not like Hardcastle. Her situation was worse than that. She *could have* liked him and was only now realizing it. He cared for Christopher mightily, had a sense of humor, was kind in a gruff avuncular fashion, and was...

Lonely. That insight had devastated her.

Hardcastle had tucked his arm around her as if daring her to protest, and she should have, but hadn't been able to. He knew exactly how to wrap a woman in his embrace, so she was protected without being confined, and without implying the least impropriety.

Ellen had slept deeply against his side and awoken feeling safe, warm, and content—also resentful, for the duke had offered her a comfort she would not know again.

He couldn't understand that, of course. When Ellen had touched Hardcastle, he'd looked a little bewildered, as if a hummingbird or a butterfly had lit on his sleeve. He couldn't know that his touch, so casually offered, bewildered her the same way.

"Uncle kissed you," Christopher said, his tongue peeking out of the side of his mouth. "When we were in the coach."

The penknife slipped, and Ellen came within a whisker of cutting herself.

"Christopher, you must not say such things. His Grace conducted himself with utmost propriety at all times, given the situation."

Christopher looked up from the owl he was drawing. In the fashion of small boys, he was fascinated with owls lately, a welcome change from the frogs and toads of earlier in the summer.

"You say I mustn't tell lies," he replied. "Uncle kissed your hair. That's not a lie. You were asleep and I was too, mostly, but I opened my eyes and saw him. He kissed your hair. You kiss my hair sometimes."

The child was asking a question Ellen hardly knew how to answer. "Lies always get us in trouble, but in this case, the truth could also get the duke in trouble. If he kissed my hair, I'm sure it was simply the same sort of gesture of affection as I've shown you. Or perhaps my hair was tickling his nose."

The truth if misconstrued could get Ellen ruined—again. A woman permitting her employer's kisses while a child looked on was a sorry creature.

Ellen would rather have been an *awake* sorry creature, though.

"I won't say anything," Christopher allowed, getting to work on the complicated task of drawing feathers on his owl. "Uncle is very dignified. Unless you want me to tell him not to do it again?"

The offer was so gentlemanly, tears threatened.

Ellen put the penknife back in the box, the pencil being adequately sharpened. "What would you say to him, Christopher?"

"I'd say to him that when a gentleman likes a lady, he should tell her that, so she knows, not sneak kisses to her hair. Ladies like fellows who are honest. You say that."

"I'm a font of useful notions. That is a very handsome owl, Christopher." A very knowing sort of owl.

"His names is Xerxes. I wish I had a real owl."

"When you are grown, you can have a mews, a real mews, with falcons in it." Ellen would not see him learn to fly his falcons, though. The realization nearly had her weeping outright.

Why had she allowed herself to grow so attached to this boy? Not well done of her at all.

"Who's that lady?" Christopher asked, sitting up. "She looks worried."

No less a personage than their hostess, the Duchess of Sedgemere was crossing the grass. She was a pretty woman perhaps five years Ellen's senior. The same governess who'd told Ellen about the sunken garden had confided that Her Grace had been the daughter of a banker and was quite approachable when the Quality weren't looking.

"Good morning, Your Grace," Ellen said, rising to curtsey. Beside her, Christopher scrambled to his feet and bowed.

"Miss MacHugh, good day, and hello to you, young sir. Christopher, isn't it? May I borrow your governess for a moment?"

Ellen's first thought was that the duchess had somehow learned of the kiss in the traveling coach and had come to see Ellen escorted to the foot of the drive, bag and baggage. Hardcastle would never have allowed that—if he'd kissed her—and as Christopher had noted, the duchess looked a trifle anxious.

"May I be of assistance, Your Grace?" Ellen asked.

"Let's admire the dratted roses, shall we?" Her Grace suggested, moving briskly along the crushed-shell walk, while Christopher went blithely back to feathering his owl. "Sedgemere's gardener was in a taking because the roses were blooming too early. Imagine the effrontery of roses blooming on their own schedule. I'm babbling."

Ellen liked this woman already. "You're worried about something."

"I'm almost too tired to worry, Miss MacHugh. I'm not very good at this duchessing business. Think of me what you will, but I need your help."

The roses were passing their prime, alas, though a few late bloomers were yet in bud. "What can I do to help, Your Grace?"

"Lady Amelia Marchman has decided not to attend my gathering. It's my first house party as the Duchess of Sedgemere, and she has one scheduled for later this summer. I do believe she's trying to sabotage my Come Out, so to speak, by making the numbers on my roster uneven."

"Ah." The warfare of women. Ellen had skirmished on these fields at finishing school, and her aunt had attempted to equip her for the greater battles to come during a London social Season.

"Miss MacHugh, I am in danger of becoming silly," the duchess went on, "and His Grace is nearly out of patience with me. I don't know many women whose consequence would make them appropriate guests at a duke's house party, and I certainly can't call on the few I do know to cover Lady Amelia's defection. I will become the first duchess in the history of duchesses to hold a house party at which the numbers do not balance."

Ellen sank onto a bench, because this request—did a duchess issue requests?— was enormous.

"You might dissuade one of the gentlemen from attending," Ellen suggested as the duchess took a seat beside her. The bench faced a small pond, in which a half-dozen serene white ducks drifted on the water.

"Brilliant notion, Miss MacHugh, but His Grace refused to countenance it. These are his school chums, his cronies from the House of Lords or their sons and younger brothers. They've already started placing bets on the Dukeries Cup race, which event is the main reason the men were willing to come. Some guests will decamp early, when they've played too deeply or grown bored, but I must at least start with an even number of ladies and gentlemen on the roster I circulate before dinner."

Such was friendship among the aristocracy that one could not ask for a favor?

"I hardly have suitable attire, Your Grace." Ellen had the manners though, as well as the French, the literature, the pianoforte. Mama and Papa had had high hopes for her, despite the costs.

"I've inquired of my housekeeper, Mrs. Bolkers, who knows everybody in the Midlands. She claims you come from an old Derbyshire family, and your uncle is an earl," the duchess replied. "I asked Hardcastle after breakfast this morning, and he left it up to you: If you'd like to be a guest at the house party, then he won't object. Nobody saw you arrive last night because you came in so late, and my sons' governess can easily handle one more little fellow."

If Hardcastle had already capitulated, there went Ellen's last, best defense against this folly.

"I should refuse you, Your Grace. Ellen MacHugh left Derbyshire under a cloud of gossip, and now she turns up five years later at your house party?"

Her Grace was not classically beautiful. Her hair was dark rather than fair, her features dramatic rather than pretty. She gazed out across the pond, just as the lead duck tipped down into the water, his tail pointing skyward. Several other ducks followed suit. The prospect was utterly undignified, but thus did ducks find sustenance.

"I'll be the duchess who returns you to the place in society you should never have abandoned," Her Grace said. "Don't steal a fellow from any of the other young ladies, don't be too witty, don't drink too much, and if you can manage to plead a headache for half the waltzes, we'll both get through this, Miss MacHugh. I will be ever in your debt, and you might even enjoy yourself."

Oh, right. Moving in society—even rural society—had gone so well the last time Ellen had attempted it.

"Are you enjoying yourself, Your Grace?"

"Endlessly, Miss MacHugh. Was the gossip serious?"

"I was seen kissing a fellow I was not engaged to." A lie, but such an old, necessary lie that it no longer felt like one.

"What a shameless wanton you are. I was seen kissing a duke I was not engaged to, and look what a miserable fate has befallen me. Let's get you upstairs, then. I have enough clothes for eighteen women, though my gowns will at least need to be hemmed if they're to fit you."

The duchess rose, while across the garden Christopher had taken to watching the ducks.

"I must report my decision to Hardcastle," Ellen said, "and gain his permission to entrust Christopher to your staff."

"Stroll with him after luncheon then. No fewer than five young ladies were eyeing him at breakfast as if they'd love to end up accidentally napping in his bed. His Grace is in for a long two weeks, as am I."

One of those young ladies would likely conclude the gathering as a prospective duchess.

"I'm in for a long two weeks as well, ma'am. A very long two weeks."

"THIS HOUSE PARTY was the most confoundedly inane notion my grandmother ever bludgeoned me into," Hardcastle muttered. "Now you tell me your uncle is an earl? Will I next learn the Regent has abdicated and winged hedgehogs grace the skies of Nottinghamshire?"

Hardcastle hadn't adjusted to the notion of Miss MacHugh leaving his employ, and now he was to accept that she was niece to the Earl of Dalton?

"I did not want to embarrass my family by my decision to go into service," Miss MacHugh said. "I had already embarrassed them enough, you see, so I took a position in Cornwall."

No, Hardcastle did not *see*.

Beneath the window of the duchess's sitting room, on a back terrace festooned with potted salvia, sat a small regiment of beauties who were little more than half Hardcastle's age. Each one was possessed of a devious mind and a large settlement, and collectively, they were plotting his downfall. They'd formed ranks at breakfast and had spent the morning going at him, like French cavalry charging a British infantry square.

Sooner or later, his lines would break, and he'd be compromised into taking a duchess not of his choosing.

In Kent, the idea of acquiring a duchess had seemed inevitably sensible. Somewhere on the Great North Road, that scheme had become anathema, while another idea—a daft, delightful idea—had taken its place.

Hardcastle quit the window before one of the enemy generals spotted him. "Explain this embarrassment you caused your family, madam. Have I harbored a bad influence in my nursery?"

A damned attractive bad influence, at that. In borrowed deep green finery, Ellen MacHugh's figure showed to excellent advantage, and her complexion was perfection itself. Her hair was severely contained, for now, and the result was feminine elegance of an order Hardcastle was not accustomed to withstanding.

"You have harbored an innocent young lady who allowed a man to kiss her," she replied. "That young lady was seen by idle gossips, which might have been the young man's intention. I left rather than let the talk grow. Nothing more, Your Grace."

With that degree of composure, she'd be a terror at the card tables. Nobody would be able to predict when she was bluffing.

"You're pretty," Hardcastle said, stepping closer. "Damned pretty."

Miss MacHugh smoothed a hand over silk skirts. "Should I apologize for that transgression, Your Grace?"

"You'll regret it," he said, trying not to stare at the simple gold locket nestled just above her breasts. "For every female pursuing me, two fellows will pursue you, and men cannot be relied upon to behave honorably, as you already know."

Hardcastle could endure the simpering females, but the notion that the strutting cocks and squealing stud colts would be sniffing around Ellen MacHugh—*his* Ellen— was unsupportable.

"I am to be the duchess's personal guest," she replied. "The gentlemen will behave themselves."

Worse and worse. "My dear Miss MacGoverness, the duchess herself is on trial here. This is her maiden attempt at managing a major gathering, and the other women will sabotage her personal guest's reception by sundown. I've met these women, and they're enough to give me an ague starting immediately."

For the first time, Miss MacHugh looked uncertain. "I told the duchess this would not work."

Hardcastle put his hands behind his back rather than find out for himself if the gold of Ellen's locket was warm from her body heat.

Perhaps he was suffering from an ague in truth. "Duchesses are formidable women and difficult to gainsay," he allowed. "I have a suggestion."

Miss MacHugh touched the locket, reminding him that he'd seen her do that before, at Sunday services when the weather was temperate.

"I will not like this suggestion, sir."

"You'll loathe it less than you'd loathe being mashed up against the wall of the linen closet when young Mr. Greenover takes a notion to acquaint you with his charms. I've yet to see him sober, but he's in line for an earldom and already controls a large fortune. Perhaps you'd like him to propose?"

She appeared disgusted, bless her. "When this house party has concluded, I will return to my family in Derbyshire."

Well, damn. If she'd been leaving him for another post, he could simply have raised her salary. Returning to the loving arms of the family daft enough to allow her into service posed a conundrum, for what could compete with family?

"So you'll tolerate my attentions for the duration of this house party?" Hardcastle asked. This strategy had come to him as he'd beheld the forces of marital inevitability gathering on the terrace below. He did not want just any duchess, and he certainly did not want a duchess who schemed to get her hands on a tiara regardless of the duke involved.

He wanted a woman who...

"Your attentions, sir?"

"I'll act as your swain," Hardcastle said, though he had no experience *being* a swain. "You'll be my damsel. We don't have to be smitten. A few glances, the occasional sighting of us walking too closely together, a waltz or two. Nothing compromising. If you see a fellow you'd like to pursue, simply tell me, and I'll do the same if one of the ladies should catch my eye."

Miss MacHugh's expression was severe indeed, as if Hardcastle were her charge and he'd just broken his slate over his knee.

"I do not like falsehoods," she said. "They grow and tangle, and become hurtful."

"My entire life is a falsehood," Hardcastle rejoined, coming near enough to study the highlights the afternoon sun put in Miss MacHugh's hair. He knew the texture of her hair, had stolen a nuzzle of it in the traveling coach. Knew the silk of it against his lips, knew the lilac and lavender scent. He knew she had seventeen freckles on her left cheek, fourteen on her right.

Hardcastle also knew his time was up. No more idle musing, no more tacitly comparing every other woman to her, no more telling himself infatuation was normal even for a duke. If he failed to woo Ellen MacHugh in the next two weeks, she'd march out of his life forever.

"My life is a study in falsehood," he said, taking up the reins of the conversation. "I'm to wear my title as if it's a great privilege, as if running twelve estates and doing what I can to keep the Regent from bankrupting the country is an endless honor. I'm to be honorable and gentlemanly without ceasing, perfectly attired at all times, never say the wrong thing, never do the wrong thing. No human man can live up to that standard."

Miss MacHugh smoothed a hand down his lapel. "But you do, sir. You are a good man and a good duke. I've recently come to the conclusion that I like you."

What in the perishing damned hell was a man to say to that?

"Then I'm not asking you to perpetrate any falsehoods, am I, Miss MacHugh? Simply act as if you like me. My name, by the way, is Gerard."

She leaned close enough to sniff the rose affixed to his lapel, then stepped back. "Gerard Juvenal René Beaumarchand Hammersley, Eighth Duke of Hardcastle," she recited. "I'm simply Ellen Ainsley MacHugh."

She was simply driving him to distraction, fingering that locket.

"My brother called me Rennie," Hardcastle said. "My father called me the despair of the house of Hammersley, though he occasionally smiled as he said it."

Miss—Ellen—peered at the gathering below, her expression disgruntled. "I will be complicit in your scheme, sir, but I foresee it ending in great scandal. Those young ladies will learn that I was governess to your heir. They will not deal kindly with me when they do."

"They will not learn of it, and in two weeks you and I will be free to quit this house and move on to happier pursuits."

Though what could be more enjoyable than pursuing her? For Hardcastle would.

He'd vowed this as she'd stepped away from him, and his every instinct had thundered at him to kiss her. She was an earl's relation, she wasn't interested in the dandiprats frolicking around the men's punchbowl, and she loved Christopher.

A tidy solution to several problems, including the predictable insurrection in Hardcastle's breeches every time she drew near.

"Very well, sir, we have a bargain." Ellen held out her hand, an elegant, freckle-free appendage.

Hardcastle took it and pressed his lips to her knuckles. "We have a bargain," he replied, keeping her hand in his.

"You're being a swain already," she said, half-amused, half-exasperated. "Am I to sit next to you every evening over cards? Give you all my waltzes?"

"You are to adore the very ground upon which I strut," he said, patting her hand. "I'll enjoy that part rather a lot. Do you even know how to bat your eyelashes?"

"You're to worship the ground I mince about on too, sir," she said, retrieving her hand. "And no, I did not acquire the ability to bat my eyelashes when I was learning French and Italian."

"Call me Hardcastle, please, or perhaps you might judiciously slip and use my name, then blush becomingly at your lapse." He'd like to make her blush. She was a redhead, and they did not blush subtly.

"And you shall slip and call me Ellen," she retorted. "What have I got myself into?"

"You have got yourself *out of* a lot of spotty boys and leering husbands drooling down your bodice, because you have me to keep them from such impropriety. You may go to sleep at night knowing you have preserved the sanity of at least one deserving duke. One question, my dear."

She glowered at him. "Yes, *dearest* Hardcastle?"

"What's in the locket? It's pretty and suits you in both its simplicity and elegance."

He'd confused her. Ellen's expression said she could not tell if Hardcastle's compliment was sincere, or swain-ly balderdash. She took the locket off over her head and opened it.

"This is a miniature of my sister. She has one of me. We're twins, though I am the elder by a few minutes."

Hardcastle dutifully took the locket, not because he needed to see a small, inexpert likeness of a younger version of Ellen, but because she'd offered to show him of her own accord. The painter, however, had been skilled with miniatures, catching the beauty of a young girl whose poise hadn't yet eclipsed her innocence.

"She's very like you, very fetching," he said, wanting to hold the locket in his palm, but giving it back anyway. "You'll see her again soon."

Drat and damn the luck.

"We're not identical," Ellen said, "but the resemblance is quite strong. I've missed her terribly."

Hardcastle knew what it was to miss a sibling. Why hadn't he realized that even governesses had family, and would miss that family? If he could have had one more day with Robin, with his parents, with even his grandfather...

"We're expected in the back gardens for Italian ices, my dear," he said, winging his arm.

Ellen dropped the locket over her head and wrapped her hand around his sleeve.

"For another two weeks, we can support this farce. Lay on, Hardcastle, and do try to look adoring."

"BLESS YOU, HARDCASTLE! You've found my Miss MacHugh," the Duchess of Sedgemere gushed. Ellen stifled the urge to duck behind the duke, for every pair of eyes on the terrace had turned to her.

"Your Grace." Ellen curtseyed deeply, while beside her, Hardcastle bowed. "Thank you so much for excusing me from the morning's activities. Won't you introduce me to the other guests?"

"But of course," the duchess said, and then Ellen was led away from the safety of Hardcastle's escort and introduced to at least thirty thousand other people, some couples, some family groups, far too many single young men, and at least one gorgeous blond duke. She encountered pleasant, welcoming smiles, leers, and from the young women intent on winning Hardcastle's notice, *un*-pleasant *un*-welcoming smiles too.

"Are you one of the Derbyshire MacHughs?" one young lady asked.

"Ellen's uncle is the Earl of Dalton," the duchess supplied. "His countess and I are fast friends, and Ellen has ever been a favorite of her aunt's. She is already a favorite of mine too."

And thus did trouble begin, as Miss Tamsin Frobisher's baby-blue eyes narrowed, and she twirled a fat, golden sausage curl around her finger.

"I seem to recall—" Miss Frobisher began.

"You will have to excuse me," the duchess said. "I am so sorry, but I must oversee the serving of the ices. Miss Frobisher, perhaps you'll assist me, and Ellen, I'll leave you in the care of my dear husband."

His Grace of Sedgemere had been silently accompanying them through the introductions. He was not a handsome man, his Nordic features were too severe for that, but when his gaze lit on his duchess, his expression softened.

"Come, Miss MacHugh, we've only the last of the bachelors yet to go," Sedgemere said, seizing Ellen's hand and positioning it on it arm. "They'll be on their best behavior or I'll kill them."

Ellen wrapped her hand around his sleeve as they traversed the steps to the lower terrace, but she already felt the flames of gossip licking at her back.

"How considerate of you, Your Grace. I'm sure Hardcastle would assist you to dispose of the remains."

"Hardcastle had better be on his best behavior too, or you need only apply to me, madam. This scheme of Her Grace's is demented, and you're either a saint or a fool for accommodating it."

"In either case, you're most welcome, Your Grace. Are all dukes so fierce, or do you and my—Hardcastle have a rivalry of some sort?"

"I consider Hardcastle among my very few friends, Miss MacHugh. Now, attend me, for my recitation will be sufficiently tedious that I don't care to repeat it. The fop on the left is Jermand Hunslinger, sot and wastrel at large, but decorative. The dandy to the right is Harold Schacter, Viscount Ormandsley, whose besetting vice is horse racing. The imbecile in the middle is Greenover. He's heir to the Earl of Moreton, has already accosted two chambermaids, and will likely not survive the next the week."

Neither would Ellen. "You'll kill him, sir?"

"My duchess will turn Miss Frobisher and Miss Pendleton loose on him. Poor sod won't know his top from his tail by Sunday afternoon."

"What a ruthless duchess you have, sir."

"They're the best kind."

SEDGEMERE STOOD ACROSS the room, impersonating a Viking guardian angel at Ellen MacHugh's side, looking quite severe, and probably laughing his arse off. Sedgemere had perfected silent mirth before leaving Eton. Hardcastle had no doubt it had served Sedgemere well through an interminable dinner too.

Miss Frobisher's pale, quivering bosom had occupied Hardcastle's attention on the left, or tried to, while Miss Pendleton's more modest attributes had been jiggled at him from the right through at least ninety-seven exquisitely presented courses.

Hardcastle had declined the blancmange and would likely never enjoy that particular dish again.

"You might smile, Hardcastle," the Duchess of Sedgemere said. "My housekeeper has been asked by four different lady's maids for a map of the guest wing, ostensibly to prevent the young misses from getting lost."

"If you gave any of them—"

She patted his hand, but the gesture conveyed none of the comfort, none of the soothing, that the same touch from Ellen would have.

"You're in the family wing Hardcastle, and so is your Miss MacHugh. Does she know you're smitten?"

"Anne, for shame. Dukes are not smitten." Though Sedgemere was. Clearly, at some point, a man who'd never been known to dance with the same woman twice had given all his waltzes to the banker's daughter. "What do you know of Miss MacHugh's family?"

"I've done a bit of research, thanks to Mrs. Bolkers's unfailing memory regarding the Quality. Ellen MacHugh never made her bow. She went to the right sort of finishing school, her auntie the countess was all ready to sponsor her Come Out, but then something happened, and into service Ellen went, far to the south, nobody knows exactly where."

"Cornwall." Literally the ends of the earth. "Her references were from Cornwall when she joined my household. Good God, now we're to endure the caterwauling and cooing."

For nothing would do, but Miss Frobisher must have Lord Ormandsley turn pages for her at the pianoforte. She played competently, she displayed her bosom for the viscount more competently still. Hardcastle's head was beginning to pound, and he was thinking fondly of rainy miles in his traveling coach, when Miss Frobisher concluded her piece and aimed a vivacious smile at Ellen.

"Won't you play for us, Miss MacHugh? I'm sure one of the gentlemen would be happy to turn pages for you."

Ellen's gaze met Hardcastle's for an instant, an *I told you so* rather than a plea flung across the parlor. A chorus of "I'd be pleased to assist," and "I'd love to oblige" rose up from amidst the puppies, and Hardcastle's headache migrated to the region of his heart.

This was his fault. What if Ellen couldn't play? What if she played badly? What if—

"I can play from memory," she said, rising gracefully and crossing to the piano. "I'm a bit rusty, but it's a beautiful instrument, and I do love music. I'll play one of my mother's favorites."

She took her place on the bench, the lamplight dancing fire through her auburn hair.

Hardcastle braced himself for some sprightly, repetitive Mozart rondo, or a crashing Beethoven first movement.

As she started to play, a collective sigh eased from the room. She'd chosen a ballad from Mr. Burns's work, "My Love Is Like a Red, Red Rose." The key was major, but the words of the poem were of farewell to a dearest love. She mercifully declined to sing, though Hardcastle knew each verse by heart.

Ellen's playing featured not showy virtuosity, but instead, a sweet, leaping melody over lilting accompaniment and sentimental harmonies. Every dissonance was quickly resolved, while every phrase spoke of loss and regret.

When the piece concluded, the room remained silent for a moment, bathed in the peace of a tender melody. The duchess led the applause and prompted another young lady to play as Hardcastle edged around the room and took Ellen by the arm.

"You play very well," he muttered, as Miss Pendleton went thumping into a tormented rendition of "Charlie, He's My Darling." "My head will soon be killing me. Might we admire the croaking of the nearest frog or the moon's reflection on a mud puddle, or some blasted thing where it's quiet?"

"I'd like that, Your Grace," Ellen replied, fluffing the folds of his cravat.

"Do that again, please, while the Frobisher creature is goggling at us, and the Sheffield heiress is for once not tossing her curls. It's a wonder the woman hasn't dislocated her neck."

Ellen obliged, rearranging lace at the same time she settled Hardcastle's nerves. "Some fresh air would be welcome, sir."

They left through the open French doors, the terrace offering relative cool and quiet compared to the crowded parlor. Hardcastle found a bench on the lower terrace, seated the lady, came down beside her, and stifled the urge to check his watch in the ample moonlight.

If he sought his bed this early, talk would ensue.

"I am ready to strangle my grandmother for insisting I attend this gathering," Hardcastle said, "and I'm ready to leave at first light, but Sedgemere is a friend, and I'd not disrespect his hospitality. Say something."

"The piano will need tuning by morning," Ellen remarked. "Miss Pendleton enjoys a very confident touch at the keyboard."

The damned chit could have drummed for a Highland regiment, but at least out here, her chopping at the hapless "Charlie" was at a tinkling distance.

"You enjoy a confident touch when your hands are on my person, Miss MacHugh. I like that."

The lady ceased fussing her skirts. "I beg your pardon, Your Grace?"

A conversational commonplace had never worn as much starch. "I said, you enjoy—"

"I heard you, Hardcastle. If you think for one moment that a casual gesture between people who've known each other for years—"

Hardcastle cradled her jaw against his palm, and Ellen fell silent. He leaned nearer, close enough to catch her scent, close enough to whisper.

"Don't scream." Then he kissed her.

ELLEN'S HEART WAS breaking about once every fifteen minutes. She saw Hardcastle teasing the duchess, a woman he clearly considered a friend, and was struck with the realization that in the past three years, she'd never once seen Hardcastle teasing anybody.

But then, nobody had teased him either.

He'd compliment a trio of companions on their embroidery and march away, oblivious to the envy directed at the companions by the young ladies they were supposed to attend.

Hardcastle was lonely, and Ellen was leaving him. He was such a good man, in his way, and after this house party, she'd never see him again.

She'd played for him, of course. Offered him Mr. Burns, a comfort in her younger years, a piece she'd be playing from memory decades hence. *I will love thee still, my dear, till all the seas gang dry...*

Hardcastle would love like that, relentlessly, deeply, nigh reverently. He'd love like a duke—

"I am ready to strangle my grandmother for insisting I attend this gathering," he said as he and Ellen gained the blessed peace of the terrace. "And I'm ready to leave at first light, but Sedgemere is a friend, and I'd not disrespect his hospitality. Say something."

Don't go, sir. Please, don't go. Not yet.

They were mere yards from the rest of the gathering. Ellen searched for a prosaic response and came up with an inanity.

"The piano will need tuning by morning," she said. "Miss Pendleton enjoys a very confident touch at the keyboard."

Her playing had sounded desperate to Ellen, as if by bombarding Hardcastle with notes, Miss Pendleton might decimate His Grace's indifference.

"You enjoy a confident touch when your hands are on my person, Miss MacHugh. I like that."

Ellen could not possibly have heard him correctly. "I beg your pardon, Your Grace?"

"I said, you enjoy—"

When in doubt, when in an utterly confused quandary, a governess always had a good scold ready.

"I heard you, Hardcastle. If you think for one moment that a casual gesture between people who've known each other for years—"

Ellen had not even begun to know this man. She'd misjudged him for years, hidden from him, in fact.

Hardcastle cradled her jaw against his palm, the warmth of his hand startling, for this was an informal house party and he wasn't wearing gloves.

"Don't scream."

His mouth settled over hers, the way calm settled in her heart when a solution arrived to a thorny problem, bringing with it rightness, relief, and a sense of revelation.

Yes, this. Exactly and emphatically, this. Hardcastle's kiss was rivetingly sweet, not a presumption, but an invitation, a fragrance that beckoned Ellen into a garden of blooming pleasures. His arm encircling her shoulders, his warmth and nearness, his hand cradling her cheek, his tongue—

Exotic orchids joined the sensual bouquet that was the duke's kiss. Heat from no apparent source glowed inside Ellen, light filled her mind where thoughts should be. The texture of his hair pleasured her fingers, and the taste of him—lavender and sweetness, from the last round of tea cakes—made her hungry in her soul.

Hardcastle could tease with kisses, drat him. Could nuzzle Ellen's ear and send all her questions and protestations begging. She tried to tease back, by nibbling on the soft flesh of his lower lip, by stroking a hand over his chest, inside the warmth of his evening coat.

That effort was hopeless. The more she touched him, the more muddled *she* became.

When the duke desisted, Ellen's heart was banging against her ribs as if a dozen unruly schoolgirls were leaping about inside her. When she would have traced her finger over his lips, he gently pushed her head to his shoulder.

"Your kisses want practice, my dear."

Indignation should have had Ellen drawing back, but a note in His Grace's voice stopped her. He was *pleased* that she had no idea how to kiss a man. He approved of her lack of experience, the wretch. As if she were the last tea cake on the tray, saved just for him.

"Yours is my first kiss, Hardcastle, and you provided me no warning." She ought not to have admitted that. He'd be impossible now, not merely an impossible man, but an impossible *duke*.

"You can't read up on how to kiss a fellow, Ellen. Not even in Latin. The business wants practice, and I'm sure you'll be a quick study." He kissed her again, a light smack on the lips. "Gets easier with practice, you see?"

He was entirely too smug about this venture, while Ellen had yet to locate her wits. She instead maneuvered artillery in place that ought to at least puncture Hardcastle's self-satisfaction.

"Are you trifling with the help, Your Grace?"

"The help isn't exactly leaping off the bench and calling for the gendarmes, is she?" he asked, his tone cooling.

"And ruin what's left of my reputation?"

The question sobered him. Ellen could feel Hardcastle's attitude change even before he withdrew his arm.

"Nobody is out here," he said, "and a simple kiss between adults does not a reputation ruin. You're not a giggling twit."

"I am an earl's granddaughter with a questionable past. Why did you kiss me, Hardcastle?"

He pushed off the bench and lounged on the balustrade a few feet away. Over his shoulder, the gardens were limned in moonlight, a fairy world suited to Christopher's owls. Behind Ellen, inside the parlor, the bashing about of poor "Charlie" came to a merciful final cadence.

"The demented women at this house party are out to capture themselves a duke," Hardcastle muttered. "You are my sole defense against their schemes, particularly now that His Grace of Wyndover has left the field, pleading the equivalent of a bachelor's megrim. It may be necessary for me to pay you marked attention, and I can't have you rebuffing my overtures."

Hardcastle's logic was a kick in the belly to Ellen's fancies. "So that was a rehearsal kiss? A theater production for the leering masses we're likely to face at tomorrow's picnic?"

His expression shuttered, and he became not Ellen's duke, not Hardcastle who'd steal a kiss to her hair, but a statue of a man, a fixture of the moonlit, fantastical garden.

"That kiss was not entirely a fiction, madam. Not on my part. If you're offended by my honest regard, I apologize. I presumed, and it needn't happen again."

Laughter spilled from the parlor. The hordes would soon descend, all smiles and sly glances. Ellen abruptly wanted to cry, but because she was not in her governess attire, she had no handkerchief tucked into her sleeve.

Hardcastle pushed off the wall and strode toward the house, pausing only long enough to gently squeeze Ellen's shoulder before he left her alone in the moonlight.

Chapter Three

"IF YOU IMPORTUNE Miss MacHugh like that again, I shall call you out, Hardcastle, and I will shoot to wound your pride, at least."

The evening was mild, and no fire had been lit in the library's hearth, so Sedgemere's threat cracked across the darkness like a pistol shot.

"If you call me out, I'll choose swords," Hardcastle replied, turning two glasses on the sideboard right side up. "You're no kind of swordsman, while my skill is indisputable. May I offer you some of your own brandy?"

"That decanter's full of whiskey," Sedgemere said, rising from a wing chair near the windows. "Anne has connections in the north who obligingly keep me supplied. The brandy's on the desk."

Hardcastle poured himself a brandy, for his nerves wanted soothing, not more passion. He passed Sedgemere a serving as well and touched his glass to his host's.

"To victory in battle," he said, reciting one of their toasts from boyhood. They'd both had ducal expectations foisted upon them too soon and at too great a cost, and that toast had covered a host of challenges.

"To honor in victory," Sedgemere replied, ambling over to the window. "What could you have been thinking, Hardcastle? Ellen MacHugh is your nephew's governess, and you were on her like a bear at a honey tree."

"I rather was." And she'd returned the compliment. "Miss MacHugh has agreed to be the object of my apparent affection for the duration of this gathering, and I shall be hers. A certain familiarity between us lends credibility to that fiction."

"Any more credibility, Hardcastle, and the woman would be having your child. I opened the French doors to my library thinking to gain some fresh air without joining the throng in the parlor, and I find a pair of minks on my terrace."

Two minks, two eager, thoroughly enthralled minks. Hardcastle took comfort from that.

"I became more enthusiastic than I intended, Sedgemere. I planned delicate forays, tactful overtures, not... not the complete surrender of my dignity." Or the complete surrender of Ellen's, for that matter.

When it came to kissing, she was a deuced fast learner, though, dignity be damned.

Sedgemere settled on the arm of the chair, moonlight glinting off the glass in his hand. "People think I married Anne for her money. Her papa is filthy rich, of course, and the settlements were indecently generous."

"People are idiots," Hardcastle shot back. "You could no more be bought by a banker than you could by the Empress of Austria." Though not for lack of trying in the latter case.

"You are an idiot too, Hardcastle, if you think by indirection to test the waters with Miss MacHugh. Go down on damned bended knee and give her the pretty words. At the very least, stop accosting her within earshot of half the gossips in London. Or leave her alone. Those are your options."

Thank God the library was without illumination. "She's leaving me in two weeks, Elias. Has given notice, and was most insistent on rejoining her family. Leaves a fellow rather…"

"At a loss," Sedgemere said gently. "Anne led me quite a dance. You'd think it's the duke who longs to be pursued for himself, rather than for his consequence. Anne stands to become wealthier than most dukes can dream of being, and I finally understood what she needed besides my passionate kisses and handsome escort."

The brandy helped. Sedgemere's company helped more. "You're uglier than a donkey's back end on a muddy day. Anne felt sorry for you, I'm sure."

Sedgemere saluted with his glass. "You're the one who set me straight, Hardcastle."

"I was half drunk, and exhausted by your violent pouting. You, a duke, sulking about like a college boy avoiding his creditors. I was on the point of proposing to Anne myself, rather than put up with more of your wallowing."

"Were you really?" Abruptly, the temperature in the library had dropped twenty-odd degrees, though at least Sedgemere had stopped handing out maudlin advice to the lovelorn.

"No, but Grandmama would have liked Anne, and Christopher adores her. What am I to do about Ellen MacHugh?"

Sedgemere, with the aplomb of a true friend, only guffawed rather than going off into whoops.

"You must charm her. The dictionary is on the table behind you, if the word is foreign to your experience. Convince her you want her in truth, despite her wild hair and advancing age, despite her humble origins."

"Her hair is perfect, and she's not a scheming twit. She's the granddaughter of an earl."

Another guffaw, followed by a snort, but Sedgemere should be allowed his diversions. He hadn't kissed Ellen MacHugh on the moonlit terrace, hadn't felt the fire and eagerness in her, hadn't endured the wonder provoked by her sheer female lusciousness and starchy retorts.

"Charm," Sedgemere said. "C-h-a-r-m. If you reach chicken, you've gone too far."

"If I reach chaste, I've gone too far. Maybe I should compromise her."

"I wouldn't advise it," Sedgemere said, swirling his brandy. "She'll be forever haunted by the thought that you had to marry her, that you married far beneath yourself. Society will never let her forget that your proposal was forced too."

"Blast you and your good sense." If Hardcastle compromised Ellen, he'd be haunted by the thought that she had married *him* out of necessity as well, not because she wanted to. "I'm taking this decanter upstairs with me."

"Better the decanter than the governess. Wedge a chair under your door when you're in your bedroom alone."

"Right. House party rules." Did Ellen know the house party rules? "Thank you, Sedgemere, and good night."

Hardcastle had reached the door, feeling silly for pilfering the brandy, when Sedgemere's voice drifted across the room.

"Compromise her, and I will thrash you, Hardcastle. Hard enough to hurt."

Sedgemere might not emerge victorious, but he'd give a good account of himself, which notion comforted on Ellen's behalf.

"I'd let you land a few blows for old time's sake, because you do so love it when Anne kisses your hurts better."

Hardcastle pulled the library door closed behind him amid more mirth from His damned perishing Grace, though what did it say about Hardcastle's ducal consequence that he envied his friend a lady to kiss his hurts better?

※

LETTERS TO EMILY always took a long time to write, and Ellen knew better than to attempt them when tired. Her mind would not settle, though, so she got out of bed and labored for half a page.

Hardcastle had kissed her, and his boldness hadn't been merely insurance against an awkward moment, when the fiction of interest in each other must be supported with a display of affection.

"I cannot fathom His Grace's motivation," she muttered, dipping her pen again and waiting, waiting for the excess ink to form a droplet, then fall back into the inkpot. "He is a surpassingly intelligent man, and more than capable of expressing himself clearly."

But Hardcastle was reserved too, possibly even shy.

Ellen was watching another droplet gather on the sharp end of the quill when a soft knock sounded at her door. By the standards of a social gathering, the hour wasn't that late. She set the pen aside, rose, and opened her door two inches.

"Your Grace?"

"No, it's Greenover, come to make violent love to you before his over-imbibing renders him entirely insensate. Let me in, madam, if you please."

The duke was, for the first time in Ellen's experience, less than perfectly turned out. His cravat had gone missing, his jacket with it, and the top button of his waistcoat was undone. His cuffs were turned back, and his rebellious hair had defeated decorum entirely.

He looked tired, disgruntled, and altogether delectable.

"Come in, Your Grace, though I'm hardly decent."

"You're covered from your pretty neck to your equally pretty toes, though the appearance of your toes must remain a matter of conjecture on my part, as I have never made their acquaintance."

Though only half dressed, Hardcastle still sounded every inch the duke. Ellen would miss even his voice, miss the clipped, ironic energy, the euphony of Oxford learning, and the confidence of bred-in-the-bone leadership.

"If you stare at my mouth like that much longer, madam, I will be forced to return the compliment, and then we'll get nothing discussed."

She'd kissed that arrogant mouth of his, been ensnared in its tender promises and bold overtures.

"You've interrupted my correspondence, sir, and the hour is late. What might I do for you?"

He locked the door, a sensible precaution, one Ellen should have seen to. "I was reminded by Sedgemere that you might not have attended many house parties. There are rules."

The first of those rules ought to be: Never allow a duke you've kissed into your bedroom late at night. Candlelight shot fire through the duke's tousled hair, and his shirt—the finest lawn—revealed the musculature of his arms in intriguing detail.

"You need not trouble yourself, Your Grace. The duchess reviewed the rules with me: Don't over-imbibe, don't steal anybody's beau, sit out half the waltzes."

He prowled over to the escritoire and capped the bottle of ink, then swept up the parings from Ellen's last efforts with the penknife and upended them into a dust bin near the hearth.

"You will not sit out waltzes if I'm on hand to dance them with you. You may also dance with Sedgemere, or with Oxthorpe, if he's joined the gathering with his duchess. I'm not referring to those rules, I'm referring to the rules of self-preservation."

Ellen knew all about self-preservation. She was leaving Hardcastle's employ partly in pursuit of that very aim.

His Grace had stopped prowling and tidying and was peering at Ellen's unfinished letter.

"A gentleman does not read another's correspondence, Your Grace." Her observation was intended to carry the whip-crack of an offended governess, not the plea of a besotted spinster.

"When you print your sentiments this large," he said, studying the half sheet of writing, "one can't help but read them from halfway across the shire. Who's Emily?"

"My twin sister. I showed you her miniature."

Hardcastle moved a branch of candles, the better to snoop into Ellen's private sentiments. "Her eyesight must be wanting, and she hasn't your gift for scholarship." He peered at the letter more closely, and Ellen's lungs refused to breathe. *"I am sad to leave my duke,"* he quoted. *"He is, in his way, very dear."*

"Right now, you are not dear at all, sir. I will scream if you do not quit my room this instant." And then Ellen would cry, because the last treasure a woman ought to be able to keep for herself was her privacy, and Hardcastle had just trodden that right into the carpet.

"Am I dear?" he asked, setting the letter down. "From you, that is quite flattering. You will be pleased to know—"

He fell silent as voices sounded in the corridor. When the footsteps faded, Ellen marched to the window and yanked the curtains closed lest the fool man silhouette himself in her window for half the guests to see.

"I will be pleased to know what, Your Grace? That you have no respect for my dignity? That you are amused by my efforts to maintain a connection with my only sibling? That you—"

Strong hands settled on Ellen's waist and turned her to face her guest. "You will be pleased to know, madam, that *in your way*, you are dear to me as well."

Ellen wanted badly to touch Hardcastle's cheek, also to throw him out of her room, for the conversation was doomed.

"In my way, Your Grace?"

"You brook no foolishness, you don't fraternize with the footmen, you cannot be intimidated, though you are never rude, and you are unfailingly kind to my nephew. You have a sense of humor, which one sees in plain sight as rarely as a falling star in a summer sky. You are pretty, damn you, and hide your beauty more assiduously than your smiles. You kiss exceedingly well for a beginner. In your way, Ellen MacHugh, you are dear."

He growled his sweet sentiments begrudgingly. His hands remained at Ellen's waist, and she covered them with her own, not to dissuade him, but to hoard his touch.

"You are ill-tempered much of the time because you are tired," she retorted. "You take your responsibilities seriously, and you are almost afraid to love Christopher, lest he be taken from you too. You are very brave, Your Grace, and protective of all for whom you're responsible. For a duke, your kisses are surprisingly beguiling."

His hands slid around her to the small of her back. Ellen's fingers rested on his muscular biceps. "How many dukes have you kissed, Miss MacHugh?"

"Only the one, and him not nearly enough to speak knowledgeably."

So Ellen kissed him some more.

SOMEWHERE BETWEEN KNOCKING on Ellen's door and realizing that he'd never before seen her hair down, Hardcastle lost track of which rules he was intent on lecturing her about. Something about wedging a chair under his chin lest he gawp the night away. Her braid was a thick skein of auburn secured with a bright green bow she would never have worn when governessing in Kent.

Keep your door locked at all times, he wanted to tell her as her lips grazed his. *Admit no one,* he thought, as her tongue took a delicate taste of him. *Never drop your guard for an instant,* his brain shouted, while his hands cupped the lady's derriere and brought her flush against him.

She let him *in,* let him taste and beg and tease and beg some more even as he tugged the infernal bow free of her braid and slipped the scrap of silk into his pocket.

"You've used your tooth-powder," he muttered, walking her back until she sat on the bed.

"You've used yours."

Then she was at him again, pulling him over her, until he was crouched above her on the bed. Some dim, despairing corner of his mind knew he was behaving badly, but being a paragon was damned hard, *lonely* work.

Being a swain apparently had much to recommend it. Who knew?

Hardcastle gently palmed a breast through Ellen's nightclothes. "I want to devour you, and you're not telling me to stop."

"I've wanted to devour you for three years, which is why—"

Three years? Three years they'd wasted with civilities and fine manners and thirty-three-day silences?

"Which is why you're not stopping me now," Hardcastle said, unbelting the homeliest quilted dressing gown ever to enshroud a man's dearest dreams. "You can stop me, Ellen. If you order me from your room, I will get off this bed and return to my chambers."

"I should," she said, brushing his hair back from his brow. "I'm leaving in two weeks, Your Grace. This folly, precious though it may be, changes nothing."

This was not folly. This was the beginning of a course they would chart together, one that would end at the altar.

"You shall not leave me," Hardcastle said, getting off the bed, lest he disgrace himself in his haste. "I did not come here intending to seduce you."

Not consciously, at least. A small fig leaf for his pride.

Ellen tied her dressing gown closed, then scooted back to rest against the headboard. She was oblivious to her braid coming unraveled, while Hardcastle could notice little else.

"You cannot tell me what to do, Hardcastle. I'm leaving your employ, and that is my final word. You are welcome to stay with me or quit the room as long as we're clear on my plans."

Less and less was becoming clear, except that Hardcastle was in the presence of his future duchess.

He began a circuit of the room, blowing out candles as he went. "You'd allow me the privileges of a lover, Ellen?"

God help him if she sought to become his mistress. Other women had offered to take his coin in exchange for enduring his intimate attentions. He'd set up such arrangements three times after coming down from university, and all three times he'd been disappointed—nigh disgusted—with the results.

"I am offering to be your lover," Ellen said, drawing her feet up and linking her arms around her knees. "Though the notion shocks me. In two weeks, I'll return to Derbyshire and resume a life with my parents and my sister. Our means are limited, and spinsterhood will be my lot."

The hell it would.

"And if I were to propose?" Hardcastle asked, blowing out the last of the candles on the escritoire. Thank God for the sophistication of the English language and the delicate possibilities of conditional phrasing.

"I'd refuse you, Hardcastle," Ellen said, without an instant's hesitation. "You are discommoded by the ladies here at the house party, and you see decades of such house parties before you. Rather than entrust your future to the first debutante who can get herself compromised with you, you're turning to a known quantity who's already a member of your household. Your thinking is practical, but I could not accept such an offer."

Good God. Her stubbornness would be admirable if it weren't so baffling. "What could possibly motivate you to refuse a tiara, madam?" He knew why a sensible woman would reject his suit—he was ill-tempered, as she'd said, much consumed with estate business, and completely lacking in... *charm*.

Ellen gazed at her toes, whose acquaintance Hardcastle was very pleased to make. Rather than take a seat at the escritoire, as any sensible duke might have done, he slid onto the bed and took the place beside her, resting against the headboard.

"I will not be your duchess of convenience, Hardcastle. You're simply having a bad moment. We all have them. I'll get you through this house party, and you can tell your grandmama you're considering possibilities. She'll leave you alone for the next two years, at least."

Hardcastle did not want to be alone. He took Ellen's hand in both of his. "I'm to content myself with some shared pleasure where you're concerned? A casual affair such as house parties are notorious for?"

She blinked at her toes. "Yes, and I will do likewise. I'll have my pleasure of you and retire to Derbyshire with some lovely memories."

What a foul abuse of a tender pair of hearts that would be. Something else was afoot here, but two things prevented Hardcastle from further interrogating the woman so resolutely rejecting his marriage proposal. First, he needed to think, to consider angles and possibilities, and this he could not do while reclining on a bed in full sight of Ellen MacHugh's exposed toes.

Second, she'd accepted his offer to become her lover. Not even a ducal paragon could give strategy his attention when faced with that distraction.

So he kissed her.

※

THREE YEARS OF living with Hardcastle had convinced Ellen of two things. First, the duke would not be rushed. Not at table, not when exchanging pleasantries in the churchyard, not when reviewing Ellen's written reports regarding Christopher's progress.

Second, when in pursuit of an objective, Hardcastle could not be stopped either.

This second attribute was a great comfort as His Grace situated himself on all fours over Ellen, kissed her, then pressed his cheek to hers, like a cat trying to inspire caresses. She should stop him, and she should order him from the room, but Derbyshire loomed in Ellen's nightmares.

Beautiful scenery, the loving arms of family, and endless loneliness. As Hardcastle's duchess of convenience, she'd be lonelier still, and yet, Ellen could not deny herself a night in the duke's arms.

She'd have decades to regret this folly, but only *now* to indulge in it.

"Shouldn't you take your boots off, sir?"

Hardcastle sat back on his heels and shot a disapproving look at her. "If you can think of boots at a moment like this, my kisses are clearly wanting in some material particular."

"You're overdressed for a *moment like this*, Hardcastle."

His gaze went to the knot of her dressing gown's belt.

Oh no you don't. "Boots off, Hardcastle. Now." Ellen used the same tone she'd apply when Christopher aimed longing glances at the main stairway's banister railing.

"Your servant, madam," the duke replied, bouncing to the edge of the bed.

"Was it so difficult to follow an order for once, Hardcastle?"

"In this bed, Ellen MacHugh," he said, yanking off first one boot then the other, "I will follow any orders you give, even the ones you can't bear to put into words."

Those were legion. He should choose a duchess he could love, one who loved him, not merely settle for a convenient woman to whom he was attracted. He should make time for amusement, play the color game in all its silly pointlessness. Laugh, smile, flirt with the dowagers, and be late for meetings. Sleep in on rainy mornings and stay up half the night reading lurid novels.

"You grow silent," he said, draping his waistcoat over the chair at the desk. "Silence is not permitted if it means you're changing your mind. That's an order you must follow, madam. You've given me leave to be your lover, and lovers talk to each other."

"You've had so many?" She hoped he'd had a few. Lovers, women whose company he enjoyed, not merely sexual passing fancies.

He pulled his shirt off, and moonlight slipped through a crack in the drawn curtains to gild shoulders heavy with muscle. Hardcastle was an avid equestrian, and often went for long tramps with his stewards to call upon the yeomanry.

He was fit and beautiful, and that was before he shed his stockings and breeches.

"I've had enough experience to know what I'm about, Ellen. You must not be nervous. Whatever encounters you've had, including the great scandalous ones that sent you into service, they don't signify."

Hardcastle stood beside the bed, as confident in his nudity as he was in all his Bond Street finery, but what was he trying to tell her?

"Are you forgiving me for having a past?" Ellen had paid dearly for that past and could not expect him to ignore it.

The duke climbed onto the bed and kept coming, a predator on the scent, until he was once again crouched over Ellen, though this time, he wore not a stitch.

"I'm asking you," he said, "humbly suggesting, in fact, that you set aside your preconceived notions, about what happens next, about yourself, about *me*, and allow me to pleasure you as a lady deserves to be pleasured."

Ellen hardly knew what happened next, though she was very sure she wanted Hardcastle to be the one to show her.

The tone of his words was imperious, while the tone of his kiss was beseeching. Hardcastle's mouth was all delicate patience and tactful entreaty as he pressed his lips to Ellen's. His explorations were the gentlest invitations, and his presence became one of sheltering warmth rather than masculine demand.

When Ellen cradled his jaw with her palm, he moved into her touch. "Tell me," he whispered. "Say what you long for."

Ellen longed for time to absorb this beguilement, for years to explore Hardcastle's unexpected capacity for tenderness. Even more tempting, she sensed he longed to lay still greater treasures at her feet.

"I long for you," she said, the most honest summary of her dreams. "Only you, all of you."

He rested his forehead against hers, and she took the moment to savor the silky texture of his hair as she slipped her fingers through his dark locks. He bore the lemony scent of a hard-milled French soap, and his back and shoulders were hot beneath her touch. In winter, sleeping next to him would be...

Some other woman's privilege.

"If you're to have me," he said, rising from the bed and turning down the counterpane, "and I dearly hope you shall, then I'd best get under the covers."

A more prudent woman would use the moment to extract a promise from him that he'd support any children resulting from this encounter. Ellen didn't bother to ask, for of course he would. The greater question was, would she even let him know she'd conceived, when his child might be all she ever had of him?

"Shall I take off my night robe?"

Beneath her night robe, Ellen wore only a summer-length chemise. The fabric had worn thin over the past five years, but Emily had helped with the white work on the hem. Sentiment thus kept near what practicality would have surrendered long ago.

"Do you want to take off your night robe, Ellen?"

Of course she didn't. She was not young, her breasts were modest when men supposedly liked an ample bosom. Her hips were generous, and she—

"My dear?" the duke asked, unknotting the sash of her robe, but making no move to take it off of her. "To be next to you, right next to you, skin to skin, heartbeat to heartbeat, would be a rare and privileged pleasure, but your wishes must come before all else."

He'd wait all night, while Ellen dithered away another three years. She wiggled out of the night robe and handed it to him, then drew the chemise over her head and scooted under the covers.

"You may hide your treasures, *for now*," Hardcastle said. Ellen expected him to toss her chemise aside, but he instead remained by the bed, running his fingers over the hem. "Part of your trousseau, I'd guess based on this embroidery. The work is very fine."

"I enjoy needlework," Ellen said. "Though it's hard on the eyes."

His Grace was the opposite of hard on the eyes. Hardcastle's belly was divided into small, rectangular fields of muscle, arranged on either side of a trail of dark hair. The trail first narrowed before widening as it went south, and then....

Then Ellen had to look away. The sight of Hardcastle's bodily anticipation of their pleasures would stay with her for the rest of her life.

He bunched the fabric of Ellen's nightgown beneath his nose. "Lavender. Lilacs. *You.*"

The nightgown went sailing to the foot of the bed as the mattress dipped. In the next instant, Hardcastle was under the covers, fourteen stone of hot, naked, unstoppable duke.

"You peeked," he said, sliding an arm under Ellen's neck and drawing her against his side. "I'm quite flattered that you peeked, and you a woman of such iron self-discipline."

"I could hardly avoid the sight of your wares right before my eyes. You gawked," Ellen countered, finding the perfect place to rest her cheek against his chest. "I wasn't flaunting anything, sir."

"You needn't flaunt your delights," he replied. "I can learn all I need to know about your various attributes by tactile exploration. You may make similar forays upon my person, and I will adore you for them."

Adoration wasn't love, but Ellen hugged the admission close to her heart anyway. "I didn't expect you to be so warm to the touch," she said, tracing a single finger down the midline of his belly—halfway down.

His reply was to take her hand and wrap her fingers around a hot, smooth shaft of male flesh.

"You didn't expect me to be so beastly aroused, but a duke is simply a man, Ellen. He's a man with more responsibilities than most, but no less human."

More human, maybe? Hardcastle's hand fell away, leaving Ellen holding... the ducal succession, as it were.

"What does one do...?" she asked, running a finger around the tip.

"One indulges one's curiosity, or—this is your only warning—two indulge their curiosity about each other."

Ellen could not have said how long Hardcastle endured her explorations, how many ways she touched and teased and tasted him, how varied were the kisses they shared. She let go of the entire burden of propriety, let go of all the tomorrows and next years, and reveled in intimacy with the only lover she'd ever have.

Hardcastle was relentless when it came to her breasts. He kissed, he fondled, he applied nuanced, maddening pressure, he put his mouth on her and drew forth groans such as no governess uttered in the company of her employer.

Ellen would have let him arouse her thus all night, except she gradually grasped that he was waiting for her permission to become her lover in the fullest sense.

She tugged on his hair, which he seemed to like. "Hardcastle?"

"My name is Gerard," he muttered, Ellen's earlobe between his teeth. "You even taste like lavender. When I put my mouth between your legs, will you taste of lavender there?"

Gracious heavens. "You would not dare."

He would, though. The reserved, sophisticated duke was nowhere in the bed. In his place was a lusty, lovely fellow who dared much and teased more.

"I can feel you blushing." Hardcastle sounded thoroughly pleased with himself as he shifted over her. "You have the most delectable ears, madam.

"Hard—Gerard, you've humored my maidenly vapors long enough. If I can't have you now, I will think you've had a change of heart."

His palm cradled the back of Ellen's head, and she pressed her heated cheek to his shoulder.

"Are you sure, Ellen?"

Now he asked that? Now, when she was so overwrought she was ready to bite him? But in this, he would be not the duke, but the gentleman, and the last piece of Ellen's heart not in his keeping slipped from her grasp.

"Now, please, Gerard."

Hardcastle braced himself on his elbows, a blanket of warmth and attentiveness. "I'll do this part, while you luxuriate in my desire and consideration, else I shall disgrace myself."

He was serious, also waiting for Ellen's acknowledgment of his pronouncement.

"I'm luxuriating, Hardcastle. You have my word on that."

"God knows, I'm desiring."

Despite that desire, he joined them slowly, with many lazy kisses, a detour here to draw on a nipple, a frolic there to nuzzle at Ellen's temple. She caught his rhythm, learned the tempo and phrasing of his passion, and of her own. Of discomfort, there was none, but along with a growing wonder, Ellen also suffered a yawning sense of loss.

Hardcastle's duchess would share this with him a thousand times, would hold him as passion crested higher and higher, would gather up the endearments lurking in his lectures and proclamations.

How could making love with him feel so blessedly, absolutely right, a long-awaited union of unlikely souls, a pleasure beyond description, and yet, all they would have was this short, drenching season of bliss, and then—

Hardcastle shifted, so he was more over Ellen, and that lined them up at a new angle, on a trajectory of sheer, mindless ecstasy. Ellen undulated into his thrusts, locked her ankles at the small of his back, and let desire pour into all the bleak questions and empty years ahead, let bliss have its long, lovely moment.

When Ellen could bear to ease her grip on him, Hardcastle was barely breathing hard, while she was panting in a near swoon.

"Now would also be an appropriate moment to luxuriate," he whispered, "for I assuredly am."

"If you move, Hardcastle, I will not answer for the consequences." Ellen would surely start crying, just as soon as she wrung herself out in his arms again.

"You move," he said, giving Ellen a lazy thrust that made her ears hum. "Play the color game. Close your eyes and see hues of passion, satisfaction, desire, and pleasure."

"I'd lose every round," Ellen whispered, smoothing a hand down Hardcastle's back to grab a muscular fundament. "For I cannot think, cannot form sentences."

"Splendid."

Splendid, indeed. Hardcastle drove her through the maelstrom again, and then once more, the last loving sweet and lazy and all the more wrenching for the deliberation with which he pleasured her. When Ellen could bear no more, he gently withdrew, stroked himself a few times, and spent his seed on her belly.

This consideration, this proof that Hardcastle would make no claim on Ellen's future, brought all the misery and loss to the fore, worse than ever because now, she knew what she'd be missing.

"I'll be back," he said, shifting off of her and tenting the covers over her middle. Water splashed against porcelain, shadows moved beyond the slivers of moonlight. Ellen bestirred herself to find her handkerchief on the night table and deal with Hardcastle's spent seed.

Already, practical reality intruded, though the temptation to cry would not leave her.

"Shall I fetch you a flannel?" Hardcastle asked from across the room.

"I used my handkerchief."

Then he was beside the bed, a looming presence. "This is clean." He put a damp cloth in her hand, then he waited by the bed, clearly expecting her to use the cloth and pass it back to him.

Intimacy upon intimacy, but Ellen liked that Hardcastle wasn't pulling on his breeches and preparing to leave her.

"Move over," he said, when the ablutions had been tended to all around. "Now comes the part where you talk to me, in which activity you have been woefully deficient thus far, Miss MacHugh."

Ellen shifted to the side, unsure if she was being scolded or teased. Hardcastle's embrace left no doubt that she was being held though. He cuddled himself around her from the back, his arm at her waist, his fingers linked with hers.

"What shall I talk about?" Ellen asked, despite the lump in her throat.

If he wanted to gossip about the house party guests, she'd muster some string of insightful observations. If he wanted to talk about Christopher, she'd manage that. They'd likely have to face each other over breakfast, after all. Small talk would be required then too.

"Tell me about home," he said, "about Derbyshire, for that's where you'll go in two weeks. It must be lovely, to call to you so strongly even after five years."

Ellen had been back in those five years. A governess was given leave, while a duke was not.

"Derbyshire is home, Hardcastle. My only sibling is there, my parents, my girlhood memories. I was happy there."

Also lonely, bewildered, and frequently invisible when Emily was in the room.

"Tell me your earliest memory. Mine was of my cat, Henry, bringing a mouse into the nursery. I thought it was capital of him to decimate the wildlife. The nursery maid climbed on a table and shrieked down the rafters."

Ellen couldn't tell Hardcastle her earliest memory, of Mama explaining that sisters always looked out for each other. She instead told him of the day she'd got her first book, a storybook with woodcuts of giants, dragons, unicorns, and princesses.

Every decent fairy tale had at least one princess. Governesses did not feature prominently in fairy tales, however.

Hardcastle excelled at cuddling, and the dratted man also had a way with a backrub, kneading Ellen's shoulders, then her hip, with a slow, confident touch that made her eyes heavy and her words difficult to find.

"Go to sleep, love," he murmured, kissing her shoulder. "You've had a long day, and we've many days yet ahead of us."

No, they didn't. They were down to twelve days now, and most of that time would be spent in polite company. Ellen closed her eyes, despite wanting to argue with her lover, and lost a final round of the color game.

She appointed herself the task of describing this encounter with Hardcastle, the tenderness and surprise of it, the pleasure and heartache. Colors would not come to her, descriptions eluded her, for no matter which way she viewed the past hour, or what aspect she focused on, all that Ellen could see was a single deep, abiding shade of love.

Chapter Four

HARDCASTLE WOKE EARLY, his body imbued with a sense of well-being in which his heart did not join. He'd left Ellen's bedroom deep in the night, unwilling to trouble her slumbers with more passion. He'd dreamed of East Anglia, a bleak and cheerless place the few times he'd visited, and he'd dreamed of Christopher.

Being a swain did not come to Hardcastle naturally, but as the morning wore on, he found that a capacity for stealth learned as a small boy was yet his. The household mail was apparently collected on a sideboard in the library, so—after sending a footman to inspect for unchaperoned females—to the library, Hardcastle did go.

"What the hell are you doing, going through my mail, Hardcastle?"

Sedgemere's question was friendly, for Sedgemere.

"Looking for a letter I might frank for Miss MacHugh," Hardcastle replied, seizing on the missive in question. Save for the direction, the epistle had no writing on the outside, much less crossed writing, and was addressed to Miss Emily MacHugh, Hollowell Grange, Swaddledale, Derbyshire.

"I frank all my guests' correspondence, as do you, Hardcastle," Sedgemere said, stalking closer. "Miss MacHugh isn't writing to a beau, is she?"

"To her sister." Even the address was printed in large letters, which made no sense.

Sedgemere snatched the epistle away. "I won't let you read her letter, Hardcastle. Not under any circumstances."

"I've already read enough of it," Hardcastle replied. *Very dear, in his way*, indeed. "Why would a woman pass up a tiara for a life of spinsterhood in Swaddledale? Where is Swaddledale, for that matter?"

Sedgemere put the letter back on top of the correspondence piled on the sideboard. "Not far south of Chesterfield. You could be there and back in less than a day, particularly if you changed horses."

"Oh, Your Graces!" Miss Pendleton stood at the library door, upon which she had not knocked. "I do beg your pardon. I thought to borrow a book until the kite flying begins. Perhaps His Grace of Hardcastle would assist me to find something to help a young lady while away a pretty morning?"

Assist her to find a fiancé, perhaps? Ellen had told Hardcastle exactly what to say in this very circumstance.

"I confess," Hardcastle replied, "I am not sufficiently familiar with His Grace's collection to be of any aid, and I have taken enough of Sedgemere's time. I wish you good day and successful kite flying."

He strode past Miss Pendleton, enjoying the consternation his comment caused.

The entire day followed the same pattern, with Hardcastle barely dodging enemy fire but for Ellen's company or guidance, until he was taken captive in the late afternoon by Miss Pendleton and her familiar, Miss Frobisher. They asked his aid choosing a suitable mount for the next day's outing to admire the lake at the Duke of Stoke Teversault's nearby estate.

By the time Hardcastle stole into Ellen's room that night, he was so hungry for her company he nearly dove straight onto the bed.

"Madam, good evening." Hardcastle had let himself into her bedroom and stood for a moment inside the door, beholding his beloved as she stared at a book before the fire. "What are you reading?"

She brushed a glance over him, and Hardcastle knew without a word being spoken, that something was amiss.

"Wordsworth," she said. "My sister Emily likes all the poems about lambs and daffodils, so I'm brushing up. You were very busy today."

Hardcastle locked the door and took the second chair facing the hearth. "I have renewed respect for those fellows who gathered intelligence for Wellington. A precarious existence lies behind enemy lines. Shall I kill Greenover for you?"

"Somebody ought to," she said, setting old Wordsworth aside. "He's a menace to the maids. The duchess now has them working in pairs to avoid his attentions."

Hardcastle nudged Ellen's slipper with the toe of his boot. "Were you avoiding my attentions this afternoon, Ellen? You were not gone from my side five minutes before the marital press gang descended."

She stared at the fire, which threw out some warmth without being a great blaze. "I cannot avoid you. You are in my every thought. I move to accept a plate from a footman, and my body reminds me of you in places a lady doesn't have names for. I brush my hair, and I feel your hands on my person. You have become an affliction for which I fear there is no cure."

"An affliction." Well, damn. He was apparently getting this swaining business all wrong.

Ellen swiped at her cheek with the backs of her fingers. "You are like the scent of roses on my favorite shawl, a sweet taste in my mouth. I did not anticipate—" She sighed mightily and tucked her foot under her. "Perhaps you'd better go, Your Grace. I seem to be in a lachrymose and difficult mood."

"You're always in a difficult mood. So am I. We like that about each other, but you're not usually irrational. Last night you called me Gerard, tonight I'm *dux non grata?*"

"Your Latin doesn't strike me—"

Hardcastle took her hand. "Talk to me, Ellen. Tell me about life as a girl in Upper Swaddlehog. Tell me about your parents, your sister, your first pony, your favorite book."

She rose, taking her hand from his grasp. "I am indisposed, *Gerard*. You needn't coax and charm me into bed, for it won't serve. I bid you good night."

Indisposed. Hardcastle knew what that meant. He'd been to university, he'd made the acquaintance of the women whose business was the education of the scholars in topics other than Latin or Greek.

"No charming or coaxing, then," he said, standing and scooping Ellen off her feet in one lithe move. "I'll simply deposit you on the bed and join you therein without further bumbling."

"Hardcastle! What are you—? Gerard!"

He was careful with her, settling her gently on the bed though the moment called for a hearty toss.

"A little insanity in my duchess will enliven the line considerably," he said, tugging off his boots. "And you have quite taken leave of your senses, madam, if you think my attentions are solely the result of animal spirits. Move over."

"Hardcastle, I cannot entertain you tonight," she groused, scooting an entire three inches toward the far side of the bed.

"You're entertaining me quite nicely, also ensuring that I get my exercise," he said, lifting her into his arms—mostly for the pleasure of holding her—then settling her two-thirds of the way across the bed. "If you need to use the privacy screen, I assure you, my delicate sensibilities won't be offended."

Well, this was amusing. Miss Ellen MacHugh, queen of the Hardcastle schoolroom and terror of twenty footmen, was gaping at him as he undressed. She'd propped herself on her elbows to have a better look, in fact, and hadn't even mentioned dousing the candles.

"Hardcastle, you are not paying attention."

No, but *she* was. "As if I could tear my attention from you, Miss MacHugh, when the livelong day I've been beset and beleaguered by your inferiors. Hounded from breakfast to brandy. Curls bouncing here, giggles twittering from over there, bosoms jiggling on all sides. Then they come at me in pairs."

"Bosoms generally do, Your Grace."

"My dear, do not mock a man clinging to reason by the slenderest thread. Get your night robe off, please."

Hardcastle pulled his shirt over his head and peeled out of his trousers. In the morning, his valet would cast martyred glances upon the resulting wrinkles, and Hardcastle *would not care.*

"Tell me about your indisposition," he said, taking the proffered night robe and hanging it on a bedpost.

"Tell me about the jiggling bosoms."

Ellen had stopped ordering him from the room, which was progress. Maybe he had potential as a swain after all. Hardcastle climbed naked under the covers.

"Nobody has used the bed warmer on these sheets," he observed. "How invigorating, as if present company were not stimulating enough. The bosoms were very pale and tended to quiver at me, like eager puppies straining to escape the bodices imprisoning them. We're not having daughters. I can assure you of this right now, my dear. My nerves will not endure such a trial."

"Hardcastle, calm yourself. We're having a liaison, or we were—we're not any longer—and children don't come into it."

Now Miss Ellen MacHugh was ordering matters on behalf of the Almighty, which even a duke knew was tempting fate.

Hardcastle rolled her to her side and wrapped himself around her. "Do you typically allow men with whom you're not having a liaison into your bed, madam?"

"I don't typically allow men anything, ever. But here you are."

Exactly where he wanted to be. "Why the tears, Ellen? Is it your indisposition? Her Grace, my grandmother, has offered a few choice sentiments regarding this indisposition. She doesn't approve of it."

"No woman does. What are you *doing* here, Hardcastle?"

"Settling my overwrought nerves, for one thing. A debutante who finishes her first Season without an offer of marriage is a ruthless, resourceful creature. Tomorrow you will do a better job of protecting me from them." He was settling Ellen's nerves too, he hoped. Stroking the tension from her neck and shoulders, easing anxiety from her fingers.

She shifted to her back. "We forgot to blow out the candles. Beeswax is very dear."

"So are you." Hardcastle got off the bed and did the honors, plunging the room into cozy shadows cast by the fire in the hearth. When he climbed back under the covers, he situated himself beside his intended, his cheek pillowed on her breast.

"What am I to do with you, Hardcastle? I cannot frolic with you, not tonight."

He'd mistaken Ellen's mood for stubborn, but a simpler explanation begged for his notice: She believed he had no use for her beyond the physical.

"You are to tell me stories, about Miss Ellen MacHugh, soon to be former governess. I'm sure the tales of Greater Goatswaddle are boring enough to put even an overwrought duke to sleep."

His arrogance must have been the reassurance she needed, for she launched into a story about picnics in the back garden, and Papa teasing Mama over breakfast, services on Sunday, and longing for a pony of her own.

Eventually, Ellen fell asleep, and Hardcastle stole from her room, intent on sticking to her side like a well-dressed cocklebur on the morrow. He had returned his clothing to the wardrobe and clothes press, and wedged a chair under his bedroom door when he figured out what about Ellen's recitation had bothered him.

Of puppies and kittens there had been numerous mentions, of Mama and Papa and the vicar and Mrs. Trimble, the housekeeper.

But she hadn't brought her sister's name up once.

⁕

FOR SEVEN NIGHTS, Hardcastle had come to Ellen's room, and he and she had developed a routine. She waited up for him, staring at poetry and wondering how on earth she'd manage when the house party ended.

He'd arrive, bristling with indignation at the latest attempt by some scheming young lady to compromise him, and Ellen would get him out of his clothes. As he shed waistcoat, cravat, shirt, and stockings, his mood would improve as well.

The prospect of losing one's liberty was terrifying. Ellen did not belittle the duke's worries in that regard at all.

She, however, had lost her heart, and at the worst possible time.

"Walk with me, Miss MacHugh," Hardcastle said, taking her elbow as she cut through the conservatory at midmorning. "Don't look over your shoulder. Hang on my every word, and I wouldn't mind if you put a bit of bosom into the conversation too."

"I have only a bit of bosom," Ellen retorted, keeping her attributes to herself. Hardcastle did this to her, made her bold and irritable. He could manage such a demeanor all in a day's duke-ing. On a governess quitting her post, the same mood came off as simply testy.

"Your treasures are abundant enough to drive me mad," Hardcastle said. "Though I'm already half insane. Sedgemere has decided we must go on a ducal progress, and sprinkle duke dust on all the local titles. In truth, Her Grace wants Sedgemere out of her hair for a day or two before the Dukeries Cup. I must oblige Sedgemere, or Anne will kill me. Consider yourself warned: Courtesy among ducal households can be a violent undertaking."

"You're leaving?" Ellen asked as they emerged onto the side terrace.

Hardcastle glanced around, and apparently heedless of who might be looking out of windows or lurking in the garden, kissed her cheek.

"Terrible timing for this outing, I know, my dear. You're no longer indisposed?"

Ellen shook her head. She was permanently disabled with longing for Hardcastle's company. Her indisposition had departed, however.

"Death is too good for Sedgemere," Hardcastle said. "I'll be back by tomorrow, the day after at the latest, and you will please be here when I return."

He'd be back the day before the house party ended. One day—most of that taken up with some silly boat race—followed by one night, after that and then... Derbyshire.

"I will be here," Ellen said. "You will lend me the ducal traveling coach for my journey to Derbyshire."

"Shall I? I've not been accused of generosity by many, Miss MacHugh."

Hardcastle was very generous, spending night after night with her, reading her poetry, regaling her with stories from public school and university. His passion was breathtaking, but this other—this simple, friendly intimacy—was devastatingly dear.

"You're generous, Hardcastle. Witness, you will not send Sedgemere calling without an ally at his side, so nobody will grasp that his duchess has banished him from his own house party."

He peered down at her. "You have the most peculiar notions. We'll take an earl or two with us, any viscounts sober enough to sit a horse or barons who've lost too much at the whist tables. The ladies will get some peace and quiet before the final ball, and the fellows who need to brush up their rowing skills can do that."

"I don't want peace and quiet," Ellen muttered as Hardcastle escorted her down the steps into the garden. "I want another week, at least, and you here, and—"

He wrapped her in his embrace, as if she were *allowed* to resent this parting, as if a part of him already belonged to her.

"Ellen, why won't you marry me?"

The question had cost him. Ellen was bundled in close, holding on to Hardcastle for dear life, and she could feel the pride and bewilderment in him.

"My family needs me," she said, which was true. "My parents are getting on, Christopher is ready for more rigorous instruction, and it's time. You must simply learn to avoid house parties, Your Grace."

His chin rested on her crown, so perfectly did they fit together.

"How would I have managed these past days without you, Ellen? You stayed with the Pendleton creature when she claimed to have turned her ankle. You put Greenover up to dancing with that forward redhead when she forged my name on her dance card. You sat next to me in every parlor where I might have found myself with a lapful of swooning debutante but for your vigilance."

This was the problem, right here. Hardcastle needed a duchess, any duchess, if he was to be spared more weeks of dodging and ducking his fate. Gratitude was not love, though, and passion was not love.

"You will enjoy this tour of the ducal neighbors," Ellen said. "Christopher will miss you."

"I ordered him to keep a close eye on you in my absence. He's having entirely too much fun with Sedgemere's ruffians, though."

All the more proof that Ellen was no longer needed in the ducal household. "I'll walk you to the stables, Your Grace."

He accepted that decision with ominous quiet and resumed their progress across the gardens.

"You will be here when I return, Ellen? No disappearing into the wilds of the Peak District, never to be seen again?"

"Not yet. That part comes at the end of the week, sir."

"The duchess in you allows you this calm. I wouldn't mind if you fell weeping on my neck, you know."

"You're welcome to fall weeping on mine, sir. I don't recommend it, though. Composure, like a reputation, is not easily regained once lost."

"More duchess-ing. Don't abandon me, Ellen. Be here when I return."

His Grace was, in his imperious and dear way, pleading.

They reached the stables, where the duke's horse stood patiently by a groom at the mounting block, and abruptly Ellen did want to fall weeping on Hardcastle's neck.

On his boots, even.

"I'll take the horse," the duke said to the groom, giving the girth a stout tug. When Ellen expected Hardcastle to swing into the saddle, he instead took Ellen by the hand and led the gelding off toward an enormous oak across the lane from the stable yard. "Madam, a moment of your time."

Ellen would never be able to refuse him anything, and grief made her reckless. "Hardcastle, perhaps it would be better if you didn't return before I leave."

"I see."

"What do you think you see?"

"I see that you are as stubborn as a duchess too. How many times must I propose to you? Your physical affection for my person has been evidenced convincingly, though on damnably few occasions. I don't think you object to my morals or even to my station. What deficiency must I address to win your hand?"

"You are not deficient, Hardcastle. You are in no way deficient, but my family needs me, and I've ignored them for too long. They love me, and they have no one else. You are fighting off prospective duchesses at every turn, but my family has only me."

Sedgemere came strutting down the garden path, his duchess twirling her parasol at his side. Before they could notice the couple in the shade of the oak, Ellen kissed Hardcastle as passionately as she dared when he was looking so thunderous.

Then she stepped back. "Safe journey, Your Grace."

"She makes no promises," the duke said to his gelding. "You will note, horse, that I am sent toddling on my way with no further reassurances of anything substantive, no real explanations, no apologies. I am a duke, though, so I shan't have a tantrum right here in the stable yard, such as *any governess* would know meant a fellow had finally been pushed too far."

"Your Grace, we have company."

Sedgemere was kissing his duchess farewell, rather shamelessly, or perhaps that was how a duke and duchess allowed a distraught guest a moment to gather her composure.

"We have company, and we are out of time," Hardcastle said. "Not even a duke can defy the dictates of time."

"I cannot deny the importuning of my family," Ellen said. "You understand duty, Hardcastle, and they are mine."

"I understand duty," he said, tapping his hat onto his head. "I do not understand you. If I'm not back in time for the Dukeries Cup, bet your pin money on Linton's boat."

He led his horse to the mounting block, swung up, and waited for Sedgemere to turn the duchess loose. Her Grace came to stand beside Ellen beneath the oak as Sedgemere's horse was brought out.

"They're a very handsome pair," Her Grace said.

"I prefer Hardcastle's darker coloring," Ellen said. "No offense to your husband."

"I meant the horses," the duchess replied. "Shall we sit by the duck pond for a moment, Miss MacHugh? I am not equal to dealing with the downcast expressions on the young ladies collectively grieving in my parlor."

There would be grieving by the duck pond, did the duchess but know it. "I am at your disposal, ma'am."

"Hardcastle has quite defied the efforts of the ladies to wrest a marriage proposal from him," the duchess observed. "You were instrumental in foiling their mischief."

"His Grace asked that of me, and I was happy to oblige."

They found their bench, and as before, a half dozen placid ducks paddled around on the pond's surface.

"You don't appear very happy now, Miss MacHugh. I apologize for sending some of the men away, but Mr. Greenover had lost more than he could afford to lose, and I could not allow the problem with the maids to worsen if I wanted my guests to sleep on clean sheets. Then too, you were not getting enough rest."

"I have never slept better, Your Grace." Never felt more safe and cared for than when sharing a bed with Hardcastle, though late night visits and cozy chats were not love.

"Miss MacHugh... May I call you Ellen?"

Oh, dear. A scold or condolences was loaded into the duchess's cannon, and either would be awful.

"Of course, ma'am."

"I am Anne, and you will think me very forward for what I'm about to say, but at night I send Sedgemere to make a final patrol of the hallways in the guest wing, and to do that, he traverses the family wing. Twice he spotted Hardcastle at your door. If you ask it of me, I will compel Hardcastle to offer for you. Sedgemere says I shouldn't, but he knows better than to expect meek complicity from me."

The ducks erupted into an altercation, with flapping and squawking and much splashing about where all had been calm a moment earlier.

"His Grace has proposed," Ellen said. "But I am needed elsewhere. He needs a wife of impeccable lineage and great consequence, while I... The very last thing I want is an offer of marriage compelled by propriety, exigencies, and ducal honor."

The ducks settled their differences, though turbulence echoed on the surface of the pond.

The duchess remained silent a moment, then fired off a broadside. "Do you love him, Ellen?"

"Endlessly, and I could not bear for Hardcastle's interest to cool in a year or two, while I'm left to console myself with his excellent manners for the rest of my life. If I marry Hardcastle, I'll trade a year of anxious bliss with him for all the years I owe my family, and be doubly miserable."

The ducks waddled onto the grass, their progress up the bank ungainly compared to their gliding about on the water. The lead duck raised his wings and flapped madly directly before Ellen, sending a shower of droplets all over her hems.

"Rotten boy," the duchess said, opening and closing her parasol at the duck. "Shoo, and don't come back."

Her Grace set her parasol aside, and there seemed nothing more to say, but one didn't hare off from the company of a duchess without being excused.

"Men are dunderheads, sometimes. Women are too," the duchess said. "We're like those ducks, taking odd notions for no apparent reason, our thoughts churning furiously while all appears serene above the surface. I cannot fault you for wanting to be loved for yourself. I put the same challenge to Sedgemere, and he figured out how to convince me of his regard. Hardcastle is no less determined and no less intelligent."

He was also no less a duke. Hardcastle wasn't the problem. "Shall we go in, Your Grace? I'm abruptly peckish, and I'd like to look in on Christopher."

"Oh, let's do repair to the nursery. We'll get up a cricket match with the infantry, and that will cheer the young ladies wonderfully."

No, it would not. Nothing would cheer the young ladies short of a decree from the Regent that dukes were allowed eleven wives apiece. Ellen soon found herself amid the noise and merriment of a cricket match anyway, though in Hardcastle's absence, all she wanted was to go up to her bedroom, lock the door, and start packing for the looming journey home.

❧

"I SAW YOU twice on my evening patrols, Hardcastle, and I wasn't even looking for you," Sedgemere announced as they brought their horses down to the walk. "Anne is ready to turn you over her knee, but I've counseled against such violence."

"Your duchess has a stout right arm, does she?"

"I presented her with three boys upon her marriage to me, Hardcastle. Everything about my Anne is made of stern stuff. Why haven't you secured Miss MacHugh's hand in marriage?"

The countryside was summer-ripe, the rise toward the Peak District visible off to the west, and yet every mile traveled was a greater distance from the woman

Hardcastle needed by his side. Ellen wasn't being entirely honest with him, and the urge to turn his horse around and gallop back to her became a greater torment with each passing moment.

"Hardcastle, I asked you a direct question using simple words. Your reply is to gaze off at the horizon looking noble and infatuated. Have you lost your wits?"

"Yes." And his heart.

Sedgemere let out a sigh of significantly longsuffering proportions. "Miss MacHugh turned you down?"

They were a good half mile ahead of the rest of the party, and privacy would be in short supply once they reached their destination.

"Ellen has refused my suit at least a half dozen times."

"Dear me, old boy. Appears you're bungling this rather badly."

Hardcastle mentally set aside the problem that was Ellen's stubbornness and focused instead on the problem that was the Duke of Sedgemere in a gleeful mood.

"Bungling should be easy for you to spot, Sedgemere, since you've done so much of it yourself," Hardcastle shot back. "I, however, am an utter tyro at the sport. Ellen says her family *needs* her, but I merely *want* a duchess, any duchess. I do believe my dearest love is trying to protect me."

This conviction grew the longer Hardcastle puzzled on the entire situation. Ellen's regard for him was genuine, of that he was certain. He cast back over three years of sidelong glances. Three years when his slightest sneeze or headache was met with an attentiveness from the staff he was sure she'd inspired.

Her regard for him had been right under his nose for years, and he'd failed to grasp that. He was similarly failing to grasp the obvious now.

"She's protecting you from *herself?*" Sedgemere said. "That makes no sense. Miss MacHugh is far better than you deserve."

And to think Sedgemere owed his present marital happiness to the patient good offices of a devoted friend and fellow duke.

"You're not helping, Sedgemere. A round of fisticuffs might restore my usual good cheer."

"Promises, promises. You have no good cheer, Hardcastle. Have you gone down on bended knee, done the pretty, delivered the maudlin speech?"

This was not good news. "A maudlin speech is required?"

Sedgemere tugged on his cravat and adjusted his hat. "You say the words, man. Ladies long to hear the words."

"I've asked Ellen to marry me in the King's English. No beating about the bush, no prevaricating—not after the first time—no dodging the issue. I've asked her as plainly as a man—if you are laughing, I will make you regret it, Sedgemere. I'm on quite good terms with your boys, one of whom is my god-son, and your estate is home to more toads than you can imagine."

"Anne is toad-proof. Put as many in our bed as you please."

"She has you in her bed. That's trial enough for any woman."

Sedgemere's smile faded to his characteristic glower. "Anne rather likes having me in her bed, I'll have you know. *Have you told Miss MacHugh that you love her?* That she is the only woman in the world for you? That no matter how little she brings to the union, no matter how much talk will result, your love is greater than any obstacle?"

"Sedgemere, have you been keeping company with Greenover?"

"As little as possible, why?"

"You have lost your wits. One doesn't make dramatic speeches to a woman of sense, as if one were any lack-wit viscount. One *shows* such a woman that she's loved. One cossets and cuddles, one reads poetry and rubs her feet. One spends time with the lady and opens his heart and his past to her. One doesn't..."

Maybe one did. Sedgemere was obnoxiously happy with his duchess, though she'd led him a dance all the way to the altar.

"Poetry, Hardcastle? You can recite Byron, but you can't say three little words?"

"Go to hell. That's three words."

"I suggest you try those with Miss MacHugh. That will enliven the house party considerably."

The words were easy—Hardcastle loved Ellen with all his heart—though his failure to give those words to her had been a dreadful oversight. She'd said her family loved her, told him that repeatedly, and he'd missed his cue every time.

Unease joined Hardcastle in the saddle. "Sedgemere, what do you know of Miss MacHugh's family?"

"She's granddaughter of the Earl of Dalton. Her aunt and Anne have a passing acquaintance. There's another daughter, but no sons."

"That's all?" Sedgemere was one of those troublesome people who never forgot anything. Not a horse's bloodline, not an article in the newspaper, not a speech in the Lords. "These people own land less than a day's ride from your family seat, and you know nothing more than that about them?"

"Does seem odd, doesn't it?" Sedgemere said. "Even if they can't afford to entertain, we'd see them at the occasional hunt ball or Christmas musicale."

A hunch blossomed into a suspicion in Hardcastle's mind. "You will make my excuses to whichever duke we're imposing on for the night. I have pressing business elsewhere." He wheeled his horse around and headed at a gallop back toward the last crossroads.

Chapter Five

"THOSE WHO WERE off visiting or enjoying the Dukeries Cup will be back in good time for tonight's gathering," the duchess assured Ellen. "Sedgemere has sent me no less than three notes confirming this scheduling, and I would sorely regret it if my duke's word were no longer trustworthy."

Ellen paced the length of the duchess's private sitting room, until she was at the window overlooking the drive.

"Sedgemere said nothing about Hardcastle needing the ducal traveling coach?" This vehicle had not been in the mews when Ellen had visited the stables with Christopher earlier in the day.

"Sedgemere did not mention the coach," Her Grace replied, sticking a finger into a bowl of white roses on the mantel. "Perhaps somebody was concerned about the possibility of rain, or a horse came up lame. Please do sit down, Ellen. You're making me dizzy with your peregrinations."

Her Grace shook droplets of water from her finger, and gave the bowl a quarter turn.

Ellen perched on the very edge of a pink velvet sofa, for one did not ignore a duchess's requests. Had Hardcastle been injured, that he'd sent for the coach? Had he decided to leave for Kent from one of the ducal residences he'd visited? How was Christopher to get home, and how was Ellen to return to her family?

"You are beyond hope," the duchess said, crossing her arms. "If you simply pressed your nose to the window glass and occasionally thumped a hopeful tail on my carpets, your sentiments could not be more transparent. I do not understand why you refused Hardcastle, if he's so very dear to you."

Ellen didn't bother pouring herself a cup of tea she'd neither taste nor enjoy. "I refused His Grace for two reasons. First, he deserves a wife whom he loves, deeply, madly, passionately, not simply a woman who's familiar to him, attractive, and useful for fending off debutantes."

This reasoning sounded tired to Ellen's own ears. This excuse. Hardcastle hadn't been much impressed with it either.

The duchess took a seat across from Ellen, her expression disgruntled. "A duke is not in the habit of yielding to mad passion, Ellen. He's a creature of duty and restraint."

No, he wasn't. Not under all circumstances. At times, he could be a creature of mindless pleasures and endless desire, a creature of genial good company and generous affection.

"A duke is but a man," Ellen quoted. "Sedgemere has told you he loves you, I'd guess. Told you he can't live without you, and no other woman could possibly be his duchess. Sedgemere's highest compliment is not that you've saved him from the clutches of the jiggling horde."

Her Grace gazed at the roses, one of which had dropped a few pale petals on the mantel. "Sedgemere has a surprisingly effusive streak," she said, rising to gather up the dropped petals and toss them into the unlit hearth. "Did Hardcastle use that term? Jiggling horde?"

"Several times, Your Grace." Ellen rose as well, because sitting still and staring down the maddeningly empty drive was impossible. "This house party opened his eyes to his own marriageability, and he panicked, in as much as Hardcastle can panic."

"Or he was brought to his senses," the duchess said. "He's besotted with you. I saw that parting kiss, Ellen MacHugh, and that was not the kiss of an indifferent man."

"That was not the kiss of an indifferent woman, Your Grace." Ellen had already established that Hardcastle had not gone directly to the boat race, as several other gentlemen had. "The more compelling reason I cannot marry Hardcastle is that I am needed elsewhere. My family needs me, and His Grace simply wants me. I want him too—desperately—but one has a duty."

"Oh, duty," the duchess said, taking a place beside Ellen at the window. "Yes, duty is a great comfort, when one is old and sore in the joints and can't find one's spectacles. A fine liniment for the conscience, is duty. What of joy? What of love, Miss MacHugh? You accuse Hardcastle of caring too little for you, but do you care for duty too much?"

The duchess's tone was nearly bitter, as if somebody might have presented her with the same choice, between her heart's desire and inevitable obligation.

"There's your duke now," the duchess said, as a rider on a dark horse came into view. "I recognize his gelding. You'll want to take tea with him in his sitting room, though a proper duchess could never endorse such impropriety. The tray will be in his room in five minutes. A woman who loved him would be there in six."

His Grace galloped up the drive, man and horse a single flowing unit of grace and power that left Ellen's heart pounding in rhythm with the tattoo of hoof beats.

"The other young ladies are in the conservatory resting after the day's earlier festivities," the duchess said. "They won't know he's back. Upstairs with you, and if you'll take a word of advice, Miss MacHugh?"

Ellen was half way to the door, but paused when everything in her wanted to race up the stairs to the duke's rooms.

"You might have given Hardcastle your heart and your intimate favors, but you must also give him your trust. That last can be harder than the other two put together, but without trust, a marriage is doomed. Now, away with you, and I'll be sure the young ladies remain occupied until Hardcastle can join you."

Ellen fairly flew from the parlor, though in the past two weeks, she hadn't set foot in Hardcastle's rooms. She knew where they were though, a mere four doors down from her own and across the corridor.

She was waiting by the hearth, the silver tea service gleaming on the sideboard, when Hardcastle came through the door, his jacket already off and his riding gloves bunched in his hand.

The door swung shut behind him. "Miss MacHugh."

Ellen slammed into him and wrapped her arms around him. "I thought you'd gone home to Kent."

"You are my home."

Then Ellen found herself in the ducal bedroom, Hardcastle's nimble fingers undoing her hooks between passionate kisses and her own efforts to divest him of his clothes.

"I missed you," she said. "Missed you awfully." She had to let Hardcastle go while he tugged his boots off, and she allowed him to remove his shirt, then she pushed him back onto the bed and attacked his falls.

Hardcastle's palm cradled her cheek. "My dear, your enthusiasm flatters me no end, but there are matters we must discuss."

"Discuss later, Hardcastle," she said, drawing his aroused length from his clothes.

"I've prepared a speech for this moment, madam. Short but impressively maudlin. I thought I'd blush to deliver it, but now I find I want to give you these words."

Ellen swung a leg over his hips and tossed her chemise onto the nearest chair. "Give me the deeds, Hardcastle. The words can wait." Especially maudlin words that likely dripped with parting sentiments, tender regrets, and swain-ly blather. "I have words for you too, words of explanation, because I owe you that much."

"I'll listen. I will always listen to you, Ellen."

So with her hands, with her kisses, with her body, Ellen told Hardcastle she loved him, and she did not want to leave him, ever. She told him how very much he meant to her, how dear her memories of him would be, how much she longed to choose pleasure over duty.

Hardcastle's response was tenderness itself as he joined them.

"You thought I could leave you?" he whispered as he gently pushed his way inside her. "You thought I could saddle up my ducal consequence, turn my back on you, trot out smartly for Kent, without a word of farewell?"

"I can't think," Ellen replied, undulating into the sheer bliss of their union. "I thought I could leave you, but—"

He surged forward, obliterating words, thoughts, logic, resistance of any type. Ellen met him, measure for measure, until she realized Hardcastle was waiting for her to surrender to their joining, waiting for her to capitulate to desire.

"I love you," she whispered, as satisfaction dragged her under. "I will always love you."

"And I love you."

Hardcastle's words struck Ellen's heart like hammer blows, bringing both pain and freedom, as a smith's hammer strikes shackles from a pardoned convict.

The pleasure was terrible in its depth and duration, a whirling black torrent that left Ellen dizzy and panting in Hardcastle's arms. His breath came hot against her neck, her heartbeat thundered against her ribs.

And then... quiet. A breeze stirred the curtain. Laughter drifted up from the lawn. A plain, brown wren lit on the windowsill, then darted away.

Hardcastle was a heavy comfort over Ellen, and sleep tugged at her awareness.

"Wore you out, b'gad," he muttered, lifting up enough to let cool air wash over Ellen's belly. "Maybe you did miss me."

"Terribly. Horribly. Wonderfully."

"Addled your wits too, apparently," he said, crouching up and nuzzling at Ellen's breasts. "I like you muddled and rosy. Addled and drowsy. You'd best get used to it."

"Hardcastle, we must talk."

He sighed a great, bodily testament to male patience. "If you insist, but you will cease reminding me of your plans to abandon me and Christopher, the two fellows who love you most in the world."

"You have learned a new word," Ellen said, running her fingers through his hair. "You'll use it indiscriminately, like a fashionable French phrase making the rounds of the ballrooms."

He glowered at her, than glanced at the clock on the mantel. "Ballrooms, bah. This evening will be interminable. You will save all your waltzes for me."

"Of course, Your Grace."

He slipped from her body, kissed her forehead, then prowled across the room to the privacy screen. In broad daylight, Hardcastle was a sumptuous argument against clothing, against allowing the sun to ever drop below the horizon.

Except he was breathtaking by candlelight too.

"Shall I tend to you?" he asked, sauntering over to the bed with a damp flannel in his hand.

Ellen snatched the cloth from him and only then realized he had spent his seed without withdrawing. Her Grace's lecture about trust popped into Ellen's mind as she got off the bed and made use of the privacy screen. Let Hardcastle look at her in the afternoon sunlight, let him memorize the sight of her as God made her.

And Ellen would trust her duke with even more than that.

"Is the door locked?" she asked.

"Holy jiggling debutantes," His Grace muttered, marching into the sitting room and locking that door, then returning to lock the bedroom door. "The drawbridge has been raised, the arrow slits manned. Now into bed with you."

"With you too, sir."

With his hair sticking up wildly, not a stitch of finery upon him, the duke of Hardcastle bowed and gestured to the rumpled bed.

"Your servant, madam."

Ellen snatched a green paisley silk dressing gown off the bedpost and shrugged into it. The fabric was cool and redolent of Hardcastle's scent—also roughly the dimensions of Her Grace's back terrace. Climbing onto the bed was an undignified undertaking, and that was before Hardcastle wrestled Ellen to his side.

"You mentioned talking," he said, kissing her shoulder. "Talking is not your greatest strength, Miss MacHugh, but I will marshal my patience and endure your conversation nonetheless."

"Much obliged, Your Grace. I have a family."

That put an end to Hardcastle's kissing and nuzzling and petting. "Go on."

"A small family," Ellen said. "My parents, my sister, and me. We're rural gentry, and when the harvest is bad, we're impoverished rural gentry. I've sent my wages home, where they've been put to good use."

"One would expect no less selflessness of a future duchess."

Ellen hit him with a pillow, then settled back against his side. "I can't be your duchess. I must be my sister's governess. My parents have had that job too long as it is."

"This would be your twin sister, Emily?"

The caution in his voice cut deeply, but Ellen had decided to trust him. Not to marry him—he'd realize that soon enough—but to trust him.

"Emily, yes. My younger twin sister. I took too long to be born, and Emily wasn't breathing when she emerged from the womb. The midwife was able to revive her, but before we were a year old, it became apparent that Emily was not entirely thriving."

"You did not take too long to be born, and I'll thrash anybody who says otherwise. Your sister is physically impaired?"

Impaired. Such a tactful word for a condition that was not of Emily's making, but created endless burdens for her and the people around her.

"Physically, Emily is quite robust. Intellectually, she is... limited. She can read some, she can play the piano a very, very little. Her embroidery is excellent, but her reasoning powers are those of a permanent innocent. She needs me."

Hardcastle flopped about, and Ellen prepared herself to be left alone in the bed. Instead, he gently shoved her to her side and wrapped himself around her.

"The rest isn't difficult to figure out," he said. "Emily is very pretty and perilously friendly. All the reserve and self-restraint you've known from childhood is foreign to her nature. She is charming, despite or perhaps because of, her lack of accomplishments."

Hardcastle grasped the situation more quickly than most did. To appearances, Emily was simply a pretty young woman, one well blessed with health and looks. She could manage pleasantries, she could behave appropriately at church services, but then in the churchyard...

"She likes to climb trees," Ellen said. "In broad daylight. She'll have her bonnet off and her skirts hiked before you can stop her. She laughs too loudly, and she—"

"Kisses boys," Hardcastle said. "Or men. You slipped, Ellen. You claimed to have fled into service because you were caught kissing a fellow, then you informed me I was the first man to kiss you. Emily was the one sharing her favors, wasn't she?"

He'd caught Ellen in the lie that others, her own neighbors, her own pastor, hadn't questioned. "Emily was very fond of this fellow, and I think he was honestly fond of her."

"The road to hell is paved with fondness. I also saw that you printed your letters to her."

Ellen could detect no tensing in Hardcastle, no withdrawing. "I lied to you, Hardcastle."

"You gave me your first kiss, Miss MacHugh. You've given me all your kisses, in fact."

His smugness was like another species of kiss, a soft, comforting warmth pressed to Ellen's heart. Dissembling in the interests of protecting family was expected behavior from his perspective.

How like a duke. How like this duke.

"The fellow who tempted Emily so badly before has moved back to Swaddledale," Ellen said, "and my parents need me at home. They're aging, and my years in service have been an embarrassment to them."

A ducal toe ran up the back of Ellen's calf. "They consider your status in *my* household an embarrassment?"

Hardcastle would get along with Papa very well, were they ever to meet. "My parents are proud, Your Grace. Emily's situation has been a trial since her birth, though they love her fiercely."

"I'm of the belief that daughters are a trial to any parents. Sons too, most likely. So I'm to send you back to Derbyshire, allow you to ensure the domestic tranquility in Mideast Hogwash, and protect your sister from the attentions of the dashing swains?"

Ellen drove her elbow back into Hardcastle's belly as she rearranged herself on her back. "Don't ridicule my family, Your Grace. Emily has apologized for her behavior and she tries very hard to be good. She was passionately attracted to Mr. Trentwich though."

"Passion must run in the family." Hardcastle shifted over Ellen, and abruptly, she was gazing into his eyes, where not a hint of levity shone. "Do you trust me, Ellen?"

"I've just told you my every deepest, darkest secret Hardcastle. You see why I must return home now? You need a duchess, not a squire's daughter with an addled sister. Let the gossips get hold of that, and the talk would never cease."

Hardcastle kissed Ellen for a while, as if he needed time to choose his words and sort options. Ellen kissed him back because she loved him, and loved kissing him.

"If you trust me, madam, then all will come right. I promise you this. Hadn't you better scamper along now and start primping for the evening gathering?"

Ellen would rather kiss Hardcastle some more. The entertainments would go on until all hours, and this might be the last private moment she had with him.

"I do not primp, Hardcastle. Come tomorrow morning, you'll send me home in the ducal coach, and there's an end to it."

"You'll make a very fine duchess," he said, settling closer. "Giving orders, making pronouncements, telling a duke how matters in his own life will unfold. Your imperious demeanor makes me amorous."

Ellen lifted her hips and met... evidence of the duke's veracity. "Simply being around you makes me amorous. I will miss you terribly."

That was the last thing she said before joining the duke in shared amorous activities, but that evening, as Ellen donned a lovely green ball gown lent to her by the duchess, a thought intruded:

Hardcastle had mentioned a prepared speech, a maudlin prepared speech, and he'd not delivered that speech. Whatever the sentiments—of parting, true love, regret?—they apparently no longer signified.

Now that Ellen had confided her situation to him, perhaps they never would.

※

"IF YOU LOOK any more fierce, even the intrepid Miss Pendleton will banish you from her dance card," Sedgemere muttered beneath the trilling of the violins.

"If I look any less fierce," Hardcastle replied, "she'll knock me over the head and drag me to her room. This house party has not gone as the mamas and debutantes planned."

"The house party has gone as Anne planned," Sedgemere said, beaming a smile across the dance floor at his duchess. "The Dukeries Cup made for some excitement today, and now we'll round out the gathering with a nice, boring ball. My duchess is very much in charity with her duke."

"For God's sake, Sedgemere. Have some dignity." The receiving line had disbanded, and yet, not all the guests had arrived. Hardcastle's own dignity was imperiled by that fact alone.

A footman sidled up to Sedgemere. "Late arrivals, Your Grace of Sedgemere. They asked that His Grace of Hardcastle be notified."

Relief coursed through Hardcastle. "I'll tend to the new arrivals. Sedgemere, keep an eye on Miss MacHugh, and do not allow Greenover within twenty paces of her."

Sedgemere offered an ironic formal bow, and Hardcastle followed the footman up the stairs to the entrance hall.

"We're here!" Miss Emily MacHugh said, bouncing on her toes. "You told us to come, and we're here!"

In her pale green ball gown, she was charm personified, not an ounce of guile in her, and thus Hardcastle deviated from protocol and bowed over her hand before greeting her parents.

"I am exceedingly glad to see you," he said, "and I know your sister will be too. The first waltz will start in a very few minutes. Do you recall what we talked about, Miss Emily?"

Emily was taller than Ellen, but she had Ellen's perfect complexion, also the *joie de vivre* Ellen kept hidden under most circumstances.

"I recall, sir. I've been practicing with Papa." She winked at Hardcastle, a slow, solemn undertaking that boded well for the rest of the evening. "Come along, Duke. I'll show you."

Sedgemere had positioned himself at Ellen's elbow, and when the orchestra had brought its delicate minuet to a final cadence, the herald thumped his staff to announce the latest arrivals.

From the top of the stairs, Hardcastle watched Ellen start forward, only to be checked by Sedgemere's hand on her arm. She was delectably attired in dark green velvet, and Hardcastle had reason to know the décolletage, though quite flattering, would reveal not a single additional freckle.

Perhaps that might change in future.

Emily tugged at his arm. "There's Ellen! There's my Ellen!" She waved enthusiastically, and Ellen waved back, more slowly.

Hardcastle waved at Ellen too, then Sedgemere returned the gesture, as did the Duchess of Sedgemere from her corner of the ballroom, and all around the ballroom, curious glances were exchanged.

"Shall we dance, Miss Emily?" Hardcastle asked. "I've been looking forward to this waltz since we parted earlier today."

"So have I! Will Ellen dance? Is that your duke friend who looks like Wotan? I have a storybook about Wotan and Thor and their friends. They weren't always nice. Loki was a rotter sometimes, but I like him too."

Emily MacHugh was exhausting in her chatter, in her mental nimbleness, in her artless observations, and she was very, very dear.

"Do you hear the orchestra, Miss Emily?"

She stopped dead at the foot of the steps and cocked her head, her parents pausing three steps up.

"Yes. I can't wait! I've waltzed before, at the assemblies, with the vicar or Papa. You are handsomer than they are, but I should not have said that."

"We'll let that be our secret," Hardcastle said. "May I have the honor of this dance, Miss Emily?"

She composed herself, though Hardcastle could feel the effort that required as she sank into a lovely curtsey.

"Sir, I would be honored." Then she bounced up and grabbed his hand. "Did I do that right? When can I talk to Ellen? I will hug her so hard she'll burst, and we'll laugh, and then she'll cry, and I'll hug her all over again."

"She'll hug you back, I'm sure," Hardcastle said. "As soon as this dance is over, you must hug her as hard as ever you can."

Emily let him lead her to the dance floor, while Sedgemere appropriated the same honor from Ellen. She shot Hardcastle incredulous, wondering glances, which he hoped meant he'd guessed correctly.

The music started, and within sixteen bars, Emily was trying to lead, laughing, stepping on Hardcastle's toes, then laughing some more. The hours he'd spent twirling her around her mother's music room had been a pointless undertaking, for no amount of patient instruction could have curbed her exuberance.

"The music will soon end," Hardcastle murmured, several athletic minutes later. "Do you recall what comes next?"

"You bow, I curtsey, and *then* we get some punch, which I must not spill on *anybody*, and I must only sip, *delicately*, like a bird at the fountain in the garden. I want to talk to Ellen first. She'll think I'm vexed with her, but I'm not. I never could be."

"Neither could I. What say we meet her at the punchbowl?"

"I like that idea. I like you. No wonder Ellen has let you be her friend. You're very sweet."

Hardcastle bowed. "As are you, Miss Emily."

She sank into another curtsey, though this time Hardcastle was ready for her when she shot to her feet and grabbed his arm.

"Ellen!" she shouted. "Meet us at the punchbowl! Bring your duke, and I'll bring mine!"

The ballroom grew momentarily quiet, until the Duchess of Sedgemere called out, "Save a glass for me!"

"For me as well!" the Duchess of Oxthorpe called, only to be echoed by the Duchess of Linton.

A hundred conversations broke out as Emily dragged Hardcastle to the punchbowl, then flew from his side into Ellen's arms.

"Oh, Ellie, I have missed you so. I have missed and missed and missed you!"

"I've missed you too, Em," Ellen said, blinking madly and hugging her sister back. "You look very pretty."

"I look all grown up," Emily said, stepping back and holding her skirts out as she twirled. "I know how to waltz. Did you see me? Hardcastle taught me this morning. He's very serious, but I like him."

"You like everybody," Ellen said, snatching another brief, tight hug. "I like Hardcastle too."

"Perhaps you'd introduce us, Miss MacHugh," the Duchess of Sedgemere said. "Miss Emily is our guest, after all."

At Hardcastle's request, Sedgemere and his duchess personally took Emily around and introduced her to half the Midlands nobility.

"I don't know whether to hug you, or smack you," Ellen said. "What could you be about, Hardcastle? Emily will think she's making friends, and instead, she'll be a laughingstock."

"No, she will not," Hardcastle said. "I've enlisted the aid of the duchesses, and they are very pleased to ensure Emily will have an enjoyable evening. She will be an original, you see, and you will be my duchess."

Emily made a lovely bow before the Dowager Duchess of Alnwitter, who then laughed heartily at something Emily said.

"You sent the coach for my family, didn't you?" Ellen asked. "You invited them in person and then made sure Emily would have a partner for the waltz."

"Are you listing my transgressions, Ellen, or reconstructing my day? If the latter, you've stopped short of the best part."

The first violinist of the little orchestra had resumed his seat and was tapping his bow on his music stand.

"The part where I welcomed you back," Ellen said, while across the ballroom Mr. Greenover, sober for once, bowed over Emily's hand.

"That was lovely too, but rather than refer to an aspect of my schedule best left private, I allude instead to what follows now. Come with me, if you please."

Hardcastle left Ellen no choice, tugging her out onto the dance floor.

"Your Grace, I'd rather keep an eye on Emily."

"I'd rather you let your sister enjoy herself, and let the duchesses enjoy themselves. Now pay heed, my dear, for you won't often see the spectacle you're about to behold. And mind you, I've already spoken with your parents, and matters regarding any settlements are quite well in hand."

"Settlements?"

Hardcastle untangled their arms and went down on one knee. He waited, because Ellen deserved for everybody to hear what he'd say to her. Within moments, a circle had formed around them, and quiet descended.

"Ellen MacHugh, dearest lady of my heart, will you make me the happiest duke in the realm—even happier than that strutting jackanapes, mine host, His Grace of Sedgemere—the happiest of all men, and accept my proposal of marriage? I will have no other but you, for you are the home my heart has longed for, the mother I would have for my children, and the wife I would have ever at my side. I love you, I need you. Please marry me, Ellen."

"Say yes, Ellie!" Emily bellowed, and the chant was taken up by the duchesses, and then by the entire crowd.

"Hardcastle, you'd best get up," Ellen muttered. "I assume you've already hired a companion for Emily?"

He sprang to his feet. "Not yet, because she'll live with us, though I expect your parents will want to visit frequently, and you and Emily will interview appropriate candidates. I'll warn the footmen about her propensity for kissing handsome men, but I don't expect them to be saints. The MacHugh women are formidable creatures."

The shouting and clapping were dying down, but Hardcastle's heart was thumping as hard if he'd just rowed to victory in the Dukeries Cup.

"You don't look happy," he said. "I have overstepped, I know, but you were determined to leave me, and I cannot very well be the Duke of Lesser Swaddlepie, now can I? Will you be my wife, Ellen, not simply my duchess—for you're right, prospective duchesses are thick on the ground—but my wife, my love, the mother of my children, and the only lady for me?"

Damnation. He'd made her cry. That couldn't be a good thing.

"Of course, I'll be your wife," Ellen said, pitching herself against him. "And you will be my husband, and my love, and the father of my children, and if you absolutely must, you shall be my duke too."

She kissed him, right in the middle of the ballroom, kissed him resoundingly and for such a protracted period that even the debutantes and drunken viscounts would realize the Duke and Duchess of Hardcastle were a love match.

When Ellen let Hardcastle up for air, Sedgemere called for a toast to the newly engaged couple and a betrothal waltz. In the minstrel's gallery, from among Sedgemere's three ruffians, Christopher sent a thumbs up, while Emily, laughing hugely, dragged a dazed Mr. Greenover onto the dance floor.

"I do love you," Ellen said, as Hardcastle offered his hand. "You didn't have to do this. A simple 'Will you marry me? I promise to provide for your sister' would have done."

Hardcastle bowed, Ellen curtseyed. A commotion at the other end of the ballroom suggested Emily was explaining to Mr. Greenover who would lead whom for the duration of the dance, or perhaps simply for the duration.

"I tried asking you to marry me, tried ordering you to marry me," Hardcastle said as he drew his prospective duchess into a cozy version of waltz position. "That left only begging, but a fellow likes to ensure the odds are in his favor if he's to make a spectacle of himself; hence, I paid a small call on your family. I did not want you to worry."

"I think we should be worried about Mr. Greenover."

The music started, Mr. Greenover yelped, Hardcastle leaned closer to his beloved. "I think we should be worried about sneaking out of the ballroom at the end of this set and repairing above stairs to celebrate our betrothal."

Ellen appeared to consider that suggestion as Hardcastle turned her down the room. She looked every inch a duchess tonight, regal, lovely, and *all his*.

"I have a better idea," she said. "Sneak me out of the ballroom *now*, Hardcastle."

"In this, as in all things, I will be pleased to heed my duchess's guidance."

Hardcastle twirled her down to the French doors, danced her out into the cool night air, and happily ever after, Ellen danced in the arms of her beloved duke.

Waiting for a Duke Like You

BY
Shana Galen

Acknowledgements

Thanks to my friend Gayle Cochrane for her help with Nathan and Vivienne. And thanks to my co-authors, who challenge me and inspire me.

Chapter One

VIVIENNE STUMBLED INTO the clearing and fell to her knees. The wet grass soaked through her skirts, but she barely noticed. Darkness still shrouded what she imagined in the sunlight were rolling green hills and manicured lawns.

Daylight was long, terror-filled hours away.

And she was so very, very tired.

She'd been running all night, running and hiding. She couldn't afford rest. The assassins were right behind her, hunting her. But for that hollow under the tree in the woods, they would have her now. She could not pause, not even for a moment.

She needed water. Her throat felt coated with sand, and it took effort to swallow. Since Masson had been murdered, she'd been constantly hungry and thirsty. She'd come this way because she thought she smelled water, and now looking out over the lawn that sloped down from the woods, she spotted a small pond with a charming bridge crossing it. The pond was not big enough to warrant a bridge, but it was probably an idea one of the British nobles had liked and commissioned. These nobles had more money than they knew what to do with.

Once, she had been the same.

Looking left and right before moving farther into the clearing, Vivienne made her way toward the pond. She had to restrain the urge to rush to the water and gulp great handfuls as soon as she reached the bank. Instead, she circled the pond until she faced the woods and her back was to the bridge. The shadows cast by the bridge in the weak light from the crescent moon would hide her, shield her, give her a moment to recover her strength.

With a last look at the woods, she removed her quiver and bow, set them against the bridge. She knelt and cupped the cool water, sniffing it and then drinking. She cupped more water, drinking and drinking until her previously empty belly roiled. Splashing water on her face, her arms, she rinsed some of the mud from her skin. Vivienne had hidden in a pigpen most of the day, and though the sow and her piglets had not seemed to mind her company, she was eager to leave reminders of the pigs behind.

She leaned against the bridge, bracing her weary body against the smooth, round stones. She'd been safe hidden under the pig muck. It wasn't until she'd tried to sneak away from the farm that the assassins had spotted her and come after her. Vivienne harbored no illusions that if the three men had caught her they'd leave her alive. They'd slit her throat just as they'd slit Masson's.

Poor Masson, she thought, closing her eyes against the sting of tears. He'd given everything he had to save her. She would not diminish his sacrifice by failing now. She had to reach London and the king. How far was Nottinghamshire from London? Hours? Days?

At the moment, London seemed as far away as the moon.

She leaned her head back, eyes still closed. She would rise in a moment. She would keep moving south, south toward London. She would not rest until she reached the capital. She...

Vivienne slept.

✿

NATHAN CAULEY, THE Duke of Wyndover, swirled the port in his glass. "I already have more money than I need. What I don't have is an heir. How I envy Hardcastle that nephew of his. Why can't I find a nephew and heir? Instead, I've a cousin in the bloody Americas. My mother is on the verge of faking her collapse in order to hurry me along."

His host for the house party, the Duke of Sedgemere smiled. "There are worse things than matrimony, Nat."

"Says the man already leg-shackled. Besides, Elias, your duchess is one in ten thousand. Where am I to find a lady like her?"

"Do you know what your problem is?"

Wyndover drained the last of his port. "I'm sure you will tell me."

"You've had it too easy. You're a duke, and not just a duke, a young duke. Add that pretty face to the package, and the ladies faint at your feet. All you need do is crook your finger."

"I object."

"On what grounds?"

"I have never crooked a finger at a lady."

Elias inclined his head, conceding the point. "My argument still stands. You have never had to woo a woman, never had to work to make one take notice of you."

"And *you* have? You're a bloody duke too, you know."

"If you think Anne merely fell into my arms, you don't know her very well. She led me on a merry chase, and I'm a better man for it."

"I'm too busy for chasing. Love and all that rot is fine for the likes of you, Elias, but I have estates to manage, solicitors at my door, stewards with rapidly multiplying rabbits."

"Rabbits?"

Wyndover waved a hand. "I need an heir, not romance."

"Then you haven't found the right woman yet. When you do, you'll welcome both the romance and the chase. You wouldn't have it any other way."

Nathan shook his head, but Elias did not stay to hear his protest. He stood. "I see Greenover is retiring for the night. There was an incident with a maid earlier. I think I'll make sure he finds his room without incident. I shall see you bright and early for the scavenger hunt, Nat."

Nathan gave his old friend a pained expression. "Scavenger hunt? Will your bride be very offended if I pass?"

"Try it and I'll call you out," Sedgemere said in a tone Nathan thought only half joking. "This is her hostessing debut. You will cheerfully attend every single event and activity, be it archery, embroidery, ices in the garden, or a scavenger hunt."

"Embroidery?"

"Be there with needle and thread."

Nathan gave a mock salute and watched his old school chum follow the lecherous Greenover out of the Billiards Room. If he'd been an intelligent man, he too would have sought his bed. Instead, Nathan poured another glass of port and settled back to watch Viscount Ormandsley lose yet another game of billiards.

The next morning came too early, and despite his tacit agreement with Sedgemere to act the dutiful guest, he was late for the start of the scavenger hunt. By the time he made it to the breakfast room, the other guests had already departed, all but a Miss MacHugh. He relaxed when he saw her. She had not fainted at his feet upon meeting him the day before. The same could not be said of two other ladies at the party—a Miss Frobisher and a Miss Pendleton. Miss MacHugh, however, had not seemed particularly impressed by him, but then he'd seen her gaze slide to the Duke of Hardcastle one too many times.

Best he left Miss MacHugh to find her own amusements this morning.

He exchanged pleasantries with her, then made his way to the drawing room to ask after the rest of the party. The butler informed him they'd already embarked on the scavenger hunt and handed him a sheet of foolscap on which had been listed a number of items he was to acquire.

"They have not been gone long, Your Grace," the butler said. "I am certain you will have no trouble catching up to one party or another and joining their ranks."

But that was the trick, Nathan decided. If he accidentally encountered the Frobisher-Pendleton party, he'd be stuck catching fainting ladies all morning and afternoon. He scanned the first items listed on the paper. A horseshoe, a feather, a pink rose, a smooth round stone for skipping.

The list went on and on.

He could find these items on his own, find them and complete the scavenger hunt without assistance or fainting ladies. He'd start with the skipping stone. It was in the middle of the list, and he imagined the teams would either begin with the first or last item and work from there.

He remembered crossing a small stone bridge upon arriving the day before. Several ducks had been swimming in a pretty little lake. He'd start there in his search for the stone. While everyone else swarmed the stables or gardens, he'd have a nice walk by the water.

Nathan started in the direction of the pond, encountering the Duke of Linton and Sedgemere's great-aunt, Lady Lavinia, returning to the house.

"Wyndover, join us," Lady Lavinia said, after the initial pleasantries. "I remember quite fondly a scavenger hunt with your late father. This was before he met your mother, and I rather think we spent more time flirting than hunting."

"Yes, do join us, Wyndover," Linton said hopefully, his voice raised so the deaf older lady could hear him.

"I wouldn't want to intrude," Nathan shouted. "I have my own plan of action."

Linton scowled, and Nathan made his escape, Lady Lavinia's voice carrying over the lawns. "Who is the object of his attraction?"

Nathan chuckled, crossing the lush green lawn quickly. Sedgemere's estate was well tended. As a man of property himself, Nathan noticed the details—the manicured flowerbeds, the way the land sloped away from the house to aid in drainage, the gravel paths that were free of weeds. He would have liked to see some of the surrounding land and meet a handful of Sedgemere's tenants, but that would have to wait until he'd played dutiful guest a few more days.

Sedgemere had mentioned archery as an activity, Nathan remembered as he neared the lake. God in Heaven, anything but archery.

At the edge of the water, he scanned the stones on the sandy bank. Several were quite smooth, but they were too round to skip well. He needed a flat and oval stone. He followed the edge of the water, head down, eyes narrowed for any sign of the perfect skipping stone. A duck quacked, and he looked out at the water, glinting in the morning sun. A drake, his mate, and a line of ducklings swam in the middle of the water, looking quite aimless. Doubtless the ducks were hunting insects for breakfast. He watched them for a moment, but when he might have gone back to his search for skipping stones, his attention caught and held on a flutter of something brown near the base of the gray stone bridge.

It looked like a clump of brown cloth. A coat a groundskeeper had set aside and forgotten? He almost returned to his quest for the skipping stone, but something made him stare just a little longer. The coat was not empty. Someone was inside it.

Wyndover stuffed the sheet of foolscap into his coat pocket and walked rapidly toward the bridge. His long-legged gait ate up the distance quickly, and the indistinct shape became clearer. It was a body lying on its side under the shade of the bridge. As he neared the form, he made out the mud caked on the coat and the matted hair falling over the person's face. Probably a vagrant who'd fallen asleep there the night before.

At least Wyndover hoped the man was only sleeping. The last thing the Duchess of Sedgemere needed was a dead body to put a damper on her house party.

"Excuse me," he said as he walked the last few steps. "Are you hurt?"

The body didn't move. The wind ruffled the brown material again, but now Wyndover all but stumbled. It wasn't a coat whipping in the breeze. Those were skirts.

A girl?

Where he might have nudged the body with his foot had it been a man, now he hunched down and examined the form. She did wear a coat—a man's coat—which was far too large for her small form. Beneath the hem of the coat, skirts covered with dry mud lay heavy against her legs, which were pulled protectively toward her belly. Her long dark hair covered her face, the muddy strands making it impossible for him to see her features.

Still, this was no lady nor a guest of the house party. She stank of shit and farm animals. Wyndover looked back toward the house. Should he fetch one of Sedgemere's servants? He winced at the thought. He could already hear the taunts from the other guests.

Leave it to Wyndover to find a girl on a scavenger hunt.

That desperate for a bride, Wyndover?

He might not need to involve the servants, but he couldn't leave her here. "Miss." He shook her shoulder gently. It was surprisingly pliable under the stiff outer clothing. He'd expected to feel little more than bird-like bones. So perhaps she was not as malnourished as he'd thought.

"Miss," he said a little louder. He shook her again.

She moaned softly and then came instantly awake. He stood just in time to avoid her swing as she struck out. She scrambled up and back against the bridge, her arms raised protectively, as though she expected him to attack. The matted hair fell to the side of her mud-streaked face, but her large green eyes stared at him with undisguised terror.

Wyndover raised his own hands in a gesture of peace. "I won't hurt you."

Her eyes narrowed. Such large eyes and so very green. They were the color of myrtle, a plant he knew well as he'd had to approve a hundred pounds for the purchase of myrtle at Wyndover Park. He'd stopped at his nearby estate before continuing to Sedgemere House, and the head gardener had insisted on showing him the myrtle, which had been in bloom with white flowers.

"Do you understand?" he asked when she didn't answer and continued to look at him in confusion. "Do you speak English?"

"Yes." She rose, using the bridge for support. "I understand."

Her voice held a faint exotic quality, a lilt that was both familiar and foreign.

She was no child; he could see that now. Although the coat hid her figure, he could see by the way she held herself that she was a woman and one of some standing. She held her chin high in a haughty manner, and her gaze swept down him with an imperiousness he recognized from more than one *ton* ballroom.

She obviously decided he was no threat, because her gaze quickly moved past him to scan the area around her. She reminded him of a hunted animal, a fox cornered by hounds. He wanted to reach out, lay a hand on her and reassure her, but he didn't dare touch her. The look in her eyes was too feral, too full of fear.

"Where am I?" she demanded, her eyes darting all around her, searching, searching. What was she looking for? What was she scared of?

"Sedgemere House," he answered. "The residence of the Duke of Sedgemere."

"Are you he?"

If she didn't know Sedgemere, she wasn't local. But if she didn't live in the area, then how had she come to be on Sedgemere's estate? He saw no evidence of a horse or conveyance. She must have walked. Another glance at the state of her clothing confirmed she must have been traveling for some time. Or perhaps not traveling but running. But from what or whom?

"No. Miss, you look as though you need some assistance. May I escort you back to the house?" Damn the taunts and teasing. The woman needed help.

She shook her head so violently that flecks of mud scattered in the breeze. "I must be going."

She turned in a full circle, obviously trying to decide which way to travel. Her muddy hair trailed down her back, almost reaching the hem of the thigh-length coat. Sections of it were still braided, indicating at one time it had been styled in some fashion or other.

"Which way to London?" she asked.

He almost answered. Her tone was such that he felt compelled to snap to attention, as though he were the butler and she the master. Something else was familiar about her. The way she spoke, that accent. She wasn't English. Not French or Italian. He'd traveled the Continent years ago, when he'd been about two and twenty. He knew that accent, just couldn't place it at the moment.

"Why don't we discuss it inside over a cup of tea?" he said. "If you'll follow me—"

"I don't have time for tea. I have to run. Hide. They're looking for me. If they find me..." She shuddered, and that one gesture said more than any word she'd spoken.

"Let me help you."

Her gaze landed on him again, ran quickly over him, and dismissed him just as quickly.

"If you want to help, tell me which way to London." She shook her head. "*Ne rien*! I'll find it on my own."

She swept past him, obviously intending to go on without his assistance. She might have climbed the embankment beside the bridge, but Wyndover suspected the exertion would have been too much for her. She would probably take the easier path around the pond and then double back and head south.

Ne rien. He'd heard that before, and quite suddenly he knew exactly where she was from. *Ne rien* was a Glennish phrase meaning *never mind* or *forget it.* Glennish was the mix of Gaelic and French spoken in the Kingdom of Glynaven.

He'd read reports of recent unrest in Glynaven. Another revolution ousting the royal family.

"Oh, bloody hell," he muttered as another thought occurred to him. He turned just in time to see her stumble. In two strides he was beside her, his arms out to catch her as she fell.

He lifted her unconscious body, cradling her in his arms. She'd barely made it three feet before she'd collapsed from what he'd hoped was only exhaustion and not something more serious. She might smell of manure and rotting vegetables, but with her head thrown back, he could see her face more clearly now. The high forehead and sculpted cheekbones, the full lips. She had all the features of the royal family of Glynaven.

But the unusual color of her green eyes gave her away—Her Royal Highness, Princess Vivienne Aubine Calanthe de Glynaven.

"Welcome to England," he said as he started back toward the house. She was light as a spring lamb, but he knew under the bulky clothing she had the full, supple body of a woman.

A beautiful woman.

She hadn't even recognized him. Other women might swoon at the sight of him, but her gaze had passed right over him, just as it had when they'd first met.

"You're in danger," he remarked to himself as he left the pond behind and started across the lawn. Not toward the house. He didn't dare take her to the house. One of the outbuildings. His gaze landed on a small shed, most probably a boathouse. He'd tuck her there and then fetch Sedgemere or his duchess.

"Princess Vivienne." He gave a rueful laugh. "Bet you never thought I'd be the one to save you."

Chapter Two

S HE OPENED HER eyes and blinked at the darkness. No, not darkness, she decided, but somewhere cool and dim. She hurt, everywhere. Her head felt as though encased in a helmet, and her legs and arms were leaden weights. She needed to sleep. She could sleep here in this cool darkness.

She closed her eyes again and everything rushed back at her—the revolution, the assassins, Masson's blood pumping out of his body...

She had to run, to hide.

She jerked up, thankful she'd been lying on the floor, because her head spun. She rolled to her side, bracing her palms on the cool dirt and hung her head. Slowly, she gained her knees and began to push to her feet.

"Where do you think you're going?" a voice asked.

Vivienne jumped, her arms buckling and almost collapsing beneath her.

"You can't even stand. How far do you think you'll be able to travel?"

She turned her head, searching for the voice's source. He stood in a corner beside a row of oars that had been hung neatly on a wall. This wasn't a prison then. She glanced quickly about her, noting the watercraft. This must be where the nobles stored their boats, little more than rowboats, which made sense, as the pond was too small for anything more substantial.

She put the pieces together, her head throbbing with the effort. She'd fainted—how absolutely mortifying! She had never fainted in her life. But she was so weak now and losing strength. As humiliating as it was to realize it, she knew he must have carried her here after she fainted.

Why? To keep her until the assassins could be contacted?

She studied him again. No, she didn't think so. He was an Englishman. That didn't mean he couldn't be in league with the assassins. They must have some Englishmen on their side, or at least willing to aid them for a handful of coins.

But this man was no farmer, no innkeeper. His clothes were too well made—a blue coat of superfine, a pale green waistcoat, a white linen shirt with an expertly tied neckcloth. He wore fawn-colored breeches and polished riding boots. The breeches were tight enough to mold to muscled legs.

She'd noticed that before—his broad shoulders, slim body, firm buttocks. But all of that was nothing when one took into account his face. He had the face of an angel. His skin was bronze, his cheeks smooth and, she imagined, soft and free of any stubble. His sunny blond hair fell over his forehead in a dashing sweep. His blue eyes were the color of the Mediterranean Sea before a storm and were framed by lashes several shades darker than his hair and thick enough that they provided a picturesque frame for eyes already striking.

No man should be so beautiful. She hunkered on elbows and knees before him and felt like the lowest worm. She would have felt lacking beside him even had she been wearing her tiara and finest gown. She didn't like pretty men, didn't like men too vain to dirty their hands.

"Do lie back down before you fall," he said.

She shook her head. "I must go. I've lost too much time already."

"You'll lose even more if you collapse on the road."

This was true. Perhaps he did want to help her, and she would be wise to accept food and water. She hadn't eaten since yesterday morning and then only a crust of bread and weak wine.

"If you would be so kind as to gift me bread and cheese, I would be grateful. I have no money, but perhaps when I reach London, I could send you—"

He waved a hand, looking quite offended. "I don't want your money. I'm trying to keep you alive, Princess."

She started and fell back onto her behind. She would have been embarrassed if she hadn't been so shocked at his use of her title.

"How do you—?"

"You don't remember me?" He stepped away from the wall, into a thin shaft of light that made a weak attempt to penetrate the spaces between the wooden boards that comprised the building's walls.

She didn't need the light to know his features. Should she know him? He did look familiar, now that she considered the possibility they'd met before. Not recently. Years ago, perhaps. But then, she met so many people, so many men.

There were no counts in England. "Are you an earl?"

"A duke." He made a sweeping bow that would have perfectly graced her father's throne room. "The tenth Duke of Wyndover."

The name seemed familiar. If her head hadn't felt as though it would crack open at any moment, she might have remembered him. As it was, all she knew was that dukes had money and power. She needed food, a carriage, a coachman to take her to London.

Slowly, she rose to her feet, intent on acting the princess even if it killed her. She wobbled, and he jerked as though he might help her. Something held him in check. Perhaps he knew her well enough to realize she wouldn't welcome his support.

"I thank you for your assistance, Duke. And since we are such old friends, I wonder if I might beg a favor."

"Old friends? You still don't remember me."

He sounded almost offended. Why should she remember him? He'd not been her lover nor had they ever kissed. They might have danced, but then, she'd danced with thousands of men in the palace of Glynaven. She closed her eyes and willed the memories away. Memories of happier times.

"Of course, I remember you," she lied. "I couldn't place you at first. I'm not at my best at the moment." That was true enough.

He shook his head, clearly doubting her. "I suppose this is no more than I deserve."

He did step forward then and took her elbow. Out of habit, she began to jerk away. Before she did so, she realized she'd been tilting to the side and his grip had steadied her, prevented her from falling over.

"Do sit down, Your Highness. I've asked the butler to send the Duke and Duchess of Sedgemere, when they return. This is the duke's land, and he is a friend of mine. I instructed the butler to be discreet. You've stumbled upon a house party."

"I don't have time to wait for your friend. I must go before they find me. They will have no compunction about killing you, killing all of these people, if it means they slit my throat in the end."

To her ears, her rapidly rising voice sounded hysterical, but he did not look at her as though she were mad. Instead, he gently lowered her to the floor, where she now saw he'd laid a burlap cloth of the sort one might use to keep dust off a boat.

"Who is after you? Do they have something to do with the political unrest in your country?"

Political unrest. Yes, that was one way to describe the revolution. That was a polite way to refer to the slaughter of her family before her eyes—her mother, her father, her siblings. They'd killed the royal family and all who were loyal to them. Vivienne had stumbled over the dead bodies of maids who'd done nothing more than launder her sheets. None of them deserved such gruesome deaths.

But the assassins were intent upon finishing what they'd begun in the revolution of ninety-eight. This time they intended to make certain no member of the royal family lived to hold any claim to the throne.

"Assassins," she said, her voice little more than a whisper. "They're searching for me. The head of the guard smuggled me out of Glynaven to Scotland. We'd made it as far into England as Nottinghamshire before the assassins caught up to us."

"And your guard?" the duke asked, though she could see in his eyes he'd already guessed.

"Dead." She looked down, blinked away the tears. "They're all dead."

She couldn't cry. Not now. Not until she reached London.

His hand covered hers, and the warmth of his skin shocked her. She hadn't realized she was so cold or so desperate for any little morsel of human kindness. His warm fingers wrapped around her hand, and her heart melted at his touch.

She couldn't allow it, though. If she softened now, she might never have the strength to reach London. She needed all her strength.

She tugged her hand away. "My hands are dirty."

He rose. Had she offended him? Quite suddenly, she did not want him to go, did not want him to leave her. Her mother had always said she was a contrary child.

"I brought you a scone," he said, bending to retrieve a plate she hadn't noticed before. "I would have brought you more, something not as rich and water or tea, but I didn't want the servants asking questions—not until I'd spoken to Sedgemere, at any rate."

Her mouth watered when he removed the linen cloth from the top of the plate and she spied the lightly browned scone, smelled the scent of cinnamon and vanilla.

"Slowly," he said, raising the plate out of her reach. She hadn't even realized she'd reached for it. "You'll be ill if you eat it too fast."

She gave a quick nod, wanting the food more than she could ever remember wanting anything else in her life. He lowered the plate, and she snatched the scone from it, turning away from him so he would not see her eat. Since she had no intention of losing the meager contents of her stomach, she broke off a small piece and shoved it in her mouth.

She closed her eyes and chewed as slowly as she could, her hands trembling from the effort not to cram the rest of the scone into her mouth.

It was the best thing she had ever tasted in her life.

She ate another small bite, then turned to the duke. "Thank you," she said, mouth full. It was the height of bad manners, but she didn't care. She could feel tears streaking down her face, tears of gratitude she couldn't hold back any longer.

He gave her a look of such pity she would have hated herself if she'd had the energy. Instead, she broke off another small piece of scone and didn't protest when he pulled her into his arms. She should have protested. She should have chastised him.

How dare you touch me without permission!

But he smelled so absolutely wonderful, almost as lovely as the scone. He smelled clean, like shaving soap and boot blacking. Comforting, normal smells. Scents she associated with her life before the revolution.

She should have stepped back. She was dirtying his clothing—very fine clothing from the feel of the wool against her cheek—with her mud-caked garments. Her body relaxed against his chest, and she sagged into him, allowing him to support her. Just for a moment. She would stand on her own again, but she could lean on this man, this duke who had known her before her life had fallen apart, for a few seconds. His arms came around her. She was petite, and his touch—light, not possessive—wrapped around her back and shoulders.

"You're safe now," he murmured. "You're safe here."

And she believed him. She felt safe. For the first time in weeks, she felt safe. She could lower her guard, relax her muscles, close her eyes.

❦

HE WAS HOLDING her. He'd never thought he'd hold her. And when he'd imagined doing so, he'd never imagined she would smell so disgusting.

But he didn't let her go. He might never have the chance to embrace her again, and he'd hold on as long as she'd tolerate it. He'd hold on forever, because it would take a strong army to persuade him to let her go now. It was obvious she needed help, and he intended to do everything he could for her. She didn't remember him, and even if she had, she wouldn't have looked at him twice. Not the way he looked at her.

But this wasn't about winning her affections. He was a gentleman. He was honor-bound to aid a lady in distress. The feel of her in his arms was almost a reward in itself.

"My bow!" She jerked back, almost tripping over her own feet. He caught her arm, held her steady. "I left it. I have to fetch it!"

Pushing past him, she started for the door of the boathouse. It opened before she could reach it. The Duchess of Sedgemere entered, her gaze flicking first to the princess and then to Nathan. She was a pretty woman and not one prone to hysterics. Her expression remained placid, despite the surprise she must have felt at seeing a strange, filthy woman in her boathouse with one of her houseguests.

"Duchess," Nathan said smoothly, moving to block the princess from escaping and simultaneously shield her with his body. "I apologize for taking you away from your guests and the activities."

"Gladstone said you asked him to send the duke or myself to you right away." Her gaze slid from him to the princess at his side. "Is there a problem?"

"Yes, but I should make introductions first. Her Royal Highness, Princess Vivienne of Glynaven, this is the Duchess of Sedgemere. It was her bridge I found you sleeping under. Duchess, this is Princess Vivienne. She's in a bit of trouble at the moment."

The duchess raised her brows with some skepticism, but she managed a very formal curtsey. "I'm pleased to make your acquaintance, Your Highness."

"Please, call me Vivienne. I'm endangering you, everyone here, with my presence. It's better if you don't use my title."

"Very well, then you should call me Anne, and I must insist you come to the house with me. You need a bath, clean clothes, and a good meal."

Vivienne shook her head. "Thank you, but no. As I said, my presence here is a danger to all of you. I want only to collect my bow and be away." She eyed the scone in her hand and ate another small bite, clearly unwilling to leave it behind.

"You can't leave," Wyndover said, surprising himself. The duchess's eyes widened, while the princess's eyes narrowed. He cut her argument off. "You're in no shape to travel to London, especially if you are being pursued by assassins."

"Assassins?" The duchess paled, but to her credit, she stood her ground.

"I will gladly accept the loan of a horse or conveyance," the princess answered, haughty as ever.

"And have the assassins take it away at the first opportunity? I think not."

Her green eyes darkened with fury. "I don't know who you think you are—"

"I'm a man who knows England a great deal better than you. You're a lone woman traveling on foot. Even traveling on horseback, you have no protection. If these assassins don't attack you, someone else will."

"I agree," the duchess said. "A woman alone is not safe from thieves or highwaymen, and the closer you get to London, the more danger you face. You cannot go alone."

"And I cannot stay here."

"I'll take you," Nathan said. The moment the words were out of his mouth, he wanted to shove them back in. What the hell was he suggesting? He couldn't take her to London. He'd traveled from Town for this bloody house party. He couldn't get involved in the revolutions taking place abroad. He had estates to manage, tenants to see to, ledgers to balance.

But he'd be damned if he allowed her to walk away from him. She'd be dead before the sun rose again. And if he had other reasons for wanting to stay with her, he didn't intend to examine them too closely.

"Fine," the princess said, surprising him. He'd fully expected her to argue, to say she didn't want him. "You may accompany me."

Nathan clenched his hands at her imperious tone.

"But you take your life in your hands, Duke. You have serfs depending on you."

"We don't call them serfs—"

"An important man like you must have fiefdoms. Can you really afford to risk your life to escort me to London? I think it's better if I go alone."

"That's out of the question."

"Fine, then fetch your carriage. We leave now."

The duchess pressed her lips together, clearly hiding a smile. She had noted the princess's dictatorial tone as well.

"That's also out of the question," Nathan said. He could dictate too. "A journey like this takes a bit of planning and preparation. Not to mention, I have no intention of traveling for days with someone who smells like pig feces—be she a princess or not."

"Why you—"

The duchess cleared her throat. "Your Highness—Vivienne—perhaps you might come inside and take the opportunity to wash and change. You're shorter than I, but I could ask my maid to hem one of my gowns or take it in a bit."

"Thank you, Duchess, but no," Nathan said. "If the assassins are tracking her, and I think we must assume they are, I want her far away from here, from your party and the guests. There are children present, and we must think of their safety."

"Then what do you propose?" Vivienne demanded, hands on her hips.

"You come with me to Wyndover Park. It's only a couple hours' ride from here. That's far enough to put distance between you and your pursuers, but close enough that I can have you there quickly. At this point, your safety is paramount."

Her expression was unreadable. It might have been the streaks of dirt on her face, but Nathan rather suspected she wasn't quite certain what to make of him. Good. He'd keep her guessing.

"How can I help?" the duchess asked.

"I want to leave without being seen," Nathan said. "I'll need you to make my excuses."

"Of course."

Vivienne nibbled the scone while he and the Duchess of Sedgemere devised a plan. She would tell Sedgemere the truth, but everyone else would be told Wyndover had an aching head and had gone to his room. During the next activity, which was a picnic in the garden, Wyndover and the princess would slip away in his coach and go to Wyndover Park. That evening at dinner, when the duke and the princess were safely at Wyndover Park, Sedgemere would inform the guests that Wyndover was called to his estate in Gloucestershire on urgent business. Wyndover Park was in Nottinghamshire, but Nathan wanted anyone who inquired after him to think he'd left the area. Otherwise, Nathan had thought it best to stick closely to the truth, and he instructed the duchess to say that a fire had broken out at one of the tenant's cottages. This was true, although the steward at the Gloucestershire estate had the matter well under control—except for the small matter of housing the tenant's rabbits—and Nathan was not needed.

"I should return to the house before I am missed," the duchess said. "I wish you a safe journey."

"Tell Elias I'll write to him with news, and accept my apologies, Duchess, for my early departure."

She waved her hand as though his absence was nothing, although he knew it would upset her numbers and cause her some difficulty. "It was a pleasure to meet you, Vivienne. I do hope we can meet again under better circumstances." She curtseyed again, and then she was gone.

Nathan leaned against the door. "I think it best if we stay here and out of sight until my coachman sends word that the coach is ready."

"I agree, but I must have my bow and arrows first."

"You always did love archery."

"And a good thing, as my skill with a bow saved me any number of times. I even wounded one of the assassins in the leg. I had hoped his injury would afford me some time, but the others seemed to come even more quickly."

"How many are there?"

"At least three, but there might be more." She motioned toward the door.

"I'll go," Nathan said. "You stay inside and hidden. Where did you leave them?"

"I slipped them off before drinking and leaned them against the stone bridge. I must have fallen asleep, and when you woke me, I didn't think to gather them."

"I'll return in a moment."

He opened the boathouse door a crack, peered out. The duchess had returned to the house by now, and no one else was about at the moment. Quickly, Nathan stepped outside and closed the door behind him. The bright sunlight made him squint, but he shielded his eyes and made his way back to the pond and the bridge where he'd seen her this morning.

He stayed alert, scanning the tree line and the lawns for any sign of movement. The pond was far enough from the house that he heard nothing and saw nothing. Finally, he returned to the spot where she'd been sleeping and circled the area, looking under the bridge and in a nearby patch of fuzzy swamp willows. He imagined her crouching beside the water to drink, tracked his gaze to where she would have set the bow and arrows.

She would have wanted them close at hand when she sat to rest for a moment. Nathan stood again where he'd found her sleeping. He could still see the indentation of her body in the sand and in the middle of that hollow, a footprint.

There was no bow, no arrows.

Nathan put his own foot beside the print. His boot was larger.

Whoever had been here had tracked the princess, taken her bow and arrows.

And the assassins would keep tracking until they had her too.

Chapter Three

"You don't know it was the assassins who took the bow and arrows," the duke said. He was seated across from Vivienne in his well-appointed coach, both of them resting on royal blue velvet squabs and using handholds of gold silk.

"Yes, I do. You are fortunate the bow and arrows are all they took." He still had his life.

"I prefer a fight to running and hiding. I would have confronted and bested them too."

He would have given the assassins a good fight, of that she was certain. Unlike Masson, the duke was prepared for an attack, and he looked like the kind of man who could hold his own. British men liked to think of boxing as a sport. In her country, it was much the same. But the assassins weren't gentlemen or bound by a code of honor. They intended to kill her, and they would do so by any means necessary.

Still, she was quietly grateful to the duke. His presence had saved her life. If he hadn't woken her, if he hadn't looked strong and formidable, she would be dead by now.

"They must have taken the bow and arrows while we were in the boathouse," she said. "If they'd come while I'd been sleeping, they would have killed me."

"Why not attack us in the boathouse? Why not kill you when I went back to the house to fetch the scone and speak to the staff?"

"I don't know."

"I will write to Sedgemere when we arrive at Wyndover Park. No doubt the bow and arrows will turn up at the house party."

She didn't agree, and the thought made the food in her belly—the duke had procured bread, cheese, and wine—sit like a handful of stones. She'd had that archery set since she was sixteen. It had been a gift from her father on her birthday, and the two of them had spent many happy hours together shooting at targets, laughing, and competing.

And now he was dead.

She closed her eyes.

To her shock, Wyndover's gloved hands clutched her bare ones. Once again, she was aware of how dirty and unkempt she was. His gloves were perfectly white, while her hands were dingy with grime.

"I can see the loss of the bow and arrows has upset you, but you don't need them any longer. I'll protect you. I won't allow any harm to come to you."

If he had been Glennish, one of her countrymen, she would have accepted his words without comment. It would have been his duty to protect her. But this man owed her nothing. Why should he risk his life for her? Why should he comfort her or dirty his hands for her?

"That is very kind of you," she said carefully. "Do you mind if I ask why?"

He did mind, at least she surmised as much when he released her hand and sat back. "Because you are in danger. What sort of man would I be if I did not help someone in danger?"

"A typical man," she said.

He folded his arms over his broad chest. The late morning sun sliced through the carriage windows, which he had insisted need not be covered, making his hair look even lighter and his blue eyes look almost clear.

"I don't agree. Most men I know would do no different."

"Then you have not spent much time at court. The men I know do nothing if it doesn't benefit them. I have been to the court of your King George when he was still well. I saw little difference."

He pressed his lips together, and she watched with an interest she could not quite control as they gradually released and became full again. She wondered what it would be like to kiss those lips, to caress those perfect cheekbones, to stare into those bluer-than-blue eyes. What kind of lover would this man be?

An unselfish one, she decided. The thought did nothing to distract her from the wayward path of her thoughts.

"I haven't spent much time at court, but I have been in Parliament for several years. Political expediency is the way of most powerful men, but that doesn't mean that they are not good men at the core."

She let out a huff of breath and looked away. Let him hold on to his naïveté. She couldn't forget the carnage *political expediency* had wrought on her country, her family.

"I'll replace the bow and arrows for you."

She jerked her head to stare at him in astonishment. "You needn't do that."

"I want to. I recall how much you enjoyed archery."

"You seem to remember me very well. Why is it I have such a vague recollection of you?"

"It wasn't for lack of trying on my part. I tried to catch your attention, but you were politely indifferent."

She smiled. "That is an apt description, I suppose."

"Very apt. I'm not particularly witty or fascinating. I suppose I didn't interest you."

Poor man. He thought he'd bored her.

"I'm afraid there is very little you could have said or done to capture my attention, Duke. Even if you had been as amusing as Leland Vibosette"—one of Glynaven's most witty actors—"I would not have sought you out."

"You find me distasteful in some manner?"

"No, not at all. I find you too much to my taste."

His brows came together in confusion. It made him look a good deal younger and quite adorable. Perhaps she had drunk too much of the good red wine he'd given her on an empty stomach.

She gestured toward his face. "I don't like men who are more attractive than I. I suppose it's vain and shallow, but I like to be the pretty one."

His brows rose again, and he stared at her for a long moment. His eyes seemed to look right through her, to the point where she wanted to shift with discomfort.

"I don't know what you look like now under the mud and grime, but if it's anything like what you looked like when I first met you, you are the most beautiful woman I have ever seen."

She gasped in surprise at his words. She'd been complimented before, of course, but never had any man's words sounded so sincere, so heartfelt. There was almost a tone of anguish in his voice.

"That's not true," she whispered. "I'm short and dark."

"You are petite, and your skin looks touched by the sun. Your hair is the most lovely shade of dark brown I have ever seen. But you are more than physically attractive. When I met you before, I found you graceful, well-spoken, and kind. Your servants could not praise you highly enough."

Her heart pounded so hard in her chest she had to press her hand to it. "You flatter me."

"No. I speak the truth. In all honesty, I would never have wanted any harm to befall you or your family. But I would be lying if I did not say I think I am the most fortunate man alive to have found you this morning. And I don't think it's merely coincidence."

"You think it fate?"

"I think I have another chance to make you see me as something more than a...*pretty* face."

"Then you have an ulterior motive for helping me too."

His eyes narrowed, and his jaw tightened. "What have I done to deserve such an insult?"

"Nothing. I did not mean to imply—"

"Yes, you did. You think I help you because I hope to take you to bed, because I want some sort of payment from you?"

She didn't answer. That was exactly what she thought. Shame crept through her, making her face hot.

"I won't deny that I would rejoice if you fell completely in love with me, if you *wanted* me in your bed. But I would help you even if you were an ugly old crone missing half your teeth."

She believed him too. The force of his conviction was entirely convincing.

He looked away from her, his eyes on the countryside visible through the carriage windows. Vivienne was not often sorry, but this was one of those rare occasions. She found she wanted him to look at her again, to speak to her with that warmth in his voice. Instead, they sat in silence for the next hour until they reached Wyndover Park.

"YOUR HIGHNESS," NATHAN said, as the coach came to a stop. "We have arrived."

He'd watched her fight to keep her eyes open, watched her lose the battle and fall asleep, her cheek resting on the squab. She must have been exhausted, because she did not move. She slept like the dead.

He wished he had a wet cloth to wipe some of the dirt from her face. He imagined she looked lovely when sleeping. Soon enough, she would be able to bathe and sleep in a bed. Perhaps that would restore her. In the meantime, he could make plans to travel to London.

Thank God his mother had left to spend the rest of the summer in Bath with her friend Lady Tribble. He did not want to have to explain his arrival with a princess of Glynaven in tow. As it was, he would have to think what to tell the staff. He had not been expected to return after the house party at Sedgemere's residence, and the staff had been reduced accordingly. That meant fewer people to trust to keep quiet.

"Your Highness," he said again, a little louder this time.

Her eyes opened, so vibrantly green, and she sat stiffly. For a moment, she looked about in confusion. Finally, she notched her chin up. "We've arrived."

"Yes. Welcome to Wyndover Park."

She peered out the window at the front of the house where the coach had stopped after making its way down the long drive. He was the tenth Duke of Wyndover, and the house was an old one. It had been refurbished every hundred years or so, but it retained some of its ancient charm—turrets and towers and crenellated parapets.

The coach door opened, and he stepped out first, holding his hand out to assist her. She took his hand, her gaze on the house.

"It's very grand," she said, looking up. "Very imposing."

"It was meant to be." He tucked her arm in the crook of his elbow and led her toward the door. "It was built for an ancestor of mine who was a baron. Wyndover

Park—it was not called that then—was the sole protection for farmers and tenants when there was an attack. At one time, there was a drawbridge and moat. Now, only what would have been the keep remains. It has been modernized, of course."

"Of course." She paused just before they reached the door where he could see his butler, Chapple, stood just inside, waiting to greet him.

"I want to apologize," she said, "for my thoughtlessness in the coach. I impugned your honor, and you have every right to be angry with me."

"All is forgiven." He waved a hand as though to waft away the smoke of discord. "I'm not one to stay angry for long, and I can hardly blame you. After what you've been through, questioning men's motives means survival."

She gave him another bewildered look. Soon enough she would take him at his word.

Nathan gestured to his man just inside the door. "My butler, Chapple. Good that you hadn't returned to London yet, Chapple."

"I was still putting the staff through its paces, Your Grace. I received word you would be returning and have made certain all of your requests have been granted. This, I presume, is the young lady who will be occupying the yellow room."

Nathan had seen the butler's gaze drift over the muddy clothes, but his expression remained respectful.

"Yes, Lady Vivienne"—he gave her a look rife with meaning—"my butler, Chapple."

"My lady." Chapple bowed.

"I hope I didn't put you to too much trouble," she said.

"None at all, my lady. May I have the housekeeper show you to your room?"

"I'd like that."

"Perhaps the footmen might bring hot water for a bath."

"Yes, thank you."

"Is there any luggage?" Chapple asked him.

"Sedgemere will have mine sent with Fletcher. The lady has none."

"We might ask one of the maids to peer into Her Grace's dressing room, but I'm afraid your mother is a good deal taller than Lady Vivienne."

A good deal wider too, Nathan thought.

"Perhaps one of the maids might have a dress she could borrow until Lady Vivienne's might be laundered and returned."

"I will see to it, Your Grace." Chapple raised his hand, and what Nathan assumed must be every servant in the house came forward. The princess was led away, surrounded by the housekeeper and maids while Chapple issued orders at the manservants in rapid succession.

Nathan's head hurt from the morning's exertions. He backed away, seeking the solace of his library. "Chapple, bring me every copy of *The Times* you can find," he ordered. "No matter how old."

"Yes, Your Grace."

"Have Cook send tea with brandy and"—what was it sick people ate to restore their strength?—"and broth of some sort to Lady Vivienne's room after her bath."

"Broth, Your Grace?"

"Just do it, Chapple. Don't stand there staring at me. I want those copies of *The Times*."

Nathan stalked away, muttering, "A man can't even request broth without his servants gaping."

Once in his library, he sat in his favorite chair beside the fire and propped his feet on a nearby table. His mother would have been appalled, but his mother was in Bath. Good thing too, or else he would have been answering all of her pointed questions about the princess rather than enjoying a few minutes' solitude and quiet.

A brisk knock sounded on the door, and Nathan dropped his feet. So much for solitude.

"Come."

Chapple entered, arms laden with newspapers. "*The Times*, Your Grace."

Nathan rose and took them. From the weight of them, he judged his butler had unearthed at least a dozen copies, if not more.

"Is the—Lady Vivienne settled?"

"I believe she is enjoying the broth you requested, Your Grace." Chapple smirked. Nathan had never seen his butler smirk before, but he didn't know how else to describe the expression on the man's face at the moment.

"That will be all, Chapple. I don't wish to be disturbed."

"Would you like Cook to send broth for you too, Your Grace?"

Nathan gave the man a narrow stare, but Chapple blinked innocently.

"No. My usual fare will be fine. I'll have it in my room, as I don't expect Lady Vivienne will be well enough to come down to dinner."

"Yes, Your Grace."

"One more thing, Chapple."

Nathan hesitated to mention additional security measures. He'd always been perfectly safe and at home in his Nottinghamshire estate. However, if assassins really did roam the countryside, searching for the princess, it was better to be prepared.

"I am not expecting any guests. Admit no one while Lady Vivienne is here. If anyone comes to call, I am not at home. I would also ask you to instruct the servants not to mention Lady Vivienne's presence here for the moment. I rely on the staff's discretion, Chapple."

The butler stiffened. "Of course, Your Grace. As you should."

Nathan went back to his chair and wished he could lift the papers and begin sorting through them. But he had better finish this.

"Lastly, I want everyone on their guard. I've...heard rumors of some rather unsavory characters in the area. I want everyone to take precautions and to alert me if they see anyone unusual or unfamiliar."

"Absolutely, Your Grace." Chapple wrung his hands together, his concern obvious. Nathan would have preferred to avoid alarming the staff, but he could not be too careful.

"Is it highwaymen again, Your Grace?" he asked, referring to the highwayman who had preyed on the shire the Christmas before last.

"No. Nothing like that. Be watchful, Chapple. That's all I ask."

When he was alone again, Nathan perused the editions of *The Times*. The first few held no information of interest, but a quarter of the way through the stack, he found an article on the unrest in Glynaven.

British citizens traveling in the country reported unrest among the populace, stirred up by various anti-monarchist groups. There had been a revolution in the late 1700s, quite a bloody one from the accounts Nathan had read. After that uprising a military government had taken power, but the people soon revolted again and demanded the return of the monarchy. Vivienne's father was the brother of the deposed king, and he had taken the throne about fifteen years before.

Nathan found another article about the royal family. It didn't mention the princess, but stated that King Guillaume was much loved. His rule had been characterized by peace, until a growing faction of revolutionaries had begun to call for his abdication. Many of them had crossed to Glynaven from France, a country that had undergone its own violent revolution not long before.

Liverpool, the prime minister, and the Prince Regent had not made any comment on the worsening situation in Glynaven. Nathan suspected they did not want to cause friction or appear to take sides. Was Vivienne fooling herself by thinking she would be safe if she reached London? Would the king really give her sanctuary, or would he wash his hands of her and leave her to fend for herself?

The king might have never acted so dishonorably, but it was the Regent who held the reins of power at the moment. Prinny was selfish and self-serving. Nathan thought it unlikely he would come to Vivienne's rescue.

Finally, Nathan found an article on the revolution itself. The paper was only a few days' old, and the actual assault on the palace in Glynaven had taken place only a fortnight before. Eyewitness accounts were still being collected, but most agreed that the rebels had stormed the castle and murdered the royal family in their beds. The bodies of the king, the queen, and two of the four princesses had been identified. Two other bodies of women were presumed to be Vivienne and her sister Camille, but the corpses were so mangled, identification was difficult. The body of a man presumed to be the crown prince had also been found, but again, due to the state of the body, identification was a challenge.

Nathan set the papers aside and raked a hand through his hair. How had Vivienne managed to escape? And what horrors had she seen before she'd fled? It was a wonder she was still alive, a wonder he'd been entrusted to keep her safe.

He heard the clock chime on his desk and looked over. It was late, later than he'd anticipated. He was hungry and tired. Nathan wanted to speak to Vivienne, to discuss her plans to travel to London. It would have to wait until morning.

He made his way through the familiar rooms of Wyndover Park and up the winding marble staircase to his room. The yellow room, where Vivienne was housed, was at the end of the corridor. It was the most comfortable of the guest rooms and had the added benefit of being far enough away from the ducal bedchamber so as not to tempt him to knock on her door.

His dinner arrived a few minutes later. Nathan ate it, but dismissed his valet after Fletcher helped him remove his coat. Alone, Nathan flung the material of his neckcloth to the floor and stood at the window in shirt-sleeves, looking out at the encroaching darkness. The sun did not set until late in the summer months, and only now did shadows begin to obscure his view of the gardens.

He supposed he should sleep and had just pulled his shirt-tails from his trousers when he heard the screams.

Chapter Four

When the alarm sounded, Vivienne had run to the hiding place. She'd been awake, even though it was long after midnight, because she'd wanted to finish a book.

Mr. Wordsworth had saved her. If she'd been sleeping, she might not have heard the alarm or not been fast enough. She was the only one of her family to make it to the small, unassuming sitting room in one corner of the palace where a hidden room lay behind the portrait of her grandfather. She'd waited anxiously for her sisters, her parents, her brother to slide the painting away from the wall and creep into the stone space with her, but no one ever came.

When she heard the clang of steel and the cries of pain, she prayed her family would come. She prayed they'd escaped through other hidden passages, though those were few and difficult to reach. Instead, she sat, shivering, for what seemed days and days while the terror erupted around her. In truth, it had probably been only hours. It had taken but a few short hours to murder the occupants of the palace, to rape and pillage, to destroy what had once been lauded as the most beautiful royal residence on the Continent.

At some point the next day, Masson had pulled her, shaking and nauseated, from the hiding place. She didn't know how he'd managed to avoid the carnage, or how he'd sneaked into the palace to rescue her. She knew only that he looked haggard and ten years older than he had when she'd seen him less than twenty-four hours before.

"Your Highness, the *reavlutionnaire* have taken over the country. If you are to live, we must sail for Britain now. Today."

"My mother?" she croaked. "Papa?"

Masson shook his head sadly. He'd been her father's adviser for over a decade. She knew he felt the loss almost as keenly as she did.

Vivienne sobbed, and Masson permitted it for a few moments, and then he took her by the shoulders. "You must be strong now, Princess Vivienne. The *reavlutionnaire* are in the taverns, celebrating their victory. They will return, and when they realize you are not among the dead, they will look for you."

Vivienne nodded and took Masson's arm. She couldn't indulge her grief, not when she was the last of her family. Not when any delay could mean not only her death but the death of Masson. At the door to the ransacked sitting room, Masson paused.

"Do not look, if you can avoid it, Your Highness. The *reavlutionnaire* spared no one."

But of course she saw—men, women, children. All dead. Blood everywhere. Gaping wounds. And eyes. So many sightless eyes.

She took no more than a hundred steps before she saw her mother's body. The queen had been trying to escape to the safe room. She'd never made it. More sightless eyes.

And then, just days ago, Masson's glazed eyes had stared at her after the *reavlutionnaire* came for her in a barn in Nottinghamshire. She'd hidden in the hayloft, and when the *reavlutionnaire* had gone out to look for her, she'd had no choice but to pass his body. To feel his sightless eyes on her.

So many eyes staring at her, accusing her.

Why aren't you one of us? Why did you live?

The voices rang in her head, and she covered her ears to drown out the sound, screamed and screamed until she couldn't hear them any longer.

One of the bodies rose up and grabbed her shoulder, shaking her. It spoke to her, but Vivienne clawed at it, fought it.

"Vivienne!"

She fell, and when she opened her eyes, she lay in bed, the sheets tangled around her, the room yellow from lamplight.

She stared at the unfamiliar face, stared at the impossibly handsome man kneeling over her. His face was so close to hers that she could practically see the dark blue rims of his irises. She felt the fine lawn between her fingers and followed her arms to where she clutched his shirt.

Abruptly, she released him, and he moved back and off the bed.

"*Je sui duilich.*"

"You have nothing to apologize for," he answered in English. His eyes were very blue and his face pale with concern.

Her throat felt raw and parched, and she realized she must have been screaming for several minutes if he had been concerned enough to enter her room.

He motioned toward the door, and several women in caps moved back. The maids must have heard her as well. She'd probably awakened the entire household. She felt her face heat and wished she could bury herself under the covers.

Of course, it was at that point she realized she was naked, and the sheet only barely covered her breasts. She ruched it up to her chin and glanced at Wyndover. His focus was on the servants in the doorway.

"The lady is fine now, as you see. A nightmare. We can all return to our rooms."

With a murmur of feminine voices, the maids withdrew. Wyndover bowed to her and backed toward the door. "May I fetch you anything, Lady Vivienne?"

She shook her head, her throat too raw to speak.

"Good night then." At the door, he paused, glanced behind him. "We need to talk," he hissed in a whisper. "I'll return in ten minutes."

And he was gone.

Vivienne fell back on her pillows. If she hadn't still been shaking from the dream, she would have been mortified that her screams had awakened an entire household. A duke's household, no less. As it was, she wanted to pull the covers over her head and hide from the memories.

But she was a princess, and she had to behave as such.

The maids had found a simple day dress for her to wear, but she didn't want to call them to help her dress. Instead, she wrapped the sheet around her body and dangled her legs over the side of the bed. For weeks, all she'd thought about was fleeing to London. London was safety in her mind.

But was it really? Would she be safe anywhere with the dreams and memories haunting her?

London was no different than anywhere else. The assassins could find her there. She would not be safe while they wanted her dead. Even King George could not protect her forever.

If he protected her at all.

A quiet tap on the door made her jerk her head up. Wyndover peeked inside, holding a lamp. Seeing her sitting on the side of the bed, he entered and shut the door soundlessly behind him.

"How are you feeling?" he murmured, keeping his voice low.

"Better." Surprisingly, she meant it. When she was in his presence, so many of her fears seemed to dissipate. "Better now that you're here," she said.

He didn't reply, but his gaze stayed focused on her, those bluer-than-blue eyes studying her face. Then his gaze slid down her neck, and she felt the heat of it on her bare shoulders and through the thin sheet over her breasts, her stomach, her hips, thighs, legs, until his gaze rested on her naked feet and ankles, hanging exposed.

"We should speak tomorrow." His gaze returned to her face. "I jeopardize your reputation with my presence."

For a long moment, she was not certain what he meant. But, of course, the English had different customs and traditions than the Glennish.

"In Glynaven, a lady's reputation is not so easy to tarnish. Virginity is not so highly prized."

"I know."

Of course he did. He had been to Glynaven.

"You're not in Glynaven any longer." He looked at the door as though contemplating withdrawing.

"Stay with me for a few moments." Panic bubbled inside her at the idea of being alone again with only the sightless eyes for company.

"Won't you?" she added, when his jaw tightened.

She might be a princess, but this man was no underling she might order about. She patted the spot on the bed beside her and gave him what she hoped was an inviting smile.

He studied her again—definitely a man who took time with his decisions—and then placed the lamp on the bedside table and stood before her. He made no move to sit beside her. Perhaps that went too far for his British sense of honor.

"I spent the evening reading accounts of the revolution. I'm sorry about your family."

She inclined her head in a gesture she'd mastered by the age of two. "Thank you."

"Was it very bad?"

When she blinked at him, he cleared his throat. "I meant your nightmare. Was it very bad?"

"Bad enough." She couldn't speak of it. Her body wanted to shudder at the mere thought of those sightless eyes. She suppressed the instinct and swallowed hard. "I am better now."

Much better with him so close, his shirt open at the throat and rolled at the sleeves. That bare expanse of his bronze neck made him somehow more vulnerable. She had the urge to touch the skin there, to kiss it and the golden stubble on his jaw. Instead, she wound her hands together, pressing her fingers tightly.

"You're safe here," he said. "I've ordered a man to be on guard at all times. The staff will keep your presence here a secret. No one has any reason to look for you here or to associate the two of us. The Duchess of Sedgemere is the only one who knows I found you, and she won't speak of it except to her husband."

She nodded. She was safe, for the moment. Finally, she raised her gaze to his. "But I cannot stay here forever, and even if I could, you would not be able to keep my presence a secret for that long. The assassins will come for me, and eventually they will succeed."

"No." He said the word emphatically, bracing his legs apart as though he might take the assassins on himself. "I won't allow any harm to come to you. I give you my word. My vow."

"How very noble." She didn't intend for the sarcasm to trickle out, but it had.

"You don't believe me?"

"Forgive me. I don't believe in anyone right now. You see, in order for the *reavlutionnaire* to carry out the attack they did, they must have had help. How else would they know how to enter the palace? How would they have found the royal chambers so quickly? My parents were dead before they had a chance to escape to the safe room. The *reavlutionnaire* knew where to find them."

"Is that how you escaped? A safe room?"

She nodded. "I was the only member of my family to reach it, and only because I happened to be awake when the attack began and the alarm sounded. But the alarm was late, too late to save anyone else."

"Members of the royal court must have assisted the revolutionaries, been part of the insurgency."

"Yes. Men and women I trusted. People I knew, no doubt. So you must forgive me if I do not trust you."

"I do forgive you. Anyone who has been through what you have would feel the same. In time, you will trust again."

That was true, but he gave her too much credit. She had always seen the worst in people, never the best, even before the revolution.

"In time, I hope you can come to trust me. I have vowed to protect you, and I always honor my vows."

"Why do you make such a vow to me? Because, as you said before, you are a gentleman?"

"Yes, and because I have fond memories of Glynaven, fond memories of your family. They were very generous when I visited the court. I want to do something to honor their memory."

If he spoke the truth, he was an amazing man. If she was to believe what he said, believe anyone could be so selfless, then he was a man she must learn to trust.

He stepped closer to the bed, and their knees almost touched. "I know you don't trust me yet, but I hope you will give me the benefit of the doubt when I say we cannot travel to London yet."

She jerked back, her gaze flicking from their knees to his face. "Why?"

"Because I must appeal to the Regent personally. Even then I have no reason to believe he will make any effort to help you. He is not a man known for doing anything that does not benefit him."

I must appeal to the Regent.

He had not said *you*, had not said *we*. It was the speech of a champion. *Her* champion.

"We can do that in person. I will appeal to the man directly."

"No. Too dangerous." The duke took her hand. His was large and warm, while hers was cold and shaking slightly. She wanted to withdraw it so he would not know she shook so, but she couldn't seem to force herself away from his heat.

"If you go to court and appeal to Prinny, we can no longer keep your presence a secret. You will be an easy target for the assassins."

"I will ask the prince to offer me protection and asylum."

The duke squeezed her hand. "And he will do so out of the kindness of his heart?" Wyndover shook his head. "He will tell you no, because it's not politically expedient to protect you. England wants no part of this civil war."

"It is not a civil war! It's an insurrection!"

"Be that as it may, we did not intervene when France lopped off the heads of most of its nobility, and we will not intervene now. Prinny will want to appear neutral as the revolutionaries have some ties with Spain and Morocco. We need those countries as allies."

Anger bubbled to the surface. She knew what he was not saying. Money and trade were at the bottom of this.

"And Glynaven is to be sacrificed so you might keep your shipping lanes open and your ships from harassment?"

"There's the temper I remember," he said with a smile in his voice. His expression remained sober, though. "I don't say it's the correct thing to do. I merely state facts. You have nothing to bargain with, nothing to sway the Regent to your side."

She began to argue, but he put a finger over her lips.

"Let me finish, and then you may rail at me all you like." The finger slid down, and despite the tingles it caused to course through her, she did not press her lips together.

"If you go to Town and approach the prince, you have little chance of success and you expose yourself to danger. What I propose is writing to His Highness and gaining his support in absentia. One of my neighbors, the Duke of Stoke Teversault, always holds a ball this time of year. He and the Regent are old friends, and the prince always attends the ball. We arrange to speak with the prince at Teversault. He will be in good spirits and that, coupled with my persuasive letter, gives us the best chance I can think of to assure your petition will meet with success."

The plan made sense. She was infinitely safer here, under the duke's protection, than she would be without a protector at court. That was, if the duke could really control his staff and keep her presence a secret.

"There is one problem you have not considered," she said.

He arched a brow.

"Whether I am here or in London, I still have nothing to bargain with, nothing to offer the prince to induce him to support my petition for protection and asylum."

"I wouldn't say that. There are those in the prince's inner circle who might be willing to persuade him...for a price." He allowed the words to hang in the air for a long moment.

He was intimating she might become a powerful man's mistress. The very thought of sharing the bed of a man simply for gain made her ill. Had she really been reduced to a state where she had nothing to offer but her body?

"But if that sort of arrangement is not to your taste, perhaps you might allow me to bargain for you."

"What can you bargain?"

"The prince needs an advocate for several bills he would propose in Parliament. I can offer to support those. If that is not enough, there's always the promise of money."

"I cannot allow you to pay for my safety."

"You could consider it a loan."

"When I have no possible way of ever repaying you?"

"Then it's a gift. Surely in your royal capacity, you have been given many gifts."

She had. And he was right that she'd never felt the need to repay the giver, although favors were certainly implied and even expected. For the first time, she did feel some obligation and a sense of duty. Wyndover owed her nothing and seemed to expect nothing in return. The more he offered her, the more indebted she felt.

Which was ridiculous. She should accept his generosity and cease questioning it. From the statements he'd made in the carriage, she could surmise he had been infatuated with her at one point. He might still be infatuated with her. He still wanted her—not that he offered assistance because he hoped to bed her in return. She knew better than to even suggest such a thing now.

But perhaps this was a means of courting her. Courting her? Did he want her for his duchess? She could not imagine why. A duchess with assassins after her would make a very poor duchess indeed.

Or perhaps he thought to seduce her...

Or perhaps he was just a kind man who wanted to help her.

Why was that so difficult to believe?

Because she'd never known kind men or women, only those who grabbed and grasped at every morsel of power they could. In the royal court of Glynaven, nothing had been free and everyone wanted something.

She did not think England was so very different. And so she would wait and watch.

"Very well, I accept your gift."

He seemed to be waiting for her to say more. When she didn't, he gave a short laugh as though chiding himself.

"You're welcome."

He'd wanted her to thank him. Of course. She should have realized.

"If you are feeling better, I will take my leave."

Her fingers tightened on his hand. She'd be alone again with the sightless eyes. She forced her grip to loosen. She was a princess, not a frightened child, and she could hardly keep the man from his rest because she did not want to be alone.

"Good night, then."

He bent, and she drew back instinctively. He caught her chin with two fingers. "It's not that sort of kiss, Your Highness."

She stilled as the soft flutter of his breath whispered across her cheek. And then, very slowly, he dipped his mouth and brushed his lips over her temple. She closed her eyes, her heart swelling at the sweetness of the gesture. It thudded hard in anticipation when his lips trailed down and kissed her cheek. She wanted to turn her head, to meet his lips with hers. If she kissed him, took him to bed, she would not have to be alone, would not have to face those sightless eyes.

Instead, she held very still, and his lips kissed the corner of her mouth. He smelled of wine and bread and the spices that had been in the broth he'd had sent for her dinner. He smelled delicious.

Desire flooded her body with heat. It had been months and months since she'd even thought about a man in that way, and the sensation surprised her. She didn't act on it, though.

She knew he would refuse her, that his honor would compel him not to touch her. But that wasn't the only reason she resisted. This was a man of honor and principle, not some rake intent on seduction. If she bedded him, it would mean something to him and, she suspected, to her.

Best for both of them if they remained acquaintances.

But as he drew back and lifted the lamp, carrying it to the door, she knew remaining just an acquaintance would be far more difficult than she had anticipated.

Chapter Five

SHE WAS STILL the most fascinating woman he'd ever known, Nathan thought the next morning as he watched her walk in the gardens. Like her, the flowers were in full bloom, resplendent with blossoms in purple, pink, red, and white.

And yet, in her ugly gray dress with a hideous white collar, she was more beautiful than all of them. The dress was too long for her, even though he supposed one of the younger maids had given it on loan. Vivienne had to hold the hem off the ground as she made her way through the paths his gardeners tended. Nathan imagined they would be thrilled someone was enjoying the garden. He had a perfect view of it from his bedchamber window, where he stood now, but he never actually stepped foot in it.

He never had time. Too much to do.

Even today was full of correspondence to answer and that most-important letter to the Regent on Vivienne's behalf. He'd spent most of the night pondering what to offer the prince, what might sway the Regent to offer Vivienne and any other refugees from Glynaven his royal protection.

Nathan could think of nothing enticing enough until he had hit upon the idea of a ship of the line. Those were ridiculously expensive to build. He would offer to build one for the prince—no, he would build three. The expense would make a dent in his fortune, but would not deplete it. If he managed his estates well—and he always managed his estates well—he could replace the funds in a decade or so.

Vivienne was worth that much to him and more.

It occurred to him as he made his way out of his room and toward the garden—the garden he never visited—that he intended to marry her. He had no reason to think she would agree. She hadn't loved him eight years ago when he'd first met her, and she didn't appear to have fallen in love with him last night.

But the truth was, he was in love with her. He'd never fallen out of love with her. That was why he'd resisted marriage all these years, despite his mother's cajoling and her reminders about *that American cousin*. He'd told his mother he hadn't met a woman who could do honor to the title she'd held for so long, and when practically every fourth debutante he met fainted at his feet, that was not wholly a lie.

On the other hand, there were many very lovely, very acceptable ladies who did not faint at his feet. They might sway a little, but they showed promising fortitude.

And yet he'd tarried. Because he still wanted Vivienne. If anyone had asked him two days ago why he did not marry, Vivienne would not have crossed his mind. He didn't think of her daily, hadn't realized she was the reason he'd put off the leg-shackling.

Until he saw her again. And then he'd known he wanted her for his duchess. Seeing her last night, sitting on that bed, her fragile shoulders hunched, her small body shaking with fear—he'd wanted her for his wife. When she'd patted the space beside her on the bed, he hadn't refused the invitation out of propriety, although that was a consideration, he'd refused it because he would not have been able to resist wrapping his arms around her and stripping that sheet away.

The sight of her bare shoulders, her small pink feet, her long dark hair falling down her back in slightly damp waves had fired his blood. And those green eyes set with determination and filled with pain. He wanted to wipe that pain away, make her eyes dark and unfocused with passion.

He shouldn't have kissed her. He'd been able to keep the kiss innocent, but it had made him want more. The feel of her soft lips on his, even if only a corner of them, made him wonder what her mouth would feel like under his.

Nathan's thoughts had occupied him all the way to the door leading to the garden, and now he paused with a hand on the knob. He had to tamp down his lust. Somehow he had to make her fall in love with him. What could he do or say to engage her affections?

Poetry?

He didn't know any poetry.

Flowers?

The garden was full of them.

Money? Title? She didn't want his money and already had a more prestigious title than he could ever give her.

The one thing she wanted was the one thing he could not give her, no one could give her. Her family back.

He stepped through the door and was immediately enveloped in the scent of flowers and soil. Bees buzzed and birds chirped and somewhere nearby one of his servants shouted.

"Dilly, where's that water I asked for?"

Nathan headed toward the section of the garden where he'd last seen Vivienne and was surprised when she stepped out before him.

"I heard you coming," she said. Her eyes were wide, and she looked a little pale.

"You thought I was someone else." He looked pointedly at her hand, where she clutched pruning shears.

She dropped them with a pretty blush that brought the color back to her skin and made her radiant. "I suppose I am a bit jumpy."

"Do you mind if I walk with you?"

"Of course not, but I don't wish to keep you from your duties."

"I have none at the moment." That was a lie. He always had duties. At present, none of them seemed to matter.

She placed her hand in the crook of his arm, and they walked in silence for a few moments. "My sister would have loved this garden," she said after some time.

"Which one?" he asked.

"Berangaria. She loved gardening."

"I remember that. She was known for her prize roses."

Vivienne nodded.

"Your sister Angelique was quite the musician."

"Did she play when you visited?" She tilted her head up to look at him, her green eyes vivid in the morning light. He realized she had no bonnet, no gloves, but she did not seem concerned.

"She played several times and sang as well. She had the voice of..." He trailed off. "A songbird. What is a bird with a lovely song?"

"The lark?"

"Yes. I'm no poet."

"I am glad. Besides, with that face, I imagine you've never needed to learn any poetry."

He waved a hand. His good looks were his least favorite topic of conversation.

"And your brother was known for his horsemanship. He gave me a tour of the stables. Quite impressive."

"Lucien never met a horse he didn't like." Her smile wobbled.

Nathan paused. "Forgive me. Does talking about them upset you?"

She shook her head. "No. I am glad to talk about them, remember them. My life has been a nightmare. Talking about them reminds me what it was like when my life was normal."

He gestured to a stone bench, took a seat beside her. "It will never be like it was, I'm afraid."

"No. It won't. And I will never forget—"

He put his hand over hers. "Tell me."

She swallowed. "You don't want to hear it. I will give you nightmares."

"Doubtful. I rarely dream of anything except account books and columns of numbers."

When she remained silent, he brought her hand to his lips, kissed it.

She looked at him, her eyes wary. She still didn't trust him, perhaps she never would. She might not be capable of trust.

"Talking about it might help," he said.

She nodded, released his hand, and looked down at her skirts.

"What did you see?" he murmured. "What plagues you?"

"Death." Her voice was quiet, little more than a whisper. "The stench of it, the sticky feel of it beneath my bare feet, the sight of it. Masson told me not to look, and I tried. I tried. But I saw some of them, and…and…"

He heard the catch in her throat and felt the way she tensed.

"Have you ever seen death?" she asked.

"Once," he said. "I was the second at a duel. The men were supposed to shoot into the air. My friend did so, but the other man did not. The ball ripped a hole in his chest, and he died on the field. Bloody, awful way to die, and there was nothing I or the physician present could do to save him."

He hadn't thought about that night in a very long time. He'd not even been twenty, and he'd thought a duel a splendid diversion. He couldn't even remember what Edmund had done to earn a glove flicked at his face. Nathan knew only that he had not hesitated when his friend asked him to stand second.

His mother had not chastised him when rumor spread that he was there. She'd reminded him dueling was illegal, but he'd expected her to be much harsher. When he asked her about it later, she told him he'd been punished enough, having to watch his friend die.

Whatever perceived crimes she might have committed, she hadn't deserved to see her family die.

She sighed, her body seeming to relax and leaning into his. His words had the effect of calming her, and he could be grateful for that much.

"So much death. I could not avoid it. And then there was my mother…" She paused and swallowed.

Nathan put his arm around her. "You don't have to say it."

She nodded. "I saw her in the corridor outside the safe room. She'd been trying to escape to safety. She'd been so close."

Her voice was thick with emotion, but she didn't cry. He wondered if princesses were given lessons in retaining their dignity no matter the situation.

He pulled her closer, and she laid her head on his shoulder. Nathan hoped none of the servants was observing them. He did not want talk about Vivienne circulating. He trusted his staff to a point, but the more plentiful the gossip, the harder to keep it contained.

"That's not the worst part," she murmured, her voice so quiet he could barely hear her. "That's not all I see in my nightmares."

"What do you see?" He could not imagine anything worse than seeing your own mother murdered.

"The eyes." Her body shuddered. "When I try to sleep, I see all those sightless eyes staring at me. "So many pairs of eyes and so many colors—brown, blue, green, hazel. All dead. I might have been another pair of sightless eyes. I feel as though I should be."

She straightened and looked at him. Nathan wished there was something, anything he could say to ease her pain.

"Why should I be alive when so many were murdered? What did the kitchen maid ever do? The laundress? If someone is to pay for the crimes the *reavlutionnaire* accuse us of, it should have been me."

"Are you guilty of the crimes?"

"Of the excesses? Probably, to some extent. Of making secret treaties and imprisoning innocent people? No."

"Your death would not have saved any of the innocents." He rose and pulled her to her feet. "Your life will ensure they are remembered."

She seemed to study the flowers surrounding them. "I hadn't thought of that. There *is* more to you than a pretty face."

He lifted her hand, kissed it. "Much more."

Nathan spent the afternoon in his library, crafting the letter he hoped would sway the Prince Regent to offer British protection for the fugitive princess from Glynaven. When he'd finished, he sent one of his grooms to London, although the prince might very well have removed to Brighton or Bath now that the Season was over.

Nathan had other work to attend to throughout the afternoon, but his mind continued to wander to the princess. He'd known she was beautiful, known she was intelligent, but the fact she'd escaped the slaughter—there was no other term for it, not in his mind—at the Glynaven palace and then made her way through the English countryside alone made her far more resourceful than he would have believed. She had inner strength as well. She couldn't stop the nightmares that plagued her sleep, but she had not shed a tear or lost her composure once in the garden when recounting the horrors she'd seen.

He knew hundreds of women, and not one could hold a candle to her.

There was a small hitch, of course. He needed a duchess, and the difference between those hundreds of women and Princess Vivienne was that the other women were literally swooning to be his duchess. Vivienne had all but told him he was far too pretty for her taste.

Well, he couldn't do a bloody thing about his looks, but he would show her he was much more than a handsome face.

"Chapple!" he bellowed, even though he had a bell pull within reach. There was something quite satisfying about bellowing for Chapple. Perhaps it was the way the butler burst into the room, eyes wide with concern.

"What is it, Your Grace?"

"Do you have it, Chapple?"

"Have what, Your Grace?" the butler panted.

"The item we discussed. The gift for the...Lady Vivienne."

"It will be delivered tonight, Your Grace."

"Good." He'd present the surprise to her tomorrow. "Tell Fletcher I'll dress for dinner now." He started toward the entry hall, Chapple following at his heels. "Lady Vivienne is aware she is expected at dinner?"

"I think so, Your Grace. I do not think she will be able to dress for the occasion, however, as she has only one dress at present."

Good point. "Then I won't change either. We will have an informal dinner. Tell Cook."

"One other matter, Your Grace."

"What is it?"

"The Duke of Stoke Teversault sent a message inquiring as to whether Wyndover Park will field an oarsman in the Dukeries Cup this year."

Damn it. Nathan had forgotten all about the annual scull race held on the serpentine lake at Teversault. At Sedgemere's house party, the Duchess of Linton had mentioned her brother would be rowing for The Chimneys this year, and William Besett would row for Teversault. Nathan was a mediocre oarsman, and he had no brothers or cousins to enter. Wyndover Park was not one of the Dukeries, but Stoke Teversault always extended the courtesy of an invitation. Nathan might have asked a friend, as he had in the past, but he did not want to endanger Vivienne by inviting guests to his estate.

"Reply that Wyndover Park forfeits this year, and thank the Duke of Stoke Teversault for his courtesy."

"I beg your pardon, Your Grace." The lines around Chapple's mouth deepened with disapproval. Chapple, like all the servants, enjoyed watching the race, especially those years when the Wyndover family fielded an oarsman.

"You heard me, Chapple."

"Of course, Your Grace," Chapple said with a labored sigh.

VIVIENNE WAS GRATEFUL for the distraction of dinner. She'd spent most of the day walking the grounds and learning her way around Wyndover Park. She might have liked to read a book, but the duke was in the library. She did not want to disturb him.

That wasn't entirely true. It wasn't that she cared so much if she disturbed him, but she didn't want to be alone with him. The way he'd held her in the garden, kissed her last night—both gestures had been sweet and innocent. The trouble was, she would have liked more of the same, only not quite so sweet and definitely not innocent.

She didn't know what was wrong with her.

She had never been free with her favors, and she had never desired a man like the Duke of Wyndover. *Ne rien!* She didn't even know his given name. It was assuredly something very pretty, like William or Charles. A pretty name to go with his pretty face.

"There you go, my lady," said the maid. The middle-aged woman had been abruptly promoted to lady's maid and tasked with styling Vivienne's hair. "You look lovely, if I do say so myself."

"It will do, O'Connell."

She did look lovely—not as pretty as the duke, but then, that bar was much too high.

"Not much we can do with yer dress. It's clean, and His Grace did say he would not dress for dinner."

"Very accommodating of him," Vivienne answered, watching in the mirror as the maid fussed with the hair-styling accoutrement. "Does he host many dinner parties?"

"Oh yes, my lady." O'Connell, who was tall with strawberry blond hair tucked in a cap, nodded. "Here and in London. I travel back and forth with the family. Not all of the staff do, you see."

Vivienne nodded, understanding the maid saw this as a mark of honor.

"He hosts dozens and dozens of dinner parties, balls, and the like. He's the Duke of Wyndover."

Obviously, the maid thought that last statement explained all.

"Who plays hostess? He has no duchess." Oh God. He wasn't married, was he? She hadn't considered that he might be married. Perhaps that was the reason he'd been so chaste in his dealings with her.

"No, my lady. Not yet. His mother plays hostess. The duchess is in Bath at present. Of course, if she hears you are here, she'll be back in an instant." O'Connell's brown eyes widened. "Not that she'll hear. We're all to remain mum on the subject."

She ought to give Wyndover more credit. "Why would she return so quickly?"

"Because she wants the duke to marry, of course. He's an only child. The duchess thought she'd never conceive, and then fifteen years after she and the late duke wed—God rest his soul—here comes the current duke. I wasn't with the family then, but to hear Chapple tell it, there was much rejoicing that day."

"So the duke needs an heir."

"If he doesn't produce one, the title passes to"—she lowered her voice—"an *American.*"

"Heavens." Vivienne barely suppressed a smile. Glynaven was on good terms with the United States of America, but she understood England's ambiguity toward its former colony.

"Why hasn't he married yet?" Vivienne asked, more to herself than O'Connell, as she didn't expect a servant to possess that information. "Surely he must meet dozens of eligible ladies at all of these family gatherings."

She'd never met the Duchess of Wyndover, but if the woman was anything like her own mother, the duke's house had been full of eligible, acceptable ladies.

"Oh yes, but none of the ladies is like you."

Vivienne turned on the stool to face the maid directly. "What do you mean?"

"I mean no disrespect, my lady!" O'Connell held her hands up. "It's a compliment. You don't swoon when you're with him. We all thought maybe he planned to make you his duchess."

Vivienne blinked. "I don't understand. Women swoon when they're with the duke?"

"All the time, my lady." O'Connell pushed a loose strand of hair back under her cap. "I can hardly blame them. I mean, look at the man. I nearly swooned when I first saw him. But that was from a distance, and Mrs. Patton—she's the housekeeper—pinched me and told me if I dared faint I'd lose my position. Now I keep my eyes down when he's near." She pushed at her hair again. "If I don't look at him directly, I don't feel quite so dizzy."

Oh, this was too much. It was a wonder the man did not have the arrogance of a king. With women falling at his feet, he should have thought himself God's gift to the fairer sex. She liked him more because he never acted as such when he was near her. In fact, he seemed to prefer to avoid discussing his good looks.

"This has all been very interesting, O'Connell." She rose, hating the plain dress she wore and knowing she should be grateful for it.

"It wasn't gossip," O'Connell said hastily. "Mrs. Patton doesn't tolerate gossip."

"Definitely not gossip to state facts." She winked, and the maid's shoulders relaxed. Vivienne liked O'Connell. Her lady's maid at Glynaven palace had been tight-lipped and always frowning. Vivienne's hair was never tidy, her dresses too wrinkled, and the maid hadn't had a tender hand with a brush.

Poor Hortense was probably dead now, and Vivienne did not want to think ill of the dead, but if she ever had another lady's maid, she'd want someone like O'Connell.

She wondered if she should meet the duke in the drawing room, then decided since the dinner was informal, he would probably be waiting for her in the dining room. Thanks to her explorations earlier that day, she knew precisely where to go.

When she entered, he stood at the far side of the table, hands in his pockets, gaze on a painting on the wall across from him. For a moment, she understood why women swooned. He was arrestingly handsome. All the golden hair shining in the firelight, those stunning eyes, that square jaw, and chiseled cheeks.

She didn't know what he looked like underneath his clothing, but he looked very, very good in it. He was all long, lean lines and firm muscles.

She moved inside the dining room, and his gaze shifted and collided with hers. She felt a jolt when he looked at her, when all of that male beauty focused on her and her alone.

He smiled, a genuine smile that somehow made him even more attractive, although less imposing.

"You found it." He crossed to her, took her hand, and kissed her knuckles. Lips still pressed to her knuckles, he glanced up at her, his eyes darkening. "You look beautiful."

She almost laughed. *She* looked beautiful? Hardly.

"Thank you," she said. "And thank you for dinner. You didn't have to go to the trouble, but I confess I am glad you did. This room is stunning."

And it was. The long mahogany table gleamed with china and silver. Above it, a chandelier glowed softly, the unusual crystal drops hanging from each sconce making a sort of rainbow on the white-paneled walls. Red roses in short arrangements sat on either end of the sideboard and in the middle of the table. One end had been set for him and one for her.

"Tell Cook to send the first course," Wyndover said to the footman.

The man disappeared, and they were alone. Wyndover pulled out the chair beside her and gestured for her to sit. Vivienne smiled and shook her head.

"What's wrong?" His brow lowered with sudden concern.

"This seat is much too far from yours," she said. "I shall have to yell across the table."

He studied her for a long moment. "You would like to sit closer to me?"

"Is that allowed?"

"Oh, allowed and encouraged. I'll have the footman move your setting."

She waved a hand. "I may be a princess, but I know how to set a table." She moved the setting herself, and a moment later, the two of them were seated beside each other, Wyndover at the head of the table and Vivienne on his right.

The footman said nothing about the altered arrangement when he returned. He merely served the soup and retreated to the corner.

Vivienne was determined to keep the conversation light, and with the servants present, she couldn't discuss Glynaven or her circumstances. She steered the conversation toward music and literature, her favorites, and Wyndover proved capable of speaking intelligently on both subjects.

He also proved a skilled conversationalist as he directed the talk toward traveling and the customs of various countries he'd visited. As she'd visited many of the same, she could add easily and with great pleasure to the subject.

They had a great deal in common, and when dinner ended, Vivienne was almost surprised to find the jasmine ice before her. They must have talked for hours, and it had seemed no time at all.

She'd drunk a little bit too much wine, as the servants had filled her glass after each sip. Her head swam pleasantly, and though Wyndover was still as handsome as ever when she looked at him, she saw more than the perfect features now.

She saw the man.

And she liked what she saw.

"Why are you looking at me like that?" he asked.

She rose a bit unsteadily. "I suppose it is because I've had a wonderful evening, and I didn't expect it."

He rose as well, taking her elbow. He must have thought to steady her, but she was not *that* intoxicated.

"What sort of evening did you expect?"

She shrugged, a gesture she would make only when in her cups, as she'd been told at least a thousand times that princesses did not shrug.

"The sort where you wax poetic on the leek soup and exclaim at the sauce on the potatoes."

His mouth turned up at the corner. It was a very nice mouth. She wanted to kiss it, but that would probably shock the servants. She scanned the room. No servants at the moment. They'd removed all but the ices and were probably in the kitchen taking a moment's respite.

"I know the sort of evening you mean. I don't think either of us had anything poetic to say about the leek soup. I must say the sauce on the potatoes was quite to my liking."

She lifted her hand and placed it against his smoothly shaved cheek. "You are quite to my liking."

He didn't blink, didn't breathe.

After a long silence, he shifted slightly. "I thought I was too pretty for you."

"Oh, you're very pretty." Her fingers stroked his cheek and trailed down to his jaw. "But I shan't be swooning, if that is your concern."

He grasped her hand. "Who told you?"

"It's common knowledge, Duke. What is your Christian name, by the way?"

"Nathan. Why?"

"I like to know a man's name before I kiss him."

He still held her wrist, and when she leaned in to kiss him, he hesitated just for a moment. Then he dropped her hand and bent as her arms circled his neck and she pulled his mouth to hers.

Chapter Six

SHE TASTED OF jasmine ices and the sweet wine they'd drunk together. She tasted better than he could imagine. And the feel of her...

He dared not put his arms around her, because he couldn't trust himself to behave. She pressed her body to him, her lush breasts pushing against his chest, her long, aristocratic fingers in his hair. Her mouth was gentle and full, and her kisses very, very thorough. He'd expected the kiss to be sloppy. But she wasn't foxed, or if she was, she was very good at disguising the fact.

She drew back, looked up at him. Her green eyes were so large they filled his vision.

"Put your arms around me. Or"—she leaned back—"would you rather I stop?"

"God, no. Don't stop."

He put his hands on her waist, pulled her body back against his. This time, he noted the heat of her. Such a small thing to generate so much heat. He cupped her face, running his thumbs over her delicate cheekbones, then brushing his lips over hers. Her mouth parted slightly, and he took her plump lower lip in a kiss, nipping it gently.

She moaned, her hands roaming his back. Nathan was aware the servants might return at any moment. They should stop kissing, but he couldn't seem to abandon her mouth. Every touch of his lips to hers made him want more. Finally, when she opened for him, where their tongues touched and tangled and mated, he swore he could hear music. He'd wanted this for so long, he hadn't thought the reality could live up to his imaginings. His very detailed imaginings.

But her lips were plumper, her mouth sweeter, the stroke of her tongue more tantalizing than he could have ever fantasized. And when her hands slid down to his buttocks, he had to release her and grip the edge of the table where he'd cornered her to keep from ravishing her then and there.

He had never wanted a woman, had never wanted anything, as much as he wanted her in that instant.

"Take me to bed," she whispered, her velvet cheek brushing against his.

Nathan clutched the table tighter, struggling for control.

"No."

She looked up at him, a brow arched. "You don't want me?"

"Oh, I want you. In another moment, I shall crack this table with the force of my want."

She looked at his hand clenching the table, then back at his eyes. "I've done something wrong. I've been too forward. I forget you English prefer your women more coy."

"No." He gripped her shoulders. "I like you exactly as you are. But if I take you"—he lowered his voice in case the servants were about—"if I take you to bed tonight, I will be taking advantage of your intoxicated state."

"I am not so intoxicated."

"Be that as it may, I prefer to give you time to reconsider."

"Very noble of you. If I do not reconsider?"

"Then you should know I want more than a night or two of bedsport with you."

"You want my affections?"

He touched her throat and trailed down to the center of her chest and that go-dawful collar. He forced himself to stop there, not to stray to the swells of her breasts. "I want your heart."

Vivienne took a shaky breath. "Perhaps time to consider is warranted."

She stepped back and out of his arms. Immediately, she wrapped her own arms around her body. Nathan could not tell if it was a protective gesture or one of thwarted longing.

"Will you ride with me in the morning? There's something I want to show you."

"Yes. I'd like that. I haven't ridden since…before."

He bowed. "Then I bid you good night. I will see you at the stables in the morning."

As difficult as it was to walk away from her, he accomplished it, not pausing until he reached his room. In his bedchamber, he leaned against the door and closed his eyes.

"Shall I leave you, Your Grace?" Fletcher asked, coming out of the dressing room. Nathan opened his eyes to study the tall, thin man soberly dressed in black. Fletcher and Nathan were close in age, but Fletcher always seemed a good deal older. He already showed streaks of gray in his dark hair, and his face had a pinched look.

"Yes. No. I don't know." Nathan pushed away from the door. "She'll refuse me, Fletcher." Nathan paced his room. "I can hardly blame her. She doesn't even know me. I must be daft to think of asking her to marry me."

Fletcher clasped his hands behind his back. "Lady Vivienne is the object of your affection, I take it."

"Damn it, Fletcher. You were with me when I toured the Continent. You know she's not *Lady* Vivienne."

"I also know the princess could do far worse than you, Your Grace."

Nathan gave the man a wan smile. "I'm not paying you enough, Fletcher."

"I would not decline higher wages, but I am paid as well as, if not better than, my counterparts. I am not flattering you, Your Grace. I honestly believe the princess would be lucky to have you. From what I know of her, *you* would be fortunate to marry her. She is intelligent, accomplished, and politically astute."

"All that and more."

"Without question."

Nathan dropped into a chair and put his face in his hands. "You make it sound so logical and reasonable, when this marriage business is anything but. What if she refuses me?"

"Then you ask someone else, Your Grace."

Nathan laughed and pushed his fingers against his tired eyes. "I don't want someone else."

"Then make certain she says yes."

THE MORNING DAWNED cloudy but dry, and Vivienne was prompt. He'd had a mare saddled for her, one of the more spirited horses, and she approved the animal and mounted with little assistance. She wore one of the duchess's out-of-fashion riding habits that O'Connell and another maid had stayed up all night to alter. It was a lovely blue with gold piping, and as soon as she climbed on her mount, she felt right at home.

Nathan rode his favorite gelding. Patch was known as such because he had a white patch on his chest. Nathan's mother had named the horse, and Nathan hadn't changed it.

He and Vivienne rode to the west. Vivienne had a good seat, and when he was certain she could keep up, Nathan gave Patch his head. The two of them galloped for a mile or so, enjoying the morning and the silence broken only by the call of birdsong. At least, Nathan should have been enjoying it. Instead, he was thinking of the instructions he'd given to Chapple. He had to keep Vivienne away from Wyndover Park long enough for Chapple to arrange everything just so.

"What is over there?" Vivienne asked, pointing toward one of his tenant's lands.

"That's the Hollands' farm, I believe."

Nathan studied the faint spiral of smoke coming from the farm and turned Patch in that direction. "Wait here."

A moment later, he neared the tenant's cottage, and Vivienne was right behind him. He wasn't surprised. He doubted she was very used to following orders.

"There's where the smoke came from."

A circle of stones ringed still smoldering chunks of wood. The fire looked to have been hastily put out and not very thoroughly. Nathan jumped down and inspected the site, then knocked on the tenant's door.

No one answered.

He walked back to Patch and was about to mount when he heard hoof beats.

"Who is that?" Vivienne asked.

"My steward."

The man removed his hat and dismounted as soon as he arrived. "Your Grace. My lady. I didn't expect to see you here." Mr. Husselbee was tanned and freckled from so much time outdoors. He had an easy smile and a friendly face. In short, he was a man who could collect rents and still find a way to remain on good terms with the tenants.

"We saw the smoke," Nathan explained with a wave of his hand.

Husselbee frowned and examined the site himself. Hands on hips, he turned back to the duke. "The Hollands are away for a fortnight. Mrs. Holland is from Dorset, and her sister wrote to say her mother was ill. I told Holland I'd feed the livestock and check on the farm while they were away."

"Then who built this fire?"

Husselbee shook his head. "I don't know. Vagrants, I suspect. I'll make a thorough tour of the ducal land after I tend to the Hollands' livestock. If I find anyone, I'll run them off with a strict warning."

"Very good, sir." Nathan mounted again. "Come by the house after your tour and give me a full update."

"Yes, Your Grace."

When they were away, Vivienne spurred her horse and rode beside him. "I don't like it."

Nathan raised a brow. "Vagrants? You should know that sort of thing is common enough. My game wardens frequently have to arrest poachers. I let them go with a warning. Times are hard. People are hungry."

Vivienne studied him, her green eyes sparkling in diffuse morning light. "That's very kind of you. I do know poachers and vagrants are common. I suppose I feared the campsite might have housed the Glennish assassins."

He saw the flash of fear in her eyes before she lowered them.

Nathan reached over and grasped her hand. "They can't have found you here. No one knows where you are. You're safe. I promised I would protect you, and I will."

She raised her gaze to his again. "I believe you."

He released her hand, and they rode in silence again for a time.

"Shall we stop there and walk a bit?" she asked, indicating a stream that flowed along the back of his property. He'd had it stocked with trout, even though he didn't enjoy fishing.

At the stream, the horses drank and grazed while he and Vivienne walked the banks. Finally, they came to a shady spot where the stream widened into a small pond. It was not quite the size of Sedgemere's pond, and certainly not big enough for boating, but he'd swum in it as a boy and had a jolly time playing pirate.

Under a willow tree, Vivienne turned to him. "Should we continue our conversation from last night?"

Nathan's heart galloped, although he'd been trying to form the right words all morning. "I...yes," he managed weakly and swore silently at his idiocy. She would be right to refuse him. Sedgemere had been right about him. He'd relied too much on his good looks and had no skill when it came to wooing women. Why the devil hadn't he memorized some bloody Byron?

"You said last night you wanted more than just my body and my affections."

Had he said that? Good God. He had been bold after the wine and her kisses.

"You want my heart."

"I do. I want more than a...a liaison."

"I'm not in love with you," she said, and his heart fell into his belly.

"Of course not."

"But I could fall in love with you."

His head jerked up, his gaze searching her face. She smiled.

"Oh, I could very easily fall in love with you, Nathan." Her hands slid to his shoulders. "Do I have leave to call you Nathan?"

"Call me whatever you want."

"I've never known a man like you," she said.

He winced. "Is this about my face again?"

She closed her eyes and shook her head. "No. This is about how kind and generous and thoughtful you are."

"In the interest of full disclosure, not all of my actions toward you have been wholly unselfish."

She laughed. "Thank God. I was beginning to think you were not human."

"I'm very human," he said as she pressed against him. "Exceedingly human."

"Is it enough if I say you have a corner of my heart? Is it enough if I say you could very well have all of it one day?"

"It's enough."

And it was, because it was not only more than he had ever expected, but he simply couldn't resist her any longer. His body was on fire with need, and—as she'd pointed out—he was only human.

He bent his head to kiss her, pulling her hard against him. Her mouth opened for him, her lips meeting his with the same passion and same intensity. He was left with no question as to what she wanted from him. He hadn't imagined he would lie with her outdoors—very well, he'd actually imagined lying with her everywhere, but he hadn't *expected* to lie with her outdoors—but he would not argue the point.

He stripped off his coat, dropped it under the tree, and allowed his hands to travel down her slim back. He cupped her bottom, brought her hips into contact with his erection. She moaned and rocked against him. Her own hands explored him—his back, his chest, his buttocks, his cock.

When she slid her hand over the fall of his riding breeches, Nathan grabbed the trunk of the tree for support.

"Your body is as perfect as your face," she murmured when he kissed her neck. "You're hard all over."

He was hard, indisputably hard. His hands skidded over her sides and up to cup her breasts. With a groan, her head fell back. Through the layers she wore, he felt her nipples pebble against his hands and wished he could see them, kiss them.

She pulled him down, settling herself on his coat. "My legs won't hold up much longer," she said, her voice husky. "You've made them wobbly and weak."

His hand slid under her skirts and up her stocking-clad leg until he reached the bare flesh of her thigh. "They feel fine to me." He kissed her again, his hand stroking her soft flesh. "Very fine."

"Don't tease me, Nathan," she murmured. "Not this time. Next time, perhaps, or the time after that. Not this time."

"I am yours to command," he answered, his hand cupping the warm, wet flesh at the juncture of her thighs.

A sigh escaped her parted lips, but her eyes—so dark now—never left his face.

He touched her, explored her gently, until she arched beneath him. Her cheeks were pink with arousal, and when he slid two fingers inside her, circled her small nub with his thumb, her eyes seemed to blur and lose focus.

"Let go, Princess," he murmured. "No one will hear you but me."

Her hips rose, and he lessened his pressure slightly. In a rush, she bowed back, a strangled cry drifting through the trees. He withdrew, studied her face. She lay with her eyes closed, chest rising and falling, cheeks stained lovely pink, and her lips plump and red.

Finally, she opened her eyes and smiled. "Nathan, do you know how to dress and undress a lady?"

He wasn't certain how to answer. He'd dressed and undressed his share, but it wasn't a subject he wished to discuss with the woman he hoped to make his wife.

"I see that you do. Good." She rose to her knees and gave him her back. "Unfasten me, will you?"

His hands fumbled at the hooks and eyes, the ties and knots, the pins and tapes. Finally, he had her out of the outer layers of clothing, and she stood in her shift.

"I don't think anyone will come this way," he said, "but I cannot be certain."

"Then I suppose I had better not stand about all day."

With a flick of her finger at the knot at her neck, the chemise came loose and slid down her body. He followed its progress hungrily. The material uncovered ripe, full breasts tipped with dark, erect nipples, a slim waist, lush hips, and plump thighs.

"You take my breath away," he whispered.

"Good." She turned and walked to the edge of the pond, her derriere as round and perfect as the rest of her. She dipped a toe in the water, let out a little shriek, then moved resolutely forward.

Finally, she'd submerged herself to just below her breasts. She turned to him, giving him a view he could have enjoyed all day.

"It's not so cold, especially once you get used to it. What are you waiting for, Duke?"

"Nothing."

He stripped off his neckcloth and pulled at his boots.

"Do hurry, Your Grace. I'm naked and wet and cold. I need you to warm me."

"I am hurrying, Your Highness. I haven't any aid, as you did."

Finally, he was as naked as she, and painfully aroused as she watched him approach.

"I should hate you," she said.

He paused, one foot in the water.

"You are the most perfect man I have ever seen. You could at least have a scar or a withered arm or some such thing to even out the face. But, no. You could be a Michelangelo."

The water was not cold, and he forced himself not to look overeager to reach her. "You act as though that is a bad thing."

He reached for her, pulling her into his arms. Her warm body was slippery and slick.

"You might have been a Botticelli," he said, kissing her neck. "You're lush and soft and—"

She wrapped her legs around him, and he blew out a breath.

"And?" she prompted.

"I can't think."

"Then don't."

Her legs wrapped around his waist, and he slid inside her quickly and more roughly than he'd intended. She didn't complain, only tightened around him and kissed him more deeply.

His hands cupped her bottom, pulling her harder against him and angling her until she slid up and down in a way he knew would give her the greatest pleasure. Her eyes widened after his first few thrusts, and her breath quickened.

"You're quite good at this," she gasped as he drove into her again.

"I suppose"—he clenched his jaw and attempted to maintain control—"you will hold that against me as well."

"Not at all. This—" She shuddered and clenched around him. "For this, I can forgive anything."

"Even my face?"

"Even that."

He couldn't hold on any longer, and he thrust hard into her, hoping it would be enough to bring her to climax. He felt her muscles clamp around him, and the satisfaction of knowing he'd brought her pleasure again was almost as good as his own release.

Almost.

Because, when they finally climbed out of the water and lay spent and sated in each other's arms, Nathan felt the one thing he had never felt with any woman ever before: certainty.

Chapter Seven

VIVIENNE WOULD HAVE been content to lie in Nathan's arms all day if her flesh hadn't started to resemble that of a plucked goose.

"You're shivering," he said, and his words alone thawed her. He noticed everything about her, wanted to keep her warm and safe.

"I don't mind. I like it here with you."

"I like it too, but I did say I have something to show you."

She rose on her elbow, faced him. "There's more?" Her gaze slid down his body—his absolutely perfect body—and the color rose in his cheeks. He was so adorable. She wanted to have him again.

"Dress, and I'll show you."

It was easier said than done, but with his help, the tedious chore was finally accomplished. Her hair was mostly dry, as O'Connell's excellent coiffure had stayed in place. Vivienne imagined it was a bit lopsided, but she didn't particularly care. Today was the first time she'd felt any real joy or happiness since the attack on the palace.

It wasn't only Nathan's lovemaking either. Being with him made her happy. She'd wakened long before dawn this morning, too excited about the prospect of seeing him to sleep any longer. She hadn't lied when she'd told him he had a corner of her heart. In truth, she'd been modest. He had captured it whole.

The prospect scared her. Everyone she'd loved was dead. Everyone who'd cared for her was dead, and the men seeking to kill her were still at large. She had no right to involve Nathan in this deadly game of cat and mouse. She had no right to care for him. Caring for him might just mean his death.

They rode back to the house, which looked impressive with the streaks of sunlight breaking through the clouds behind it. Nathan led her to the back, but instead of turning in the direction of the stables, he motioned toward the lawn. In the middle of the long expanse of green bordered by pink and purple flowers, she spotted three targets made of straw and painted with red circles in the middle.

A groom took her mount and handed her down, and she joined Nathan and his butler.

"Duke, I didn't know you had an interest in archery."

He smiled, the smile of a man with a secret. "I don't. I know you do." He held out a hand, and the butler reached into a sack at his feet. He pulled out a quiver of arrows, followed by a bow, and handed them to Nathan.

"What do you think?" the duke asked.

"Very nice." She stepped closer to better appreciate the fine craftsmanship of the bow. "May I?" she asked, indicating the arrows.

"Please."

She lifted one out and nodded approval at the straight line of the shaft and the high quality of the fletching.

"For a man with little interest in archery, this is an extraordinary set."

"It's for you."

She jerked her head up, uncertain she'd heard him correctly. "Me?"

"Yours was...lost. This is a replacement."

"But this is too much." She'd never given a second thought to the cost of things before, but since the attack had left her with nothing, she'd begun to think of money more and more. That didn't stop her hand from curling around the handle of the bow. She itched to try it, to pluck the string to see if it sang.

"Go ahead," Nathan said. "These targets are for you."

A thrill of excitement raced through her. Archery had always been one of her favorite pastimes, one at which she excelled. Now she fitted the bow around her hands, took a moment to accustom herself to the weight and the feel of it. Then she pulled an arrow from the quiver and pointed it at the target on her right.

"Not that one," Nathan said.

She glanced at him over the bow.

"Start on the left."

Strange request, but she didn't argue. She shifted until she faced the new target, notched her arrow, and pulled back the string. With a satisfying *twang*, the arrow soared toward the target, hitting the red center circle just to the left.

"Very good, my lady," the butler remarked.

Vivienne narrowed her eyes, calculating her error. She squared her shoulders and, facing the center target, pulled another arrow from the quiver. She made a slight modification in how she held the bow and let the arrow soar. It hit the center dead in the middle.

She allowed a small smile to curve her lips.

"If you'll excuse me, Your Grace," the butler said, and started back toward the house. Vivienne hardly saw him go. She turned to the last target and positioned the bow, then pulled another arrow from the quiver.

She was aware Nathan stood beside her, feet braced apart and arms crossed over his chest. He shifted slightly, and she had a moment to wonder what he was nervous about before the target consumed her focus.

She narrowed her eyes, pulled the string of the bow back, and let the arrow fly. It made a small *ping* when it hit.

"I hope I didn't break the tip," she said. Without waiting for his answer, she marched across the grass and examined the center of the target.

Something gold glittered in the filtered sunlight. Her arrow had pierced it through.

She pulled the arrow from the straw, and the small circle came with it, balanced precariously on the tip of the arrow. Vivienne's heart lurched.

It was a ring—a ring with a rather large diamond in the center surrounded by green stones she assumed must be emeralds.

She jerked around, almost bumping into Nathan, who had come to stand beside her. Before she could say a word, he bent to one knee.

"The ring was my mother's—not her wedding ring. She still wears that. It was a gift from my father on my birth. I always think of you when I see it because of the emeralds. They're almost as beautiful as your eyes."

"Does this mean what I think it means?" she asked, her voice shaking. Every part of her shook now—her legs, her belly, her hands.

"I want you to be my wife, my duchess. I know this may seem sudden. You don't know me very well, but it's all I've wanted for the last eight years. I never forgot you."

"I don't know what to say," she finally managed.

"You could say yes."

The look in his eyes almost melted her. She could see the love in his face, in the way he looked at her. She'd seen it in the way her father had looked at her mother. But did she feel the same, or were her burgeoning feelings only infatuation or, worse, gratitude for his kindness?

"I..." she began, uncertain what she would say. At the moment, her English all but eluded her.

He held up a hand. "Or you could tell me you need more time."

When she didn't answer, he winced. "Or you could tell me no." He rose slowly, brushing the grass from his breeches.

She took his hand, looked up and into his eyes, bluer even than the sky on this cloudy day.

"The answer is most definitely *not* no." She pressed the ring into his palm. "But it's not yes either. Keep this for me? I hope when I am ready, you will offer it again?"

"Of course." He stepped back, pocketing the ring in his waistcoat. The air around him was formal now, and how she wished she could bring back the easy mood of their morning.

"Thank you for the bow and arrows. I would say you have no idea how much it means to me, but it occurs to me that perhaps you do understand."

"I do," he said, and the answer seemed to encompass more than her thanks for the archery set. "Stay and practice as long as you like. I have some business to attend to."

"Oh." She had hoped they might spend more time together. "Will I see you at dinner?"

"Of course. And I've asked one of the maids to take your measurements. The housekeeper assures me she's an adequate seamstress. Perhaps in a few days, you will have several more gowns. Tell the maid what fabrics you like, and they will be ordered from the town or from London, if they are not available here."

"You are too generous."

"I have more money than I can spend. A few dresses and an archery set are hardly largesse. And, as I said, I'm not entirely unselfish. I want you to fall in love with me."

With those words, he bowed and started back toward the house.

"Nathan," she called after him.

He paused and turned back to face her.

"I'm falling."

THE NEXT DAYS were filled with pleasant morning rides and scintillating dinners. Vivienne was all Nathan could want in a woman and more. He'd vowed not to take her again until after she'd agreed to be his wife, but he could hardly resist when, laughing, she pulled him into an empty stall in the stable, or when she opened her bedchamber door at night and tugged him inside.

She was passionate, witty, energetic, and diverting. He'd never enjoyed himself as much as he did when he was with her. He'd never laughed so much, talked so much, craved someone's touch so much.

It wasn't only her touch. Just the act of seeing her or hearing her voice made his heart swell and lift.

Since the day of the proposal, he had not brought up marriage again. She knew his desires, and she would give him an answer when she was ready. In the meantime, he began to look for a response to his request from the Prince Regent. She didn't ask directly if he'd received an answer, but he often saw a hopeful look in her eyes. He shook his head when she raised her brows in question, and they waited.

One morning, about a week after the proposal, the two of them were met by Mr. Husselbee as they walked back to the house.

"Your Grace." He gave a bow. "My lady." Another bow. "I trust there have been no more signs of vagrants in the area."

"None," Nathan answered. "Did you catch the men?"

"No. I tracked them to the edge of the property and lost the trail. I think they must be long gone and someone else's problem now. The Holland family has returned and reported nothing in their house or shed was disrupted."

"Very good."

Vivienne touched his arm. "I will leave you gentlemen to discuss crops and farms and livestock. Excuse me."

Nathan watched her go, then asked Husselbee to join him in the library.

Husselbee sat in the chair across from Nathan's desk and elaborated on the condition of the estate. Finally, he took a breath, let it out, then took another.

"Is something troubling you, Mr. Husselbee?"

"Yes, Your Grace. I'm not certain how to proceed. You see, ever since one of the maids ordered those fine fabrics from the town, there's been talk. Who are such fine fabrics for? I don't blame the girl, Your Grace. She didn't say anything to set tongues wagging, but you know how people are."

"Can't we say they are for my mother?"

"Not in the proportions ordered, Your Grace. Your mother is tall and, er, ample compared to Lady Vivienne."

"I see."

"And there's more talk, Your Grace. Usually when you are in residence, you host some of the local gentry for dinner or a garden party. No one has been invited to visit, and you've been here almost a fortnight."

"I understand, Husselbee. Unfortunately, I don't have a solution for you at this time. Lady Vivienne has fallen into some unfortunate circumstances—through no fault of her own—and it is best if we keep her presence here a secret for the time being."

"Yes, Your Grace. I'll do my best for as long as I can."

Nathan knew that couldn't be for much longer.

He went to sleep late. He'd had another engaging dinner with Vivienne, and when she'd hinted she would welcome a visit from him after the servants had gone to bed, he had politely refused.

He wanted a wife, not a mistress. Oh, he liked bedding her well enough. She was enthusiastic and imaginative. But he wanted more than bedsport. He wanted a wife, a partner, a mother for his children.

He had thought she would give him an answer by now, and there had been times he had looked at her and seen something in her eyes. He'd held his breath, certain she would ask for the ring again—the ring he kept always in his waistcoat.

But she had not asked, had not declared her love for him, and because she hesitated, so did he. He wanted to hold her in the aftermath of their lovemaking, stroke her hair, and tell her he loved her. But he didn't dare push her or pressure her to say more than she was willing.

And so he waited far longer than usual to go to bed. He'd dismissed Fletcher so his valet could rest, and Nathan did little more than shed his coat before falling into bed. He didn't even bother to toe off his boots. It wasn't the first time he'd slept in his clothes, although it was more comfortable when he was foxed.

Still, he fell into a deep, dreamless sleep, only coming awake slowly at the pinch in his neck.

He opened his eyes and stared at the man bending over him. "Don't move, or I'll slit your throat."

Nathan didn't move.

"Good. Now tell me where she is, and we'll let you live."

"Where who is?" Nathan croaked.

"Princess Vivienne."

Chapter Eight

H<small>E HADN'T COME</small> to her. She'd waited, the lamp burning, her heart thudding, for what seemed hours. At midnight, she realized he wouldn't come. She could hardly blame him. He wanted an answer to his proposal. He deserved an answer, and she hadn't given it.

She'd wanted to give it so many times—wanted to tell him *yes, yes, yes*. She loved him, couldn't help but love him, despite that too-handsome face and perfect body.

And because she loved him, she had not given him an answer. Because she loved him, she couldn't bear to put him in danger.

But perhaps the danger was over. The assassins must have given up searching for her by now. They'd be expected back in Glynaven, undoubtedly had superiors to report to. Perhaps she could give Nathan the answer he wanted. The answer she wanted.

And she did not want to wait until the morning.

She climbed out of bed, naked, stumbled over the bow and arrows she'd left by the bed, and found her shift on the Chinese screen. She pulled it on, considered lighting a lamp, and then decided she knew the way to his rooms well enough without it.

The moment she stepped into the corridor, she knew something was amiss. The hair rose on her arms even before she saw the shadow across from his room.

Clamping a hand over her mouth, she dove back into her chamber, closing the door silently and locking it behind her.

They'd found her.

The assassins had found her.

They hadn't given up after all. They were here, and this time they would kill her.

The sightless eyes flashed in her mind again—all those eyes and the blood on the carpets, sticking to the bottom of her slippers. She couldn't bear to see it all again. She couldn't shoulder the guilt of bringing death to any innocents at Wyndover Park.

She had to go. She had to flee before the assassins found her and slit her throat.

She staggered toward the Chinese screen and the boots set neatly behind it. She did not care about a dress, but she could not run without boots. She knew that well enough. She'd bent to pull them on when her mind froze, and even in her panicked state, one word broke through: Nathan.

She couldn't leave him.

Vivienne shook her head.

He was dead. He had to be. They'd already killed him. She could save only herself now.

But her hand dropped away from the boots, and her gaze tracked to the bow and arrows near the bed. Even if he was dead, she couldn't leave him. He would never have left her. He would have given anything to keep her safe. If there was a chance he still lived, she had to go to him.

Snatching the bow and arrows, she readied an arrow and tiptoed back to the door.

Silently, she turned the lock and eased the door open. The hinges made no sound, and if she lived, she would thank Mrs. Patton for that later.

Peering around the doorjamb, she saw the corridor was empty. For a moment, she hoped she'd imagined the shadow and the man's form, but then she heard the low rumble of men's voices coming from Nathan's room.

Keeping against the wall, she crept down the hallway. Her heart beat so hard, her chest ached, and she was almost dizzy from the fear. As she neared the room, she heard the most terrifying sound yet—Glennish.

If she'd had any doubts before, she had none now. These were the assassins, and they had Nathan.

Alive.

She knew that because she heard him answer them. "I don't know what you're talking about," he said. "I don't know any princess."

"He lies," one of them hissed in her native tongue. "Kill him."

"Slit his throat, and we'll find her ourselves. She's here."

Nathan would die. For her.

Vivienne stepped into the doorway, arrow nocked and ready. She assessed the situation quickly. Two men were near the door, and the third had a knife to Nathan's throat where he lay on the bed.

"Touch him, and I'll shoot you through."

One of the men by the door jerked toward her, and she swung her bow toward him. "Don't do it," she said in Glennish. "If you know anything about me, you know I can kill all three of you before you can shout for help. If there were anyone who would help you."

She swung her bow back to the man kneeling over Nathan. "Get off him and back away slowly."

"I'll cut his throat and then yours, *Princess*."

"Get off him!" she shouted, afraid to wait too much longer, knowing every moment she waited was another moment closer to Nathan's death.

The assassin didn't move.

God! God! God!

She didn't want to kill him. She'd never killed anyone, man or beast.

But her gaze collided with Nathan's. His eyes focused on her, still alive, still full of love. She couldn't allow his to become another pair of sightless eyes that haunted her.

Twang.

She loosed the arrow, heard the sickening *thunk* as it struck flesh. She yanked another from her quiver just as quickly and swiveled to face the last two assassins.

NATHAN PUSHED THE dead weight of the assassin off and jumped to his feet. Vivienne stood across the room, arrow trained on the two men intent on killing her. Both had drawn their knives—long, sharp weapons—and Nathan had no doubt they would use them on her and anyone else in their way.

He had to help her, but for the first time in his life, he felt utterly helpless. He had no weapon, no means to rescue her. She'd rescued him.

At an imperceptible signal, the assassins separated and began to circle the princess.

"Don't move," she ordered in Glennish.

The assassins ignored her. Despite her claims, she couldn't shoot them at the same time, and if she fired at one, the other could attack. Nathan took a step toward the one closest to him. The man brandished his weapon.

"Stay back," he ordered.

"Nathan, be careful!"

He'd distracted her, and the assassins were now on either side of her. She had to pivot from one to the other in order to keep her arrow trained on them. She was fast and agile, but she couldn't hold them off forever. Nathan pressed his weight onto the balls of his feet, preparing to throw himself at one assassin, thereby removing one target. He'd probably end up dead and without an heir. The bloody American cousin would have the title.

His poor mother.

Nathan lunged just as the dressing room door opened. He caught the distracted assassin about the waist, and the two tumbled to the rug. Nathan got in a good jab to the man's back before he rolled and brandished the knife in Nathan's direction.

"Let him go," Vivienne said, her voice full of command.

"I'm fine," Nathan answered. "I can take him."

The assassin jabbed at him, narrowly missing.

"Or not," Nathan muttered.

"I believe she meant me, Your Grace."

Nathan's head jerked at the sound of his valet's voice. "Fletcher!"

His valet stood in front of the other assassin, the man's knife a steel slash across his exposed neck.

"I heard a sound and thought you might require assistance, Your Grace."

Goddamn it all to hell. "Let him go!" Nathan shouted in Glennish, kicking out to prevent his own attacker from coming closer. Thank God he still had the boots on. The knife grazed his calf and would have split his skin open without the protection of the thick leather.

"Lower the arrow," the assassin holding Fletcher told Vivienne. The assassin was dark and short, holding his knife like a seasoned warrior, whereas the one Nathan fought was younger and moved with less certainty.

"Let him go," Vivienne countered.

"Shoot him, Vivienne," Nathan said, kicking at his assassin again. This time, the knife did pierce his boot, and warm blood trickled down his skin.

She shook her head, her eyes never leaving the assassin's face. "Release him. I don't want to kill you."

"I'll kill him, then you," the assassin hissed. "Put down your weapon."

She hesitated, and her arm wavered.

"No!" Nathan yelled. Their only chance was to kill one of the assassins. "Kill him!"

"I can't!"

The dark assassin pulled his hand with the knife back, and Fletcher closed his eyes.

※

VIVIENNE CLOSED HER eyes and let go. She half prayed the arrow would miss, though it would mean the death of an innocent man.

But she didn't miss. Of course she didn't miss. She never did.

The assassin screamed as the arrow plunged into the side of his face, the side exposed over Fletcher's shoulder. The man's knife clattered to the floor, and Fletcher went down on his knees, looking like he might fall over from the shock of it.

There was no time to help the valet, no time to render any aid to the wounded assassin writhing on the floor. He'd be dead in a moment or two. Dead because of her.

She pushed the thought aside and reached for another arrow, swung to Nathan.

But the third assassin was gone.

Nathan swiped the blood from his calf away.

"Your Grace," Fletcher wheezed. "You're hurt."

"I'm fine." He rose to his feet, looking a little unsteady but solid.

Vivienne felt unsteady too. She wanted to collapse, to cry for days, to run into his arms and bury her face in his chest. Instead, she gestured with the arrow toward the open bedchamber door.

"We have to go after him." She didn't add what she'd been thinking: before he murdered innocent servants.

"Not without a weapon." Nathan pushed the dead man on his bed over and yanked the knife from his hand. "Now I'm ready. Follow me."

Without waiting for her agreement, he started forward, pausing at the door to sweep his gaze in both directions.

"Fletcher?"

"Left, Your Grace."

"Stay put, Fletcher." Nathan glanced at her over his shoulder. "Coming?"

He didn't tell her to stay. He didn't expect her to wait for him, like a helpless girl. This was her battle too, and he knew it, respected her need to end this herself.

Oh, how she loved him.

"I'm coming." She raised the arrow again and followed him into the corridor.

Nothing but shadows and the distant sound of a clock's pendulum swinging back and forth with a quiet ticking. At the first doorway, which was closed, Nathan put a finger to his lips and lifted the latch. He pushed inside, knife raised, and she followed, swinging her arrow left and right. He parted the drapes, opened the tallboy against the wall, and peered under the bed.

"Empty," Nathan declared.

She moved back into the hallway, and he followed.

"There's only one more room this way, a servant's closet."

"And that door?" She pointed to a doorway made to look like the wall's paneling.

"The servants' stairs. I'm betting he took those."

"I think you're right. He wants to escape."

"He wants to kill you. I don't think he's given up yet."

She agreed with him on that point as well. He started for the end of the hallway, but she grabbed his arm and pulled him back.

"Nathan."

He gave her an impatient glance, then looked over his shoulder at the door. Vivienne placed a hand on his cheek. That earned her his full attention.

"Just in case I don't have another opportunity, I want to tell you I love you."

"You will have another opportunity. But I love you too."

She smiled. She couldn't contain the burst of joy that raced through her. "Do you have the ring?"

"What?"

He must think her mad, and perhaps she was. This was no time to discuss marriage, and yet, she'd seen how quickly life as one knew it could come to a crashing end. Now might be the only chance she ever had.

"Your mother's emerald ring?"

He stared at her for a long moment, then his hand passed over the pocket of his waistcoat. "Are you saying you'll marry me?"

"Yes. I was coming to tell you when I interrupted that tête-à-tête in your room."

"I much prefer your company at any rate." He pulled the ring from his waistcoat. "I don't have time to do this properly."

She waved his protest away. "Put it on my finger. That's as proper as I need or want."

He took her hand, slid the ring on her finger clumsily.

She kissed him quickly, ran her thumb over the unfamiliar piece of jewelry on her hand.

"Now, let's go catch an assassin," she said.

HE WOULD DIE. She'd finally told him she loved him, finally agreed to be his wife, his duchess, and now he was off to his death. Life was full of injustice. Nathan just hadn't ever had so much of it thrown his direction.

He led her down the servants' stairwell, emerging silently onto the house's ground floor. He mentally outlined the geography of the house. Short corridor leading to the expansive vestibule in front of him, door to his library, which led to a parlor on his left. Door to the music room, which opened to a large sitting room on his right. The dining room was on the other side of the vestibule.

"I'll take this side, you take that," Vivienne said.

"Hell no. Stay with me." He would not let her out of his sight. "Let's start in the library."

He opened the door, crept inside, keeping his back to the wall. Vivienne followed, closing the door behind her. Smart woman, he thought. No one could come in or out without alerting them.

Nathan jerked his head toward a couch facing the fire. He doubted the man would be lying on it, but he motioned for her to cover him while he checked behind the curtains. The two of them moved silently toward their corners.

Just as Nathan tugged the drapes open, he heard the *swish* of an arrow. He turned just in time to see the assassin raise his knife and hurl it.

At him.

Nathan jerked to the right, and the knife clattered against the window inches from where he'd stood.

"You missed!" Nathan yelled.

"So did she," the assassin answered.

Vivienne was already readying another arrow, but the assassin didn't wait. He flung himself at Nathan, and the two men rolled to the floor, Nathan's knife tumbled under his desk.

"Nathan!" Vivienne shouted. "I can't get a clear shot."

The assassin's fist collided with his nose, and Nathan smashed his forehead into the man's nose while the assassin kneed him in the breadbasket. The two tumbled over each other again and again, overturning tables and lamps. He smashed the assassin with an antique bowl and stumbled to his feet. For a moment, he thought he'd won, but the man was up again and plowed him in the face.

Nathan saw darkness right before his head hit the floor. Vivienne's scream brought him back, and he moved his head right before another fist slammed into it. The assassin pulled the punch but too late. His fist hit the hard wood of the floor.

Nathan grabbed his neck and pushed him off, using his elbow to pop the assassin in the mouth. When the man was down, Nathan hit him again. And again.

He would have punched him a third time, but Vivienne stayed his hand.

"It's done," she panted. "He's unconscious."

Nathan gained his feet, putting his hands on his hips and drawing in gasps of air. It hurt to breathe. It hurt to think. It hurt to exist.

"And my father made me take fencing," he said between breaths. "I told him those lessons were a bloody waste of time."

Vivienne gave him a bewildered look. "What did you want to take?"

"Boxing."

She nodded, drew in a breath. "All of our children will be pugilists."

"Even the girls?"

"Especially the girls."

He opened his arms, and she fell into them. He didn't care if the servants were gathering in the doorway now, if Fletcher was calling for a doctor, if somewhere above a maid screamed.

Vivienne was in his arms. His princess.

His duchess.

Epilogue

"He's an insufferable *muc*," she said, using the Glennish term for *pig*. The door of the Grecian parlor at the residence of the Duke of Stoke Teversault closed as the Prince Regent made his exit.

"I will not argue." Nathan leaned against one cream and dark lilac wall and watched her pace. His wife's ire was stoked now.

She was his wife. *His wife*. After they'd dealt with the business of the dead assassins and the live one, they'd received a letter from Prinny summoning them to an audience at the Duke of Stoke Teversault's ball. Nathan had already planned to attend and to approach the prince, who never missed the annual affair, but he'd thought a formal audience a good sign. He should have listened to Stoke Teversault. The duke had cautioned him against reading anything into Prinny's invitation. Nathan had hoped Stoke Teversault was just being...well, Stoke Teversault. He was naturally sober and restrained. Fortunately, Nathan had the foresight to procure a special license and marry Vivienne before the ball.

Prinny might offer his protection, but she'd have Nathan's in any event.

"Can you believe the way he spoke to me?" she said, striding across the parlor and then back again. Through the open windows behind her, he could see the famous row of lime trees that lined the house's drive. "He acted as though it was my father's fault he and my mother were killed. As though anyone deserves to die that way!"

"He's afraid," Nathan said, moving toward her and laying his hands on her shoulders. "He knows but for luck and the grace of God, that could have been him."

She turned into his arms. "He's allowing me to stay in the country only because of your gift." Her eyes narrowed. "What exactly was this gift?"

"A small token of my fealty." Three ships were a token indeed. "But you are the Duchess of Wyndover now. He couldn't make you leave even if he wanted."

"And so there's to be no outcry over the massacre at Glynaven Palace, no public condemnation."

"Not from England, but you've written dozens of letters to other world leaders. Surely one of them will condemn the actions of the revolutionaries. Perhaps Spain or Russia."

"Perhaps."

He wrapped his arms around her, looked into her lovely eyes. The music from the orchestra Stoke Teversault had hired for the ball swelled and carried on a breeze scented with flowers. "I cannot give you public condemnation. But I can give you revenge."

She stiffened. "What do you mean?"

He touched his forehead to hers. "Happiness."

"Happiness?"

"Did you think I would suggest we hire mercenaries and order the revolutionary leaders slaughtered?"

"It would be a nice gesture."

"You don't want that." Although he imagined a small part of her did, and he could hardly blame her. "Why not be my wife, have children with me, grow old with me? The revolutionaries who tried to kill you, to kill off the royal line, will always know they never succeeded. Our children and our happiness will be the best revenge."

She heaved a sigh of resignation. "You make sense, as usual."

"I am an extremely sensible man."

"You must be to tolerate all those swooning females. Three fainted in your path on the short walk to the ballroom."

He scowled, clearly not wanting to speak of the incidents.

"I'm certain the heat overcame the ladies, nothing more. This ball is a crush."

"*I'm* certain it was one look at your pretty face. Oops!" She fell against his chest. "I accidentally looked directly into your eyes. Help!" She arched back so he was forced to catch her. "I shall faint." Her hand brushed her forehead.

He lifted her off her feet and swept her into his arms. "In that case, perhaps we'd better retire to the bedchamber Stoke Teversault thoughtfully supplied. You'd better lie down, wife."

"Take me to bed, husband."

"With pleasure."

Duchess of Scandal

BY
MIRANDA NEVILLE

Acknowledgements

Thanks to Caroline Linden and Megan Mulry for their support and advice; to Daniel James Brown for writing *The Boys in the Boat* and inspiring the Dukeries Cup; and to Grace, Shana, and Carolyn.

Chapter One

HE WAS A fool to come back to The Chimneys. As he neared the entrance to the estate, the Duke of Linton almost told his coachman to turn around. Last time he made this journey, Althea had been with him, the sweet young bride whose beauty and bright spirits had captivated him and led him to select her against common sense and the advice of his family. Last time he drove along this road, he'd thought of little else but the approach of night and his new wife's bed.

Which was an object lesson in the danger of quick decisions and allowing desire to overcome reason.

He did not change his order to the coachman, and he did not dwell on the three weeks of his honeymoon when he thought he would be happy. He tucked his disappointment into a hidden chamber of his heart and looked forward to a few quiet days.

When the coach stopped before the wrought-iron gates to the park, Linton opened the window and glanced out. A couple of small boys tore through the thick laurels adjacent to the gate. The larger of the two tackled his junior to the ground, and they rolled around together, squealing like a pair of piglets.

Linton had been a child here, many eons ago, though he had played next to the main house and usually alone, having only a trio of older sisters, the plague of his life. He'd have liked a brother to wrestle with. He dismissed a pang of regret that no sons of his own would ever romp on the lawns of this or any other of his twelve mansions.

A woman, followed by a couple of little girls, emerged from the neat brick lodge and opened the gates. The last thing Linton noticed, as the coach rolled forward, was a washing line pegged with numerous garments flapping in the breeze. What was the world coming to when the small clothes of his servants' families disfigured the pristine entrance to a duke's estate?

It was a small annoyance and quickly forgotten in anticipation of seeing The Chimneys. When they turned the corner into the avenue, the graceful Queen Anne house came into sight, all mellow brick and golden stone, perfect in its proportions and dominated by the four giant chimneys that gave it its name.

Nine days he had, with almost no business to conduct and no one to bother him. No callers, no secretary, and certainly no wife. Nothing to do but walk, read, or anything else that took his fancy. Maybe a spot of fishing.

Descending the carriage in what were, for him, high spirits, he greeted the elderly butler. "Good afternoon, Binney. I trust I find you well this fine day."

"Your Grace." Binney seemed shocked. "We weren't expecting you. Will you be staying..."

Linton silenced him with a twitch of the ducal eyebrows. Each one of his residences was kept in a state of readiness for his arrival, even this one that he never visited. Why were his servants questioning him? His secretary had tried to argue when he'd announced his decision to make a detour to Nottinghamshire on his journey to Longworth, his principal estate in Berkshire. Although the duchess had made The Chimneys her domain, he had every right to come here whenever and for whatever reason he wished and stay for as long or short a time as suited him. None of them could complain he neglected his duty—not that it was any of their damn business. "I'll settle this boundary issue with Sedgemere myself," he'd told Newton firmly. Tomorrow he'd ride over to Sedgemere House and talk duke to duke about a pair of tenants fighting over a fence. Or maybe he'd wait a few days, until after he'd done some fishing. He could do with a little peace and quiet after a long parliamentary session.

Entering the hall, he found he could not after all forget his last visit to The Chimneys. He'd chosen this house for his honeymoon because it was his favorite, smaller and more intimate than the vast Longworth. He expected to hear Althea's laughter and see her leaning over the banister, beckoning him with her smile, when he came in from riding. But of course she was not here. The three weeks, during which he'd hoped his conventional marriage would flower into something sweeter, had been followed by disillusionment and fiery quarrels. Six months later, the Duke and Duchess of Linton were in a state of almost complete estrangement that had, over almost five years, slipped into armed neutrality. Now they lived in separate houses when they could, and when they couldn't, for a couple of months during the Season, they nodded with bared teeth should they happen to cross paths at Linton House in Grosvenor Square. They had different interests, moved in different circles, and led separate lives.

A pall fell over his spirits and, to cap his lost holiday mood, the light through the great window over the staircase turned gray. He needed to stretch his legs after hours in the carriage, but a walk or ride didn't appeal when it was likely to rain. Like all his houses, The Chimneys was equipped with a room where he could build up a sweat and exorcise his frustrations.

After an hour of hard work punching the leather bag of sand, he was pleasantly exhausted. He ordered hot water brought to his rooms and planned a quiet dinner with a book for company. Perhaps, daring thought, he wouldn't even bother to change into evening dress.

He opened the tall casement windows of his bedchamber and breathed in country air, rested his eyes on the white dots of sheep grazing in the park. At first he barely registered the murmur of female humming in the adjoining room—there were always servants going about their business—until the timbre of the voice penetrated his consciousness. He strode over and flung open the communicating door.

"Linton!" Althea, Duchess of Linton's voice was musical as ever but far from pleased. "What are you doing here?"

"I might ask you the same thing, madam. You are not supposed to be at The Chimneys until the fourteenth of the month. You will have to leave."

"You are mistaken. I've been here since yesterday, and I'm not going anywhere. This is my house."

"The Chimneys belongs to me."

"Of course it's yours. I am well aware that I have nothing of my own. Yet, by our agreement I spend the summer here, and the last time I checked July was summer. You are supposed to be in Berkshire, and *you* will have to leave."

"You told Newton you wouldn't be here."

"I told him nothing of the kind. You're saying that because you have come to torment me."

"Are you accusing me of prevarication? I assure you, madam, that the Dukes of Linton do not lie."

They were squabbling like a pair of children, and unless he stopped it, the exchange would mushroom into the kind of bitter argument that had plagued the early months of their marriage. He leaned back on his heels and reassembled his shattered temper, because, as always, it was up to him to behave with dignity. "There has been a misunderstanding, Althea. I trust we can spend one night under the same roof without a quarrel."

But for her expression, she might have been the girl he'd married. In a white muslin gown with her red-gold hair tied in a careless knot, she was lovely, more so than ever, and her beauty caught at his throat. The beauty had always been there. It was why he'd foolishly chosen a very young girl of small fortune and from a tainted family for his bride. He'd made the mistake of assuming he could possess this beauty and charm and that she would be a proper wife for a Duke of Linton.

Daggers darted from her eyes, contrasting with the simplicity of her attire. Then she gave a swift, sharp nod, and her mouth relaxed from its defiant pout. They stared at each other in a skeptical truce.

"Will you dine with me, Linton?"

His pleasure at this surely grudging invitation surprised him. Was he such a fool that a few yards of white cloth made him forget the past? The true Althea was the one tricked out in extravagant silks and satins, adorned and bejeweled, her hair braided and curled into the rococo absurdities of the London hairdresser, her eyelashes blackened. His moment of weakness was only a false recollection of happier times.

"Country hours?" he asked.

"Of course. I don't like to keep the servants up late."

She didn't mind it in London when he'd return from dining out to find a crowd of fashionable ne'er-do-wells and fribbles lolling around his dining room table, draining the contents of his wine cellar. "As you wish," he said. "Speaking of servants, do we have a woman in the lodge now? Or was her husband absent this afternoon?"

"Mrs. Trumbull is the widow of your tenant John Trumbull."

"I remember he caught a fever last year."

"Her children were too young to take over the farm, and she couldn't manage alone. I gave her the lodge. She seems just about capable of opening and closing the gate without the help of a man."

It was the right thing to offer the widow a house and employment, and he might have thought of it himself had he been consulted. Instead, she made him feel obscurely guilty. "She hangs washing in front of her house," he said.

"And where else, pray, would she hang it?"

"I don't know, but it's unsightly and spoils the approach to the park."

The light of combat brightened her green eyes. "So to avoid offending your sensibilities, you would have her children go dirty?"

"I didn't say that."

"You change your linens at least once a day, don't you, Linton?" He felt his cheeks darken at the indelicate question. "Where do you suppose your shirts and stockings and drawers are dried?"

"Somewhere I can't see them."

"Indeed. Every one of your twelve houses is furnished with a kitchen courtyard where the mundane operations that keep you fed and clothed are conducted away from your fastidious gaze. Perhaps you'd like to build such a facility at the lodge so that the Trumbull children's small clothes will no longer offend you."

"That would be absurd."

"Precisely." Walking around him, she opened the door wide in a clear gesture of dismissal. "I shall see you at dinner, and despite our rustic ways we do change for the evening." With an exaggerated sniff, she wrinkled her nose. "Lucky you have a good supply of clean shirts."

She was close enough for him to catch the subtle rose perfume she favored and the scent of her freshly laundered garments. Mortified, he realized he was in his shirt-sleeves, the garment hanging loose to his knees. Worse, it was still damp from his exercise, and he probably stank like a ferret. A little laugh of derision followed him as he stalked out and slammed the door behind him.

ALTHEA WATCHED HER husband retreat under her scornful onslaught, but as soon as the door closed, her throat closed over her mirth. Shoulders slumped, she gasped as though she'd been running. So much for the quiet restraint she had fought for, and largely attained, when dealing with Linton in recent years. Not that she regretted what she'd said about the lodge keeper and her laundry. Bentinck Travers, Duke of Linton, was much too hoity-toity, without a notion of the daily challenges faced by mortals who had not been a duke since the age of ten. Not to mention that he was entirely in the wrong. As usual, she had provided Linton's secretary with a list of her movements and engagements for the summer, complete with dates. She'd told him she'd be at The Chimneys on the fourth of July, and that was precisely when she'd arrived. Linton had no business bothering her here when he had his choice of eleven other mansions to honor with his glorious presence.

Fidgeting at her dressing table, she picked up a hairbrush here, a rouge pot there, and slammed them down again. Seeing him here, where they'd spent the only happy three weeks of their five-year marriage, had shocked her into the kind of childish taunting she should have long outgrown. And now she'd cracked her crystal pin tray.

Coming to The Chimneys for the first time felt like yesterday: the thrill of arriving at a house (one of many) where she would be mistress, the anticipation of long hours alone with the husband she hardly knew. Dazzled by the attentions of the handsome, reserved duke who improbably had courted her, she'd looked forward to falling in love with him. He must love her, she'd reasoned. There was absolutely no other reason why he'd chosen a young lady as insignificant as she was.

She flung herself onto her bed and buried her head in the pillow, the bed he'd once shared with her and the pillow on which he'd laid his head after their couplings. She'd been so young and anxious and eager to please her grand new husband, twelve years her senior, and she'd thought she had—poor little simpleton. Entirely ignorant of marital relations, after the initial shock she'd found it... pleasant. She'd liked feeling close to him and enjoyed his obvious satisfaction.

She'd wanted to make him happy and thought he felt the same. He'd seemed pleased with her, both in bed and out. During the day they'd walked and ridden and conversed. She'd begun to detect tiny fissures in his well-fortified reserve.

The day they returned to London everything began to change and it had become clear that he didn't love her and never had. He'd been cold, critical, and neglectful.

Working herself into a rage was not the best idea when she had to sit through a meal with him, surrounded by servants. Neither did she want to weep and present herself with reddened eyes. Sniffing hard, Althea got down from the bed and rang for her maid. She hadn't planned to change when she expected to dine alone, but now she had to.

"Which gown, Your Grace?" the maid asked.

Her first thought was a pale yellow silk with a lace overdress, but she settled on her plainest evening gown, a fine white cambric figured with a whisper of lavender thread. When first married, she'd been thrilled to patronize the most fashionable modistes with what seemed to her a limitless budget. Tonight she had looked forward to a couple of months in the country without constant attention to her toilette.

Throughout her girlhood, she had yearned for London. She believed that if she could live there away from her oppressive family, she would be perfectly happy. Balls, excursions, *people*, were the sum of her ambitions. Lately those entertainments had palled. Perhaps all pleasures did after a time, a melancholy thought.

She fastened a chaste string of pearls about her neck, and at the last minute, lest her husband think she'd turned puritan, she dabbed rouge on her pale cheeks and touched up the kohl on her lashes and brows. Linton, she had no doubt, would be immaculately turned out in one of his soberly correct ensembles.

Her lips twitched. He hadn't been so correct this afternoon with thick brown hair all over the place and his damp shirt sticking to his chest. As a matter of fact, he'd looked rather fine. She knew he boxed and fenced regularly and could guess at the musculature beneath the well-tailored garments. But she'd never seen it. He used to come to her bed wearing a dressing gown, and their relations were conducted under covers, in the dark, and in silence. His state of undress confirmed what she knew from the tentative touches she'd essayed between the sheets. The Duke of Linton was a splendid figure of a man, and he was as well-formed at thirty-five as he had been at thirty.

And it meant nothing to her. Not one little thing.

Chapter Two

LINTON CAME DOWN to dinner chastened. He'd extracted Newton's memorandum from his document portfolio and read it three times; each time it read the same way. *The duchess to Chimneys the 4th of July.* Not the fourteenth, the fourth. He'd misread it, and Newton had tried to warn him. He had no one to blame but himself for the awkward situation.

He must be meticulously polite and get through the evening without inciting conflict, or allowing her to set off his temper with her verbal pinpricks. And tomorrow he'd leave for Berkshire. The estate there had decent fishing too. He didn't need to be at The Chimneys. Except for that one matter with Sedgemere, which he didn't like to leave unsettled. He could ride over first thing, speak to Sedgemere, and be on the road by noon.

At first all went well. They conversed about uncontentious matters: the affairs of The Chimneys estate (avoiding the vexed question of washing), news of ducal neighbors (Sedgemere's bride, a banker's daughter), and the prospect of summer entertainments.

"And there's the Dukeries Cup," she said.

Linton nodded. Once upon a time, the annual rowing race had been the summit of his summer. All the mansions in the vicinity would be alive with whispers about the fancied competitors, and the betting was fast and furious. The rival houses took the race seriously, and the handsome prize added spice to the contest. But no one needed the money, and the real incentive was the right to crow over the other dukes. And to have fun. But he didn't have time for fun. Life wasn't supposed to be fun. He bit his tongue on the suggestion that he should return to The Chimneys for the contest.

"The new Duchess of Sedgemere has invited a large party and intends to give a ball," Althea said, while the servants removed the covers and brought in the second course.

"You'll enjoy the company." He definitely wouldn't return this summer. They'd managed to get through half an hour amicably, but more time together would be tempting fortune.

She still looked different from the London Althea; from his vantage point at the other end of the table, he could objectively admire her unspoiled appearance. He even had to admit that the darkened brows and lashes added emphasis to her lovely but pallid coloring. Accepting a serving from the footman, she said nothing, then looked up through her dark lashes in a blend of apology and defiance.

"I'll have Nick to entertain me. I expect him in a few days."

Linton took a drink of wine to calm the instinctive irritation. There was no reason Althea shouldn't invite her twin brother, wastrel though he might be and a major cause of dissension between them. "Anyone else?" Nicholas was one thing, Nicholas's friends quite another. A more worthless set of parasites...

"I haven't invited anyone else," she said.

All right then. "How is Nicholas?"

"Well." He let it go at that since further questions might lead to a request for money to pull the young scoundrel out of yet another pickle. Linton had made it clear in the past that if Althea wanted to waste her very generous allowance on her brother, she could do so, but he wouldn't contribute another penny.

"I'm glad to hear it." And glad to hear she wasn't planning to fill his house with every budding rakehell in London. He ate a spoonful of syllabub.

She broke the uneasy silence. "What do you think of the unrest in the north of England?"

"The activities of the Radicals cause considerable concern in Westminster. What do you know about it?"

"Don't sound so astonished. I read the newspapers."

That was news to him. In the days when they'd been in the habit of conversing, she'd talked of nothing but gowns and parties. Her eyes would glaze with boredom when he tried to explain the business that occupied him in Parliament.

"What do you think?" He expected his challenge to be met with a retreat into frippery.

"I think low wages and the high cost of food create hardship for the poor. Children are starving, and the government should help them."

"I wish I could snap my fingers and create an ideal world. Political economy is a difficult subject." She was looking at him in a way that confused him. She seemed genuinely interested, but it was equally possible she wanted to goad him into an argument. "The ministry is more concerned with quelling unrest than examining its causes."

"And I suppose you agree with them."

He declined to be goaded. "Not all the Tories march in lock-step. In my opinion, neglecting the problem is asking for trouble. The streets of London are teeming with misery and discontent, and it's even worse in the north."

She wrinkled her forehead. "Do you mean you wish to help the poor to prevent unrest, not because you think it's right to relieve misery?"

The question made him uncomfortable because he wasn't sure of the answer. His wife was a lot subtler in her ideas than he had ever suspected. "Does it matter? Doesn't it come to the same thing?"

"In practical terms, yes. But intentions are important. I would prefer you to leave Mrs. Trumbull's laundry alone because you see the justice of her need to dry her children's clothes, not because you don't wish to quarrel with me and spoil your dinner."

"I wondered when we'd get back to this." Her artful twisting of the argument amused him, but he kept his expression impassive. "Will it spoil my dinner if I insist on the removal of the washing? Will you throw your napkin across the room and storm out?"

Once such provocation would have resulted in her doing that very thing. Now she retained her composure and smiled sweetly. "No. After you leave, I will tell Mrs. Trumbull to keep her washing line."

"In that case, let her keep it with my good will. I shall rejoice in my magnanimity and the knowledge that I have contributed to the cleanliness of the little Trumbulls."

"Perhaps you'd like to go over and scrub their shirts."

"Touché. I don't have to concern myself with the practicalities of housewifery, and I am grateful for it."

This was the most bizarre discussion he'd ever had. The closest he'd come to the indignity of labor was learning to groom his pony as a child. The idea of a duke washing his own clothes, let alone anyone else's, was too ridiculous to contemplate. And yet he was enjoying himself.

She was intelligent, his wife, and far more mature than the flouncing eighteen-year-old who had come to London and run wild, thumbing her nose at the *ton* and her older husband. She had been, it occurred to him, like a child dressed in her mother's clothes. Now she had grown into them and, incidentally, looked very fine. Ignoring her studiously for over four years, he hadn't noticed she'd become a woman.

A very beautiful woman.

Stirrings of desire teased him. She was his wife, and they were under the same roof. He could knock on the door of her room, go to her bed, hold her delectable, fragrant body against his... But pride, if no other reason, required that he fight off lust for a female who had turned him away from her bed.

∽

ALTHEA WENT TO the drawing room, leaving Linton to his wine, without an exchange of harsh words. The only tense moment had come when she told him Nick was expected, and perhaps she shouldn't have brought it up. But whatever Linton said, and he'd favored her with long harangues in the past, she would never feel bad about supporting her twin. Nick was the only person in her life who had loved her without reservation. Since the day of their birth, they'd formed a united front against an unkind world. It wasn't Nick's fault their father had hated him, hated them both, but being a boy, Nick had borne the brunt of Sir George Maxfield's revenge against his erring second wife. On the day of her wedding, their elder half brother, Geoffrey, the new baronet, had given her away to Linton and washed his hands of them both. "Nicholas is your responsibility now," he'd said coldly. She had taken him at his word, not out of duty but from love.

Hoping Linton wouldn't join her—she wasn't sure they could maintain the façade of politeness without servants in the room—she sat at the piano and picked her way through a waltz. Her playing had never been better than acceptable because her father and brother refused to pay the salary required by a superior governess. Neither did any of the faded gentlewomen entrusted with her education stay long. The Maxfields, father and son, were disagreeable employers, as well as miserly ones.

During her third and improved attempt, she became aware that Linton had come in and was watching from behind her. Making no comment when she botched a tempo change and gave up in a discordant clatter, he leaned over her shoulder and leafed through the sheet music on the piano. The brush of starched linen against the skin of her upper back, the heat of his breath on her neck, made her feel prickly. It was years since they'd been at such close quarters.

He selected a Mozart duet and spread it open on the stand. "Shall we try this?" He used to be a fair pianist. They'd played for each other during their honeymoon, though never together.

"Only if you will take the high part. It's too difficult for me without a lot of practice."

"Move over."

She slid left to make room for him on the padded bench, keenly aware that only an inch or two of space lay between their respective thighs, and pretended not to notice him as she studied the first page of music.

"Shall I count?" he said, and her attention slipped to his hands, large and shapely, flexing over the keys.

She gulped. "Please take it slowly."

"For now. One, two, three."

She came in half a second behind, but caught up when he got to the first complicated passage. Concentrating fiercely, she managed not to make a complete fool of herself and started to enjoy it when she realized his performance was no better than hers. She kept playing when her arm knocked against his. "Sorry!" she cried when their hands crashed together. "Don't stop," he called back and made a particularly tricky flourish sound like broken china. Occasionally in harmony, more often out of step, they limped to the end of the movement. By a miracle, they finished almost together and looked at each other. He was smiling. The creases in his cheeks, so rarely seen, transformed his austerely handsome face.

"My fingers are rusty," he said, waving them at her.

She almost blurted that they were still strong and very capable. Once, they'd touched her, quite intimately. Turning back to the piano to hide her blush, she leafed back to the beginning. "Shall we try it again?"

They did better this time, both of them, though his improvement was greater than hers. She managed to keep pace, and the final chords came in satisfying concert.

"Bravo!" he said. "We should congratulate ourselves."

"You should. Do you play much nowadays? I never hear you."

"That's because we are seldom at home together." Was that a veiled barb? "The answer is, not often. I don't have time to practice."

"And I have all the time in the world, yet my skill is far less than yours." He demurred modestly, but they both knew she was right. "You do everything better than I do. It makes me feel inferior."

"Why?" He looked startled, and she felt the same way. Not because of the sentiment, but because she had dared to express it. It might be the first honest thing she'd said to him without having her tongue loosened by anger.

"You're good at everything. You run your estates, you earn the respect of people in the government, you excel at sports. You even play the piano better than I, though you hardly ever practice."

"I wasn't aware we were in competition."

"Of course we aren't. I would lose every time."

"Do you wish to pit yourself against me?" In a sense, she had. She'd never bowed down under his constant criticism. Nothing she did ever satisfied him, but she refused to be cowed.

She shook her head. "No. I don't enjoy competing."

"Except at cards." A note of iron entered his voice. One of their worst rows had resulted from a gaming debt. She hadn't admitted that it was Nick's debt that she'd taken on herself because Linton had refused to bail out his brother-in-law again.

"I don't play cards much anymore. Another thing I don't do well."

Politeness demanded he contradict her, praise her for some virtue, invent one if he had to. "Ladies are not expected to excel," was all he could manage.

Except as mothers. The thought must be in his head, as it was in hers. During six months of relations, she'd never got with child, and now, she supposed, she never would. Apparently, he was resigned to letting his cousin eventually inherit. He'd surely have divorced her had he not been horrified by the idea of a scandal. That was why he'd never sought a full separation.

"Most ladies boast of their accomplishments, like speaking French and Italian, painting in watercolors, or embroidery. My only skill is the piano, and you have seen how well I do that." She'd own up to her many inadequacies, but she was not to blame for her barren state. She had stood the constant carping on her extravagance and wild behavior, but she'd drawn the line when she learned he maintained his mistress after their marriage.

ALTHEA TOSSED BENEATH the covers, unable to forget the occupant of the adjoining chamber. Whether from his damp shirt or the forced contact on the piano bench, he'd unsettled her, made her aware of yearnings in her body she normally suppressed. Naturally, she had indulged in flirtations, another cause of complaint from Linton. All women of fashion did, as she had discovered as a wide-eyed young bride let loose in society for the first time. It had meant nothing, and he ought to have known it. He could have flirted with her himself, kissed her hand, laughed at her witticisms, whispered extravagant compliments in dark corners. Instead, she had to submit to his constant disapproval. A month after their honeymoon, she was certain she could do nothing to please him. Not even in bed.

At first he was gentle and considerate, and she felt cherished in his arms. But when they returned to London, he visited her room less frequently. He often had evening engagements that excluded her and came home after she was asleep. Once she and Nick made friends of their own, among the younger fashionable set, it was she who yawned her way through the front door of Linton House in the small hours.

There had been just one time. They had attended a dinner at his sister's house. Althea had been on her best behavior and managed to ignore the stinging darts of Lady Mary Poole, who had made no secret of opposing their marriage. Linton told her, over a glass of wine in the library, that she had pleased him and kissed her when she withdrew to bed. Glowing at his unusual praise, she eagerly anticipated his arrival in her room. For once, all the undefined expectations of the physical side of marriage were met. As she trembled in his arms, his caresses made her vibrate with a strange longing. She reveled in the weight of his body on hers and the heft of his member when he entered her. She sensed the climb to an unknown pinnacle that both frightened and thrilled her. Though he finished before she crested the summit, she nevertheless felt a rare delight. Daring to wind her arms about him, she fell asleep with her head on his chest, happier than she'd ever been in her life.

She woke up alone, and the sunny morning was ruined by a blazing row over a dressmaker's bill she couldn't pay because she'd given most of her quarter's pin money to Nick. A few days later, one of her new, sophisticated friends told her about his mistress.

"I know about Mrs. Veney," she told him, hoping he would deny it.

He reddened with anger. "Mrs. Veney is none of your concern. It is grossly improper for her to be mentioned between us."

"You pay for her house in Molyneux Street and her servants' wages and no doubt all her bills," she stormed in the face of his affronted serenity.

"That is my affair."

"So I have heard," she retorted. "Keep her if you insist, but don't expect to share my bed again."

He took her at her word and left her alone for a few days. When he finally came to her room, she told him she expected to suffer from headaches every night for the foreseeable future. Funnily enough, it turned out to be true. The final disintegration of their relationship drove her to an orgy of dissipation, marked by wild escapades and the imbibing of a great deal of wine. Tired of waking with a dry mouth and pounding brain, she eventually moderated her behavior and achieved a kind of serenity in the suspended state of her marriage.

Now, confound him, he'd shattered her hard-won poise by invading her haven. His very presence had her thinking of the ecstasy that she'd heard about from married ladies of her fast set and had never experienced. Never would experience. Her healthy twenty-three-year-old body ached to be kissed and caressed and loved, and she could weep with frustration for the bliss that would never be hers unless she broke her vows and risked the scandal of pregnancy.

Since the only husband she would ever have lay a few yards away and didn't do her the least bit of good, perhaps she would succumb to one of the many lures thrown out to her by the rakes of London. And that was something more to weep about.

Chapter Three

Waking late, as listless as though she'd drained a bottle of champagne at dinner instead of one glass of wine, she read the note delivered with her chocolate.

Madam.

I must see Sedgemere this afternoon, so I will trouble you for another night at The Chimneys. Meanwhile, I have gone fishing.

Your etc.
Linton.

Althea didn't know whether to be glad or sorry. They'd managed to spend the evening with civility. But could they repeat the feat? Past history indicated that a second dinner alone together would end in strife.

After breakfast, she dealt with correspondence forwarded from London and went outside to consult the head gardener. A long, soothing discussion about the control of aphids left her in a more optimistic frame of mind. On her way back to the house, she spotted the approach of a familiar vehicle, a glossy curricle with spanking yellow wheels. Nick had arrived early, but he was not alone. The sight of his companion sent a pool of bile to her stomach.

"Allie!" Nick jumped down and swept her into a hug. "Aren't you pleased to see me?" Unusually, she realized she was not. He put his hands on her shoulders and set her at arms' length. "Country air must suit you, for you're looking in the pink."

She wished she could say the same for him. He seemed pale and drawn, with dark rings under his eyes, and a shadow of beard marred his beloved face.

"I am glad you are here, of course. It's just that I wasn't expecting you for a few days."

Nick's insouciant grin didn't fool her; something troubled him. Traitorously, she wished she didn't have to deal with it now. Her peaceful summer was threatened first by her husband, now her brother, and most of all by Nigel Speck.

"Duchess," said the odious man, who'd been observing the twins' greeting with a mocking smile. "I hope you have room for me in your little house."

"Any friend of Nick's is welcome, Mr. Speck," she managed to grind out without spitting. She'd like to slap his smooth, smirking face.

"Why so formal?" Nick asked, with forced jollity. He knew she was displeased. "You've been Allie and Nigel to one another for years."

"With Her Grace's permission," Speck said.

With Her Grace's good will, you may call me Your Grace and take yourself off, was what she wanted to say, and cursed Nick for putting her on the spot. She stretched her lips into a thin smile and let them read it how they would.

"It's good of you to have Nick and me for the summer, Allie," Speck said. "The house parties at the Dukeries are legendary, and I've always wanted to be invited."

You haven't been. "Come inside, and I will have a room prepared for you."

Having let a footman show Speck upstairs, she pulled Nick into the morning room. "Why did you bring *him*?" she said. "I told you last year that I didn't want to have anything more to do with him."

"You never told me why," Nick said.

"There's something unsavory about him." *To say the least.*

She'd never told anyone about the night at Vauxhall. When she first met Nigel Speck, she'd been charmed. He seemed the epitome of worldly sophistication, his outlook a mixture of ennui and sarcasm she'd never encountered in her sheltered life. Not precisely handsome, he held a forbidden allure. She was flattered when he flirted with her, and she flirted right back. But she'd never been the particular object of his attentions until last year. That night she'd found herself alone with him in a deserted walk and the quality of his compliments made her uncomfortable. When she tried to laugh him off, he'd persisted, grasping her in a steel grip and forcing a plundering kiss on her unwilling mouth. He called her a tease and said he knew she wanted him. Not sure how she'd managed to escape, the experience left her terrified, and worse, feeling soiled.

She couldn't shake off the feeling that the miserable episode had been her own fault. Certainly Linton would think so. Perhaps it had been a mistake not to tell Nick, but she hadn't wanted to even think about what had happened, let alone talk about it. Nick was such a hothead, he'd probably call Speck out and end up at best with a scandal and at worst injured or dead. Her hints about Speck's character apparently went unheard.

Nick wore his sheepish look. "As a matter of fact, Allie, you were right. I wish I'd listened to you."

"Then why did you bring him here, for heaven's sake?"

"He insisted. I owe him money. I lost to him at piquet."

Althea groaned. "Oh no! You promised!" Nick's talent at cards didn't match his enthusiasm, and piquet was his worst game.

"I know, I know, I'm sorry. If you lend me the money to pay him, he'll go away."

Lend! She felt no desire whatever to succumb to his winning smile. "How much?"

He named a sum that made her gasp. "How could you, Nick?"

"Please, Allie. Just this once. I'll never do it again."

The twins had inherited nothing from their wealthy father beyond a sum from their mother's marriage settlement, providing Althea's dowry and leaving Nick a modest income, which he augmented by handouts from his sister and his own wits. Rather small wits, she thought uncharitably. It was time Nick grew up, and she wondered if she had helped him by bailing him out a hundred times.

"You'll have to retrench and pay him over time," she said. "Staying here for the summer won't cost you anything. He can go back to town and wait."

"It's a debt of honor. You know they have to be paid at once. If we send him back to London, he'll tell everyone, and my reputation will be ruined."

"You should have thought of that before you gambled more than you could afford."

"I was sure my luck would turn."

"It never does, as you should know by now."

"I know you are right. I promise I'll never do it again."

Althea paced the room, contemplating the dilemma. If she paid Speck, he'd go away. If she sent him off empty-handed, he would make trouble for Nick; he could also spread rumors about her. She had enough money, just, but it would leave her account almost empty, and she had sworn never to apply to Linton again.

Oh God, Linton. He'd be back from his fishing any time now.

She wanted to tell Nick to pack his so-called friend into his curricle, her gift to him on their last birthday, and roll on back to London. But she'd never let him down before. Besides, the idea of changing her brother's careless outlook on life had taken hold. She wanted to do something that would help him in the future instead of providing a temporary bandage in the form of a bank draft.

"I have an idea. You can enter the Dukeries Cup. The prize is enough to cover your debt, and a little more." She explained about the annual rowing race. "The Chimneys hasn't entered anyone in the race for a few years, but you can practice on the lake here, and I am sure you can win."

"I haven't done much rowing since I left school."

"You used to win all the races then. You have weeks to prepare, and I don't suppose the competition is very great."

"I suppose I can give it a try. It'll be good to get out onto the water." His wan cheeks flushed a little, and he looked more enthusiastic than she'd seen him in months. The exercise would do him good. "What about Speck?" he asked nervously.

"Will he wait if you explain?" She supposed she'd have to pay the monster herself if Nick didn't win the cup, but she'd keep quiet about that. Her brother needed the incentive to work hard.

"You heard what he said about summer at the Dukeries."

Her heart sank. Three weeks and more with the odious Speck in the house, wondering if he awaited her behind every corner.

"Just make sure you don't leave me alone with him."

"What has he done?" Nick had finally woken up to the fact that she really didn't like the man.

"Nothing," she said hastily. "It's merely that I find him repulsive." She had plenty of servants at The Chimneys, so he couldn't maneuver her into a dangerous situation as he had at Vauxhall. She could manage.

"I'll lend him my curricle, and he can spend the days while I'm training calling on the other dukes. He'll enjoy that." He kissed her on the cheek. "Thank you, Allie. You always come up trumps."

"One more thing, Linton is here."

"What the devil? He's supposed to leave The Chimneys to you. I shall remind him of that fact."

The notion of Nick speaking sternly to the Duke of Linton would have made her laugh, but for the irony of what he had done. By inflicting Speck on her, he'd inconvenienced her far worse than having her husband here for a day or two. Whatever Linton might do, she didn't have to worry about him trying to kiss her in dark corners. Not even in earlier times when she would have welcomed it.

"It's just for tonight," she said wearily. "Promise me you'll behave and not provoke him?"

"I've never done anything to him, and it's not my fault he doesn't like me," Nick said a little sadly, and with new evidence of his utter obliviousness. "But don't worry, I'll be as bland as a white sauce."

~

THE BEST SPOT for trout lay over a mile from The Chimneys. Linton chose to go on foot to enjoy a couple of hours of fishing in which he let the business of casting occupy his mind, luxuriating in the respite from the demands of duty that filled his life. The stream had been neglected. Overgrown bulrushes that kept snagging his line needed to be cleared, and he should see about having the stock of fish replenished. But why go to the trouble when he wouldn't be here?

He stowed his fishing tackle with regret that his brief holiday was over. He missed this place. Could he persuade Althea to choose another estate as her country house? Or he could visit The Chimneys more often *with* her. Last night they had managed to be polite, even amiable. The pleasures of angling receded from his brain to make way for vivid images of the hour with her on the piano bench. Of the scent of her, the weight of her thigh against his, and the way her soft cool hands brushed his.

Desiring Althea was nothing new. Though not the only motive for wedding her, it had been a strong one. He did not think he'd been bewitched by a pretty face as his sisters claimed, but his judgment of her character had turned out to be mistaken. What he didn't know was if the maturity and intelligence she'd displayed last night were real. Had she changed inside as well as out?

He pulled the reins of his racing brain. Unthinking haste was what got him into the disastrous marriage that twenty-four hours earlier he'd believed—*known*—to be irreparable. If their current rapprochement lasted a few days under the same roof, there would be time enough to consider reconciliation. He'd see how things went day by day, until Nicholas Maxfield arrived.

If nothing else resulted, he might at least catch a fish larger than a minnow. Hurrying homeward, he found himself whistling, satisfied with his sensible and measured decision. After disposing of the fishing gear and changing into dry clothes, he went in search of his duchess. Maybe he'd ask her to accompany him to Sedgemere House to call on the duchess while he talked to the duke about their tenants' dispute.

Maybe not. When the collapse of the Linton marriage was one of society's nine days' wonders, the whispered gossip as he entered a room affronted his dignity. He could imagine the speculation if they were seen in public together. He decided to put off his call until tomorrow and see if she wanted to go for a stroll.

He found her in the morning room drinking tea with a snake in the grass. Correction: a pair of snakes, and one was a viper. He didn't really mind Nicholas, idle and feckless as the young man was. At Nigel Speck, he drew the line. Unpleasant rumors swirled around the man's name. Although Linton didn't know him well, to look at him was to hate him.

"Linton!" Althea's voice emerged high-pitched and artificially welcoming, recalling the beginning of some past arguments over her indiscretions. "Look who's here. Nick has brought a friend down for the summer. Do you know Mr. Speck?"

Speck bowed with oily affability that made Linton want to use him as a punching bag, rearrange his sleek features, and wipe away his ingratiating grimace. "A surprise to see you, Duke, but a most agreeable one, of course. We are glad to share the duchess's company with her husband, are we not, Nick?"

A new suspicion swelled in Linton's chest. He knew Speck had been one of Althea's flirts, but he'd never thought there was anything particular between them, or between his wife and any of the gallants who frequented her circle. Foolishly, perhaps, he'd always believed she'd remained innocent of the ultimate betrayal. Heedlessly indiscreet, yes, but not adulterous, not least because she knew he would never acknowledge a bastard child. But there was always the possibility that she had been careful, or lucky.

He schooled his expression to casual disdain and answered Speck's greeting with the meanest of nods.

Nicholas seized his hand with a big smile, so like his sister's. They were ridiculously alike, the twins, Nicholas a handsome masculine counterpart to Althea's delicate beauty. "Linton, my dear fellow. I'm glad to see you. What a pity it'll only be for one night."

"Madam," Linton said. "A word with you." Althea shrugged at her brother and let Linton lead her into another room. "I do not like Speck," he said.

"I don't see how that's any of your business. I can ask any guests I wish to my house."

"I agree," he said, struggling for patience in the interest of amity. "I would *request* that you not entertain men of poor character."

She paused, apparently considering the matter. "I'm sorry, Linton," she said finally. "I don't wish to quarrel with you, but I cannot accede to your *request*. He is a friend of Nick's and as such welcome. I don't see how it matters to you, since you are leaving tomorrow"

Linton didn't want to quarrel either. Neither did he like the idea of Althea under the same roof as that specimen of seedy manhood. Speck might be a gentleman by birth, but Linton would wager he didn't have an honorable bone in his body. "I'm not leaving tomorrow. I intend to stay a week, very likely more."

"Oh!" He wasn't sure if Althea's exclamation was one of surprise or displeasure. He feared the latter, but that was too bad. He wasn't going anywhere.

"Very well, Linton. You may stay. But so does Mr. Speck."

Chapter Four

A LTHEA HAD BEEN pleased when Linton said he'd remain. If only he knew how much she wanted to obey him for once and send Speck away. During the nightmare of dinner, she changed her mind. Only Nick gamely tried to keep the conversation going by revealing his plan to compete in the Dukeries Cup, although not the reason for it. Once that topic dried up, she had to fend off the flirtatious sallies of Nigel Speck without giving him an overt set-down. Linton sat at the end of the table, silent as a judge, observing the byplay between her and her unwelcome guest.

She wasn't going to put up with this for long. Either Linton must leave, or Speck, preferably both.

Desperate to survive the remainder of the evening with a minimum of conversation, she suggested a table of whist. As bad luck would have it, she drew Speck as her partner. Playing with more than her usual lack of attention, her side was soon down by many points. Things would have been worse but for the skill of her partner, who forgave her mistakes with a charming forbearance that infuriated her and, on one occasion, caused her to revoke.

"Allie!" Nick said. "You had a club left, but you trumped my ace last time they were played. You owe us three points."

"Never mind," Speck said. "It's only a friendly game, and clubs and spades look alike. It's not your fault. Since we're only playing for penny points, it's no great matter. Don't be so hard on your sister, Nick. No one expects someone as pretty as she is to be an expert at whist."

Althea clutched her remaining cards to foil the urge to throw them at him.

"Three points." Linton, a silent but overbearing presence during the game, noted the penalty on the scorecard. His unhurried scrutiny passed over the other players, one by one. "I propose we raise the stakes," he said.

What was he doing? Did he intend to beggar her? Nick, scenting a lucrative evening, agreed enthusiastically.

"Why not?" Speck said. "Shall we say sixpence a point? What do you say, Duchess? The cards have been against us, but I have faith we can come about."

What did it matter if she lost a few pounds instead of shillings? She hoped their deficit would be enough to cause Speck a little embarrassment and Nick would win some much-needed cash.

"Paltry." Linton enunciated the word in what she always thought of as his ducal voice, the one that placed him above lesser creatures. "I'd propose a guinea, but that might be too rich for your blood. Ten shillings is a nice round sum, high enough to add spice to the contest, but not enough to cause anyone serious embarrassment."

She stared at him in amazement, remembering the lectures she'd endured from him about high play. It was all very well for the Duke of Twelve Estates to say ten shillings a point was nothing. If the stakes had been that high before, she and Speck would owe almost one hundred pounds. Linton merely raised his brow, his harsh, aristocratic features as inscrutable as ever. He dominated the room with his height, his sober evening clothes, and impeccable white linen, making the other men seem mere boys.

Speck pulled a polished gold snuffbox from his pocket and offered it around. Nick and Linton refused, and after he took a sniff, he laid the box on the table next to his brandy. "I'm in," he said. "Ten shillings it is. My turn to deal, I believe."

Whatever Linton was up to, he'd aroused Althea's pride. She wasn't a total incompetent at whist when she tried, so she concentrated on her cards and tried to forget her husband's puzzling behavior. She and Speck won some hands, lost others, and by dint of some brilliantly lucky risks on Speck's part, they were up by twenty pounds after an hour.

Linton called a break. "Will you ring for refreshments, madam?" He made some small talk as they waited, commenting affably on the course of the game. While the servants served tea and cake, he reached for Speck's snuffbox. "A pretty thing, quite old. I prefer an unadorned box, myself. Some of the French designs are overly elaborate, I always think. Is it a family piece?"

Speck seemed nervous at being addressed by the duke in a friendly manner. "No," he said, flicking a reptilian tongue over his lips. "I don't recall where I got it."

"Won it at cards, perhaps?"

"Perhaps."

"It's rather in the way here. I'll put it over here." Linton set the box on a side table.

They played on, and now the luck was on the side of Linton and Nick. "Almost even," Linton said, adding up the score. "It's getting late, but we should play one more hand. What do you say to fifty guineas, win or lose?"

Nick and Speck, who had drunk a lot of brandy, agreed. The evening had taken on a fantastic character, and Althea felt reckless as well as confused. Her husband remained calm and unusually cordial, but she couldn't shake the feeling that he was up to something. Was he trying to provoke her so that he could berate her later as an irresponsible gamester?

"Fifty guineas it is," she said, tilting her chin defiantly. "Your deal."

The cards lay evenly, and it came down to her at the penultimate trick. With all the trumps out, her discard was crucial. She stared at the two cards in her hand, trying to remember what had been played. Her partner, whose courtesy had slipped badly once they started losing again, almost snarled at her. Heart or club? Which should it be? The clock ticked away the seconds, and she couldn't remember. About to throw down a card at random, she looked up and found Linton regarding her intently. Hoping for her to get it wrong.

Then he smiled, not an unkind, mocking smile, but one of reassurance and encouragement. Her mind cleared, and she remembered. She set down the knave of clubs, and her queen of hearts took the final trick and the hand.

She barely registered a crow of triumph from Speck and one of despair from Nick. Linton grinned broadly. "Very well done, Althea," he said, and she flushed. Although she didn't understand why, she had won his approval for *something*.

Linton turned to Nick. "Don't worry, Nicholas. I'll cover your loss. It's worth it."

FIVE YEARS AGO, Linton had at first been pleased that Althea had her brother to escort her around town. Parliamentary duties had pressed, and he really should have postponed the wedding, but he hadn't wished to. Back in London, he had little time to spare for his new bride. Paying heed with half his mind, he gathered they indulged in such benign youthful activities as visits to Astley's Amphitheatre and feeding the ducks in Hyde Park. He had a rude awakening one evening when Althea came downstairs to meet Nicholas attired in a costume borrowed from her maid. They were off, she told him blithely, to dine at an inn near the East India docks. Strictly forbidding Nicholas to expose his sister to such an ungenteel and dangerous place, he'd left for an evening debate in the House of Lords. They went anyway, and of course someone saw them, and the party of worthless bucks who made up the party. He'd had to listen to a lecture from his sister Mary about how she was right and his wife had caused a scandal.

The incident resulted in the first huge quarrel with his wife, with Althea defending Nicholas and dismissing the peril that made Linton cold with fear. It was a miracle she hadn't ended up violated and murdered. He blamed Nicholas who should have protected his sister.

Now he wondered if hadn't been too hard on Nicholas, who had, after all, been only eighteen, little more than a boy. He resolved to try to be more tolerant. He stood on the bank and watched Nicholas row up and down the lake. Althea was right about her brother being a good oarsman, despite a few problems of technique.

Nicholas noticed him when he stopped to rest. He sweated profusely, more than he should from exercise alone and far more than the cool day warranted. Too much easy living and hard drinking in town had softened him. He'd have to work hard to get up to full mettle and defeat Lord William Besett, who, according to Sedgemere, was the favorite to win the Dukeries Cup this year.

"Linton," Nicholas gasped. "Could you pass me that jug of water, please?"

Linton handed him the pitcher sitting on the bank and watched Nicholas drink in great gulps. "Hard going, is it?"

"About as I expected," the young man replied, on the defensive.

"You're dipping the oars too deep. You'll move more water with a shallower stroke. And you should keep the blades at an angle."

"What do you know about it?"

"I was in the Monarch Boat Club at Eton, and rowed at Oxford too."

"I doubt the Monarch can teach anything to the Isis Club at Westminster."

"If the Westminsters row like you, the Etonians will take you every time."

Nicholas's belligerent look dissolved into a grin. "I seem to recall that we beat Eton last time we met, and mine was the fastest time." He had recovered his breath and his cheek.

"And I won the Dukeries Cup, so why don't you try it my way?"

Nicholas handed back the water jug and took up his oars. "All right, I'll give it a go. I haven't checked with a watch, but I know I'm slow."

"Start at the end of the lake, and I'll time you."

Linton was in a good mood. He and Sedgemere had come to satisfactory terms about their tenants, but better still was his triumph the night before. He had established that Nigel Speck cheated at whist. Whenever Speck dealt the cards, he could see their reflections in the shiny surface of his snuffbox, so during every fourth hand he knew exactly who held what and was able to execute extraordinary feats of play. Really, Nicholas and Althea were a pair of babies not to have spotted the oldest trick in the book.

Better yet, Linton had observed her carefully, and he believed, though he couldn't be entirely certain, that Speck made Althea uncomfortable. At first, during that dismal dinner, he'd been sure her embarrassment at Speck's unctuous compliments were caused by her husband's unwelcome presence. Yet, not once in the whole evening had he intercepted a look between them that indicated any intimacy. Quite the opposite. If he was right, Althea was as displeased by Speck's visit as he was, and the only question was why she allowed it. Indulging Nicholas as usual, he supposed. It also occurred to him, given her obvious indifference to card playing and discomfort with high stakes, that her previous losses were, in fact, her brother's.

The latter was ready. Linton took out his watch and shouted for him to start. After an impetuous beginning, Nicholas was immediately in trouble. With the oars at the new angle, he lost his rhythm, dug too deep, and caught a crab, landing on his back in the rocking scull.

"Damn it," he shouted. "This isn't working."

"Keep trying. Better still, I'll show you." Linton stripped off his coat and waistcoat and loped to the boathouse to launch the other scull.

Well over a decade after he'd last set foot in a boat, it was instantly familiar: the sway as he lowered himself onto the bench, the creak of wood in the rowlocks, the resisting water when he first dipped the oars. He lined up his hands, bent at the waist, and pulled. Too deep, just like Nicholas. An adjustment, another pull, and he moved forward. Taking it slowly, listening to his oars lapping through the rippling lake, he lined up with Nicholas in the middle.

"Do you see how my blades are set?"

Nicholas adjusted his position under Linton's direction, and they surged forward side by side, Linton calling the strokes. Once they found their rhythm, he increased the pace. God, he'd missed this. There was nothing like the power of muscle over water. He went smoothly now, enjoying the burn of arms and shoulders, stomach and legs. Some muscles he hadn't used in years protested, but he rowed through the ache, turning smoothly at the end to glide the full length of the lake. After three lengths, he pulled up and waited for his companion, who had fallen behind, to join him. Nicholas had mastered the new stroke, dipping his oars at just the right depth. As he continued to train, his speed would improve. For the first time, Linton thought the lad might be capable of winning, if only he could keep at it, not let his fickle, frivolous interest wander.

Nicholas looked discouraged. "You beat me."

"You did well."

"You're years older. I should be able to beat you easily."

"Youth isn't everything. I'm stronger than you, and I drink less."

"I was sober as a judge last night." Linton raised his eyebrows. "Almost as sober. I suppose I could do with a glass or two less."

"If you're wise, you'll give up brandy until after the race. And take only one glass of wine with dinner."

"How will I keep my strength up?"

"By eating more. Talk to your sister about beefsteak for every meal. You need lots of bread, not too many sweets and other rich foods, and absolutely no strong spirits. Now let's talk about rowing. Speed and endurance aren't enough. You need brains too, if you're capable of exercising them. The Dukeries Cup requires strategy." Linton warmed to his subject, and Nicholas looked interested, even hungry for information. "Above all, it's won or lost on the turns, and yours are too slow and too wide. The lake at Teversault is three-quarters of a mile long, and the course is four full lengths. It's narrow at each end, so the oarsmen have to turn around in little more than the length of the boat, and they have to do it quickly. You need to practice turning until you can do it neatly and in seconds."

Nicholas nodded without a trace of the sulkiness he sometimes displayed when offered any kind of advice. "Show me."

WITH LINTON CALLING on the Duke of Sedgemere and Nick at the lake, Althea needed to get out of the house before Nigel Speck found her, so she went to see how Nick was getting on. His brandy consumption during the whist game had worried her, and she feared his drive to compete would be short-lived. He'd left early, before she came downstairs, and she was proud of him for getting out of bed and going to work, even with a pounding head. He could use some sisterly encouragement.

A strange sight greeted her as she descended the gentle hill to the lake. There were two boats on the water, turning in tight circles like a pair of deranged insects. Coming closer, she saw that one of them was propelled by her husband.

She sat on a hummock above the bank and watched, unnoticed by a pair of men engrossed in their aquatic twirling. After a while, they stopped to chat, a little way from the shore. Without making out every word of a discussion about rowing and racing, she could hear Nick's enthusiasm and Linton's deeper, measured tones. They seemed on the best of terms, something that had not happened since the eve of her wedding, when eighteen-year-old Nick, just out of school, had been awed by his about-to-be brother-in-law and proclaimed him a great gun. Linton had proven more of a rapier, constantly pricking at Nick for extravagance and slashing him for perceived poor behavior. Over the following months, Linton grew more censorious, Nick more defiant. By the time Linton and Althea made the final break, it was much, much better not to have them in the same room.

Look at them now, enjoying one another's company, the way she'd hoped when the magnificent Duke of Linton, the biggest catch on the marriage mart in decades, had offered for the humble Miss Maxfield. Geoffrey had warned her not to expect much by way of a husband; the most she'd aimed for was a man who wasn't actually cruel. Nick and she, it must be admitted, had gone a little mad when the delights of London first beckoned, and they were free from the restrictions and malice of their half brother. With Nick, in recent months, it had gone beyond youthful glee. He was in danger of becoming truly dissipated.

He had more color in his cheeks than she'd seen in months, and Linton, well, Linton was just as underdressed and even more disheveled than when he'd entered her room two days ago.

Having apparently come to an agreement, the oarsmen were ready to move again. Linton pushed his damp locks from his forehead and, in one sweep, removed his shirt and tossed it onto the floor of the boat. Whether he heard her gasp, or happened to look her way, he noticed his audience.

"I beg your pardon, Althea. I didn't see you there," he called, and reached for his discarded garment.

"Don't worry," she called back, standing up. "I'm enjoying the view." She fanned herself. "It is awfully hot."

He gave her a look she couldn't read and, thankfully, left his shirt where it lay. "Do you have a watch?"

"No."

"Mine is in my coat. Could you find it and time us?"

Going through Linton's pockets made her self-conscious. The coat smelled of him, and rifling through the contents—coins, a slender pencil, some papers—seemed intimate and... wifely. She found the watch and took up position on firm ground above the marshy edges of the lake.

"Wait until the second hand reaches twelve and call the start," Linton ordered. "We'll do two lengths of the lake. Ready, Nick?"

The sight of a pair of well-formed gentlemen plying the oars was delightful. To be honest, she paid only cursory attention to Nick. It was Linton who riveted her: the smooth play of his muscles as he worked the oars, his chest moving to and fro as he rowed away from her, and then, as he made the turn and approached again, his bare back and broad shoulders. The sight of such exertions made her feel quite warm and distracted her from her duty. Not wanting to bungle the task and add or subtract minutes, she kept her eyes on the watch face and let her eyes stray to the lake only once every half minute.

One minute twenty-nine, thirty. She looked up as the two boats streaked past, Nick in the lead by a nose. Both boats made the turn neatly—now she understood what they'd been practicing before—and they raced back toward her, backs straining as the pace increased. She couldn't tell who was ahead, but she thought Linton might have edged out Nick when they passed her at an invisible finish line.

They laughed and panted as they pulled up. "How long?" Nick called.

"Two minutes forty-three seconds."

"Not bad for the first day," Linton said. "You'll have to be faster at Teversault, and more important, you'll have to keep it up for almost twenty times longer."

"That sounds like a lot," Althea said.

"The lake at Teversault is a monster to row. It's what makes the Dukeries Cup a great contest."

"What was the time when you won?" Nick asked.

"Twenty-six minutes and seventeen seconds."

"You won it?" Why had her husband never mentioned it? "When was that?"

"In my distant youth."

"You didn't look like a poor toothless old man on the water just now."

"I was twenty years old, but there's life in me yet. I doubt I could keep going for three miles, however."

"But you'll keep training with me, won't you?" Nick asked. "You helped me a lot today, and you know the Teversault course. You're staying until the race, aren't you? Please say yes."

That meant another three weeks of Linton around the house and in the next bedchamber. Another three weeks of awkward dinners and unwanted card games. Also piano duets and bare chests and the occasional encouraging smile. Her husband's presence was fraught with problems and possibly even more dangerous to her state of mind.

"I think I can spare the time." He spoke to Nick, but he was looking at her.

Chapter Five

"I HEAR THE Duke's Arms at Hopewell-on-Lyft is a decent place to raise a jar of ale and cast the dice." Speck, obviously bored, was looking for livelier entertainment than he found in the drawing room at The Chimneys.

"Don't fleece the rustics," Linton said.

"What do you mean by that?" Speck asked casually. He was an expert at deception, but Linton detected his tension. The man was clearly worried that Linton had rumbled his game with the snuffbox. Linton merely raised his brows. One of the advantages of being a duke was that he never had to answer a question if he didn't want to.

"Which duke is it, of the Duke's Arms, I mean?" Nick asked. "There are so many in these parts."

"Oxthorpe. Hopewell is his village."

"So are you coming, Nick?"

"You can take my curricle, but I'm for bed." He yawned. "I haven't been sleeping well lately, but tonight I'm tired."

Linton knew something troubled Althea's brother, but several hours at the oars had a way of making other worries recede. True to his word, Nicholas had confined his indulgence to a single glass of claret, and his state of exhaustion had a healthy cause. Linton was pleasantly tired too.

Speck left to deprive the local farmers of their hard-earned pay—Linton hoped he'd be caught cheating and beaten to a pulp—and Nicholas excused himself with more yawns, a kiss for Althea, and a handshake for Linton, who expected Althea to follow her brother.

She sat down again, hands folded in her lap. He leaned back on a sofa, working his stiff shoulders and admiring his wife, pretty in pale green. She had a quality of stillness, he realized, unexpected in such an animated woman. Most ladies in his experience occupied their hands with some kind of needlework or fiddled with their shawls.

"Thank you for helping Nick," she said after a pause.

"It's nothing. He needs something to do besides running around London causing havoc and drinking too much." Not wanting to reopen the old quarrel, he softened his voice. "Why does your older brother let him run wild, Althea? He should set him up in a profession."

"Geoffrey doesn't like Nick. He won't help him." She stared down at her lap. "Because of our mother."

The subject of the second Lady Maxfield had never been raised between them, although he'd heard plenty from his sisters. The sorry tale of the baronet's wife who'd run off with her husband's steward had been hushed up, but Lady Mary Poole had a peerless ability to nose out scandal. He'd sworn to himself before his marriage that he would never discuss the distressing past with his bride.

"It was hardly his fault."

Her head jerked up, eyes glistening like polished jade. "Do you blame me? Do you think I am like her?"

"Of course not. It happened when you were mere infants. What were you, two years old?"

"Three. We were three. My father said we had inherited a fatal flaw."

"Nonsense. Our faults are our own, not those of our parents. Do you even remember her?"

"No."

"It must have been hard for a young girl without a mother. I miss mine too. The Chimneys was her favorite house, you know, which was why we always came here for a month or two in the summer after my father died. He preferred Longworth."

"Was she like your sisters?"

"Not a bit, thankfully. She was kind and not very forceful and disliked pomp."

"Not at all like your sisters then," she said with an impish grin.

"None of them has any taste for the simple life." He smiled at the memory of his gentle, rather vague parent. "My mother used to feed me sweetmeats and tried to protect me from them."

"Poor child. A mere boy, and a duke too. You must have needed lots of protection from those girls." Her teasing seemed almost affectionate, and he liked it.

"They saw their little brother as a pestilence best crushed underfoot for the offense of causing joy to my parents. If you didn't know, and you must have guessed from the ghastly turbans that Mary uses to disguise her gray hair, I arrived many years after they'd given up hope of an heir."

"I'll refrain from comment on Lady Mary's millinery."

"I seem to recall less than complimentary remarks in the past." He could have bitten his tongue. The last thing he wanted was to start a quarrel. The disparaging, and well-deserved, criticism of Mary's hats had come in the context of a row about Althea's dressmakers' bills. He didn't want to revisit that argument now. He didn't even know why he'd made such a fuss then. He could stand the expense, and Althea always looked charming, if a little too dashing for so young a lady.

To his relief, she didn't remember, or ignored the provocation. "What was your father like?"

"He was occupied with his own affairs. I was under the care of tutors and didn't see him much. Then he died."

"He sounds better than mine."

"He was an honorable man. There was never any reason to be sorry for me."

They exchanged tentative smiles. He felt like an explorer, picking his way gingerly into new territory, careful of pitfalls ahead yet eager to reach an unknown but potentially marvelous place.

"We never talked like this when we were married," she said.

"We're still married."

"You know what I mean."

He wasn't sure why he confided in her now. When they wed, he'd been aware of his great condescension in choosing a young girl of respectable family, but much lower than his rank merited. He'd expected gratitude and obedience to his will. What a fool he'd been. Instead of an adoring wife, he'd discovered a rebellious hellion; instead of a faithful helpmeet, he'd married a woman who always put her brother's needs before those of her husband.

"Anyway," she said. "Thank you again for helping Nick."

Always Nicholas. Surely he wasn't jealous of that wayward boy?

Yet today he'd thought Althea's twin wasn't beyond hope. He was a promising oarsman, and if nothing else, Linton owed him gratitude for getting him back in a boat with a pair of oars in his hands. Even if parts of his body ached like the devil. He shifted his arms.

"Are you in pain, Linton?"

"Just a little sore. Rowing uses some muscles I haven't exercised in a while."

"Your shoulders seem to be troubling you. Would you like me to rub them?" She looked at him with artless concern, while the prospect of her hands on him stirred a different kind of ache.

"If you don't mind, I believe that would help."

"Don't get up." She walked around behind him and held his upper arms in a light grasp. "I won't do much good through your coat. You'd better take it off."

His heart beating a tattoo, he removed the garment with her assistance.

"The waistcoat too."

He'd never undone buttons with less care. About to offer his shirt too, he decided better not. Her touch on his skin might make him do something he'd regret. She laid light fingers either side of his neck, making him shudder with anticipation.

Then she walked away, and he almost cried out his frustration. He wanted her hands on him now.

Roaming the room, she found an ottoman and dragged it over to the fire. "Sit here and lean on this." She arranged his arms on the back of a small chair. "Now I can reach everywhere," she said, her cool tone not matching the lascivious images that possessed his mind at her words.

She began gently, working nimble fingers from his shoulders inward to his neck and over the upper part of his back. "This will have to go," she said, and unwound his starched neckcloth.

He closed his eyes, the better to savor the sensation of being undressed by unseen hands. Enthralled, he shivered when she unlooped the top button of his shirt and her fingers skimmed over his collarbone.

"Are my hands too cold?"

"No, they're perfect," he managed to say. *The shirt too*, he managed not to say. Contrary to his instincts, he ceded control to Althea.

She started at the base of his head, using her fingertips with a light but firm pressure, progressing down the sides of his neck and pulling down his shirt to work on the upper part of his back and between his shoulder blades. She settled on a spot below the nape of his neck he hadn't known hurt, circling her thumbs with increasing strength that pained and soothed at the same time. "Yes, there," he rasped.

"Be quiet and still. Don't think."

Think? Was she mad? He was awash in pure sensation: her scent, her breath on his neck, a soft loose curl that brushed against him when she leaned in for a special effort.

Then she stopped.

"Don't stop."

"I'm afraid I'll have to pull down your shirt. I can't reach your shoulders and arms, and the effect isn't the same through cloth. Do you mind?"

Mind? He nodded numbly, keeping his eyes open so he could see her hands reach down to unfasten the rest of the buttons. She pulled the garment down, but there wasn't enough slack, and it got caught on the angle of his shoulders. Without a thought, he grasped the placket in each hand and ripped it all the way to his waist.

"Linton!"

"As you remarked lately, I have many shirts." Only two days had passed since then, which was hard to believe, so differently did he feel about her, a hundred miles from the sour resentment with which he'd found her at The Chimneys.

She laughed softly, drew the ruined garment down to the crook of his elbows, and began to rub his shoulders and upper arms with strong, smooth strokes. He relaxed blissfully into the motions.

"Why did you give up rowing?" she asked.

"After I won the Dukeries Cup, it seemed the right moment to stop. I came of age that year and into the full responsibilities of the dukedom. Being a good oarsman requires a lot of time. I fit bouts of boxing and fencing in between my duties in Parliament and seeing to the estates."

"You are always busy." His aching shoulders melted beneath her ministering touch.

Too busy for a man with a young bride, he realized. If he'd given her more attention when they returned to London after the honeymoon, made time to introduce her to the delights and temptations of the capital, maybe she'd have approached the delights with moderation and resisted some of the more pernicious temptations. That wasn't how things worked in the *ton*, where men of his stature went about their business without their wives hanging on their sleeves.

"Did you feel I neglected you?"

Her fingers stilled. "No," she said cheerfully. "I had Nick for company."

Bloody Nick. Always bloody Nick.

Though she continued to work her magic on his arms and shoulders, his state of euphoria had abated a measure. Not, however, his inconvenient state of desire. His mind filled with earthy images involving himself, his wife, and somewhere soft and horizontal. Damn it, he didn't want to want her like that. It upset the life he'd resigned himself to.

"Why don't you divorce me?" she asked. He jerked his head around to look at her. "Why, Linton? I'm a dreadful inconvenience to you."

True, though at this moment not in the way she meant. He returned to his leaning position, and she continued her strokes.

"Divorce is difficult and requires an act of Parliament."

"With your influence, any obstacle would be a bagatelle." She snapped her fingers, and he missed her touch.

"There'd be a lot of talk." That was the excuse he always gave his sisters when they urged him to dispose of his erring wife and find a lady to produce an heir.

"So it's the scandal?"

"Partly, yes. Such an action would be ugly."

"Partly?"

"I haven't sought a divorce because of what it would do to you. In my position, I'd weather the scandal, but you would be ruined. You'd never be received anywhere again." He was embarrassed to admit it; it sounded sentimental and weak. Certainly Mary would say Althea deserved it.

"Why would you care about that?"

"Because you are my wife. I married you and vowed to care for you. Nothing changes that, even if we never speak to one another again."

"Oh," she breathed and said nothing more.

Perhaps, he thought wryly, she'd taken him at his word and silence would reign forever. She did, however, continue to rub his arms and shoulders with a firm touch that seemed to penetrate deep into his muscles, until he felt boneless and more at peace in his body than he had in years.

There was one more thing that would make it perfect. Did he dare? His spongy brain sought the words to proposition his wife. Was he mad?

"Is that enough?" she asked in a tone that gave him no reason to believe her mind was moving in the same direction.

"Maybe a minute more. Just there, yes. How did you learn to do this?"

"Life at home was very dull, so I used to read a lot, anything I could find in the Maxfield library. There were very few novels but quite a few travelers' accounts. I don't know why, because my father never went anywhere. I read about what is called *massage* in French in an account of the Orient. I used to do it for Nick, and he always liked it."

Of course he did, lucky devil. Linton's sisters had never possessed such a splendid skill.

"And now I fear I must stop, for my hands are tired."

"And I no longer feel as though I'd rowed ten miles." He stood and stretched. "Thank you, Althea."

She tilted her head sideways with a twisted half-smile. "It was nothing. Do you want me to help you into your coat?"

"Given the state of my shirt, I won't bother."

She gave a laugh that was half gasp. "Do you realize the servants will think we've been fighting even worse than usual?"

Flinging his coat over one shoulder, he touched her hand. "That is further from the truth than at any time in five years."

"I know, Linton, and I am glad." But she backed away from him, the lovely line of her profile partly hidden behind the curls that had come lose during her *massage* exertions.

He pinched his lips together and hesitated, trying to read her thoughts. "I think I'll go up now. May I escort you, or do you have things to do here?"

"No. Let's go to bed."

A triumphant fanfare rang in his ears until he considered her tone of voice. She couldn't possibly mean it in the way it sounded. There was nothing remotely erotic or even flirtatious in the way she looked at him, waiting for him at the door.

He accepted a candle from the footman on duty in the hall and lit the way to their rooms, stopping at the entrance to hers from the passage. Not from his room. "Thank you," he said again.

"Thank you, Linton. For Nick."

"You've already thanked me."

"I suppose we can't stand here all night thanking one another." She raised herself on tiptoes and kissed his cheek. "Good night."

In his own chamber, he crept over to the connecting door, hearing the murmur of her conversation with her maid, envisioning the removal of her gown, the fall of her petticoats, the slide of silk stockings down her limbs. His hand reached for the doorknob, and he snatched it back.

Tomorrow he'd go back to the lake with Nicholas and make him work until he won the Dukeries Cup. Then he'd find the young man something useful to do, preferably far away. And then... and then he didn't know what he'd do.

Chapter Six

THE SEAT IN the brick alcove was Althea's favorite fair-weather retreat when she wanted to read, or merely think about things. She had much to think about, but half an hour failed to make any sense of last night, or of anything that had happened since Linton came to The Chimneys. His behavior confounded her. He'd changed so much, or perhaps he was the same and she had never known him.

She'd offered to massage his shoulders because she wanted to touch him. She admitted that now. There hadn't been the least need to half undress him in the drawing room, for heaven's sake. It made her blush to recall her removal of his cravat and the bold way she'd undone his buttons. When he tore apart his shirt, she was ready to go up in flames.

She'd invited him to bed. *Let's go to bed*. The moment the unconsidered words dropped from her lips, she knew what she'd implied, though it wasn't what she'd meant. Except that when he failed to respond to the ambiguous suggestion in the most obvious way, she'd felt disappointment. As she undressed, she thought about him coming to her room, caressing her, bringing her to the joy that had eluded her during their married life.

He could do it, she was sure. He knew things about pleasing a woman that he hadn't practiced on her.

He kept them for his mistress, she supposed. She hadn't heard a word about the house in Molyneux Street in years, but she had no reason to believe that Linton had dismissed Mrs. Veney. Or hadn't found a replacement for her. Althea might behave like a wanton and live like a nun; her husband was doubtless the opposite, a monk in public and a satyr behind the doors of his mistress's house.

That was going too far. It was absurd to imagine her dignified husband leaping on a woman and ravishing her.

On the other hand, he had ripped his shirt.

She'd thought she was now indifferent to Linton's infidelity, but the idea of him ripping off his clothes and touching his mistress made her burn with the same anger and hurt she'd suffered when she discovered he still kept a mistress when he married her. She could never forgive him that.

And yet her treacherous body yearned for him.

Well, it could yearn for someone else, for the nameless, faceless lover who often occupied her waking dreams in the lonely hours of the night. Lowering her eyelids, she pictured herself in a bed, no, in a fairy bower of flowers in a summer's wood, moss soft beneath her back. He came to her quietly to waken her with a kiss and whisper poetic words of love while he caressed her. Then in her mind she heard a sharp ripping sound. In her daydream, the unknown hero had turned into her husband, the Duke of Linton. Without his shirt.

No no no no. That was not what she intended. Ridiculous too, since Linton was the last person who would ever speak in poetry. But her imagination refused to be governed, and no matter how she tried, her husband seemed determined to invade her mind. Very well, then. It wasn't real. She wanted a dream kiss, so Linton would have to do. Dreaming about kissing her estranged husband might be pathetic, but it was hardly sinful. No one had to know, least of all Linton himself. It would be her secret.

She removed her bonnet to enjoy the sun on her face. Her pale skin would redden and freckle if she wasn't careful, but five minutes wouldn't hurt. Closing her eyes again, she relaxed and didn't feel the hard bricks against her back. She lay in a pair of strong arms—she now knew those muscles very well. In seconds he would kiss her. She felt his breath close to her mouth, uncannily real. "Kiss me," she murmured.

The brush of those lips on hers was too real to be a dream.

Her eyes shot open to find the odious face of Nigel Speck almost mashed into hers.

With a shriek, she pushed him back and leaped to her feet. "How dare you," she shouted. "You vile man."

"My dear duchess. Allie. You asked me to kiss you."

"Not you, you brute." She scampered backward to get away from even the possibility that he would touch her again.

"Dear me. I wonder whom then? Were you expecting a caller while your brother and husband are playing with boats?"

"Go away."

"I wouldn't like to leave a lady unkissed when she so clearly wants it. Come, Allie, let us finish what we started at Vauxhall."

"I didn't start anything. I'd sooner be kissed by a snake."

"That's not the message I receive from you. You invited me to your house."

"Never, and well you know it. I let you stay only because of Nick." She shuddered with loathing. "I don't care how much money Nick owes you. I want you to leave at once, this morning. If you don't go, I shall tell my husband."

"I don't know what you mean."

"You attacked me."

"That is not at all my recollection of events. We went to Vauxhall in the same party, and you invited me to come away from the boxes and walk with you. We left the crowds behind, and you led me into a deserted walk. You're a very beautiful woman, and I'm not a man to refuse such an invitation. We kissed, many times, but you started it. I am far too modest a man to initiate advances to a duchess. You let me touch you through your gown, and you pressed yourself against my hardness. I could hardly believe my luck, and I was right to doubt. Tease that you are, as soon as I accepted the goods so brazenly offered, you thrust me aside with a mocking laugh and left me wanting."

Her mouth fell open in the course of this outrageous recitation. "That is not what happened. You're a liar as well as a lecher."

"Who do you think people will believe if our stories were told side by side? Who would your husband believe?"

"He will believe the truth," she said with a good deal more confidence than she felt.

"Truth is what people believe, Allie. You've hardly gained the reputation of a saint. *The purest treasure mortal times afford, is spotless reputation; that away, men are but gilded loam or painted clay.* Shakespeare said that, clever fellow. And what goes for men goes even more for ladies. Your clay, Duchess, is painted in very bright colors."

Althea hesitated. It was bitterly unfair that Speck's attack at Vauxhall, one of the most horrible nights of her life, should rear its head when her relations with Linton were improving. She couldn't be sure he'd believe Speck's accusation, but he might, and so would others. Any number of people had seen her after she'd fled from Speck and sought the safety of the rotunda. She had made up a story for her friends about tripping in the dark and getting ensnared in a bush. Now she wished she'd told someone, but the same consideration had kept her silent: Everyone would believe she had asked for it.

"Very well, Mr. Speck, you may stay until after the boat race." She had to dig her nails into her palms to stop herself from slapping his sly, triumphant face. "But do not *ever* lay so much as a finger on me again."

"I never touch a lady who doesn't want me."

"Now stay out of my way. If you even attempt to get me alone, Linton will learn all, because I shall tell him myself, and he will ruin you."

Chapter Seven

ALTHEA CAME DOWN to the lake to cheer them on and hold his watch, but she showed more enthusiasm for Nicholas's performance behind the oars than his. Understandable, since her brother was the competitor. Nicholas had shown himself to be a talented oarsman, and Linton couldn't complain about his diligence. He'd never have thought the young man had so much determination. Still, it was more than two weeks until the race, and it would be no surprise if he slacked off.

"Fifteen seconds faster that time, Nick," Althea said, "even in this wind. Well done!"

And I was only a second behind, Linton wanted to say. *Pay attention to me*! "Are you cold up there?" he asked her.

She huddled in her shawl. "A little. I think I shall go in."

The next day it rained. Though no reason to forgo their practice, they had to manage without a timekeeper. He entered the house late in the afternoon having rowed better than ever. His dormant muscles had loosened and were regaining their old facility, but they'd pushed themselves today, and everything ached. He knocked on the door between their rooms.

"Good Lord, Linton, you aren't dressed yet."

"Neither are you." Her shift, stays, and petticoats covered her as thoroughly as an evening gown, but the lace-trimmed silk gave him ideas, and a pain in a new place.

"The vicar and his family will be here in half an hour."

"How long will it take you to finish your toilette?"

"Maybe ten minutes. I only have to put on my gown."

"I can be ready in five." A gross exaggeration. "Could I beg you to rub my shoulders for a few minutes?" He managed what he hoped was a winning smile. Begging and cajoling were not things he'd often had to do. If ever.

"A quick one," she said.

Her maid regarded them with curiosity. "You may go," he told her. And when Althea started to object, "I will help you into your gown."

"Dictatorial as ever, Linton," Althea said.

"Dictatorial? I was begging."

"You're not very good at it. Sit here."

She placed him on the padded stool in front of her dressing table. The mirror let him see her standing behind him and, when she leaned over, gave him a splendid view of the tops of her breasts.

"Shall I remove my shirt?"

"We haven't time."

The massage didn't feel as good through cloth, and it was over far too soon. "We must dress," she said, giving his shoulders a last kneading.

To prolong the moment, he laid his hand over one of hers. "I wouldn't have expected you to invite the vicar to dine with you."

"Why not? I do it several times every year."

He did the same at each of his estates, but he couldn't see Althea in company with Mr. Foster, an expert on local ancient monuments, of which he was a prime example, it being a miracle he could still climb the steps of the pulpit.

"I'll have you know that I like the vicar's sister Mrs. Widmerpool immensely. She enlivens meetings of the church floral committee."

"I'm having difficulty seeing you in those surroundings."

"I don't see why. I provide flowers from the garden, and may I inform you that I am quite skilled at arrangements?"

"I had no idea."

"I pass my time in innocuous activities when I'm not busy with mischief and debauchery." She tried to pull away her hand, but he held it fast.

She saw his remark as critical, which was far from his intent. "That's not what I meant." The last thing he had in mind was a scolding. He was rather desperate to kiss her.

"Go to your room at once," she said. "I'll call my maid to help me. We don't have time."

So he didn't even have the pleasure of fastening her gown, though, in truth, he'd rather be undressing her.

∽

AT DINNER MRS. Widmerpool, who made a study of the publications of Mr. Debrett, subjected Nigel Speck to a probing interrogation.

"Are you one of the Dorsetshire Specks?"

"Sir Donald is my cousin," Speck said with the air of false modesty with which he boasted of his distinguished relation at dinner each night. "Larchmont is a magnificent house. Have you seen it?"

"I've never been to Dorset," Mrs. Widmerpool said, implying that the county wasn't worth honoring with her presence. "You are not Robert Speck's son, are you?"

"No."

"A third or fourth cousin, I suppose. A mere speck on the family tree, one might say." She chortled. "Are you often invited to Larchmont?"

Linton caught his wife's eye down the length of the table. She appeared to be struggling to suppress mirth.

Once she could speak, she changed the subject. "Tell me, Mr. Foster, will you go to Teversault to watch the Dukeries Cup race?"

"I never miss it. I remember when His Grace won by almost a hundred yards, one of the most extraordinary feats of rowing I ever witnessed."

"I think that says more about the competition that year than my own skill," Linton said.

"You are too modest," the vicar replied. "None of the other houses had a strong entrant that year, but your time remains a record for the race."

"It could be broken this year. My brother-in-law is rowing for The Chimneys and promises to put up an excellent time. Do you know who else is racing?"

"The Duke of Stoke Teversault's brother Lord William will try to win for the fourth time in a row."

"That has never been done."

"He's a very strong young man."

Linton saw that Nicholas looked worried. "Do you know William Besett, Nicholas?"

"I raced him once in London. He beat me soundly."

"You never told me you rowed in London, Nick," Althea said.

"Just once, with the Star Club. I was thinking of joining, but it didn't come to anything. You know how it is. Other things came up."

Other things being drinking and gaming and leading his sister astray.

His wife turned to the vicar and looked so beautiful his breath caught. A base craving roiled his loins, and something more. Tenderness. Tenderness for the young girl she'd been before being spoiled by the worst London had to offer, and for the lovely woman she'd grown into.

For now he'd settle for a look, but she favored the vicar with her smiles.

"Mr. Maxfield is fortunate to have His Grace as his guide," Mr. Foster said. "Winning on the lake at Teversault requires strategy and knowledge. I assume you will practice in situ."

"I sent a message to Stoke Teversault asking if we could take our sculls over there tomorrow. Nicholas and I have the use of the lake for the day. Will you come with us, Althea?"

"I'd like to see Nick row the famous serpentine lake, and," she added, causing his chest to swell, "to see the site of your triumph."

If he didn't kiss her soon, he was going to die. Desperate merely to touch her, after dinner he proposed they play the Mozart duet.

They made a decent job of it. Althea had mastered her part, and Linton had to make several deliberate mistakes to achieve the accidental meetings of their hands that he craved. They finished with a flourish and looked at each other. Amid the applause, he kissed her hand, and she did not snatch it away. Then Nigel Speck ambled over to the piano.

"Congratulations. I had no idea you were such an excellent player, Duke."

"Why would you? I don't know you," Linton said.

Ignoring the snub, Speck leaned over Althea's shoulder. "And you, Duchess, have improved much since I last heard you."

She slid off the bench and moved out of Speck's orbit. Out of Linton's too, but not before he caught the look of disgust on her face. "I didn't know you had ever heard me play, Mr. Speck."

"You entertained us with some songs after dinner at Linton House. I have never forgotten the delightful occasion."

"Oh yes," she said. "I believe you did dine with us once."

"Us?" Speck said. "Linton wasn't there. As he just remarked, we were not previously acquainted."

That was enough. Linton was now certain that Althea merely tolerated Speck for her brother's sake. Whatever there might have been in the past between them, she disliked him now. The thought of *anything* between Althea and Speck made him want to smash something. It was time to take action and get rid of the worm.

He'd done nothing about his discovery of Speck's cheating because he wasn't certain how Althea would react, and he didn't wish to start an argument. In the past her response to perfectly reasonable requests had been unpredictable. This time he wasn't going to ask. Speck had upset her, so Speck must go.

SPECK HAD RUINED her evening with his innuendo about his visit to Linton House, the only time he'd set foot in the London residence.

As she prepared for bed, Althea remembered the dinner. Linton had been away, and she'd invited her coterie: Nick and some of his young bachelor friends, including Speck; some dashing young couples; and a couple of young married women who, like her, were in the habit of going about alone when their husbands were occupied with their own affairs. Things got a little merry, as they often did, and after dinner she was persuaded to accompany some singing. Her simple playing was good enough for the rum-ti-tum of raucous drinking songs. It was all in good humor and ultimately innocent. She could imagine how the account of the evening would sound with the embellishments of Speck's cloven tongue.

She'd enjoyed having Linton as host with her tonight. She used to dread the dinners she'd attended with him in London, where she'd feel young and stupid among people of the highest rank and political influence. Nothing she said ever seemed to be right. She'd look for him, longing for his support, but he was always deep in conversation with some important person. Once, when she tried to explain, he had brushed off her concern, telling her she was doing well enough and would learn to be more comfortable. Little wonder she had preferred to racket around town with Nick and his friends.

During that first massage, when he asked her if she had felt neglected by him, she denied it. Perhaps she should have told him the truth.

Tonight she hadn't felt stupid, except sometimes when she intercepted a hot glance that addled her brain. He wanted to return to her bed, she was sure of that. She was almost sure she wanted to invite him. The prospect of Linton as her lover enticed her; having him back as her husband filled her with doubt.

A knock at the door made her leap to her feet. Linton. What was she going to do?

He was fully dressed and not looking at all amorous.

"I have come to tell you," he said, "that I have asked Mr. Speck to leave tomorrow. I do not feel that he is a suitable person for us to introduce to our guests."

"I see," was all she could manage. Had Speck said anything to Linton about her?

"Are you displeased?"

Displeased? She was delighted not to have the horrid man in the house. "No," she said faintly.

"Good," he said.

It didn't appear that Linton knew about Vauxhall, for surely he'd be furious. If he believed Speck's tale, he might be so angry that he'd divorce her, whatever he'd said before. There had been times when she was in low spirits and wouldn't have cared. If she was to be a scandalous duchess, she might as well do it properly. Things were different now. Hope of a better future had crept into her heart.

"Where is he going?" If he returned to London, she'd feel much easier, but she couldn't believe he'd leave the neighborhood before he'd collected on Nick's debt.

"I will deliver him to the Duke's Arms, and after that I neither know nor care." He stared at her, apparently waiting for something, but she had nothing to say. "I'll say good night then."

"Good—" Before she could finish, he strode over, took her by the shoulders, and planted a firm kiss on her lips. Oh Lord, she had forgotten how good his mouth could feel. She wanted a longer, deeper kiss, and that wasn't all. But before she even had time to respond, he withdrew, wished her good night again, and returned to his own room.

※

ALTHEA CHANGED HER mind about joining them at Teversault. Instead, Speck came with them in the carriage, a very poor exchange. But they dropped him at the Duke's Arms, and Linton hoped never to set eyes on him again. He'd gone easily enough when Linton mentioned the shiny snuffbox, though he claimed innocence. It was true that he hadn't actually been caught marking the cards or hiding an ace in his sleeve, but he knew Linton could damage his reputation. That was exactly what Linton intended to do once he returned to London. In the meantime, he was merely relieved to have him out of the house.

A cart had delivered their sculls earlier, so Nicholas and Linton went straight to work, practicing the serpentine lake's tricky curves and tight turns before a run-through of the three-mile race. Linton was gratified to complete it without killing himself and only a few minutes behind Nicholas, who rowed superbly.

Resting on one of the lakeside benches, they shared a picnic of bread and cheese washed down with small beer. Linton had never felt so fondly of his brother-in-law. They talked of past races at their respective schools and Linton's at Oxford.

"Why didn't your brother send you up to university?" he asked.

"He said our father had done enough for me by paying for me to go to Westminster. When I finished there, he handed over my inheritance from my mother and told me to leave the house. Our father didn't care for Allie and me, because of our mother, you know, and Geoffrey was as bad."

Linton never knew the father, but he thought Geoffrey an unpleasant man and was glad Althea wasn't close to him. Taking care of the future of your dependents was the decent thing to do, family animosities aside. Nicholas was too young to have been thrust into the world without the benefit of masculine counsel.

"Yet he provided for Althea."

Nicholas emitted a short, unamused laugh. "Only because she made him. Even Geoffrey couldn't toss out his sister. People would have talked. He tried to marry her off to some old neighbor, but she dug in her heels. Allie was always the strong one—not like me—and Geoffrey knew it. So he bought her a few new gowns instead of the old rags she wore and ponied up for the Season in London." Now he was grinning. "I can just imagine how Geoffrey must have felt when she landed the catch of the Season. She always said he hoped she'd have to settle for a nasty old man with the pox."

"No danger of that. I had plenty of competitors for her hand."

"Geoffrey may have been annoyed by her good luck, but it meant he could finally wash his hands of me. Told me before the wedding that I could go to Allie if I wanted anything and told Allie I was her responsibility."

Unfortunately, Althea hadn't done her brother any favors by cosseting him. Linton accepted that she'd acted out of love, but Nick needed to be his own man. The efforts he put into his rowing showed that he was capable of hard work and persistence. A little self-absorbed and lacking in confidence, but he was still young, and Linton had found a new tolerance for the weaknesses of youth. Once the Dukeries Cup was theirs, Linton would find him an occupation since Maxfield would not.

"I'd have paid for you to go to university. Sooner that than your gaming debts."

Nicholas had the grace to look ashamed. "I daresay I wouldn't have gone. I was enjoying London too much. I'm not much of one for responsibility myself."

Linton could have agreed, but Sir Geoffrey's was the greater fault. A boy didn't acquire a sense of responsibility without guidance and example. Sir Geoffrey certainly hadn't provided the latter.

"I'm pretty worthless, I'm afraid. Only thing I was good at was rowing, but that time I rowed for the Star Club I was drunk. That's why I lost to Besett. Or perhaps I would have anyway. He's strong."

"If I have anything to do with it, you'll beat him. But to get back to you and Althea, why didn't she tell me this and ask me to help you?" He had a nasty feeling his young bride had been too frightened to confide in him. He was beginning to wish he'd done things differently.

Nicholas gave the matter his consideration. "I expect she was ashamed to admit that Geoffrey was such a shabby fellow. Or perhaps—yes, I remember her saying something like this once—she didn't want you to think she'd married you only for my sake."

Linton had assumed, at least after things went wrong, that Althea had accepted him for mercenary reasons. "Why do you think she married me, then?"

"She didn't want a man like our father or Geoffrey, and she said you were a good fellow. She trusted you."

The words lightened his heart. The lovely, willful girl had trusted him to treat her well. He understood her better now, her unreasonable support of Nick, even her extravagance after living with a pair of misers. How dare the Maxfields, neither of whom was short of a guinea, dress their daughter and sister in rags? Little wonder a spirited girl like her would go a little wild when free from their cheeseparing tyranny and defy a husband who did nothing but criticize her. She'd thought him a good fellow, trusted him, and he had let her down.

He was ready to be a more tolerant husband, but he didn't know if she could regain the liking and trust with which she'd entered their marriage. He wondered if he would have another chance to win her love.

Chapter Eight

TWO WEEKS OF festivities at the houses of the Dukeries began with an afternoon affair at Sedgemere House. The new Duchess of Sedgemere had assembled an enormous party from her own houseguests and those of the neighboring estates. On arrival they learned the principal entertainment was to be a scavenger hunt, which Linton muttered was a silly idea. Althea thought it sounded fun.

She was aware that the united appearance of the Duke and Duchess of Linton aroused intense curiosity among the guests. All eyes were on them as they joined the party on the terrace. Were they together or not? They didn't feel united to Althea. Linton hadn't offered his arm when they approached their hosts. Looking like a happy couple would hardly be a true representation of the state of affairs, but she could have used the sanction of his approval when entering the lion's den of polite society.

When the Duke of Sedgemere expressed his pleasure at Linton's prolonged stay in the county, he merely replied that he was here for the Dukeries Cup, not a ringing endorsement of his duchess. He then wandered off with Sedgemere. The Duchess of Sedgemere was a kind and gracious lady, but clearly as nervous as Althea would be, giving her first important gathering, and had many guests to attend to. She presented Althea to Lady Susan Frobisher and her daughter Miss Tamsin Frobisher, a golden-haired giggler, and the latter's bosom friend Miss Pendleton. The two younger ladies stared as though in the presence of a fantastic creature; they knew all about her. Althea had met Lady Susan before, at the house of her sister-in-law Lady Mary Poole.

"What a surprise to see you here, Duchess." Lady Susan's eyebrows shot up toward her forehead, forming deep wrinkles, cracking a badly applied layer of powder. Since Lady Mary had berated Althea for her eyebrow blacking, she rather enjoyed this evidence of cosmetics on the face of one of her critics.

"No great surprise, since I spend every summer at The Chimneys."

"I mean with the dear duke. We dined together with the Pooles only a fortnight ago, and he said nothing of coming to Nottinghamshire."

"I daresay he doesn't feel he needs to inform you of his every movement."

Lady Susan showed her teeth. "Of course not. It's always a pleasure to see him so content with life after all the distress he has suffered. I haven't seen you in town this age. I trust you haven't been unwell." Meaning that, like her friend Mary, she hoped Althea would contract a double dose of smallpox and measles and die.

"I have rarely felt better."

"Some ladies thrive on late nights. I need my beauty sleep."

"I am sure you do." Althea smiled sweetly. "How are you, Miss Frobisher? Did I hear that you are betrothed?" Immediately, she was sorry for her question, since the young lady remained unwed after three seasons. As she knew better than most, the sins of the mother should not be visited on the daughter.

But like Althea, Miss Frobisher was more than capable of committing her own trespasses. "I think it is better to wait and make sure one contracts a compatible marriage, not merely one of worldly advantage."

Althea would have agreed with the sentiment, had the young lady meant it. But she'd noted the way the latter's eyes darted whenever a gentleman hove into view and how they brightened when the gentleman was especially eligible, like the Dukes of Stoke Teversault or Wyndover. Wyndover was ridiculously good-looking and could set any lady's heart aflutter, but Althea would wager a goodly sum that either Miss Frobisher or Miss Pendleton would accept a one-legged octogenarian if he were rich and a member of the peerage.

She bit back another uncharitable response. She too had been a young thing desperate to find a husband, probably even more than these ladies, who at least had parents who cared for them. Who was she to blame Miss Frobisher for wanting the security and stature that a woman could gain only through marriage? Althea had thought herself the luckiest girl in the world to attract the attention of the wealthy and attractive Linton. And she had hoped for compatibility, even love, as well as the advantage of escaping her older brother. Whose fault it was that the marriage failed no longer seemed important. The fact was, through her own behavior, she had lost her right to be an accepted member of the kind of female society gathered here today.

The gentlemen, on the other hand… Viscount Ormandsley was making eyes at her. Worst of all, she spotted Nigel Speck hovering at the edges of the party. How he'd received an invitation she didn't know, but it meant he remained in the neighborhood, a lurking threat to her peace of mind. If ever she had needed the support of a husband, it was now.

She turned away sharply and looked for hers. Linton was in deep conversation with a cluster of fellow dukes. What did dukes talk about when they congregated? Surely not the shortcomings of their social inferiors. Why comment that cats could see in the dark or that water was wet?

Partnerships and groups were forming for the scavenger hunt, and no one had asked her to join theirs. Despite his dismissive remark, she hoped Linton would suggest they play together. She tried to catch his eye, but he remained engrossed and didn't look her way. Another minute and she'd be forced to spend the whole afternoon with the Frobishers.

A burst of masculine laughter arose from the group around Ormandsley. She excused herself from the ladies and joined the viscount, and some other young men, all of whom she knew in London and some of whom she even liked. Jermand Hunslinger, for instance. The Bavarian ambassador's half-English nephew drank too much and was as idle as a midsummer day was long, but he was amusing and good-natured and exceedingly good-looking.

"Gentlemen," she said. "May I join your side for the scavenger hunt?"

∽

LINTON WAS IN a good mood that the prospect of an idiotic game couldn't dull. He was in the company of friends he'd known all his life, on a fine summer's day. Rushing around in search of meaningless objects might even be fun in company with Althea. If he had her alone, who knew what might happen? Snatching a kiss while rifling the garden shed for a trowel or some such thing. The scavenger hunt suddenly seemed less absurd and rife with possibilities.

He stood with a huddle of dukes. Was there a collective noun for his ilk? Huddle would do well enough. There were fewer duchesses in the Sedgemere gardens, and his was by far the prettiest. He surveyed the other ladies in his view, including the group she had joined, and breathed a deep sigh of satisfaction. Lady Susan Frobisher was a tartar, as befitted one of his sister Mary's best friends, but of high *ton*. It was good to see Althea at ease in her proper setting.

The dukes, of course, were talking about the Dukeries Cup, which would cap the social season, followed by a ball at Sedgemere that night.

"It's splendid that we have a full field this year," Stoke Teversault said.

"Pity Sedgemere doesn't have a better entry." That duke shook his head sadly. "Bourne agreed to come down and row, but he sprained his wrist last month, and he's not up to strength."

"My cousin John Fletcher is little better than a dabbler," Oxthorpe said. "I doubt he'll even finish the course."

"William won handily last year, but he refuses to practice," was Stoke Teversault's contribution to the litany of pessimism.

Any of these statements might or might not be true. Disparaging one's entry was part of the tradition, as everyone tried to get the best odds in the betting.

"Nicholas Maxfield looks strong," Sedgemere said. "He's the man to beat."

Spying on the opposition was also part of the game. Practices were supposed to be private, but doubtless the bushes around the lake had been bristling with observers when he and Nick did their trial runs. Linton had already talked to his head groom, a veteran observer of years of races, about scouting the opposition as they took their turns.

"I don't know where you got that idea," he said. "Nicholas hardly out-rowed me, and I hadn't handled a pair of oars in years until last week." He bent over in exaggerated decrepitude. "Whatever I could do at the age of twenty, these old bones are scarcely up to the demands of three miles." He looked over at his wife and felt like a boy of twenty again.

After another ten minutes of enjoyable posturing, he realized that the party was dispersing in groups. The hunt was up, and he needed to claim his partner. But Althea was nowhere to be found among the chattering swarms of brightly clad ladies and their escorts, until he heard her musical laugh. Swiveling, he was just in time to see her slipping between a pair of large rhododendrons, followed by three men. He recognized them. All men, all young. Hunslinger and Ormandsley were worthless fribbles, but innocuous. Greenover, on the other hand. He might be the heir to an earldom, but he had a nasty reputation.

The arrival of the Duchess of Sedgemere and a diminutive lady of extreme old age halted his pursuit. It was all he could do not to paw the ground like an eager racehorse while courtesy forbade him from ignoring them.

"Duke," the duchess said, and laughed. "I could be addressing anyone, couldn't I? Your Grace of Linton, I should say. Since your wife has joined another party, would you be good enough to lend Sedgemere's Great-Aunt Lavinia your escort? She doesn't have a partner."

He cast about wildly for a plausible excuse and failed miserably. Instead of charging off into the shrubbery, he accepted a list of the objects to be retrieved and offered Lady Lavinia his arm.

Sedgemere and Stoke Teversault smirked at him. He had no doubt the pair of them had taken preventive action to avoid the same fate. "Take care of Auntie," Sedgemere whispered. "She's a family heirloom. And don't, whatever you do, leave her alone with that lecher Greenover. I'm sorry we had to invite him, but we all have some rotten branches in the family tree. No woman of any age is safe with him. Don't worry," he said in response to Linton's glare. "She's so deaf she can't hear anything less than a shout. Lucky your lungs are in good fettle from all that rowing."

He thought he was being terribly amusing; Linton found nothing to laugh at. The good manners that he regarded as essential to the functioning of decent society had become a curse.

"What's on the list, Linton?" Lady Lavinia seemed bright enough, like a small and slightly decrepit bird.

Summoning patience, he read from the sheet of paper, inscribed in an elegant hand. "A horseshoe, a feather, a pink rose, a smooth round stone for skipping, a puce ribbon, a sprig of heather, a hen's egg, a silver ladle, a stick of sealing wax, and a pair of spectacles." Wonderful. The list was designed to send them hither and yon all over the house and grounds. The last should be easy, at least. "Do you have your spectacles with you?" he roared.

"I'm deaf, not blind," the old lady said with a cackle. "We'll have to steal them from the butler's pantry."

"Good. That'll take care of the ladle too." He planned a strategy that would cover the ground with the least waste of time and effort. The stables for the horseshoe, the garden for the plants, then the butler's quarters, which were no doubt close to the kitchens for the egg. No need to make a side trip to the hen house, wherever that was, as long as they were lucky enough to find a feather somewhere along the way. The other objects should be found indoors, except the skipping stone. The lake. Perhaps they should start there, and then Lady Lavinia would be exhausted, and he could find her a comfortable place to rest and leave her to find Althea.

"Can you manage the walk to the lake?" He seemed to be speaking loud enough to make himself understood.

She cackled again. "I'm deaf, not lame. No need to go there, though. There are plenty of stones in the paths in the sunken garden."

What a splendid old lady! He'd enjoy her under other circumstances, when he wasn't wishing he had Althea as his partner instead of the oldest guest at the party. At least Lady Lavinia wasn't Lady Susan Frobisher. "That'll take care of the rose too. Do you have any idea where to find heather? I wouldn't think it common in Nottinghamshire."

"Nonsense, Linton. We'll get a piece of leather when we go to the stables. I don't know where we'll find a leg."

"Not a leg. A hen's egg."

Lady Lavinia went on without hearing him. "Old General Mosley at the Willow House had a wooden one, but he died years ago. Pity. A very handsome man, and he hopped around on that leg like a young rabbit."

Without too many more misunderstandings—he finally convinced her that there was no need to call on the late general's nephew in hope that the wooden leg had been stashed in the attic—they managed to collect most of the items on the list. During their wanderings, they encountered other players, but never once the Duchess of Linton. Her party must have taken a different route, and doubtless made the long walk to the lake since she lacked his partner's useful inside information.

"Your wife's a beauty," Lady Lavinia remarked as they left the kitchen with an egg in hand, along with a basket to carry their booty. "And a nice gal too. Whatever quarrels you have with her, you should make up. Serves you right for choosing such a young 'un, but youth is an affliction from which we all recover, more's the pity." She cackled loudly.

She was right. He should stop worrying, because Althea was a sensible woman now and quite capable of fending off Greenover. Besides, even a rakeshame wouldn't assault a lady in the presence of two other men. Damnation! Why hadn't she made sure there was a lady in her party? Gallivanting around the place with three men was just the kind of indiscreet behavior he abhorred.

Correction: two men. Leaving Sedgemere's study with sealing wax in hand, they met Ormandsley and a couple of others laying bets on the Dukeries Cup. She was alone with Greenover and Hunslinger now, or maybe with only one of them, and he wasn't sure which was worse: to think of her fighting off the former or flirting with the handsome German. Then Greenover joined the betting party.

She was alone with one man.

"One last thing to collect," Lady Lavinia said gleefully. "I do believe we'll win, and Anne has promised a handsome prize."

Linton didn't give a damn about the prize. "Do you happen to own a puce ribbon?"

"Hideous color. Never wear it, but Susan Frobisher loves it. Her dressing room will be full of puce. Gowns, bonnets, slippers, and the dreadful turban she wore at dinner last night."

"Ribbons?" Normally, he'd hesitate to invade a lady's chamber with larceny in mind, but these were desperate times.

"Of course. I know the way."

They weren't the only ones to have noticed Lady Susan's taste for that noisome shade. A door off her bedchamber was closed, presumably leading to the dressing room, but not empty. He heard a man's laugh, followed by a feminine shriek and words from a voice he knew only too well. "For Lord's sake, stop tickling me." More shrieks, then the door flew open, and his wife emerged, followed by Jermand Hunslinger, also laughing maniacally. Clutching an ugly length of ribbon to her stomach, she would have fallen had her pursuer not grabbed her waist to steady her.

"Linton," she said, mirth fading away. Shock and guilt were written all over her face.

"Madam," he said. "I will speak to you alone, if you please."

Seizing her wrist, he pulled her away from her unresisting swain, dragged her out into the passage and into an empty room where he turned the key in the lock.

⁂

ALTHEA HAD BEEN having a wonderful time. Once she got over the disappointment that Linton hadn't invited her to join the hunt with him, rushing around the beautiful Sedgemere grounds in search of unnecessary objects was fun, especially when Nick joined their group and the dull Ormandsley and lecherous Greenover became bored and went off to find liquid refreshment. At one point she, Nick, and Hunslinger had hidden in a shrubbery and listened with glee to Linton shouting at his elderly partner. How sweet he'd been, patiently trying to make himself heard by the tiny old lady. Her team hadn't been above using their eavesdropping to avoid a walk to the lake. All was fair in love and scavenger hunts, according to Nick.

Raiding Lady Susan's wardrobe had seemed particularly amusing. By this time, Nick was pretending to compete with her for the prize and tried to tickle the puce ribbon away from her. She'd torn out of the dressing room to find Linton looking absolutely furious. He found her antics reprehensible, it seemed. Why did he object to such innocuous fun?

And that wasn't all. Once he'd locked them in another room, she rubbed her bruised wrist and waited for the expected scolding. It saddened her that he hadn't changed a bit.

It was far, far worse. Towering over her at his most haughty, he spoke with dangerous calm. "Will you explain, madam, why I find you hidden in a bedroom closet alone with another man?" She was too shocked to speak. "I knew you for an unrepentant flirt, but this is beyond anything. I suppose I know what would have occurred had I not happened by." Whiteness around the mouth proclaimed his anger, but it could be nothing to the disappointment that possessed her. Her vision blurred with rage.

She declined to defend herself. "Divorce me then," she said, tilting her chin. "I don't care."

"Now that you've given me indisputable cause, I may act on your suggestion."

"Do it then, and I hope you enjoy the scandal. I doubt the hypocrisy will trouble you. You convict me of adultery on the slenderest of evidence, while everyone knows that you keep a mistress and have for years."

"I do not keep a mistress."

"Really? Mrs. Veney who was *not my affair* is no longer yours either?"

"For your information, Stella Veney died three years ago."

That took the wind out of her sails, but only for a second. She didn't wish anyone dead, though she'd often thought unkindly of Mrs. Veney, but Linton was the target of her ire. "I am sorry for your loss. It doesn't change the truth that you had her in your keeping both before you married me and afterward." Delivering the speech without shouting cost every piece of composure she possessed. Linton hadn't made her this angry in years. "I am aware that the world would think me a fool for caring and expect me to turn a blind eye. You told me so yourself. But the fact remains that you are an adulterer, and I am not, and you make me sick." Her voice broke on the last words.

She would not cry, and she would not let Linton see how much he had hurt her. Hurrying to the door, she fumbled with the key.

"Stop!"

She ignored him and met Nick and Lady Lavinia in the passage. Irrelevantly, she noticed that the old lady was holding the infamous ribbon.

"Are you—?" She cut her brother off with the palm of her hand.

"I am unwell," she said with a loud sniff. "I will call for the carriage to take me home and send it back for you."

"But, Allie. Are you all right? Do you want me to come with you?"

"No." She suddenly felt almost as angry with her brother as she was with her husband. "I wish to be alone."

Chapter Nine

THE STARLIT NIGHT with a crescent moon was perfect for love and rowing. Linton was rowing, up and down the lake for an hour and more, ignoring the agony in his shoulders and trying to forget the pain in his heart.

It had taken five minutes to learn that Nicholas was both chaperone and tickler in the supposedly compromising situation. By that time it was too late and Althea was in the carriage, bowling down the drive. Since Lady Lavinia insisted on claiming the prize for the scavenger hunt, he'd had to tolerate the congratulations of the party, the anxious (and avidly curious) enquiries about his wife's health, and make small talk for two interminable hours until he could go home. Althea had locked both her doors and wouldn't answer his knocks, nor Nick's.

"Tell her you're sorry," Nick had said when, in desperation, Linton confided his mistake. "Allie's not a girl to hold a grudge."

She was holding one tonight. Knowing he would never sleep, he went to the lake.

Fool, fool, fool, his mind chanted in time with the oars.

Jealous fool, the lapping water jeered at him.

For that was what he was. Jealous of her youth and joie de vivre that he had lost or never possessed, jealous of the gaiety of her young friends, jealous of the unstinting love and loyalty she gave her twin, and jealous of every man who ever looked at her.

Digging his oar too deep at the turn, he caught a crab and ended flat on his back. As he recovered his balance, the prow rammed into the rushes. He couldn't even row properly. Lucky Nick was competing and not he. Having righted the scull, he set off again, attending only to his rhythm, the play of his muscles, the ripples on the silent lake. When he passed the point across from the small hill on which Althea had stood and kept time, he saw that he had a watcher, dressed all in white, almost formless in the dark. It must be a ghost.

Linton didn't believe in ghosts.

Since he was rowing at some speed, the shadowy form faded into the distance, and he wondered if he'd conjured the specter of his wife from his own yearnings.

Linton wasn't the kind of man to conjure anything. He had no imagination and acted only on evidence. Some of which turned out to be wrong. Making the turn perfectly, he sped back, resisting the temptation to look over his shoulder. He pulled to a halt in the middle of the lake, next to the hill.

She was still there. Althea.

"Linton!" She stepped forward.

"Take care!"

Too late. She misstepped in the dark, slid down the dewy grass, and splashed into the water, feet first.

Abandoning oars and boat, he scrambled over the side and swam to the bank. "I'm coming."

She floundered and splashed and shrieked a few words unbecoming to a lady. Reaching her before she sank, he grasped her by the waist and managed to get her up the slope to firm ground. She lay on her back, arms stretched out, eyes closed, completely still. Was she dead? She couldn't be. He must have reached her in time.

"Althea?" No reply.

He recalled seeing a man resuscitated from drowning by someone breathing into his mouth. On hands and knees, he leaned over her.

She opened her eyes. "I can swim, you know."

He hadn't known. There were so many things he didn't know about her.

"Besides, the water is only a foot deep at the edge."

She smiled up at him with parted lips, and he decided to try the mouth remedy. Just in case.

Her lips were cold and wet, her breath was hot, and the pent-up frustrations of weeks, months, and years went into his kiss. He cupped her head, feeling damp hair and warm skin against his palms, and feasted on her, ravishing her mouth. If this was the last kiss he ever had from her, it would be a good one.

She raised her arms, but instead of rejection, she clasped his head and drew him closer. Her tongue met his, and he was lost to further thought. Nothing in the world existed but Althea: the ridges of her teeth against the tip of his tongue, the texture of her mouth, her taste of sweetened lake water. His thumbs traced the angles of her cheekbones and explored the whirls of her ears. Shapely ears that he would kiss later when he could bear to relinquish her lips. Her hunger seemed as great as his, her kisses as devouring, while his eager hands traced the column of her neck, descended to her shoulders, reaching under clinging muslin to find cool, satin-smooth skin as alive and vibrant as she. The ache in his loins heated and grew.

It had been so long.

When she shivered, he reluctantly lifted his head. "You are cold. You should go in."

"I am a little cold," she said. "I wonder what we should do." Her wicked smile expanded his desire to unmanageable proportions.

"I'll warm you." The night was cool and his clothes even wetter than hers, but his body was a furnace from exercise and lust.

Gathering her close, they went on kissing, but her gown and his shirt intruded. "I think we'll be better off without these." To encourage her, he tugged at the neck of her gown and undergarments, barely exposing a taut nipple. First, he breathed on it, then took it in his mouth and sucked. Her pelvis bucked against his. "I can do that all over you, and you'll be as warm as toast in no time."

"Linton," she said on a breath, and that was invitation enough.

"Sit up."

Her loose gown came off easily enough, but the wet lacings of her light stays refused to yield. The need to drop fervent kisses on her neck and shoulders didn't help his concentration. "The knot is wet."

"Do you have a knife?"

"No," he croaked, and cursed his useless ducal existence that made it unnecessary to carry tools. This couldn't be over. It must not be.

"Never mind," she said, and twisted around to throw her arms about his neck and wrestle him to the ground in a tangle of limbs and wet skirts.

He shoved the muslin up her legs and found them bare. No stockings, the minx, nor drawers, and she was here, and in his arms. His questing hand found her miraculous center, warm and wet but not from the water. His head burst with triumph and his breeches with the need to enter her, now, without delay, and relieve his protesting cock.

He made himself slow down by making his mind register the discomfort of wet breeches and the night air cooling his damp back. He was determined that she would find fulfillment, with or without him inside her, preferably both.

His mouth on her breasts, fingers playing inside her, his thumb stroking the core of her pleasure, he did things he'd never thought proper for his virginal bride. Earth could offer nothing better than listening to Althea's gasps of delight, feeling her breasts grow firm as he sucked, the blissful writhing of her hips, and the clenching of her inner muscles on his fingers.

One thing better. *Wet breeches*, his mind screamed. *Don't care*, his cock answered back.

Before he exploded, she came with a long shudder and a deep sigh. "Linton," she murmured as she melted beneath him. "Now, Linton. I want you."

He might have lost a button or two as the fall of his breeches fell faster than bails off a cricket wicket, then, at long last, he was inside her. What an idiot he was to have cared what she did and given up the chance for this. He should have let her go her merry way and come back to him at night so that he could bury himself in her and drive himself to bliss. *Mine, mine, mine*, went a drumbeat in time with his thrusts. *Mine forever*, he thought as she moaned and rolled her head and dug her nails into his shoulders. *Mine forever*, as one delicious quiver after another embraced his accelerating thrusts.

"Althea," he shouted for every creature in the park to hear as he expelled his seed and collapsed, panting as though he'd rowed farther and better than ever before.

They lay still for a few minutes, his head tucked into the crook of her neck, her hands resting lightly on his back. Replete and sleepy, he wanted only to rest in her arms, but his brain insisted on being curious when his body felt only satisfaction.

He looked at her, pale and impossibly beautiful in the dim light. "Why?" Just one word.

"I believed what you said. The Duke of Linton never lies." She was talking about Stella Veney, he realized. He hadn't given that part of their quarrel another thought. He opened his mouth to tell her his former mistress meant nothing to him and explain why he had continued to pay for her keep after they separated.

"Don't say anything." She placed a silencing finger over his lips. "When we talk, we argue, and I don't want to."

Disinclined to argue about *anything*, he kissed her softly, pulled her close, and fell asleep.

He woke up alone. Had he dreamed the whole wonderful night?

But he was covered with a canvas boat cover that lived in the boathouse, and his breeches were unfastened.

It was dark, and he could still see the stars and the moon, but a faint lightening on the horizon across the lake told him dawn approached. It had been a perfect night for love and rowing, and he had done both. He had made love, and for the first time in his life, he was in love.

Chapter Ten

ALL DAY LONG as she went about her duties, Althea felt as though she held a special secret close to her breast. Last night, unable to settle, she'd pulled on an old gown and walked to the lake in search of answers. Finding Linton had been a surprise, but what occurred afterward was an answer of sorts and satisfied her for now.

More than satisfied her. She hugged herself in glee, causing the gardener to ask her if she was cold on an unusually warm summer day.

After dinner, she and Linton played the piano for Nick. They'd almost mastered the Mozart, and she was not without hope that many more duets lay in their future. But she wasn't certain. She excused herself and retired to her rooms, evading Linton's suggestive glances. He had said good night with a gallant kiss on her hand and looked disappointed. He wouldn't be for long.

Through the connecting door, she heard him moving about the room. Once he dismissed his valet, she smoothed her long hair for the last time, hung a gauzy silver shawl over her arms so that it did not cover one inch of the skin exposed by her nightgown of white cotton so fine it was almost transparent, and slipped into his room.

He stood in the middle of room in a dark red dressing gown. His eyes gleamed, and his jaw dropped. She'd never thought much about her husband's mouth before. When she was in the mood to admire him, she noticed the whole man, or more recently his upper body, but those lips could do wonderful things, as she now knew. She smiled in anticipation.

"Althea." He held out arms she was eager to fall into.

First, business.

She folded her arms and imitated his tone when speaking to his secretary. "It has come to my notice, Your Grace, that you are in need of a mistress."

His brow creased as he tried to make out what she meant. "I don't want a mistress. I have a wife, and you are all I need or want." A good answer but not quite good enough. Her husband had a lot to make up for.

"I haven't much enjoyed being your wife, Linton. After last night, however, it occurred to me that I would enjoy being your mistress. In my experience, wives are treated to formality, scoldings, and—for the most part—attentions in the bedchamber that are somewhat cursory."

His Grace had the grace to look abashed. "I am sorry for that, but—"

She cut him off. "I told you last night I didn't want to discuss the past."

"We—"

"Listen to me, please. I have a proposition for the future. I don't have much knowledge of the perquisites of a mistress, besides a smaller house in a slightly less good part of town than the wife, but I like the idea of it. I imagine that instead of formality, a mistress enjoys intimacy. Instead of scoldings, she is treated with flirting and compliments, and as for the other, I would like to find out. As you have often pointed out, I like to enjoy myself, and it seems to me that mistresses have more fun." Her speech so far received nothing but a blank stare. "I am applying for the position."

She looked back at him with a confidence she was far from feeling, waiting to learn if the cool duke obsessed with propriety would respond or the slightly crazed man who played piano duets and exchanged amused glances and made love to her under the stars. She wanted the latter badly and wouldn't take back the former under any circumstance.

"Would a mistress rub her protector's shoulders?" He spoke with perfect gravity and a lurking smile.

Her heart skipped. He understood her.

"A very grateful one would," she said, tilting her head.

He glanced around the room. "Unfortunately, I don't have any jewels on hand."

"There are other ways to earn gratitude besides material gifts."

"I will bear that in mind."

Images of other ways flooded her mind and scorched the air. Her shawl dropped to the floor. "Do you have any more questions?"

"Would a mistress be available to me during the day or only at night? Would she, for example, attend dinners with the vicar, and picnics, and scavenger hunts, and balls?"

"You shock me, Linton. Such dull occasions are the purview of the wife. The mistress only does things she enjoys."

"Would a mistress watch me rowing?"

She nibbled her finger while she considered the matter, and his exaggerated composure wavered. She trusted he would be earning her gratitude in the near future. "While you are training your wife's brother, it would be grossly improper for the mistress to be present. The mistress would only be there when you are alone, particularly when the night is warm and the stars bright."

"So my mistress would be a secret between ourselves?"

"A delicious secret. Especially if she were very grateful. Oh! What are you doing?"

Linton, practiced pugilist and fencer that he was, could move fast when he had to. He picked her up and carried her to the bed. "A mistress needs to keep up her strength and mustn't squander it on unnecessary walking."

"I didn't know that, but then, I am new to the business. I'm afraid you would have to instruct me in many matters. Am I to understand that I have passed the interview and won the position?"

"With flying colors."

She sprawled on the mattress with glee and rising excitement. It appeared that Linton was as naturally talented at this game as he was at other sports. What he would be like with practice… "Let us come to terms. I have told you what I expect as your mistress. I daresay you have demands of your own."

"I hope you won't find me too demanding, but I have certain requirements."

Being ordered around by him suddenly didn't annoy her at all. "Tell me."

"For a start, I don't like my mistresses guilty of excessive adornment, and you, my dear, are wearing far too many clothes."

"My abject apologies, Your Grace. Is it my duty to remove them or yours?"

"Do I need tools?"

"There are no stubborn laces on this garment."

"Then allow me." He patted the bottom of the bed. "Come and sit here."

She obeyed him and raised her arms so that he could pull her nightgown over her head, as one might undress a small child. His expression made her feel anything but childish. She sensed neither shyness nor shame while his burning gaze roamed over every inch of her exposed body, even between her slightly parted thighs.

"I've never seen anything so beautiful," he said, reverently caressing her naked breasts. "You are perfect in every way." Being praised, even in her role as mistress, soothed a little of the hurt caused by his disapproval of his wife.

"Am I permitted to beg for a kiss?" she whispered.

"Begging isn't required."

"But I might enjoy it. Please, please, Your Grace. Kiss me now."

He complied, on her lips, deeply, and any other number of other places. She discovered that she was particularly receptive at the base of her neck and around her ribs. Falling back on her elbows, she positively purred, and then began to laugh, and so did he, nuzzling her belly and taking hold of her hips when she pretended to struggle. Mistresses really did have more fun. When he fell to his knees between her flailing legs and planted a kiss right on the curls of her mound, she gasped with shock and a kind of appalled longing.

"Shh. Let me. I think you will like it."

Oh Lord, did she like it. She shrieked when he parted the tangled curls and the hidden opening with his thumbs. She moaned when his tongue found the sweet spot and the right rhythm, just as he did with a pair of oars. She called on the Almighty and her duke as strong, even strokes carried her toward a heaven just outside her grasp, until she tumbled into bliss with a divine explosion even more intense than the one his fingers had set off the night before.

For a long moment, or many minutes, she lay supine and boneless. "That was..." She had no words to describe it, so she stroked the dark head resting on her belly and played with one of his ears. "I like your ears," she said idly as full consciousness returned. "They are just the right size and lie flat against your head, not flapping in the breeze like some men's." It was lovely being able to say whatever silly thing entered her head.

"I endeavor not to let anything flap," he said, resting back on his haunches and offering a fine view of his private parts to her fascinated eyes.

"I wouldn't call that flapping, but it's certainly buoyant."

He held out his hand. "Come to bed with me. You can help me do something about it."

She went willingly, and to her surprise he settled on his back, propped up against the pillows. His... prick, as she'd heard it called by drunken young men who'd forgotten there were ladies present, appeared well named, straining toward the flat ridges of his stomach. Was he expecting her to reciprocate what he'd done to her with his mouth? She wasn't reluctant, but she was distinctly nervous. Kneeling beside him, she touched it gingerly, then snatched her hand back when it twitched.

"Like this." He showed her how to hold it, firmly, and how to move her hand. It felt strange in a wonderful way, both soft and hard, and alive under her fingers. Better still was his gratification, signaled by disjointed approving words. "*Like that. Umm. Yes. Aah!*"

She explored the slightly bulbous head, marveling that it had been inside her on many occasions and she'd had little idea what it looked like. How could he have kept his wife in ignorance of such an interesting part of him? A drop of fluid seeped from the tip. Dipping her head, she tasted it and found it odd but pleasantly salty.

Linton gazed at her mouth as though he'd discovered the Holy Grail. "You don't have to do that," he said huskily.

"Is it one of the duties of a mistress?"

"If the mistress wishes. The mistress should never do anything she finds distasteful."

She licked her lips. "I think it might make *you* very grateful."

"It would. By Jupiter, it would. But not now. I have a different plan."

"I thought you were lying down to take a nap."

"Not at all. I have a requirement. I want you on top."

She thought about it for a moment, then gave a drawn-out *oh*. "That does sound like fun. Let me see if I can do it without instructions."

It turned out, she could, quite easily, and it was the most marvelous feeling, taking him deep inside. Holding on to his beautiful broad shoulders—the benefit of regular exercise!—she controlled the pace, adjusting her position and movements to find the angle that pleased her most. His beatific grin told her that she pleased him as much. And when they were both done, ecstatically done, she lay against his chest with his arms around her.

"Linton," she began.

"What?"

"Do your mistresses call you Linton, or is it always Your Grace?"

"I might invite a mistress of whom I was particularly fond to call me by my given name."

"Bentinck." She tested the name on her tongue. "Bentinck."

"I would be honored if you would use it. No one in my entire life has called me that."

"I am not at all surprised." She couldn't possibly share a bed with a man named Bentinck without laughing. "I shall call you Ben."

"Ben," he said. "Ben. Short, undignified, and plebeian. Whoever heard of a duke called Ben?" But he was smiling. "I like it immensely."

"It shall only be when we are alone. The special name your mistress uses."

His throat gulped. "Thank you," he said, and drew her down for a kiss.

∽

LINTON ROSE EARLY the next day and went to the kitchen garden where he filled a small basket with strawberries, tied a white rose to the handle, and sent it up on Althea's chocolate tray with a note. *My dear duchess. Please accept my humble offering. Yours etc. Linton.*

Not Ben, but Linton. This was a gift for his wife, not his mistress. He had nothing to complain about having Althea play the strumpet at night, but he'd spoken with complete, if understated, conviction when he'd said he didn't want a mistress, only the wife he had. He had listened to her pithy enumeration of his shortcomings as a husband and acknowledged their justice.

The first time he set eyes on Althea Maxfield, he had thought her the most beautiful creature he'd ever seen, and he had wanted her. Being a duke and well aware of his value on the marriage mart, he had no doubt that he could have her. He went through the formalities of courtship: two dances at every ball, hothouse flowers the next day, a few drives in the park. He'd made no attempt to win her affection; it hadn't even occurred to him to try. He was Linton, and she would accept him. And so she did. He was gratified, naturally, that this rare beauty would be his. He also felt the enormity of his condescension in selecting her over more eligible debutantes.

Now he must woo her as he'd never troubled to before, in hopes that eventually his wife by day and his mistress by night would become one—one woman who loved him.

The thought of being loved by Althea made him feel soft inside and as mighty as an emperor, or a duke. For her, he'd slay villains and wild beasts or row ten miles.

But he knew that he wouldn't win her love through the exercise of power. He'd tried that before and failed dismally. He had to convince her by gentler means, through skills he'd never had to cultivate.

That afternoon, he asked her to show him the changes she had made to the gardens and praised her plans for the new hothouse. Praise was no hardship: She had a true talent for the possibilities of the landscape. He couldn't wait to unleash her on Longworth. At every opportunity in the next days, he deferred to her wishes. He sent her flowers, carefully chosen bouquets of her favorite flowers—which he knew from listening to her carefully and remembering what she said—delivered with little handwritten notes. In London, he had had his secretary order something from the flower seller accompanied by his card. *The Duke of Linton.*

He was Linton by day, but at night, he was Ben. One day, he hoped, she would always call him Ben. Even in public, dignity be damned.

At night, she was his mistress—intemperate, abandoned, catering to his every whim with unfeigned enthusiasm. By day, she was his wife—charming, clever, and joyful, as she had always been, but he hadn't the wit to recognize it. Also a little cool with him. He looked for new ways to show himself an ideal husband.

When they attended events at the other ducal houses, he wanted everyone to know about their reconciliation. If she'd let him, he'd have sent out cards. "The Duke and Duchess of Linton are pleased to inform you that they are no longer estranged."

"It's our secret, Ben," she said one night in bed when he asked her to reveal the improvement in their marriage. "I enjoy having all those people speculate as to whether we're about to reconcile or split apart for good." Then she fell upon him and did delectable things with her mouth, and he'd have agreed to anything.

One evening they dined at the home of the Duke of Oxthorpe, Killhope Castle, whose austere magnificence was tempered by gorgeous floral arrangements. It turned out Oxthorpe was a connoisseur of horticulture and offered to show Althea his conservatory. Jealousy was out of the question—the reserved duke was devoted to his wife. Besides, Linton had conquered such irrational impulses. After half an hour, he sought them in the conservatory because he missed her.

He entered an oval paradise bursting with blooms. Exotic vines he couldn't possibly name scaled marble columns. The riot of color and perfume dazzled his senses. At the far end, peering at a pink flower, stood the somber figure of Oxthorpe, and Althea, perfection in bright green, the fairest bloom of all. He had not previously been given to fanciful metaphor, either in his speech or thought. Althea had made him poetic.

She looked up. "Linton! We are talking about rose blight."

He half listened to the utilitarian discussion while his mind wandered to matters of an earthy but very different sort. She was dainty in her silks, but he knew and loved the indelicacy she displayed when they were alone. He beat back a vision of raising her skirts and taking her on a bed of rose petals with the first stars of the summer night glowing through the glass ceiling.

One of his omissions as a husband, according to Althea, had been compliments and flirtation. He'd done his best, but elegant trifling did not come to him easily. He had to rack his brain to rise above the pedestrian. When a footman demanded Oxthorpe's attention, Linton stole closer to Althea, placed his hand on her slender, silken-clad shoulder, breathed in her scent, headier than any flower, leaned in to whisper in her perfect pink ear, and... nothing. So he did what he wanted and kissed her there. She did not pull away, but shivered in the way that signaled her arousal and curved her bottom into his breeches. He had to step back before Oxthorpe noticed.

"Excuse me, Duchess," the other duke said. "I must postpone our interesting talk, for *my* duchess requires my presence in the drawing room."

"I will look forward to it," Althea replied, cool as sherbet, with no sign that her own husband had put his tongue in her ear seconds earlier. "If you don't mind, I will remain awhile and show Linton your orchids."

Once alone, she turned to him with a quizzical look. "Well, Ben?"

Ben! He knew what that meant.

"Someone may come in."

"I must confess I found it strangely stimulating to be kissed when Oxthorpe and his servant might turn our way."

A lifetime of discretion fought a moment of searing desire and lost. "Over there. Behind that curtain of vines."

"Mimosas."

"I don't care what they are called."

They found a marble shelf, warm from a day of sunshine through the roof. Ruthlessly removing some pots, he raised her skirts while she fumbled with his buttons. He swung her onto the convenient ledge and checked her for readiness, but she was having none of it and pushed away his hand. "Now, Ben," she said, low and urgent. "I want you now, hard and fast."

He might not be capable of a graceful compliment, but hard and fast he could manage. Too fast, he feared. Encased in her heat, he was ready to explode in seconds. A brutal thrust, another, a dozen more, and her head fell back on a cry that shattered his tenuous control. They clung to each other, panting hard, forehead to forehead, until they burst out laughing.

"We're mad," she said.

"Someone could have come in."

"Maybe someone did," she chortled.

He just didn't care.

He fastened his breeches; she smoothed her skirts; he offered her his arm. "Shall we return to the drawing room?"

"Oxthorpe has given me some fine ideas for the hothouse at The Chimneys," she said languorously. "I hope you will approve of them, Linton."

He was Linton again, but he wanted to be Ben, all day and all night, every minute. He cursed the hours he devoted each day on the lake. But when he steered Nick to victory, Althea would be grateful, and he'd wave her brother off to London, or somewhere else far, far away. Then he'd have all the time in the world to convince his wife that they belonged together always, day and night.

Chapter Eleven

On the eve of the race, they retired early. Linton always wanted to retire early these days, and he told Nick sternly that he needed sleep.

"I want a breath of fresh air first," Nick said.

"Make it quick." Nick hadn't touched a drop of wine for a week and Linton trusted him to be sensible. He didn't want to waste any more time getting to the mistress portion of the evening.

Valets and maids could be a confounded nuisance. He and Althea would be able to shed their clothes much faster without the help of servants. He was almost bursting with impatience by the time they were alone together in her room.

"Now," he said, ready to scoop her up and throw her into bed.

There was a knock at the door and, damn it, without waiting for an answer, Nick crashed in. Displaying not the least surprise at finding Linton in Althea's room, he burst into speech. "I can't row tomorrow."

What bee had got into the boy's head? "Last-minute nerves are to be expected, Nick," Linton said with as much tolerance as he could muster. "You are going to win."

"I have to withdraw."

"Dozens of people have laid bets on you. I wagered one hundred guineas with Sedgemere at evens. The honor of the house rests on your shoulders."

Althea approached her twin and examined his face carefully. "What is it? This is more than a case of nerves."

Nick sighed. "I've been a fool."

"Probably." Linton wished Nick would get on with it and go away.

The younger man slumped onto the settee at the end of the bed and hung his head. Then he swallowed hard and met Linton's critical eye. "I don't know if Althea told you, but I brought Nigel Speck down to The Chimneys because I owe him money."

"She didn't, but I guessed as much. Why else would any of us put up with a weasel who cheats at cards? Is that what happened?"

"Perhaps," Nick said, the light dawning. "But it doesn't matter. Althea wouldn't give me the money this time and suggested I enter the race. The prize is enough to pay off Speck. Tonight he sent me a note asking me to meet him outside. He has been staying at the inn, waiting for me to pay him. He asked me to lose, on purpose. He's bet a lot of money on Lord William Besett at very good odds. He said if Lord William wins, he'll forgive my debt *and* give me a portion of his winnings."

"Nick! You didn't," Althea cried.

"Of course he didn't," Linton said. "You said no. You can win on your own merits and be rid of the man."

"I can't. That's what I've been trying to tell you. When I refused, Speck said some things that made me so furious I hit him. I think I've broken my hand."

"What did he say?" Linton now noticed that Nick was cradling his right hand on his lap.

Althea tugged at his arm. "That's not important. Poor Nick. Does it hurt dreadfully? Show me."

Nick's hand was swollen and turning black. Linton was inclined to think it wasn't broken, but there could be no question of rowing the next day. "I'm letting all those people down. Their wagers will be forfeit if The Chimneys doesn't field an oarsman."

"You said The Chimneys," Althea said. "Do you mean they were betting on the house, not on you?"

"What's the difference?"

"By tradition, all bets are on the house," Linton explained, "whoever is competing."

"If someone else rows for us, will the bets stand?"

A wild thought entered Linton's mind to be instantly dismissed. Apparently, he was not alone. Althea and Nick looked at him with pleading in their identical-twin eyes. "You can enter, Linton," Nick said.

"Of course he can," Althea said. "I've watched you, and your times are almost as good as Nick's."

"No one knows the strategy of the race better than you."

"You'll win, and that disgusting pig Speck will lose a fortune." She held his shoulders and regarded him with faith, and pride, and love. "Please, Ben."

What could he say but yes?

While Althea took Nick off to get his hand bandaged by the housekeeper, Linton returned to his room and got into bed. Mentally, he prepared himself. He knew he had the stamina, but could he summon the speed under competitive conditions? Could his thirty-five-year-old body outstrip the younger muscles of Lord William Besett? He closed his eyes and rowed the course in his mind, noting the crosscurrents, the bends in the serpentine lake, the tricky turns. If he couldn't win, he'd give it his best shot.

Althea interrupted his planning with a soft kiss. "Move forward. I'm going to rub your shoulders. We need you in prime condition."

"How's Nick's hand?" he asked, while her fingers performed their magic.

"He'll mend." She worked the muscles of his arms for a while. "Linton," she began. "Ben. Nick told me what Speck said. It was about me. You are not going to be pleased."

"Hush," he said, reaching back to clasp the hand that was kneading a sore spot in his neck. "I'll deal with Speck later. As you said, I must be in prime condition for tomorrow."

Leaning against his back, she crossed her arms over his chest and kissed his neck. "Whatever happens, I shall be proud and so very grateful. What else can I do to help?"

"There is one thing, alas, you can't do."

"Oh?"

"There are lots of different opinions about the best way to train for a race, but one thing is almost universally agreed on. No sexual intercourse the night before. I must conserve every ounce of strength."

"I could do all the work," whispered Eve's serpent in his ear.

"Go to bed, baggage. Or better yet, lie down with me and sing me a lullaby."

"Yes, Ben."

∽

THE LAKE AT Teversault had been formed by damming the River Lyft in the middle of the last century. In recent decades, when the present duke's father instituted the annual race, extensive excavations had been undertaken to improve the course. The middle section of the lake, where the race began and ended, was the broadest, wide enough for all the competitors to line up without danger of jostling oars. The shoreline curved sharply on either side, and the earth removed to create that expanse of water was mounded up to form a small hill in the S of the curve.

Spectators from all walks of life lined the three-quarters of a mile length of the lake, but the hill, from which almost the entire lake was visible, was reserved for the ducal parties and their friends. Althea, as Duchess of Linton and wife of her house's oarsman, was given a prime position. Refusing a chair, she preferred to stand with her injured brother among the excited members of the *ton*. Nick's injury and replacement was the main topic of discussion. It was generally agreed that Linton had no chance. Lord Bourne, rowing for Sedgemere, was fancied to come in second, and there was some healthy side-betting on whether John Fletcher for Killhope or Linton for The Chimneys would finish in third place. Lord William Besett was the runaway favorite, and the odds on his victory had shortened to less than evens. No one was prepared to bet against him now, and Nigel Speck, hovering on the edge of the elite crowd, looked unbearably smug.

"Bloody sporting of Linton to give it a go," Lord Ormandsley said. "Too bad I put all my money on Maxfield and now I can't get odds on Besett to hedge my bets.

Anyone want to wager me a hundred guineas against Lord William? All my blunt's on the old man, and he hasn't a chance."

"He is not old," Althea whispered furiously to Nick.

"No," her brother said. "He's a damn good oarsman. I wish I had a few pounds."

"Anyone?" Ormandsley asked again. "I'll give you odds. Ten to one."

"I wouldn't bet against Besett if you gave me twenty," someone jeered.

"Come on, fellows. Twenty to one. You can't lose at that price." And everyone laughed, because that is exactly what they were sure would happen.

"I'll take it." A dozen heads swiveled around to look at Althea.

"I say, Duchess," Ormandsley said. "I didn't see you there. Beg pardon if I said anything to offend."

"I'm not offended. I expect to win a great deal of money from you."

"Who'd have taken you for a loyal little wife?" For a moment, the men's attention veered to Speck, then back again. Althea knew that they knew (or thought) her relationship with Linton was chilly, but they were, for the most part, gentlemen and would never refer to the fact in her presence.

"Damn bad *ton*," someone muttered.

Althea ignored Speck and held on to Nick's arm in case he was tempted to do something foolish. He'd told her what Speck had said, exactly what she'd suspected. Later on, she would tell Linton herself, before Speck had a chance.

"What will you bet?" Ormandsley asked. "Five pounds?"

"Five hundred." Her stomach churned. Never in her life had she wagered such a sum, and if Ben lost, there'd be no new gowns for a year. If she won, she'd have ten thousand pounds. Nick could pay off Speck, and she'd make him invest the balance in the funds to give him a respectable income. Linton had talked to Nick about taking a position as steward at one of his estates. Linton would also, she was certain, come up with the money for Speck if she asked him to. But she wanted to do this by herself, although the plan did depend on Linton's efforts with the oars.

Ormandsley grinned, certain that he'd win back some of his money. Little did he know how good Linton was. "Done," he said. "You're a sporting lady after my own heart."

She felt a little sick, about the race, not the viscount's potential loss. He was a rich idiot who could well afford it. But she knew Ben was nervous. She had watched him sleep for a long time last night before curling up beside him in the small hours. This morning, she had bustled around him like a good wife, making sure his beefsteak was cooked just how he liked it and pouring his coffee herself. He was quiet during the journey to Teversault, apart from a brief discussion of strategy with Nick. Before he left to join his competitors at the boathouse, he drew her out of sight behind the carriage.

Their eyes met for a long moment. "Wish me luck."

"If you wish," she said, putting her arms around his neck, "but you don't need it."

"I am probably about to make a fool of myself."

"Not in my eyes. Never in my eyes."

She rested her head on his chest for a while. The strength in his arms and broad shoulders gave her confidence. "I know you are going to win," she said, and tears of pride welled against his coat.

"I must go. I'll see you after the race." He walked off briskly, but looked back after a few yards.

"Good luck, Ben," she said, and waved. *I love you.* She wished she had said the words aloud.

The four competitors arrived on the opposite bank, carrying their oars, and followed by servants bearing the long, narrow sculls. They were dressed in tightly fitting shirts, linen breeches, and light half boots made of jean. Each man wore a different-colored neckerchief so the spectators could distinguish the rowers at a distance. The garments revealed a selection of fine masculine physiques that Althea was too much on-edge to appreciate. Linton was the biggest man, but there was little difference between him and Besett, except for ten years. Bourne and Fletcher were both slighter, but to Althea's worried eyes, they looked healthy and fit and with less bulk to move. Nick had explained that superior strength more than carried its own weight, but she couldn't quite believe it.

After a little ceremony conducted by Stoke Teversault, the host, the rowers settled in their boats, lined up evenly spaced across the breadth of the lake, and awaited the judge's order to begin.

Besett started fast and immediately drew ahead, Bourne and Fletcher right behind him, Linton far back. By the time Besett reached the end of the lake, Linton was only halfway. Althea clutched Nick's arm. "He's far behind," she whispered. "There must be something wrong."

"It's all right," Nick said. "He's conserving his strength and letting the younger men tire themselves out. Also, where the lake narrows at the end, there's only room for one boat to turn at a time. Bourne and Fletcher wasted their energy, because now they have to wait for Besett. It's all going according to plan."

∽

IT WAS GOING as Linton had expected when he glanced over his shoulder to see what was happening with the boats ahead of him. While Bourne and Fletcher floundered at the turn, he maintained his steady rhythm. He felt good. As Besett crossed his path going the other way, he had a chance to assess his competition. Besett was a strong and skilled oarsman, no question. But his strokes were a little careless and dug too deep. The effort put into displacing the extra water would cost him over three miles.

Linton made the turn neatly and quickly, all his practice with Nick paying off. Because he was well back, he had no interference from other boats and picked the fastest route around the two big bends in the lake. Familiar with the ways of the lake from birth, Besett did the same and lengthened his lead. Linton resisted the urge to increase the pace of his strokes. He knew he had only one prolonged spurt of speed in him, and he must wait for the right time to use it.

On the second full passage along the lake, he passed Fletcher and then Bourne. His boat nosed ahead of the latter just below the hill, and he heard the applause. Althea was up there, and he fancied he heard her cheer, but he couldn't think about that now. He concentrated on maintaining the coordination of breath and movement. By the time he reached the second-to-last turn, he was gaining on Besett. His chest was ready to burst, his thighs protested, and his shoulders and arms burned with the deep, throbbing pain that every oarsman experiences during a long race. Rationally, he knew that his opponent must be in the same state, but insidious doubt could not be denied. He let up his pace a fraction, while Besett made the turn and followed him, ready for the last push. He had to be ahead by the last turn or he had no chance. He couldn't make up the ground on the final dash to the finish line. Leaning forward, arms extended, he readied himself to take the full length of the lake as fast as he was capable.

Fatigue dropped away, and the ever-present pain faded to the recesses of his mind. His oars skimmed the water without an iota of wasted effort, and he achieved the heady sensation that he and his boat were one and they were flying. Just past the big curve at the hill, he saw the stern of Besett's scull in the corner of his eye.

∼

ALTHEA COULDN'T LOOK when Linton finally caught Besett and the two boats streaked past, side by side. "Who's ahead?" She clutched Nick's arm.

"Hard to say at this angle, but I'll tell you one thing, Besett made a mistake. He's let Linton have the inside position on the next curve." He craned his neck. "By Jove, this is close. If Linton gets to the turning point first, he'll win."

Others thought the same. There were competing groans and cheers and jostling for the best view, and a few more bets on who would make it to the far end of the lake first.

"Linton has it," someone shouted, and Althea's heart soared.

"No, Besett's ahead." She closed her eyes tight and prayed.

Then a cacophony of cries and chatter, and she couldn't bear to know why. She no longer cared about Nick, or Speck, or the five hundred pounds. She wanted her husband to win because she loved him and she wanted his triumph.

Nick shouted something and grabbed her by the waist. "He did it, Allie. Linton nosed Besett out at the turn, and now Besett has to wait, and Linton'll have at least a boat's-length advantage in the last half mile."

But Besett hadn't won the Dukeries Cup three times in a row by giving up at the last. When the sculls rounded the last curve, he had made up some of the lost ground and was gaining fast.

LINTON HAD NOTHING left to draw on. His only hope at this point was to keep his strokes even, hold his pace, and pray that Besett's stamina was equally depleted. The best and worst thing about having the lead was being able to see the other boat. He watched helplessly as, stroke by stroke, his opponent's scull drew even. Besett was rowing a little wildly now, but the man was strong as an ox. Why wasn't he tired? Linton knew the answer to that. The man was only twenty-five years old.

There was nothing he could do about his years, but he would not be defeated by fear and envy. Doubt could lose a race as surely as exhaustion. He looked deep into his heart and demanded the impossible from his tiring body.

By this time he was beyond knowing how frequently his strokes came. They needed to be faster, that's all, and conquer the few hundred yards of water that lay between him and victory. Pain could no longer be ignored. It blazed red hot and set off an explosion of lights behind his eyes. Forward and back he moved, faster and stronger, not surrendering to the agony, but embracing it.

The next thing he knew, a riot of human noise penetrated his consciousness and told him the race was over. He dropped his oars and slumped forward in blissful relief that he could stop. A glance showed Besett in the same position a few yards over. The other man looked up and nodded. What did he mean? He held up his hand to indicate an inch between his thumb and forefinger. It had been that close. Then Lord William bowed to him, and Linton knew he must have won.

Chapter Twelve

THE DUKE AND Duchess of Linton were waltzing. They'd performed the dance just once, before they were married, when the waltz was quite new in London and still regarded as shocking. Althea remembered it well, because it had been the first time Linton touched her beyond a chaste clasp of hands or a decorous offer of his arm. Being so close, his gloved hand on her waist, had aroused an indefinable and confusing elation. She had kept her eyes on his waistcoat and wondered what it would be like to be married to him.

Now she knew, and it was wonderful. She also recognized the waltz as a prelude to a more intimate intercourse and wondered if everyone whirling around the Sedgemere ballroom felt the same way.

"Why do you smile?" Linton asked.

"Because I am happy."

"There was something more. I saw it in your eyes."

"If you must know, I was wondering how many of the dancing couples are thinking about going to bed together."

He looked around them. "Hardcastle is regarding Miss MacHugh with a certain look in his eye. I have my doubts about Lady Lavinia, yet she will gladly tell you she is deaf but otherwise in possession of all her faculties. I doubt many will be as fortunate as I, or do I presume?"

"You have the world's best mistress."

"I have the world's best wife too."

"I wasn't always, I know. I behaved badly in the past."

"You have nothing to apologize for. Your faults were nothing compared to mine. I had no idea how to treat a bride, especially one as young and lovely as I was lucky enough to win. I was too cognizant of my own importance and so ridiculously proud that it never occurred to me that you had a right to know that I continued to support Stella Veney only because she was ill. She came to me soon after our marriage and told me she had a consumption and her new protector had abandoned her. In light of our past connection, I felt a responsibility, as I would to any dependent."

"I wish you had told me."

"Other men of my rank keep mistresses, and if I chose not to, it was no one's business but mine. What a fool."

"I'm glad you did not, Ben. It hurt me, especially since I knew I did not satisfy you. After our honeymoon, you seemed not to care about me at all. I think part of my wild behavior was an attempt to draw your attention."

"And all I did was withdraw." He drew her a little closer. "Let me assure you of one thing. When we married, I didn't know your true value, but you always satisfied me, though not as well as you do now."

"We have both learned to do better, in so many ways."

"Dare I hope that we shall continue to do so—"

One of those momentary silences that sometimes falls over a large gathering cut off Linton's words. They were forced to notice that the waltz had come to an end.

"Let's go outside," Althea said, tucking her arm into his in a way that bordered on the indecorous.

But they were mobbed by a group of gentlemen who wished to congratulate the winner of the Dukeries Cup and bombard him with questions about how he won the race. She let her husband enjoy his moment, happy to be at his side and without any need to draw his attention. She knew she would have it later.

Even the sporting set had to stop talking when the Duke of Hardcastle proposed marriage to Miss MacHugh in the middle of the ballroom.

"Good show," Ormandsley proclaimed. "I had twenty guineas on that match. Help me pay my loss to you, Duchess. Not that it wasn't worth it. I never saw a better-run race, even at Newmarket."

"I'm glad to be compared to a horse," Linton remarked.

"Damn it if I don't start betting on the oars more often. I hear they've started regular racing at Oxford. By the way, have you seen Speck? I need to collect from him."

No one had. Speck had vanished without making good on his losing wagers on Lord William Besett. Though a pleasure to hear him universally excoriated, Althea drew Linton aside. She didn't think telling him about Vauxhall would make any difference to them, but she wanted everything open between them.

He regarded her with such undisguised affection that her throat dried up. "Where are we going?" he asked.

There wasn't a convenient alcove or curtain or flowering vine to be seen. "The French doors."

All too often at balls, any cool spot was crowded. She'd timed their exit well, for a new dance was in progress, and they had the terrace to themselves under an almost full moon. In the shadow of a potted orange tree, Linton embraced her. She put her arms about his waist and looked up at him. The rigid duke had vanished to be replaced by Ben and his marvelous smile.

"I am afraid this spot is too public," he said.

"I am shocked, Ben, shocked. You have a wicked mind. All I had in mind was a kiss."

"I suppose I can oblige you." He did so, long, deep, wonderful.

"I will never get tired of your kisses," she said when they came up for breath.

He took her right hand in both of his and laid it over her heart. "Will you accept them forever?"

"Yes."

"Hardcastle went down on one knee in front of all the guests and proposed to his lady. Would you like me to make a public declaration?"

Althea realized that he would do so, if she demanded it, but she knew that he would much rather not. "I won't subject your dignity to such a display. I am more than content to have my husband, the very proper Duke of Linton, in public, and my lover, Ben, when we are alone. I love them both."

"Damn it, Althea. I meant to say it first."

He looked so happy she hated to spoil the moment. "There is something I need to tell you, but I wanted you to know that I love you." But she'd left her confession too long, and a group of the betting men, armed with glasses of brandy, joined them on the terrace.

He laughed boyishly and grabbed her hand. "Come with me. There's something I have been wanting to say in public these two weeks."

"Duchess," Linton said, bowing to Sedgemere's bride, who stood with her husband, and Hardcastle and his new fiancée. "I wish to thank you for a delightful ball. I know that most of your guests will be leaving soon, but the Duchess of Linton and I would like to invite whomever remains to a dinner at The Chimneys tomorrow. Next year we shall arrange something less impromptu."

The duchess accepted warmly and looked pleased.

"Will you compete in the Dukeries Cup again, Linton?" Sedgemere asked.

"I have retired, again, from competition. My brother Nicholas Maxfield will row for The Chimneys next year. He has accepted a position as steward at my Yorkshire estate, but I shall make sure he has time to prepare. I put you on notice now that he is the man to beat. Who knows? Maybe a son of mine will follow in his father's footsteps and win the Dukeries Cup." Linton had made as public an announcement of their reconciliation as he could without putting a notice in the newspapers or sending out cards.

Just when Althea felt she could never be unhappy again, her heart sank. Nigel Speck entered the ballroom. He elbowed aside several of the men who were trying to collect on their wagers and insinuated himself into the group surrounding Linton and Althea. All his sleek smugness had vanished to reveal the ugly truth of his soul.

"Speck," Sedgemere said. "A number of gentlemen are anxious to speak to you. I trust you have come to make good on your debts of honor."

"As soon as Maxfield pays me an old debt, I shall do so, assuming he is a man of honor himself. I don't see him here."

Linton placed a warning arm on Althea's shoulder, but she would not remain silent when her twin was impugned after he had worked so hard to make a fresh start. "Unlike you, he is. You'll get your money. This worm," she informed the listeners, "tried to persuade Nick to lose the race. That's how Nick's hand was injured."

The minute she said it, she knew it was a mistake. Speck was beyond self-restraint. "Shall we tell them why your brother hit me, Duchess? How he was defending *your* so-called honor? Shall we tell them about our delightful tryst in the dark at Vauxhall?"

This was her worst nightmare. She must make her confession to Linton in the presence of his peers. Some things were definitely not better done in public. She opened her mouth, searching for the right words to describe that night before Speck produced his venomous version, when she saw that her adversary was sprawled on the floor, out cold. Linton had moved so fast she didn't see the punch. He stood with hands hanging at his sides, breathing hard and glaring at her unconscious tormenter.

"Splendid hit," someone said.

"Excuse me," Sedgemere said. "I must call my servants to remove this piece of vermin from my duchess's ballroom." Before he left, he took Althea's hand and bowed. "I deeply regret, madam, that you have been subjected to such unpleasantness under my roof."

The other ladies gathered around, offering sympathy and refreshments, but Althea only wanted her husband. She had known he would defend her, but would he forgive her? She turned to him with her arms outstretched in a kind of plea.

"Althea," he began, and winced when she took his hand. "Don't do that. It's as well I don't have to row tomorrow. I injured my hand on Speck's jaw."

∽

THE DUCHESS OF Sedgemere led them to a withdrawing room and sent in a servant with hot water and towels. While Linton soaked his hand, Althea began to tell her story.

He tried to stop her. "There's no need. I don't believe there was anything between you and that maggot—you wouldn't have the poor taste—and if there was, I don't want to know."

"Thank you," she said, her eyes brimming. "And thank you for standing up for me, but I want to explain. I don't want any secrets between us." She described the events of a night at Vauxhall Gardens a year ago. "I never mentioned it to anyone, not even Nick." The sadness in her voice wrenched his heart. "No one would believe I hadn't asked for his advances, and he knew it."

"You should have told me. I would have sent the bastard to the right about."

"Would you? When we had scarcely spoken in years? Perhaps. But you would have blamed me too."

He searched his conscience and had to agree. He'd have been furious at the carelessness that resulted in such a compromising position. At best, he'd have scolded her for indiscretion. "I would have been wrong."

"I brought my reputation on myself, Linton. Everyone was very kind tonight, but they know *something* took place. Even the truth doesn't put me in a good light."

"It was my fault," he said savagely. "If I'd been a real husband, you would never have been put in such a situation, because Speck wouldn't have dared, regardless of whether I was there that night. And I would have been."

He reached for her, injury be damned, but she fended him off and took his right hand in hers with infinite gentleness, applying a towel with soft dabs, then bringing it to her lips and kissing each knuckle. "I was so frightened. At the time, and later in case anyone found out. I was a fool."

"Come over here," he said, leading her to a sofa and drawing her onto his lap. He tucked her head into the crook of his neck and stroked her hair with his good hand. "Let me tell you something. It doesn't matter if you were a fool. A gentleman does not take advantage of a woman. A gentleman always takes no for an answer, however much it may pain him."

Angling her head, the look she gave him reduced his heart to warm treacle. "You must be the most wonderful man in the world, Ben. I have felt so horrible about that night, and having to entertain Speck was dreadful, but you've made me feel light inside again. I wasn't wrong, and as long as I have your support and love, I don't care what anyone else says."

God, he loved her. And, by Jupiter, he'd never actually told her in so many words. "I…"

She started kissing him, and he gave a mental shrug. He had all night and a lifetime to say those three words, and for now, he was otherwise occupied.

An Unsuitable Duchess

BY
CAROLYN JEWEL

Acknowledgments

Thank you to all the people who make me a better writer, especially these awesome people; critique partner Carolyn Crane, editor Robin Harders, and copy-editor Joyce Lamb. Thanks must also go out to the authors in this anthology who are so wonderful to work with, Grace Burrowes, Shana Galen, and Miranda Neville. There's the usual crew of private thanks too. Marguerite, for being my fan and sister, to my son Nathaniel, my nephew Dylan, and my nieces Lexie and Hannah.

Chapter One

Teversault, The Dukeries, Nottinghamshire, England
July, 1819

STOKE'S ABILITY TO strike terror into the hearts of mere mortals was a talent too useful not to keep in good order. Five steps into the Grand Falcon saloon, so named because of the eponymous birds carved into the molding, and a pocket of silence had formed around him. He stood motionless, searching for his brother because she would surely be with William. Though a hair over six feet tall, Stoke did not think of himself as tall on account of his brother being six feet three-and-a-half inches of lion-hearted masculinity. A credit to the Besett line.

None of the strangers here, and there were many, had so far guessed he was a Besett. *The* Besett. In respect of looks, Stoke was at the edge of unattractive, a fact of which he was acutely aware. Besetts, male or female, were either dark-eyed and hawkish or blue-eyed and leonine. He was of the hawkish Besett. William was of the leonine. William was beloved for his wit and humor and easy manners. Stoke was feared on all accounts.

There. At the other side of the room. As he headed for his brother, all but the least observant among his guests moved out of his way. This reaction had been the case for so long he no longer realized it was unusual. Nevertheless, the saloon was crowded enough that walking a straight line was not possible.

He walked forcefully, propelling his lean-muscled body through space as if a current of air carried him and no one else, a Besett hawk making his way past peacocks toward one Besett lion. He reached them in due course but halted some feet short of where William held court. The Hunter sisters stood on either side of his brother. The women were the younger siblings of a protégée of Stoke's, presently in Paris and attached to the British Embassy there. He willed away the unwelcome thud of his pulse at the sight of Mrs. Lark. There was no point allowing it.

She had never been much in terror of him, but he'd been unable to close the distance between them, either. By habit, he was a man who observed from afar, who must see the eagle's-eye view of a problem before plunging to grasp in metaphorical talons the required solution. He did not act until he was certain. William saw his quarry and pounced. Half a minute later, his prey would be a bosom friend.

Mrs. Lark was quick-witted, generous, and always believed the best of everyone. Like William, she threw herself into friendships with no hesitation. He'd spent too long observing her, understanding her. His caution and prudence, in the matter of the former Miss Hunter, had proved fatal to his hopes, for she'd blithely danced out of his view and into the arms of another man.

This was her first visit to Teversault in all the time since her family and his had become connected. He'd last seen her a year ago at one of the assemblies in Hopewell-on-Lyft, though he'd not danced with her despite her being out of mourning. They'd barely spoken, and why should they have? He had no ability to make himself into the sort of man who would suit her.

Grief no longer shadowed her eyes, and she'd regained some, though not enough in his opinion, of the weight she'd lost. She had always been a tidy woman who much resembled her elder brother, and so she remained. She was not tall enough for a man his height and certainly not for someone William's size. There was no disguising the generous curve of her bosom, all the more apparent because she was quite small and slender everywhere else. Her hair was irredeemably orange, far too pale to be called red. Her alabaster skin made her freckles all the more obvious. The cleft in her chin was charming, but had the effect of making her mouth appear decadent. Though he could not see from where he stood, he knew her eyes were the color of cognac held to candlelight.

She was a decade younger than he, twenty-three. Married at twenty-one, widowed less than a year later. William, resplendent and too handsome for his own good—he was of the lion line, after all—rested a familiar and possessive hand on her shoulder.

"Revers," William had just said, raising his voice to be heard over the noise. "These are the young ladies I've been telling you about." Lord Revers bowed. "George, this is the Viscount Revers."

She curtseyed. "My lord."

The saloon was filled with guests, more than in any previous year for these series of summer parties across the estates that made up the Dukeries. This circumstance was the weight of tradition, alas. Balls, fêtes, routs, picnics, the Dukeries Cup race on the serpentine, all to culminate in a grand ball which the Prince Regent himself was to attend. One was no one without possession of the right to say he, or she, had been a guest at one of the Dukeries parties.

"Revers, this is George." William grinned. "Mrs. Lark."

Revers looked bored but took her hand and bowed over it. As he did, his attention slid to the other sister. Just as well, as far as Stoke was concerned. "Delighted to meet you, Mrs. Lark."

"George." William thumped her shoulder. "Everyone calls her George."

George. As if she were a man. As if it were proper for anyone to call her that except her most intimate friends. She'd only just met Revers. The man had no business addressing her as anything but Mrs. Lark.

"Lord William." She tapped his arm with her closed fan. "Not everyone." Then she smiled. "Likewise, my lord."

She had no idea what transformation took place when she smiled. No idea at all. Revers did not release her hand. Instead, he cocked his head. When he spoke, his words and manners were smooth and liquid. "Lord William's been talking for years about the delightful women of Uplyft Hall." He put his free hand over his heart. "At last we meet."

She drew her hand from his, by smile alone transformed from unexceptional to ravishing. A woman a man wanted under him in bed. God knew Revers was rogue enough to be thinking how to get her there. "At last, sir."

"A pox on you for not introducing me sooner Lord William." Revers had a reputation for liking the ladies too well. There had been indiscretions on his part. To George, Revers said, "I'll make up for time lost, I promise you."

Still with that smile, she laughed. Revers was fascinated. This was her gift, that when she smiled, one was convinced there was no finer, kinder, or more desirable woman than her.

"Miss Hunter." William brought the young lady forward. He beamed as if he were introducing a beloved sister to a man he hoped would agree they'd be an excellent match. "Will you allow me to introduce Lord Revers?"

The young lady extended a hand with less poise than he would have expected from one of her beauty. Golden hair, blue eyes. An oval face without a single freckle. "Yes, please."

"Kitty, this bold fellow here is Lord Revers." The Lord only knew how long Revers would have stared had not William brought Miss Hunter closer yet. "Revers, this enchanting creature is Miss Kitty Hunter."

Kitty blushed and put her hand on the palm Revers extended to her. The viscount bowed over her hand. "Delighted to meet you as well, Miss Hunter." He looked her up and down. "Such beauty. I am enrapt. Enthralled by the perfection before me."

George darted an assessing glance at Revers. He was handsome enough to present a danger to youthful virtue, which no doubt George well understood. He was also possessed of a title and a fortune, and one forgave too much in the face of that.

William kept his hand on George's shoulder. "George, Kitty, you've met everyone who matters. You might as well retire for the day." The remark was uttered in a breezy, thoughtless manner without consideration of there being anything forward about calling the women names that ought only be used by family and one's most intimate friends. His brother glanced around the room but did not, for whatever reason, see him standing not five feet away. "Except for that dashed brother of mine, of course."

"Are you sure he's here?" George asked. Careless. Not particularly interested in the answer.

"Hiding in his room, I expect." William glanced at the ceiling. "You know how he despises parties."

"Yes," she said. "I do recall."

Stoke wended his way closer. As well make himself known to them before someone spoke ill of him. He put a hand on William's shoulder and did not smile. "Here you are. I have been searching for you these ten minutes at least."

"Stoke!" William shook his head of tawny hair that had not one single curl. "You've been searching for me? Well, I've been looking everywhere for you. Ten minutes, you say?" He drew George's hand through his arm and placed his hand over hers. "You ought to have been here an hour ago."

"Business detained me."

George curtseyed with an elegance she had acquired during her marriage, for she'd not had that polish when he knew her before. Her eyes were as remarkable as in his memory. He'd not forgotten how clear they were. He could not help but admire them as if he had. She took a breath and held it for a moment—composing herself? Perhaps, for her smile faded. She extended her hand. "How lovely to see you again."

He touched her fingers, nothing more. Orange hair. Freckles. That decadent mouth and lush bosom. "Mrs. Lark. Welcome to Teversault."

"Thank you." She smiled, more reserved with him than with William, whom she'd known for at least a decade. William and her brother were friends from their days at Eton and Oxford. William had been to Uplyft Hall a dozen times before the day Stoke had agreed, reluctantly, to drive William there on his way to Nottingham.

There was nothing extraordinary about her. Nothing at all. Yet the jolt of arousal at seeing her again was unwelcome and inappropriate.

He took Kitty's hand and bent over it. "Charmed to see you again, Miss Hunter. Welcome, both of you, to Teversault. I hope you enjoy your visit."

"Thank you, Your Grace." Quite a pretty young woman now that she'd outgrown her schoolroom days.

"It's more beautiful here than I imagined, and I assure you I imagined a great deal." George threw one arm wide in a gesture that included the whole of Teversault. "Hugh and Lord William did not do it justice. Nor you, Your Grace." Miss Hunter widened her eyes at her sister, and George moderated her enthusiasm. "I mean to say, this is a house of taste and elegance."

He studied her, working out how she could be at once undistinguished and intensely appealing. The curve of her bosom, the shape of her lips, that cleft in her chin, the clear, pale brown of her eyes. Put all together, and he never failed to think of darkened rooms and bodies sliding along sheets. One day some rogue was going to decide that he wanted to know if she could be persuaded to put that mouth to corrupt uses.

She looked to his brother. "Lord William promised us a tour later."

William put a hand over his heart. His handsome, charming brother must have had such thoughts about her. How could he not? The idea that George and William were suited made his stomach tighten in an unwelcome manner. "So you shall have one," William said. "I keep my promises, George."

William's gaze connected with his, and it was appallingly apparent that his brother was in a fair way of fancying himself in love with George and that he was matchmaking for Revers and the younger girl. William fell in love with a different woman every fortnight, it seemed. So Stoke told himself. There was no cause for concern. He would be out of love before the prince arrived.

His greater worry was how determined Revers would be in pursuing Miss Hunter. The women were under his protection here. If Revers thought to seduce either of them, the viscount would find in him an implacable enemy.

Chapter Two

At Teversault, even the door hinges moved as if they knew they'd best open crisply and with respect. They had certainly better, hadn't they? George led her sister into a parlor twice the size of the one at Uplyft Hall. Both of them stopped, awed by their surroundings.

The parlor, smaller than the saloon they'd gathered in earlier in the day, had a view of the famous tree-lined driveway and a portion of the front lawns. Sunlight glittered off the distant serpentine. Cream walls were trimmed in dark lilac with touches of gold, colors repeated in the carpet and upholstery. If only she could pack up the colors and decorations and take them home with her to Uplyft Hall. One of the windows was open, and it was late enough in the day that the fragrance of the Nottingham Flycatcher growing on the outside walls scented the air.

"What if we've come to the wrong room, Georgina?"

"We haven't. I asked for directions before I knocked at your door. Besides, Lord William said we were to meet in the Grecian parlor, and behold." She pointed upward. A panoply of the gods of Olympus gazed upon them, arrayed in brilliant color and drawn with unnerving realism. One could but pray Zeus would refrain from throwing thunderbolts at such imperfect mortals as walked beneath their painted eyes.

"You might have mentioned that."

"Kitty. Dear sister. You've no need to be nervous." She faced Kitty and adjusted one of the tiny bows around the sleeve of her gown. Not even the duke could deny Kitty's beauty, inside and out. "You are too lovely not to be universally admired."

"Georgina." Kitty squinted and tipped her head to one side. "Your hair is crooked."

"No it isn't." She put a hand to her head and found that, yes, the cascade of curls at the top of her head was not where it ought to be. Attempting to repair herself made matters worse, for she could feel her hair shift.

"Stop. Let me fix you."

"Please."

Kitty pushed around pins and the like, which was not difficult since George was much shorter. "There." Kitty considered her. "Better now."

She patted her head. She was forever falling apart, much to Kitty's dismay, and the best intentions in the world did not stop her peculiar gift for unintended disasters of wardrobe. "I too am perfect."

Kitty plucked straw from the side of George's skirt and huffed. "You promised you'd stay away from the stables."

"And so I did."

Kitty shook the straw at her with familiar anxiety. Even as a child, defects in one's dress, manners, or deportment had caused Kitty no end of distress. Nothing could be done about their modest antecedents, but for Kitty, to be held in high regard in all other respects was like water and air. A necessity. "You've been to the stables." She removed more from George's skirt. "Honestly. You're not to be trusted."

"I am. I am the most trustworthy sister you have. On my honor, I have not been." She shrugged when Kitty held up the straw. "I visited the kennels."

"Not one word about horses or hounds, Georgina." Kitty, whose taste in all things was innate and irreproachable, believed George's shortcomings were due to a lack of attention to detail rather than unchangeable fact. "Not in front of Lord Revers or the duke. Please. Best behavior. You promised."

"I only went for a moment." She smoothed her skirts and gave them a little shake in case there was more straw.

"You need only a moment to become completely undone."

"Alas, true." George had every intention of visiting the kennels again, and the stable block as well to confirm the duke's horses were as healthy and gorgeous as Lord William claimed. She took the straw from Kitty and dropped it into her pocket. She could have sworn she'd managed to brush off all the detritus of her visit before she returned to the house. "There are puppies. Adorable puppies. The kennel master let me play with them. You cannot expect anyone to resist puppies."

"You could have waited for me." If she had, Kitty would have prevented her from going, and they both knew that.

"I was outside not somewhere inside. You were upstairs putting on that lovely gown. Why shouldn't I have a look at the hounds while you were otherwise engaged?"

"You know what I mean." With their brother Hugh in Paris these past two years, the management of the farm and lands attached to Uplyft Hall had fallen to George. She'd learned a great deal about property management during her marriage, and she now spent hours in conversation with their own steward and the managers at neighboring estates, discussing the latest problems, ideas, and innovations. Her new bull, a Lincolnshire Red procured winter before last, was producing excellent offspring, and she had high hopes for the second generation. Two farmers had recently asked about breeding rights, and wasn't that a vindication?

She crossed the room and, staying sideways to Kitty, slid a hand along the top of the marble mantel. Marble columns on either side of the fireplace soared upward with chimney glass in between that reached all the way to the ceiling. Twin marble Titans held up the mantel. "Did you ever see such a fireplace as this?"

"I won't allow you to distract me. When do you think of anything but horses and dogs and cows?" Kitty shook her head in despair. "Or the best time to plant turnips?"

"At the moment, I am thinking of Greek gods and marble fireplaces." She faced the edifice in question and, hands on hips, admired the pink-veined marble. On the mantel itself was a statue of Hermes. "Therefore, Kitty, you could not be more—"

Lord William's familiar voice rumbled through to the parlor. George looked over her shoulder, smiling, and then quickly not smiling at all, for Lord William was not in conversation with himself.

"—mistaken." Let his companion be Lord Revers, who was so charming, wealthy, and taken with Kitty.

"Please, please, behave while you are here," Kitty said. "No talking about bulls or hunting dogs or the proper method of mucking out stalls."

"I promise." She picked another bit of straw from her skirt and put that in her pocket with the others. Perhaps she ought to have looked in a mirror before she returned to the house. Not that it would matter much. She wasn't bad looking, she knew that, but she hadn't Kitty's beauty or brilliant eyes. Since she had no intention of marrying again, she felt not the least inclination to *behave*, as Kitty said, for any reason but decency and her sister's peace of mind. She'd had her chance to dance with handsome men and to be flattered and found interesting. Now, it was Kitty's turn, and Kitty must, could only be, an absolute triumph.

The door hinges whispered with the utmost respect. As George and Kitty faced the entrance, the Duke of Stoke Teversault strode in. Lord William followed on his heels.

What a fierce man the duke was. Once upon a time, his icy gaze had filled her with trepidation. Since her husband's death, her opinion of him as cold-hearted and unpleasant had altered greatly. She'd not seen him but once or twice since that terrible time in her life, but marriage and tragedy had given her new eyes. Not cold, but reserved. Not unpleasant, but quiet and direct to a fault. There was a center to him, a solidity that one could rely upon. He would never act against his conscience.

Where once she had preferred a man who was robust and active, she now saw much to admire in the duke's lean body. His features, which she'd once thought too sharp and uneven, were, in fact, commanding. His self-mastery, once mistaken for hauteur, was the sign of a man who understood himself and was satisfied with the accounts.

Her changed appreciation of Stoke Teversault, she understood, was the result of maturity and experience of life, yet also, she must admit, in respect of his appearance, a puzzling state of affairs. A man who held honor and duty above all else was a man who must be admired, no matter how difficult he was to like, this was no mystery. But she'd always preferred men who inhabited the social whirl, handsome men of fashion such as Lord William or Lord Revers, who amused and flattered and made one laugh. She had no ready explanation for why, when she saw the duke, parts below came alive with unseemly interest.

Today, as ever, the duke's attire was sober to the point of plain. Black trousers, black shoes with silver buckles, a black coat, and a black waistcoat embroidered with tiny silver dots. A black tie wound around his white neckcloth. He was deliciously forbidding. To gaze upon the Duke of Stoke Teversault was to see a man born to coronets, castles, Orders of the Garter, and robes with ermine tails.

"George!" Lord William crossed the room, arms outstretched, and she was in his embrace before she could react. He swept her into a mock waltz. Her stomach swooped as he whirled her past the windows, and she breathed in the sweet scent of the Nottingham Flycatcher.

"Lord William." She managed, at last, to extricate herself from his arms and take several steps back. He'd whipped her around so fast she was short of breath. He grinned at her in that puppyish way of his that never failed to smooth the path for him. She couldn't help smiling back. "How delightful to see you after"—she consulted the clock on the mantel—"only an hour and a quarter."

"A long and sorrowful eternity, George." He'd ended up close to Kitty, and he leaned over and kissed her sister's cheek. "What a pretty blush. Is that not a pretty blush, Stoke? Kitty, delight of my heart, how are you? It's been an age since I saw you." He looked over his shoulder at her. "George, did I remember to write you that my favorite bitch whelped as I said she would?"

"You did not."

"I'm sure I did."

"Perhaps your letter was lost in the post. Or you wrote to Hugh and not to Kitty and me. But never mind, I've been to the kennels and seen the puppies. They're rascals all four."

"Two females, two males, as perfect as anyone could like, which I am certain you saw. By the time you go, old enough for you to take one home if you like. Pick of the litter."

From the corner of her eye, George saw His Grace raise his eyebrows. He kept his hair too short for her tastes, but she shivered inside when his penetrating eyes connected with hers. Oh dear. Perhaps that hadn't been quite the thing for Lord William to say. Surely, the duke knew his brother would forget his offer before it was time for her and Kitty to return home.

Lord William had Kitty in his arms now, though his attention remained on George. "The kennel master will know which one best suits a Hunter of Uplyft Hall."

"Thank you."

"That's excellent. Is this not excellent, Stoke? Miss Hunter." His eyes softened, and George shot another glance at the duke to see what he made of his brother's tenderness. Not much, it seemed. "What a treat you are to mine eyes, Kitty. I never knew a woman could be as lovely as you." He gave Kitty another kiss on the cheek. "I've missed you."

Kitty gazed at him, besotted.

The duke's frown deepened. Well, what had he thought would happen? That his brother would call at Uplyft Hall during all this time and never notice that Kitty was sweet and beautiful and all that was generous? Did he not know his brother at all? Apparently he did not. She hoped to see Kitty through this visit without a great disappointment. In matters of the heart, Lord William was inconstant.

"Stoke. You ought to say something, or are you saving your breath for the grand tour of Teversault?"

"This is the Grecian parlor," the duke said. "So called because of the Ionic columns there, and the fresco on the ceiling. Painted by a student of Piero himself." He pointed and, in practiced tones that were not the least warm, continued his well-rehearsed speech. "The mantel was carved from a single block of marble. Winged Hermes was made from marble quarried from the same location. The carpet is said to have been looted from a palace owned by Darius the Great, but that is rank speculation."

"The very best sort, if you—"

Kitty elbowed her, not discreetly enough.

George coughed. "Goodness. Something in my throat. Forgive me, Your Grace. Do go on."

The duke did something with his eyebrows, some minute twitch of displeasure, that convinced George he did not like her any better than he ever had, which was not very much at all.

Chapter Three

AT HALF PAST seven the next morning, a maid directed George to the morning room, and thank goodness, for she'd otherwise have stayed lost for who knew how long. She had her back to the open door as she thanked the maid, then whirled and entered at her usual brisk pace. Today, she meant to explore the whole of Teversault on her own.

"Oh," she said. She slowed, then stopped. "Oh my. Magnificent." She barely glanced at the sideboard where the aroma and arrangement of food—eggs and bacon, fresh bread, strawberries, and jellies—put a sharp edge on her hunger. She went to the window, arms wide to embrace the scene. "Teversault," she pronounced to no one but herself, "must be the most beautiful place in all of Britain."

Behind her, a chair moved across the wooden floor. Slowly, she looked to her left, willing that sound to mean anything but impending embarrassment. She was not so fortunate today. Of course not. This was her fate where the duke was concerned. He did not care for flighty women, and she knew for a fact he considered her a soft and feckless female. Which she had been before she was married.

Stoke Teversault stood at the top of the table, a napkin in one hand, the morning paper beside his plate. He did not smile. The duke, like Kitty, found her too frequently undignified. So be it. Life was made of beauty, moments to be strung together and remembered so that one had them close in less happy times. She delighted in beauty, reveled in it and allowed her heart to crumble in the face of humbling perfection. God, she believed, lived in such moments as this. Edward had told her she wore her heart on her sleeve, and that was true. She did. Edward had loved her for it, and that, too, was written on her heart.

The fit of the duke's buckskins revealed powerful, leanly muscled thighs. Not as slight a man as she'd imagined, then. His midnight blue coat lent his eyes a soulful cast, and his buff waistcoat provided more color than he usually wore. She could not look away from him. His eyes entrapped her, robbed her of breath.

"Good morning, Mrs. Lark." His mouth twitched. She was sure of it. Kitty, if she were here, would be horrified. "I share your high opinion of Teversault."

"A happy circumstance, Your Grace." Events in Hampstead Heath when Edward's death had left her bereft had stripped away her ability to see him as His Grace the Duke of Stoke Teversault, personage of Great and Terrible Consequence. When she looked at him now, she saw a man who made the floor vanish from beneath her feet. She shoved aside her inappropriate reactions and sensations and managed to say with creditable carelessness, "I bid you good morning, Your Grace."

He dropped his napkin on his chair and went to her, dignity and restraint oozing from his pores. "Allow me to fetch you a plate."

One did not refuse a duke, and never this one. He extended his elbow. For several seconds, she stared at the blue wool of his sleeve, baffled as to what he meant by such a gesture.

"I had rather not guess at your preferences for your morning repast, though I would be happy to bring you a selection, if you'd prefer."

"Oh. Well. Yes. I mean, no. Please don't go to any trouble." She placed her hand on his arm. He walked, sedately, to the sideboard. A footman who practically blended into the wall handed the duke a plate. She examined the array of delicious, aromatic food. Eggs poached, fried, and scrambled, three kinds of preserves, and sausage cooked to perfection. Delicate ladies did not pile food on a plate and eat every bite, but she wanted to. She was ravenous.

"Eggs, ma'am?" he asked. "Toast for Mrs. Lark, John. I hope that was not presumptuous of me."

"No. That is, rather, not at all, Your Grace." She adored a perfectly poached egg and these looked perfect. She wanted some of everything. In the back of her disordered and distracted thoughts, she knew that would not improve his poor opinion of her. What would Kitty do? There was her answer. "Toast, thank you."

"Is that all?"

"Yes."

"I seem to recall from previous encounters that you never lacked for appetite."

"I've reformed." The butter was stamped with the duke's coat of arms, but he'd already taken some that included a corner of the escutcheon. There were fresh strawberries, bright, gleaming red, and so plump her mouth watered looking at them. Blackberries and gooseberries too and clotted cream.

"Have you?" Miles and miles of desert sand enfolded his words. Ten thousand miles of hot and arid dunes.

"Yes. I have."

She sat at his right with her toast and the dab of butter Kitty would have allowed herself. She resented him and Kitty for the bareness served her. She also resented the footman. In fact, she resented the entire household for the expectation that she be a properly delicate female.

His plate had one and a half poached eggs on it. He had toast with butter melted over the entire top and three sausages. Three.

She poured herself tea and remembered, at the last moment, to ask him if he wished for more. He did. The morning *Times* was at his elbow, and while she essayed to appear so frail of appetite that toast was a challenge for her constitution, she surreptitiously read his paper upside down and partially sideways.

At Uplyft Hall, Hugh's papers were still delivered. The butler ironed the pages for her every morning, and she pored over them with her breakfast, which was more than toast and an atom of butter. Meanwhile, His Grace addressed himself to his meal with no sign of appreciation.

"Have you plans for the day?" he asked.

She was going to die from lack of poached eggs. She had visions of distracting him long enough to take one of his sausages and ended up in the uncomfortable situation of being both hungry and amused at the thought of snatching food from the duke's plate. She ought to dare all and take his paper too. "Plans?"

"Yes." He took a sip of his tea. "Plans. Activities. Outings. Such as will edify you or improve your character."

"Yes. I have—" She was infernally aware of her sexual response to him. It was unfortunate. Beyond unfortunate. It was highly improper—she was improper. Entirely unsuitable for such company as his. "I strive always to improve my character."

"Perhaps I've not made myself clear." He picked up his fork. "I refer to something that you hope to do today, as opposed to some uncertain time in the future."

"Oh. That sort of plan."

"Yes."

"I thought I'd read." Lie naked beneath him, her legs wrapped around his hips? Her resolve to be delicate wavered in the face of her unassuaged hunger.

"Have you a volume in mind?"

She gaped at him. What was this inquisition? Her mind went blank. What would a delicate young lady want to read? Something boring. Something educational or inspirational. "A...history."

"Of?"

What was the dullest possible thing she could read? "Of...of...botany."

His expression smoothed out. Thank God one of them could manage this conversation. "Teversault has an extensive library. Please feel at liberty to browse."

"Thank you." She took a bite of toast and chewed with no enthusiasm. As toast went, the bread was excellent, but there wasn't enough butter. She stared at her plate and forced herself to swallow. Toast was all Kitty ever had for breakfast. How did anyone survive on toast alone?

She imagined jumping to her feet. She could claim she'd seen a mouse, and then, when he went to investigate or, more likely, when he was distracted with his footman investigating, she could take his last sausage and—

"Are you unwell, Mrs. Lark?"

She let out a short breath, defeated. "I cannot do this. Kitty will never forgive me, but I cannot."

"I beg your pardon?" He'd been about to cut into his sausage, but he stopped, silverware in his hands. His fingers were long and slender. He had strong, dexterous hands.

"I promised I'd behave. Be proper and ladylike, but I am neither of those things. I'm not scandalous, I don't think, but I'm not dignified. Not like Kitty. Or you."

His eyebrows rose as he completed a neat slice across his sausage.

"I've tried to be delicate and refined, which is what all gentlemen prefer in a lady, and where has it got me?"

"At Teversault?"

She tossed her napkin on the table. "I've been plotting how I might snatch that sausage from your plate. Because I'm famished." She rushed on. It felt good to speak without artifice. "It's better you accept the truth about me, except I suppose you already know."

"Do go on."

She pointed at his plate. "I love poached eggs and sausage and those berries, I could eat them all, and there isn't near enough butter on my toast. I don't care how dainty and feminine it is to eat only tea and crusts. I've never been dainty, as you well know. You once lectured me on the subject."

"Did I?"

"I'm sure you don't recall, but you took me to task for my lack of delicacy."

"Extraordinary that I'd do such a thing."

"You were correct."

"As I often am. I am, for example, correct when I say that you are dainty."

She snorted and tried, too late, to recover.

The duke continued as if he'd not noticed. "If one defines dainty as slender and small, then you are dainty."

"I can't help that." She threw her arms wide. "I am not quiet. Nor subdued. Kitty says I smile too often and laugh too much, and I know, sir, that you think the same. I enjoy food and good drink and when I see a view like this"—she indicated the windows—"why, I feel it so strongly I am unable to stop myself from saying so."

"True."

"It's worse. I have no plans to read about botany."

"I am astonished."

"My plans this morning, sir, are to walk all the way to the end of your driveway, I might even run for the sheer joy of it, and I shall count all the lime trees, and then I shall beat your brother in a footrace, and I'll play with your puppies and take sugar to the horses."

He did not say a word. Not one. She felt her cheeks burning, and at the same time, her stomach clenched. Teversault, like the man before her, was dignified and grave and steeped in centuries of nobility, and she, why, she was none of that.

Eventually he said, "A footrace."

"Yes." He was not the sort of man to slip between the covers naked or leave a bed sweaty from exertion. What a pity that was.

"I am perfectly happy to live at Uplyft Hall with Hugh when he comes home at last, with whomever he marries. I ask you, how many people have relations they must tolerate for the sake of the happiness of a loved one? Oh, good God!"

The footman who had been so excellent at blending into the wall had taken it upon himself to fill a plate with eggs and sausage for her, and he'd bent over her shoulder to remove her toast and set this new plate before her, followed by a bowl of berries immersed in a cloud of clotted cream.

"Please. Enjoy your meal, Mrs. Lark." Stoke Teversault retook possession of his fork and ate a bite of sausage.

She placed her napkin on her lap and did exactly that. She tasted one of the poached eggs and moaned. When she'd swallowed, she whispered, "Perfection."

"My chef is gifted."

"He is. He is." She ate steadily, savoring the flavors and textures. The smoothness of the eggs, the tension and release as her knife sliced into the sausage, the herbs and seasonings that had been added to the meat. In between, she sipped her tea. She nodded at his paper. "Is there news of the French legation? Every morning I scour the *Times* for any mention of Hugh. Since I haven't my own paper here, I hope I may persuade you to search for me. Or give me the pages you are done with."

"I should be delighted to assist you." He picked up the paper and opened it. He spoke the correct words, but there was a rigidity to them that suggested he'd taken offense. This was ever her fate, to offend him with her lack of delicacy.

Having eaten every last morsel on her plate, she drew the berries toward her and ate a spoonful. Again she sank against her chair. "I have eaten a mouthful of summer."

He held his paper to one side and glanced at her, eyebrows raised.

"Sublime summer, Your Grace." She sat straight again, closed her eyes and took another spoonful. When she'd finished the mouthful and allowed the experience to settle on her, she decided she could survive sight. Stoke Teversault was watching her intently, because that's how he did everything. She put down her spoon and set her elbows on the table and her chin on her clasped hands. "Do you know what I adore?"

"I expect you intend to tell me."

"White raspberries. I had them the summer I was married. My husband brought them back from Wiltshire." The incident had taught her much about how to get on in a marriage. She and Edward had formed an even stronger bond, for George had learned that receiving a gift with delight had made the gift as delightful to Edward to give as for her to accept. "Edward and I, Mr. Lark, that is, we had blackberries at the end of our rear lawn that he told me he never could eradicate, try as he might. When I tasted them, I told him he must never try again. You've never had better blackberries than that, I promise you." She plucked one of the blackberries from the cream. "These are nearly as sweet as ours were."

"Nearly?"

"Your strawberries are better. I confess that." Now she felt odd for having mentioned Edward. She oughtn't have, nor should she have been prattling on at all. "Have you found anything shocking? In the paper."

"I would not tell you if I had."

She stirred her berries and cream. "I suppose nothing shocks you."

"On the contrary. There is a great deal that shocks me."

"Such as?"

"The poor manners and laziness of our youth, for one."

"Our parents said that about the young—us. And their parents said that about the young in their day. It never ends."

"Your poor opinion of my blackberries, for another." His dark eyes were focused on her, and she ended up staring at her bowl for fear he'd see too much in her expression, for she was thinking of naked dukes.

"Would you rather I lie to you?"

He snapped out the paper. "I shall look for news of your brother."

"Thank you. That's very kind." She meant that sincerely and hoped he believed it of her. "More tea?"

"No, thank you."

She finished eating while the duke scanned the news. She watched him while he read. The planes and angles of his face, the shape of his mouth. The breadth of his shoulders. His features and body converged into an ineluctable whole that was nothing like Edward. Her husband had been shorter than the duke, less wiry, and more prone to smiles. Edward had been handsome. Handsomer even than Lord William, with blue eyes and blond hair, and she missed him desperately. She could not comprehend why a man so different from Edward would cause this constriction of her heart.

What, she wondered, as she sat at the table with the dark and quiet duke who could never be called handsome, would he be like as a lover? In her mind, she saw and felt the sweep of his bare palm along her thigh, the drag of his fingers after, the slide of his sex into hers, with all the slippery, throbbing, glorious feelings that came with such contact.

She did not dare look at him. He'd know. He'd take one look at her and see her thoughts. A whirlpool appeared in her teacup. Lord. Lord. What was she to do about this? She spooned in some of the cream from her berries.

"Mrs. Lark. What are you doing?"

She picked up her tea, annoyed by his offended tone. "Adding cream." She took a sip and considered the impact. A hint of the berries which was nice. The fullness of the cream diluted by the tea was—what did she think? "I believe it needs more."

"More."

"Yes." She added two large spoonfuls and stirred.

"That is an abomination."

"Half measures never do." She added the rest because he was so horrified. The remaining tea was now pale tan and thick. "It's the color of my freckles."

"Delightful."

"It is." After another sip, she stared into her teacup. "That's quite good."

"I don't believe you."

"Why not? Clotted cream is delicious, the berries make it sweet, and the tea renders it bracing. Here." She extended her cup to him. "In the interest of scientific inquiry."

"I've no intention of drinking anything that looks like a potion brewed of your freckles." No smile appeared on his hard, stern mouth. Not a whisper of a smile, yet she had the oddest, most peculiar suspicion that he was, in fact, playing along.

"Coward."

He leaned back and looked down his nose at her.

"What else am I to think?"

"That I've better sense than you."

She drank more.

He reached over and took the cup from her. He studied the contents, then took a sip. "Gah. As well drink cream."

She took back the cup. "You don't wish to admit I've invented a new drink."

"Cream? Not new, Mrs. Lark. We have been drinking it since the domestication of cows."

"Cream tea."

"There is no such thing."

"There is, but your objection is noted." She took a long drink, in part to hide her smile. "Now, Your Grace, I thank you for your hospitality." She rose, and so did he. "I have activities to engage in, sir, that I hope will improve my character."

"Pray God they do."

Chapter Four

STOKE SAT ASTRIDE his horse at the mouth of his driveway, watching a figure in white and pink heading toward him. He had this morning seen just such a gown. The woman wearing it raced along the edge of the drive and touched each of the lime trees to her left as she passed them. No one but George moved with such exuberant life. Nor was that mass of pale orange hair easily contained or disguised. He stayed, stupidly, mounted even when she was near enough to see him.

She slowed, looked guilty when she did see him, then came to a halt and curtseyed. She cocked her head and smiled, resigned, or so it seemed to him. Not the smile that had taken his breath the first time he saw it, but his spirits lifted all the same. She was not a suitable match for him. No woman of her liveliness could be happy with a man of his temperament.

He ought to touch the brim of his hat and go on his way. That would put an end to the relaxation between them that was the result of this morning's interactions. He ought not allow her to think they had anything more than acquaintance in common. She would never find in him a man who would delight her.

She wasn't the least out of breath, despite having been running along his driveway. Touching his trees. Her smile struck straight to his heart. He did not move, though he knew that was no wise decision. He did not want to stop watching her. In all his life, he'd not met a woman so vigorously alive as she was.

Stoke was aware that he might have been married but for Edward Lark. Lark had been at Eton with William and Hugh Hunter. Two years ahead, but much admired by his schoolmates. He was the third son of an old and respected family from Devonshire, distantly related on the distaff side to Lord Bolingbroke.

He'd joined the army after school and been to Spain but in the interlude that ended with Napoleon's escape to France, Lark had inherited a modest but not insubstantial fortune from an aunt. He'd resigned his commission and come to Scylfe to celebrate his good fortune with William.

At that time, Stoke had been there too because, as he'd learned, Hunter and his sisters were there, and he had begun to entertain improper thoughts of Miss Georgina Hunter. Had Lark arrived even a day later he might have found Stoke had lost his head and got himself engaged to the woman. For what young lady, he'd thought, would refuse an offer from a duke?

Edward Lark and George had hit it off instantly. Like George, Lark had thrown himself into friendships upon no evidence at all that there would still be a friendship the next week. The Hunters delayed their departure a week, then another week, and during that time the two had become inseparable. A month later—a single month—Stoke had sat in a place of honor as that damned interloper married George. The marriage had been the very definition of rash behavior soon regretted. Except, as he well knew, she regretted nothing. The lesson he ought to have learned—that George was not the duchess for him—had not sunk in.

She walked partway around him, just to the side, and pushed back the brim of her hat. "Is he very fast?"

"Yes."

"Has he a name?"

"Third To Left."

Her forehead creased and then smoothed out. She let out a laugh. "That's excellent. You're teasing me. I didn't know you could." She was so young yet. He could not get out of his head his awareness that she had been married. She knew what went on between a man and a woman. "What miracle is this, that you'd tease me?"

"Perhaps you've been inattentive."

"Perhaps I have been. Will you tell me his name?"

"Neptune." Edward Lark had taken her to bed, and her experiences since then had not dampened her spirits in the least.

"That's a splendid name for this fellow. Do you race him?"

"Certainly not." She was all eyes on his horse, and he had the very inappropriate thought that he would like it very much if she looked at him like that.

"He's a beauty. May I pet him?"

"Thank you. Yes. If you like."

She stroked Neptune's head, but had to go on her toes to do so. Stoke found himself with a view of her bosom. "I wish I had some sugar for you, you magnificent beast."

Stoke dismounted and held the reins in one hand. The distance from here to Teversault was a mile and a half along that drive lined with lime trees a hundred years old. There was another line of trees to the right and, in between, a footpath shaded by the trees. "How many did you count?"

She blushed, and that was charming. The dimple in her chin ought to be a flaw, along with her strong nose, but neither were. In some ways they were a better match now, as unacceptable matches went, now than they had been before she met Lark. Time and her marriage had given her the confidence of maturity and experience. She was no longer too young for him. "I oughtn't have said anything this morning."

"You would have expired of hunger if you hadn't." He led Neptune toward the path. With her, Stoke could keep a decent walking pace, and even so, she often ran ahead two or three yards. Did she ever stop moving? During one of the interludes when they were walking side by side she clasped her hands behind her back and said, "What was it like growing up here? I can't imagine it at all."

"Pleasant."

"You would say that. You've never known any other way of living."

"Nor do you know any way of living but as you have."

"Lord William says you have been solemn since the day you were born, but I don't see how that could be."

"I have always had duties that admit of little leisure or lightness of spirit."

"Yes. I can see how that would be so." She skipped ahead and walked backward for several feet so that she faced him. It wasn't, he thought, as if she was so very different from other women. He knew her better than most women of his acquaintance because he had spent long hours in contemplation of his feelings for her and in whether it would be appropriate for him to act on those feelings. His answer to that had come too late. "I counted nine hundred and ninety-seven lime trees."

"There are one thousand forty-two."

"No."

He speared her with a look. "I have documents that prove you wrong."

"I'll have to walk this way tomorrow and recount them. Again the day after that." She extended her arms and turned in a circle, head tilted toward the dome of trees. "I adore this tree tunnel. The light is so lovely filtered through the leaves."

He joined her on the path, leading his horse. "Tree tunnel."

She stopped turning. "Yes. A tunnel made of trees. It's heartbreaking."

"You seem quite cheerful in the face of such sorrow."

"Everything beautiful is heartbreaking. I had rather embrace beauty and be brought to tears than turn away."

"These trees make you cry. Have I understood you?" By some miracle he had not yet offended her.

"Yes." She fell back in step with him. "You say that as if you mean, 'oh, that woman. She is incurable.'"

"Best be less relentlessly cheerful if you wish a different reaction from me."

"Who wouldn't be cheerful on such a day as this? It's July, and I have no responsibilities at all but to look after Kitty, *and* I've discovered your cook is a genius." She leaned toward him and gave him a conspiratorial smile. "I'm going to talk him into betraying all his secrets to me and give them all to the cook at Uplyft Hall. Then, when Hugh comes home, he'll never think to ask what I've done with the property in his absence. So, you see, I have good reason for cheer." They kept walking. "Why, even you are cheerful today."

"Never."

She lifted a hand, one finger pointing skyward. "I have observed you, Your Grace. I know the nuances of your expressions. The subtle movement of an eyebrow. The darkening of a glance. The hint of movement at the edge of your mouth. The twitch of an eyelash. You, sir, teased me."

"I deny any such thing took place."

She pretended to study his eyebrows, which meant they stopped walking. "I see much in the curl of your lip."

"There is no nuance to me."

She clasped her hands behind her back once more and rocked back on her heels. "On the contrary. You are by nature stern and proper, but now we've spent enough time together that I have learned you as I expect few others have."

"How have my eyebrows edified you?"

Her smile softened. "I have learned that duty matters to you more than most anything."

"One needs no special insight for that observation, I hope." They stood too close for his comfort. He could lose his head. Was on the verge of it again. Part of him wished to fall. Perhaps she did read his expressions, for he was thinking about his hands on her naked skin. Her cheeks pinked up. She was no innocent. No longer.

She glanced away, then back. "Have I ever thanked you for all you did for me when my husband died?"

"Yes."

"Not properly." She swallowed. He had discomfited her, as he so often did with everyone who spent time with him. "If it hadn't been for you, I don't know what I would have done. You came to my aid, and gave me comfort. You think I don't know of the hours and hours you spent seeing to details. I know you intervened with his family and his father." She hesitated. "Perhaps you got on with him."

"I don't recall." He hadn't at all. He still remembered his fury at the discovery that Lark's father was determined to leave her with nothing.

"What I mean to say, just this once, with the god of the ocean as our witness, you terrified me too until then. You never did much care for me, yet you came to Hampstead Heath, and I was both grateful and humbled."

"Mrs. Lark." He held himself quite still. "I have never disliked you."

She drew a breath and let it out. "Couldn't be bothered to, is that it?"

"You allow others to call you George."

"Your brother started that. As a jest. And then it stuck."

"Did your husband?" He was jealous of a dead man. This was unacceptable, that he should be so disordered. "Surely Lark did better by you than that."

"He got the habit from Lord William." She frowned. "I like it. It's amusing. It makes me smile to think people are fond enough of me to call me George. They say it affectionately, you know."

"A lady ought not be called by a man's name."

Her eyes lit up with a smile, and God help him, he could not breathe for wanting her. "Lord William calls you Stoke. Do you feel that's unseemly?"

"He is my brother. And the Dukes of Stoke Teversault have been called Stoke by their intimates for five generations."

"I have been called George for five years."

"Mrs. Lark—"

She peered into his face.

"Kindly leave my eyebrows and lashes out of this discussion."

"You can't say it, can you?"

"What?"

"George. You cannot say George when it would refer to me."

"Certainly not." In his most reprehensible imaginings he whispered that name, low and soft. "We are not on terms that would permit me the liberty of calling you George or Georgina or any other name that is not Mrs. Lark."

She waved him off. "I give you permission to call me Georgina."

More than anything, he wanted to call her George. The intimacy dizzied him. He was aware that his course was obvious. He ought to lance her with a glare and say nothing. He was capable of stopping conversation dead with a single look. He'd done so several times, hundreds of times. The mere fact of him walking into a room could bring every soul inside to silence.

"Say *Georgina*." She grinned. "You've earned that right. Whisper it if you cannot bring yourself to speak the word. I won't take a similar liberty. I'd never."

"I thank you, but no."

"I'm sorry for that. But I can't stop others from calling me George. Besides, it's only Lord William and my family." She looped her arm around his, and they resumed walking. "And now Lord Revers."

"Lord Revers?"

"He's a charming man. I like him a great deal."

"The last time one of William's friends began calling you George, you were married to him a month later."

Chapter Five

STOKE WOULD RATHER walk through fire than leave his private office. He stared at his watch-face but was unable to make the time anything but half past two and advancing. Half past two meant he ought to have left an hour ago. Thirty-one minutes past two meant he could no longer delay his obligations to his guests, be they strangers, relations, or acquaintances.

A gentleman of rank did not shirk his responsibilities, even when there were a dozen pressing tasks that required his attention. He snapped the watch closed and brushed his thumb over the falcon engraved on the cover before he slipped it into his waistcoat pocket.

There could be no regrets for doing one's duty. One did. No more could be said on the subject. He rang for his valet and moments later, Daniels glided into the anteroom Stoke used as an unofficial office. He did not meet callers here, nor his secretary, nor the chief household servants, for that matter. Nevertheless, he preferred this room in his wing of the house for managing his personal correspondence and reading.

On coming in, Daniels frowned to see Stoke in his shirt-sleeves, waistcoat unbuttoned, coat tossed over the back of his chair. "Will you be joining the festivities, Your Grace?"

He sighed. "Make me presentable, if you would."

Stoke came around to the front of the desk so that Daniels could have at him. He valued the servant's stoicism about events such as this. He was indeed in some sartorial disrepair. Daniels set a small leather case on Stoke's desk and reached for his coat. Daniels was never in disrepair. Stoke trusted his valet's discernment in all things related to a gentleman's proper attire.

His valet of the last five years had not lost the brawn of his fighting days. He'd come to England fifteen years ago, a free black man eager to prove his mettle in the ring. Which he had done. After modest successes culminating in retirement from the art, he'd declined to return to America. Instead, he went into service, hired by an acquaintance of Stoke's. Upon seeing the improvement in the man's appearance and in need of a new valet, Stoke had hired Daniels away by offering both the step up in employer and a doubled salary.

He held out his left arm. Daniels unrolled Stoke's sleeve and refastened the cuff. Same with the other. He'd only to stand there while his servant put his clothes to rights and helped him into his coat. Again from his leather case, Daniels produced hairbrush and comb and smoothed the imperfections of Stoke's hair. Stoke insisted his hair be cut short to prevent the appearance of unruly curls. The next process involved a lint brush put to thorough use.

With his American manner of speaking not the least affected by his years in England, Daniels said, "Sit, and I'll polish your shoes."

Stoke looked down. "Not necessary, I shouldn't think."

There was a moment of deep silence that, when it happened over incidents like this, never failed to make Stoke worry that Daniels would resign his position if he didn't cooperate. Daniels pursed his lips. "There's a crowd downstairs."

He shuddered at the thought. "Your point?"

"It's an ill reflection on me if you look anything but perfect."

"Oh, very well." He sat, aware that Daniels was a master of managing Stoke's moods. Thank God there was someone who tolerated him.

With swift, sure strokes, Daniels buffed Stoke's shoes. He did not care for anything gaudy, but Daniels had convinced him that silver buckles did not go too far. In truth, Stoke had become used to the improvement in his appearance since he'd hired the man. Satisfied with the result, Daniels gestured for Stoke to stand. The valet straightened his cravat again and readjusted his coat sleeves. "There. Now you may be seen and no one will think you ought to find a new man to do for you."

He and Daniels shared a lean, dry humor, so neither of them spoiled the moment with a smile or laughter. "You are quite welcome."

"Your Grace."

Stoke nodded and headed for the door. Daniels arrived first and opened it for him. The most direct route to his destination was to his left into the west wing of the house, down a short flight of stairs, to the right along another corridor and to the grand entrance hall with its view of the driveway, the banisters carved by Belgian craftsmen in 1432 and walnut panels from a French villa taken as the spoils of war by one of the hawk Besetts the century before the carving of the banisters.

Stoke, offended by the crowds of people he did not know who presumed unwarranted intimacies by their presence here, and weary because he'd been up since before six in the morning, soon stood at the edge of the side lawn where there were more guests today than yesterday. The fortnight of merriment moved from estate to estate to estate, and there were times when Stoke was convinced the Dukes of Oxthorpe, Sedgemere, and Linton conspired to send everyone here.

He had envisioned today's picnic as a sedate interlude in which the invited guests of the four dukes would consume an excellent repast and then stroll the grounds to view his newly constructed orangery, admire the gardens or, for the ambitious, follow a portion of the lime-tree-bordered path beside the driveway.

Most of his visitors remained on blankets painstakingly laid out by his staff. Footmen had delivered each group its own wicker basket of delicacies prepared by his chef and a kitchen staff of thirty, half of whom had been hired for this summer series of entertainments.

For those who preferred a less natural setting in which to dine, there were tables close to the house with canvas umbrellas as protection from the sun. This year's boisterous and over-represented contingent of the young and the unmarried had eaten quickly, if at all, and were now gathered on a portion of the lawn farther from those still picnicking.

This group of young ladies and gentlemen had previously included William. William had left the field of play to join him for reasons he trusted would soon be made clear. "Are you in training for the Dukeries Cup?" Lord Ingleforth asked William. "I've money on you." He shook his finger at William. "Oxthorpe has laid down a packet on Mr. Fletcher. I expect you to win. We shall have words if you don't."

"I'm looking for a fourth victory this year."

Years ago, at one of these infernal parties, Stoke's father had organized a single scull race on the serpentine. Some wag had called it the Dukeries Cup, and with that the race became a tradition. As had the betting. A good deal of money was wagered on the contestants. He always put a hundred pounds on William, a strategy that had, three years running, been quite profitable.

"I'll go out on the water tomorrow." William pretended to row a stroke, using the tennis racket he held in one hand as if it were an oar. Green stained the top of the racket, and two blades of grass were stuck in the upper strings. This was due to William having involved himself in the game being played on his lawns. William continued to propel an invisible scull across invisible water. His brother had rowed at university and had rarely lost. "I could race the course with my eyes closed. I'm not worried about the competition."

Stoke did not care to see tennis rackets being used as if they were oars or shovels, and it was all he could do to keep himself from snatching away William's racket and striding out to the field to demand everyone stop abusing equipment that did not belong to them. Laughter rose up from the lawns—male and female, for they had included ladies in the game. He told himself the inclusion of both genders made sense. There would be opportunities to exchange looks and impress others with one's agility, grace, and prowess. Quite likely some of the participants would one day trace their marriages to this day.

Their travesty of a game involved tennis rackets and balls, a wicket, and metal hoops from an ancient set of pall-mall. He doubted whether anyone had touched the pall-mall equipment since the previous century. He had but the vaguest recollection of his father allowing him to swing a mallet as tall as he was. Which was the truth, seeing as he'd been no more than two or three at the time.

There was a great deal of unsedate dashing about and much laughter. He told himself young people had a right to their high spirits, though he had never been such a youth. The game reminded him of a medieval melee, with knights fighting for their lives. It appeared the rules were being made up on the spot. Further, and more to the point of his disquiet, George was in the thick of it. Could one fault so young a widow for her play? She was twenty-three. Younger than Lord Revers, William, and Miss Paltree. Young enough that if she had never been married at all, no one would think twice of it. She wore a light blue frock and, at the moment, was sprinting after a ball with such speed the long ribbons tied at her back streamed behind her.

What others called her, if not Mrs. Lark, was none of his affair. There was no reason for him to care in the least. George waved her tennis racket, laughing joyously as she reached the ball and whacked it in the direction of one of the metal hoops. She was happy. Since the night he'd held her, inconsolable, he'd hoped she would recover, in some scant degree, from the heartbreak of her husband's death.

Ingleforth cleared his throat. "There's a lively female. Who is she again?"

"Which?"

"The one Revers keeps chasing."

He shaded his eyes and examined the field of play. Ingleforth meant George. "That is Mrs. Lark. Her brother is Hugh Hunter of Uplyft Hall."

"Hunter. Hunter."

"From Hopewell-on-Lyft."

"I knew a Charles Hunter. Is that his girl?"

"Yes."

Ingleforth shaded his eyes, too, and peered across the lawn. "Can't make head nor tails of what they're doing."

"Through no defect of yours, my lord. There is no logic to their game."

"It seems the ones with the rackets are attempting to drive the balls through the hoops."

Someone else asked, "Why do only some of them touch the wicket?"

Stoke sent the man a withering look. "For pity's sake, at least ask why a wicket at all."

"I assumed because it was necessary."

Stoke ceased paying attention to their speculation. George's bonnet had flown off during a far too vigorous run, a full-out sprint that involved her touching the wicket and swatting a ball in the direction of a player who did not have a racket. She clapped a hand to the top of her head—too late to do any good—and whirled. Her hair was too long for the current fashion and coming loose from its pins. She darted after her hat and then, in hoydenish fashion, lunged and used her tennis racket to pin it to the ground.

From the lawn, her victorious shout floated to him. Did she not understand she'd ruined her hat? William put his hands around his mouth and shouted, "Well played, George, well played! Double points for the hat!"

She looked their direction and waved. Then she whirled, hat in one hand, racket in the other, and dashed into the fray.

His brother loped toward the field, then came back and stood for several moments facing him, hands on his hips, thoughtful. "You ought to play, Stoke."

"I think not."

William looked over his shoulder at the game. Half the players now had pall-mall mallets, while the other half were in the process of destroying the tennis rackets. George had fetched another handful of metal hoops and was pacing off steps before she pushed a hoop into the ground. "We're having a grand time."

"I can see that."

"George calls it lawn-mall."

He cocked his head and affected boredom. Such had always been her nature. She invented amusements where there were none, and it was a rare game she did not amend with her own version of the rules. Her penchant for invention was what had first drawn his interest. "The players are mauling my lawn."

William stood beside him and leaned a forearm on Stoke's shoulder. "She's a fetching thing," He waved at someone on the playing field. "You ought to have come downstairs to say good morning to her. We were hoping you'd join us."

"I was otherwise engaged."

"Two minutes to say, 'Hello, delighted to see you, George'?"

"George is no proper name for a woman."

William turned serious. "Why do you dislike her so?"

"I beg your pardon?" he said as if there were no water anywhere in the world. "I do not dislike her. Excuse me. Mr. Amblewise has agreed to lead a discussion on the sin of deception and the merits of honesty. Join us. I'm sure you'll find the subject improving."

"Oh well, as for that." He coughed once. William had got through school by relying on the intellectual prowess of Hugh Hunter. He wasn't stupid, merely an indifferent student far more interested in physical pursuits. "I'm sure I would. Very disappointed of course, but I've made other plans, and I shouldn't want anyone to think I'd not been honest about considering myself engaged."

"Of course not."

"You could join us after."

"For?"

"George hid treasure somewhere on the grounds." He dug in his pocket and pulled out a quarter sheet of foolscap. "She's made a map, you see, and we're to fortify ourselves with sandwiches and such and see who finds it first."

He gave William another searing look. "Could not your quest be delayed until after the discussion?"

William swung his racket in a looping oval with enough force to make an annoying whoosh. "Treasure, Stoke. Whoever finds it keeps it." He laughed heartily. "I intend to win."

He refused to look in the direction of the lawn where that misbegotten game continued. "What sort of treasure?"

"Who knows? She did not say except to tell us it was treasure. She's been devilishly clever. All the maps are different." William waved his racket. "Have a look." He thrust his sheet of paper at him. "She's left out most of the directions. We're to logic out the rest." He swung his racket again. "Too bad Hugh isn't here. He'd take a look at it and have the answer in a blink."

"You will need an alternate strategy."

William cackled. "I have one."

"Is that so?" Stoke glanced at the page. She'd drawn a large letter N on the left side with an arrow pointing to the right. He recognized the block that represented the house itself, the meandering S-curves of the serpentine, his orangery and a few other monuments. Some were connected by lines that wandered about the page or never ended anywhere. "If all of you have accurate maps, there will be a crush at the site of the treasure."

"I've no worries on that account. I'm faster and taller than most everyone. I always win at races, and this, my dear brother, is yet another race I'll win." He swung the racket again.

"Perhaps I ought to ask Mr. Amblewise to speak on the subject of hubris." He handed back the paper.

William waved off the map. "I don't need it."

"How will you win without it?"

"There's no need to bust my noggin interpreting puzzles. I'll leave that to the likes of you and Hugh. I'm taking one of the hounds and giving him her scent. I'll follow her trail and"—he waved his free hand—"treasure."

"Is that not cheating?"

"There's no rule against it. I daresay George will think it clever of me."

The group on the lawn began shouting. William shouted back. "I told you he wouldn't."

He winced at the pain of William's bellow. His hearing, like his vision, was acute.

"Are you sure you won't come along?"

"Quite."

"Enjoy your discussion, Stoke." He loped off to rejoin the mad game that by now looked rather dangerous. Someone was going to get a mallet to the head. Stoke watched a while longer before he headed inside.

Amblewise's discussion proved a dull affair. The conversation soon left the main topic and became lost in predictions about the upcoming Cup. William was the heavy favorite. When the subject turned to Sedgemere's ball, which was to take place the evening of the race, Stoke made his excuses.

There was always work waiting for him. In the corridor outside, he thrust his hands into his coat pockets and encountered the paper William had given him. Ah yes. The map George had made. He studied it to be sure he'd not mistaken his earlier interpretation. He hadn't. Intellect would defeat a bloodhound.

He set out for the orangery, an octagon he'd built onto the existing house, taking down most of one wall and building a double door where much of that wall had been. He'd left the terrace to serve as the new floor. Outside there were now white arched, glass-paned doors and walls, precisely the striking result he'd intended. Two of the doors were open to the afternoon sun.

He went inside and referred again to the map to orient himself. There, in an orange tree in an urn by the door, at a height just above where George's head would reach, hung something that gleamed gold.

Someone had affixed a string to one of the branches and to that a gold chain from which there dangled a golden apple the size of the tip of his thumb. Treasure, indeed.

Chapter Six

HER GOLDEN APPLE was gone. How was that possible when none of the treasure seekers had returned with it? George frowned at the tree. This was most mysterious and upsetting.

Beside her, Lord William frowned as well. "Could you have put it in another of the trees and forgotten which one?"

"I'm sure I did not. It must have fallen." She eyed the ground around the urn in which the orange tree grew but saw nothing. She leaned over to examine the soil. Still nothing. She made a wider search of the area around the tree. The urn sat on the paving stone that made up the floor here. If the apple had fallen, it was possible it had rolled a considerable distance.

Meanwhile, Lord William went to the orange tree at the other side of the entrance and examined that. His was a good instinct, she decided, though if he found it there, it meant she'd lost her mind.

"Anything?" she asked.

"Nothing. You're sure it was an apple?"

"Yes. Absolutely sure."

Lord William rubbed chin and then the side of his face. "Gold, you say?"

"Yes." She joined him at the other orange tree and craned her neck. "I couldn't have reached so near the top."

With a sheepish grin, he said, "You're such a wee thing, George. And I'm a giant."

"You are."

They crouched and searched around the urn in opposite directions. When they met halfway around, she stood, bedeviled by the disappearance of the apple. "Nothing," he said.

For some minutes she tapped her foot. "I fear we must assume we will not find it here. Either it is lost or someone has it in his possession and is not telling us. I cannot imagine that, though."

Lord William slowly nodded. "I concur. Perhaps one of the servants or a public visitor came across it and thought someone had lost it."

"Yes." She brightened at this very reasonable possibility. "Like as not, it's been returned to one of the staff as a found item." This query was put to a nearby groundsman who, having replied in the negative, was dispatched to inquire of the household.

"Have no fear, George. He'll return with your apple, I'm sure of it."

Admittedly, her invented games sometimes went awry, but none as badly as this. The participants had vied for treasure, and someone deserved the prize. She did not want anyone to be disappointed. "Suppose the apple is not at the house? It might be lost forever."

"Let's choose an alternate means for determining the winner." He laughed. "Whoever devised the cleverest plan for finding treasure via hunting dog?"

"And award what prize?" She went through a mental inventory of her possessions, but there was nothing she could substitute.

"A coin?" William patted his pockets. "I'm sure I've a penny or two."

"A penny. At least my apple was gold."

He took his money purse from his pocket and shook a handful of coins onto his palm. "Three shillings, sixpence." George watched him look for more. "I was sure I had a guinea. I've been saving it. That's a shiny bit of something to award."

"Lord William, you are an inspiration!"

He put away his purse, astonished. "I am?"

"You brilliant man. We'll put a shilling in a box and tie it with red ribbon to present as a medal. I'll write a commendation to go with it. We shall call it the Dukeries Commemorative Shilling."

After a moment considering the idea, he nodded. "With some sealing wax to make it official."

"Oh, yes. I like that idea." She grinned, pleased beyond measure at this solution. One could do a great deal with this. "Do you suppose your brother would allow us to use his seal?"

"It's difficult to say with him. I've a seal. We'll use mine."

"Now." She tapped her chin, cured of her previous despair. "How are we to determine the winner? Do we know if any of the searchers came here? Besides you, I mean. We shall have to interview the others and select a winner from among those who came here. Or near here."

Lord William stood straight. "I had the best, cleverest plan, George. Revers didn't think of anything half as clever. I'd have won if the prize hadn't gone missing."

"That may be true, but, Lord William." She gave him a stern look, but the poor man looked positively downcast. "You cannot be the winner when you are assisting me in choosing another prize. That is a clear conflict."

"As well choose someone at random." He stared in the direction of the house. "As long as it's not Revers."

"I'll be sure everyone understands your brilliant thinking saved the treasure hunt. Don't sulk." She patted his chest. "You saved us from disaster. You are a hero, and you know how ladies adore a hero."

He brightened and brought his attention back to her. "They do, don't they?"

"Indeed, Lord William. Indeed." She laughed, for doubtless he was imagining the ladies about to be impressed by him. Teversault at present had a surfeit of pretty young ladies in attendance so this could only be an advantage for a man like him.

"Do you adore a hero?" His blue eyes stayed on her face.

"I am a lady. Of course I do." She took a step back, for her neck was getting a crick from staring up at him, but he closed the distance between them. She'd have backed up again, but the orange tree behind her prevented that. "Perhaps our treasure hunt and the Dukeries Commemorative Shilling will become another tradition."

"Perhaps it will." After the oddest pause, Lord William bent down, for what purpose she could not imagine. An advance was not among the possibilities she considered, but in point of fact, he pressed his mouth to hers, and not in brotherly affection.

It wasn't that he didn't kiss well, she thought he did, but she had no visceral reaction other than alarm and astonishment, and she knew well that a kiss from the right man was profoundly visceral. She leaned back, one hand lifted. "Lord William, I—"

He gave her a sideways look, not the least abashed. In fact, he looked cheerful. "I like you, George. A great deal."

"And I you," she said. "You are my friend. My brother's good friend." A man who'd been kind and who had never, as most handsome men did not, paid *that* sort of attention to her. His being a hero seemed to have gone to his head.

"Hugh wrote that I ought to marry you." He beamed at her. "What do you say?"

"Marry?" She edged away from him. He couldn't be serious about this. There was nothing of the impassioned lover about Lord William. He looked and sounded as if he were proposing they take a stroll about the grounds. A servant walked past the windows, but it wasn't the groundsman they'd sent to the house. The man kept walking and was soon out of sight. "Hugh put that notion into your head?"

"He's never given me bad advice before."

"I fear he has this time."

"We get on, you and I. You're pretty, and once I looked at you—I do like your figure." He held out his hands, forming a circle with them. A space, she realized, he meant to represent her waist. "I can overlook that you're so tiny compared to me."

She bit back a laugh because he was not serious. Lord William never was. He was correct, though. They did get on well. If she were to remarry she could do far worse than the brother of a duke. What a pity she did not want to marry him. "That's good of you to say."

He studied her for a while, as serious as she'd ever seen him. This she found concerning, that he should be so serious. "You didn't feel anything when I kissed you."

She shook her head.

"I took you unawares." He put his hands in his pockets and settled his weight on one hip. "That must be why. I don't normally kiss a woman without making her faint from passion."

She laughed, as he'd meant her to. Her amusement did not change the fact that she did not wish to marry him. There was Kitty to consider as well since she suspected her sister was too fond of him by far.

"I wouldn't mind a wife I admire and who makes me laugh." He moved closer again. Oh dear. "I've been thinking about it for days. Ever since Hugh wrote me."

She licked her lower lip. "I don't want to be married again. I don't think."

"I don't want to be Edward to you. No one could be that." He pressed her shoulder, a warm and friendly gesture. "Hugh wants to know you're taken care of, and I would like very much if his mind were easy on that account."

"I wish he hadn't put such thoughts in your head." Blast her interfering brother.

"Why? When I read his letter I thought, why wouldn't I be happy married to George? She's jolly and amusing, and I like spending time with her. You."

She stared at the tips of her slippers, then raised her chin. He was handsome. Yes. But there was no spark between them. Lord William was not the Besett brother who tied her heart and stomach into knots. "You didn't feel anything either."

He gave a deep sigh. "I wasn't sure I was going to kiss you at all, but I saw you looking at me, and I thought, why not?"

"It was a pleasant kiss," she said. His face fell. The last thing she wanted was to hurt him. "There's nothing wrong with pleasant kisses."

"George, kisses ought to be more than pleasant." He drew himself up with a determined look. "By Jove, I'll not have you think I don't know how to kiss a woman!"

He was handsome and splendid, and they had so much in common. They loved being active and outdoors. They were mad about horses and dogs. She took his hand and pressed it between hers. "I don't think that at all. I'm sure you kiss wonderfully when your heart's in it."

He stared at her, and she recognized that look. It was the look that said he expected to win at everything, from boat races to kissing. Good Lord. An offer of marriage was not a contest to be won. "We ought to try again, don't you think? The kissing."

She didn't, actually. Then again, what if he was right? What if they never found out they suited because they'd given up? As he'd pointed out, he'd taken her by surprise. It didn't make sense to feel so little when a handsome man kissed her. "Very well."

He slipped an arm around her waist, and she put her hands on his shoulders. She did not doubt he was an energetic lover. How could he not be? She looked into his blue eyes. To kiss him required that she rise up on her toes. She imagined doing so, but her limbs refused to cooperate. How odd. How odd that she was relieved.

He lowered his head, and she closed her eyes in preparation. He didn't kiss her, so she opened her eyes just as he closed the distance, and it was just so very awkward. His mouth touched hers, gently, and for half a second, she thought she felt something. The sensation fizzled out.

He did kiss well. He did. She knew he did. She enjoyed his kiss in a detached sort of way. She understood passion. She had felt it with Edward, and just now passion was nowhere on the horizon.

He drew back. "Well, George?"

"I—"

"That was better, don't you think?" He waited a beat then ran a hand through his thick, golden hair, but he wasn't smiling. He looked perturbed. Distressed.

"Oh, yes. Very much so."

"George." He gave a long, loud sigh. "You know that's nonsense."

"I'm sorry."

"It's me. It has to be."

"No, it was me."

"I'm enthusiastic about kissing a pretty woman but—Not you."

"I'm sorry. So sorry."

"Don't be. Don't be at all."

"I'm not your usual sort."

"No." He gazed at her. "I like a woman with some substance there." He fluttered a hand in the vicinity of her bosom. "And you—Much to admire there, George."

"Thank you. There's much to admire in you as well."

"Yes, I know. It's, it's..." He scrunched up his face and then burst out with, "It's as if you were my sister, and a man can't kiss his sister. Not anything like properly."

"You mustn't think it's your fault. It's mine too. I think there may be no one else for me but Edward." That wasn't true. One other man affected her the way Edward had, and that man was a hawk not a lion. With him, there were no roars meant to impress, only a swift strike that left one breathless and weak at the knees.

He touched her cheek, but she saw a flash of relief in his eyes. "You and Lark were meant for each other. I never saw any two people fall in love so fast in all my life." He let his hand fall away. "I want that for myself. To meet the person who completes me. You should want the same."

"We tried." She patted his chest, more than a little relieved to have come to this point. "You and I. We tried, and now there can be no question we are destined to remain friends."

"Yes." He grinned, and the awkwardness melted away. "That's so."

"We'd best go inside and explain to the others that someone has absconded with my treasure."

"Yes. Let's do that."

They returned to the house and found a box, paper, and ribbon for the new prize. William dripped blood red wax on the box and pressed his personal seal into it. In her opinion, the result was quite effective.

The participants in the hunt were in the music room as agreed upon for the post-treasure-hunt celebration. Whilst they were waiting, no laggers had appeared with her apple, and the housekeeper had give them the disappointing news that no apple, gold or otherwise, had been turned in to the household staff. There followed a great deal of discussion and the proffering of ingenious and ridiculous theories about the disappearance of her apple, but there was general satisfaction with the decision to select an alternate means of winning and the awarding of a new prize.

With great pomp and circumstance, and a rousing speech about valor and honor, Lord William produced the Dukeries Commemorative Shilling. George awarded the prize to Miss Paltree, for careful questioning had elicited the information that she had arrived at the orangery in time to see Lord William departing with the bloodhound.

After this, Kitty sat at the piano and played a march suitable for the bestowment of a distinguished, coveted prize. She gave up the bench to another young lady who played and sang very well indeed, and after that, Miss Paltree played the harp with Lord William accompanying her on the piano and really, could a day be more perfect than this one thus far? Aside from the mystery of her missing treasure.

Revers said, "Will you sing for us, Miss Hunter?"

Lord William thumped the piano bench. "Come, Kitty. I'll find something here for you to entertain us with."

Kitty returned to sit beside Lord William. Her fingers rippled over the keys as if born to them. She'd always practiced more than George. "Do you have 'A Trifling Song' or 'I'll Love Thee Night and Day, Love'?"

"What about 'O, Life is Like'?"

Kitty played the opening melody. "A pretty tune."

"Yes, yes. That's here." He settled the music before her.

Kitty acquitted herself beautifully. When she'd done, Lord William said something to her, and she smiled and played a Bach cantata from memory. Her sister was talented, and Lord Revers and the others came to attention. At one point, Lord William ceased watching the others to concentrate on Kitty. George wondered if he'd already forgotten he'd proposed marriage to her not an hour past.

The song ended, and Kitty said, "Your turn now, Georgina."

"George, you must," Lord William said. "There's no such thing as a musical recital if we don't hear you." He riffled through sheet music until he found something he liked. "'No One Shall Govern Me.' One of your brother's favorites."

"Do you have 'Is There a Heart'?" Kitty leaned over Lord William's shoulder. "Yes, there it is. Georgina, you know the words?"

"I do."

Kitty played the opening chorus, and George stood beside the piano and hummed along with her sister's introductory notes. The Hunters were a musical family, and George did love to sing. Adored it. She had a good voice, possibly better than good. She glanced at Kitty and her sister nodded, and really, all they were missing was Hugh as she launched into the song. She didn't hold back. She never could. The tune was beautiful and lovely and she never could do anything but her absolute best. If the words reminded her of Stoke Teversault no one need know.

Is there a heart that never loved
Or felt soft woman's sigh?
Is there a man can mark unmov'd
Dear woman's tearful eye?

The moment she finished, Kitty began another favorite of theirs, again from memory, so Lord William had no pages to turn. He stayed beside her on the bench, though. George sang that one, too, and Kitty added a counterpoint and Lord William joined in because he'd been at Uplyft Hall many times for a musical evening and knew the song well.

When they were done, amid much applause and requests for more, Kitty laid her hands on the keyboard. Underneath the applause, she said, low enough that only George and Lord William heard, "I miss Hugh. I wish he were here."

Lord William put an arm around Kitty's shoulders and hugged her. "I as well, Kitty. I as well. We'll have a week's celebration when he's home from Paris."

They relinquished their place at the piano to give others a turn to play. While they'd been singing, other guests had come in, so places to sit were scarce. George hung back, pleased that Kitty was so much at ease now. Lord Revers joined Kitty and Lord William. George, watching from a distance, rather fancied the viscount's regard for Kitty had undergone a marked change. Not mere admiration, but genuine respect for more than her looks.

A prickle of awareness went through her, and she turned toward the door.

There in the doorway, dressed in dark, dark clothes and with his stern and disapproving look, stood the Duke of Stoke Teversault. He was staring at her, but that wasn't what had her staring back. He'd added a second fob to his watch, a golden apple that dangled from a golden chain.

Chapter Seven

DURING THE SEVERAL minutes it took her to traverse the twenty yards between her and the duke, he seemed carved in place, for he did not move even once. She felt they were the only two in the room, even though they weren't.

With the music done and aspirants to additional performances dispersed, the level of conversational noise had increased considerably. With every glimpse of him, desire pooled in her, shocking, yet not to be denied. Whatever interior fire had driven him to the state of his body—lean, strong—his was a form honed to serve the intellect behind his stark eyes.

When they met, not even half the way, she curtseyed and steeled herself against that assessing gaze that since she'd come here had never failed to carve out a pit of nerves in her stomach. No handsome man had ever made her feel so helpless. His waistcoat was dark bronze silk shot through with gold thread. A hawk's head was engraved on his buttons. Short hair because he had no vanity. Plain clothes for the same reason. *Here is the man I am. Take me or leave me as you will.*

"Your Grace."

"Mrs. Lark." His eyes challenged her.

"You have my apple."

He tapped his ear and shook his head.

She leaned in and raised her voice. "Your Grace, you have my apple."

Again, he shook his head, impatience in the curt motion. "Come, Mrs. Lark." He touched her elbow and guided her toward the door. She expected he would veer left, but he did not. His hand remained on the back of her elbow, guiding her out of the parlor. It was already quieter out here, so she could not disagree with his remedy.

When they were several feet down the corridor she said, "You have my apple, Your Grace."

"I do not know what you mean." He walked fast enough that she had to take long steps to keep pace.

She frowned at his retreating back, baffled by a response that was an outright lie. She hurried after him. "There, on your watch. That is my apple."

He turned his upper body toward her. "Is it yours? I think not."

"I think so."

"We'll settle the matter presently." He gave her a meaningful look and fell silent when several young ladies passed them. He walked away from her again. "I should like a word in private with you."

"Oh. Well." She was so astonished she stopped walking. He did not. She caught up. She wasn't foolish enough to think her attraction to him was returned in any way. "May I ask on what subject?"

"A matter that requires the privacy lacking anywhere in this house that I could take you with hope of decency."

There was nothing in his voice or expression to suggest he meant anything other than his plain meaning. Yet, the suggestion that there could be impropriety floated between them. "Very well." She increased her stride and banished such ridiculous ideas. "If it's necessary."

"It is."

"Where are we going?" she asked when he opened a door to the outside.

"Where we will not be overheard." They veered away from the gardens where there were at least thirty people admiring the colors and greenery. He took a path away from the house and toward a grove of mammoth oaks she had been intending to explore.

"How far are we going?" She was wearing silk, a gauzy white lace shawl, and a hat that offered no protection from the sun or the breeze. "Will we be long?"

"If I were to escort you to my private quarters we would be seen and remarked upon in a manner that does us no credit. Half the people here today are friends of Sedgemere's or others whom I do not count as allies."

"I accept your premise that gossip is to be avoided at all cost." She picked a windblown leaf from her hair. "I haven't a cloak or a shawl, Your Grace."

He gave her another of his *save me from this woman* looks and then, God in heaven above, he stopped walking and stripped off his coat.

A thousand, no, a hundred thousand butterflies soared in her belly. The man moved with bewitching economy and assurance. "It does not make me warmer, sir, if you also do not have proper attire."

In chilling silence, he draped his coat around her shoulders and tugged the upper collar close. When she reached to hold the fabric herself, he jumped back as if he were afraid of pestilence. Gallant of him, and a kindness snatched away by that retreat. Well. There was not even a moment to misunderstand him. He could not bear to touch her.

He resumed walking. His coat was warm, and it smelled like him, and she was glad to have it, for he was walking toward the shade. Something heavy in one of the pockets tapped against her leg as she followed.

"What if I no longer wish to accompany you?" The man who had been so newly charming to her while they walked the lime-tree avenue was nowhere in evidence. What had she done to turn him so cold?

He faced her. "That is your right, Mrs. Lark. If you wish, I will escort you back to the house."

What choice had she, really? None, if she wanted to know what he intended to say to her. At least he'd chosen a scenic direction, though, in fairness, there were few places at Teversault that were not scenic. No would-be lovers the two of them. On this promenade, he was a general and she a lowly foot solider about to be upbraided for some heinous breach of decorum.

Two liveried footmen stood guard at the U-shaped entrance to the grove of trees, a demarcation of a part of the grounds not open to the public. Both servants were as tall or taller than the duke. He meant business in posting these men here. If she'd come here by herself she'd have thought twice about getting past them.

She imagined herself on a secret campaign, marching through enemy territory, facing certain death. They were well into the trees, their mission involving the fate of England... From the occasional stump amid the gigantic oaks, she deduced there had been deliberate culling and shaping of the grove over the years. There were other signs that this area had been tended to appear wild without actually being so. There was very little of the usual bramble, and closer to the path, the leaves had been swept away. The path itself was covered with freshly laid crushed gravel.

Another imaginary scene came to her. Far more apt, she decided, than a general and a loyal soldier. "I am put in mind of the story of Sleeping Beauty."

He was not amused. "You are no princess, ma'am."

"I wasn't implying I was, sir."

"Nor am I a huntsman with secret orders to return with your heart and eyes in a box."

After several more steps, she muttered, "If you were, you would not tell me, would you?"

He stopped and turned sideways, his far arm extended along the path ahead. "Behold. The scene of your gruesome death."

She only just avoided walking into him. They had emerged into a glade where the sun glinted off a pond, though not a natural one. It was a large rectangle, with a low curb overgrown with moss all around. In places the ledge was covered by the reeds growing at the edge. The path widened to accommodate a series of iron benches painted glossy black and facing the pond. On the opposite side of the water, an expanse of well-tended meadow extended into the surrounding trees.

She moved past him, holding on to his coat, enchanted by the view. "It's not fair of you to bring me to such a beautiful place when you intend to make me unhappy."

Ducks and swans floated on the water, and she saw the flash of a pheasant tail at the far side of the glade. She headed toward the water. "I wish I'd known this was here, I'd have brought bread for the birds."

He stopped at the edge of the pool and stared at the green surface, his face in three-quarter profile to her. It was unsettling to see him without his coat. Not just unsettling. Dangerous. She was drawn into the intimacy of his undress. She thrummed with sexual tension. Now that she'd experience of life and men, she was able to identify her reaction. Animal attraction. Unwarranted, yes, since he did not share her feelings. Think what would happen if he did. Have mercy on them both, for they would be reduced to ashes. She would, at least.

Desperate to break her mood and his silence, she asked, "Do you swim here?"

He picked up a pebble and skipped it along the surface of the water. "I did as a boy. William too, when he was old enough."

His shoulders were broad, and she could not help but see the flex of muscles when he released another pebble. When the silence bore down too hard, she coughed to remind him she was here. He sorted through the pebbles in his hand, tossing unsuitable ones just as he judged, and rejected, unsuitable people. "Is the water cold?"

"That is dependent upon the weather." He let out a breath and faced her. "We will be private here, I assure you." Fearful anticipation took over as her predominant state of mind. His eyes were so cool she had no idea what he might say. Anything at all, though she suspected what he intended to say would not be pleasant for her. "Mrs. Lark."

"Has something happened to Hugh?" She spoke too fast, and fear pushed her voice into a higher register than she liked. She could but brace for the worst possible news.

His eyebrows shot up. "No, ma'am."

She rested a hand on her upper chest, half on his coat, partially on her throat. Eyes closed, she gave thanks for that. "I could not think what else might require such solitude as this."

"From your murder to this." He shook his head. "Your imagination is too easily stirred."

"You are not standing here with no idea what horrible news must soon be imparted."

"Point taken." His dark lashes lowered so that she could not see his eyes. The tiniest quirk flashed at the corner of his mouth, a rare smile or a mark of his displeasure? She was not certain which. A smile from him could, would, lead her to her doom. "Allow me to relieve the worst of your fears then. I am not going to murder you."

"Thank you."

"Nor have I news of your brother."

"Then why did you bring me here?"

"I thought you would find this place beautiful."

She adjusted his coat, baffled by this encounter. The garment was too big on her shoulders, and it was heavy too. "I would enjoy the prospect more if I were not in a state of utter terror."

He bent for another pebble or two and weighed them in his palm. "What are your intentions toward my brother?"

She gazed at him, nonplussed, and then she wasn't. She mentally counted to five so that she would not say words she would regret. "Friendship, Your Grace."

In all her life, she had never been in such a peculiar position as this. She owed him a great deal. It was due to his influence that Hugh had his position and a bright future. Stoke Teversault had come to her assistance during the very darkest time of her life. Yet, he had never, but once during that time shown her anything but icy disdain. Once, in his arms, once with her soul stripped bare, and he'd sunk into the marrow of her bones.

"Nothing else?" he asked dryly.

"No, Your Grace." An awful explanation for his questions and dire manner occurred to her. He'd seen Lord William kissing her and believed she had designs on his brother. "I love your brother. I do."

Those were the wrong words. Or, rather, she said the correct words in an incorrect order. He went still in that way she'd come to recognize. That stillness meant he was especially alert. It meant his emotions would be impossible to divine. That stillness meant that when he struck, the blow would be deadly. He could decimate her with a look, a word. With silence.

"You've no idea the power you have over me," she said softly. The ducks were waddling ashore without sign of fear. The swans had come closer too.

"Since I believe I have none, I must agree."

She told him the unvarnished truth. "If I were in love with Lord William, with anyone at all, no matter how desperately, I would give him up if you asked me to."

The barest of hesitations preceded his response. "For what reason?"

"I owe you nothing less."

"Why?"

"Have you really no idea? Why, for everything you did for me after my husband died. For everything you have done."

He took a breath. "You say I have the power to destroy your happiness. That may well be, but your power over me is no less brutal."

"I do not understand you."

"If you were in love, I would corrupt myself."

"I'm not in love. I'm not." He did not wish her to marry Lord William. He meant that if she'd confessed that she did, he would use the power she'd given to him and demand she abandon his brother. "This is so simple, Your Grace. You've brought me here for nothing. I admire and respect your brother for his friendship with Hugh and with my sister and me. There are no warmer feelings between us."

He rubbed a thumb over the pebbles he held. "I don't believe he agrees with you."

"I assure you he does." The man who'd held her when she was devastated by grief did not exist. Perhaps he'd never existed except in her imagination. But, she remembered his arms around her, his soft, *Hush, darling.*

"You've known William half his life. You cannot be blind to his many qualities."

At that, she had to laugh. "If length of acquaintance is of any importance to such emotions as love then, if you're right, in ten years I'll be in love with you."

"My condolences for such a grim future."

"Grim indeed, Your Grace. In ten years, you'll wish I had married your brother."

"No, Mrs. Lark. I will not."

She walked to one of the benches and sat, staring at the swans on the still, green water. The left side of his coat went *clunk* as whatever was in the pocket landed on the bench. She lifted that half of his coat. "What do you have in here?"

"What else but a box?" he said. "For your heart."

"You'll just throw my eyes into the trees, then."

He stood to one side of her, too somber. "Mrs. Lark."

He'd brought her out her to warn her off Lord William because he'd judged her unworthy of a Besett. She wanted Kitty to have the best possible chance at marriage, to see something of society before she begged Hugh to fund a Season for Kitty. Until then, where but at Teversault would her sister have the chance to meet men of fashion and *ton*? "You might have saved yourself a deal of trouble" she said, "by asking your brother not to invite us. Did you two never discuss the guest list?"

"You are not unwelcome at Teversault."

"So long as we know our place." This was beyond perverse to intend to do whatever he asked and at the same time resent him for not liking her. Those two things were not related. She made the mistake of looking the duke square in the face. Her stomach tightened, and she hated herself for the reaction. So foolish to find him so attractive when he wasn't. His coat slipped off her shoulders. She ignored it. "You ought to have put us below stairs so we'd know how to behave."

"There is a servants wing." He was enigma. She'd joked about reading his expressions, but she couldn't. Not when he was like this. "Not a below stairs."

"I—" Her words stuck in her throat. "I don't know why—" She wiped at the corner of her eye. "You've no obligation to like me, but I confess, it seems to me you've no reason to dislike me either."

"I spend far too much time saying that I do not dislike you."

"Worse." She gripped the button-side of his coat. "You don't even care." She lost the power of speech. He'd been so helpful to her, and all she wanted was to give back something, to make him some repayment. Since Edward had died, she'd got tangled up about him with no way she could see to unravel the mess. She gave in to her tears, turning away from him and folding her arms on the top of the bench to hide her face from him.

"This is unacceptable. Cease immediately."

George lifted her head long enough to see him standing exactly where he had been. "Go. Go away. Leave me to my abject misery."

He sat beside her and did something with his coat. If she had any luck at all, he really would put her heart in a box. Instead, he touched her shoulder.

She kept her face away from him. "Leave me be."

"My handkerchief."

She moved her head and saw a square of silk inches from her face.

"I cannot abide a woman's tears."

"No. No, you wouldn't." It was ridiculous for her to feel this way. She took his handkerchief and pressed it to her eyes. "Thank you. You needn't stay." He did not move from the bench. He wanted her reassurance that she did not intend to lure his brother into an unsuitable marriage. She took several calming breaths and sat back. "I do not want to marry your brother, and I daresay he does not wish to marry me." She squeezed his handkerchief. "There. You may rest easy now."

"Thank you."

She stared at his watch chain and the two fobs dangling from it. The silver lozenge he always wore and the golden apple she'd intended to offer up as treasure. She pointed. "That is mine."

He raised one eyebrow. "I won your game. Therefore, the prize is mine."

"The game required a map. You did not have a map. Ergo you did not play; ergo you did not win."

He leaned over her, stretching an arm across her. "Your pardon."

Her breath hitched. Whether he noticed, she could not tell. He extracted a folded half sheet of foolscap from his coat pocket. "As you can see, I had the requisite map. Though perhaps it's not genuine. Examine it and tell me if it is."

She glanced at the paper in his hand. "Yes, it's genuine. Where did you get it?"

"William. Therefore, under the rules, I did participate. In addition, I found the treasure. It wasn't difficult." He touched the apple. "Therefore, I won."

She blinked at him. "Well," she said slowly, "it's too late. We awarded a different prize."

"If you've reneged on the original prize, I'll claim another." He detached the gold chain from his fob and held it out. She stared at the apple turning slowly in the air. "Has my touch poisoned it?"

"No." She looked up, and her heart thudded he was so close. She could scarcely think. "You cannot invent prizes to win. What if you decided you'd won a chest of gold or a diamond necklace?"

"I've no use for a diamond necklace."

"Nonsense." She lifted her chin, afraid to look at the apple he still held. "They make excellent gifts for one's mistress."

"What gifts I give to a lover is my choice to make. Not yours." He took her hand and dropped the apple onto her upturned palm.

"I was pointing out that you do have a use for a diamond necklace."

"Point conceded."

She regarded the apple with some dismay. If she weren't wearing gloves, she'd feel the warmth of the metal. He'd said it wasn't poisoned, and of course it was not, but she could not shake the conviction that just holding it meant more of him was twisting its way into her, never to be capable of removal.

"If you haven't a chest of gold or a diamond necklace, you'll have to think of something else."

She held out the apple. "It's yours."

He wrapped his hand around hers so that they were both holding the apple. He braced his other hand on the back of the bench and loomed over her. For one soaring, pulse-pounding moment, she was sure he meant to kiss her. Worse, even worse than that, she moved toward him while her world tilted out of balance, with Stoke Teversault the only man who could put it right. They were too close. Then not close enough, and he did not kiss her.

She turned away. Humiliated.

"This is not the time or place," he said.

She held out the apple again. "You won it fairly."

He leaned against the bench, one leg outstretched, and regarded her with his impenetrable gaze. "Keep it."

"I don't want it."

"Why? It's a pretty bauble."

"It was a gift from Edward's father." Stoke's eyebrows shot up, and she hastened to explain. "He gave it to me as a reminder of woman's original sin. I've long thought of giving it to someone who would have pleasant associations with receiving it. Now I've tried, and I can't even do that. It's too awful."

He sat up enough to take it from her. "Did I say it was a pretty bauble? I see the poison now. I'm sorry I wore it."

"You can't believe how I despise that apple."

"I can imagine." Stoke closed his fist and, then, in one explosive movement toward the pond, he hurled the apple over the water. It arced in the air and plunged down, down, down, sunlight glinting off the metal.

She stared at the water and the ripples spreading out where it had landed. "Will I offend you if I say I shall be in love with you in a considerably shorter time than ten years?"

"Not in the least."

Chapter Eight

GEORGE TENSED WHEN she saw Stoke Teversault walking the path to the pond. She wished she hadn't decided to come here, but she had and now it was too late to hide. She could be as cool as he could be. She would be.

It was her plan to pretend she'd not seen him, and then, when he saw her, he could decide to walk away. He would return to the house, and no one need admit that there was no repairing the break between them that had existed since the day she'd told him she was not in love with his brother.

She was prepared to have him avoid her as he had these past two days. He continued walking. Why? Why hadn't he taken the chance when he'd had it? He was a clever man. He would know he could turn away. It wasn't too late yet. She kept her eyes forward, but she could hear him coming nearer. Now, she thought. Now, he must realize he was at the very limit of where he could retreat with their pretense of ignorance intact.

"Mrs. Lark."

She did not love Lord William but that had not been enough to fix whatever had gone wrong. She would rather go back to his disdain of her than endure knowing she had made this painful for him. She hid the rest of the bread she'd cadged from the duke's chef in her reticule. "Good morning, Your Grace."

He stood on the path, unmoving.

She steeled herself, but the words she'd rehearsed a dozen times flew out of her head. "I wish I could fly or turn invisible. Or could travel back in time to never make a fool of myself."

"I beg your pardon."

"But I have. Made myself foolish to you, I mean. We shouldn't have come. Kitty and I." She sank into the drama that had overwhelmed her these past days. "I should never have let Lord William convince us to come here. I did so want Kitty to have a chance to meet fashionable people. With Hugh away, we don't see many gentlemen worthy of her. I was selfish for I so wanted to see Teversault for myself. I ought to have known you would prefer we not come here." She drew breath. "Therefore, I've decided that we shall leave."

"Mrs. Lark. There is no reason for you to leave. You have not troubled me in the least."

She stared across the water, then looked at him, determined to make things right between them. "Except when you feared I meant to marry your brother."

He held her gaze, and her stomach swooped. "I am a difficult man to know and more difficult to befriend, I'm told."

"I can't think who'd dare tell you something like that." The birds had stopped singing, as well they must. What creature would risk displeasing Stoke Teversault?

His smile was pained. "You needn't leave on my account, unless what you mean to say is that you cannot tolerate me."

She dug her toe into the gravel then realized she oughtn't. "I did not say that."

"If you leave, I will think you believe it."

She stared at him, perplexed. He was serious. She narrowed her eyes at him and then smiled and extended her hand to him. "Good morning, Your Grace. How delightful that you should decide to walk here at the same time I did."

For the space of two heartbeats, he did not react. Then, he took her hand and bent over it. "A happy coincidence, indeed."

"Lovely morning, don't you agree?" she said when he'd released her hand.

"Yes." He stood beside her and watched the water with her. The swans and several of the ducks had swum away one she'd stopped throwing them treats. "Not too warm."

"Not yet. Perhaps later, though." She was going to learn how to behave with the duke if it killed her, and she thought it would. "I do prefer cooler weather. Don't you?"

His arrival brought the birds to the edge of the pool, with the ducks being quite vocal.

"Yes." He drew a hunk of bread from his pocket. The noise from the birds increased. "Better for the nerves, one hears."

"Yes. Nerves." She didn't want to look at him but she did. He looked especially fashionable today, with his beaver hat and a greatcoat of chocolate wool. "One does wish to avoid a case of the nerves."

He tore off bits of bread and tossed them onto the water. The swans floated close, necks arched gracefully. He turned his head to her, and she froze, and then hated herself for being caught in his gaze. His nose was too long and too boney, his cheeks too sharp, and his mouth was as hard as his heart. "Greedy beggars."

"Yes, they are." She forced herself to reply when she'd rather stare at his face and ponder why she found him so attractive. "Beautiful, greedy beggars."

He tore off more bits of bread and extended a handful to her. "Would you like to feed them?"

George opened her reticule and took out the bread she'd shoved inside. She held it up. "I came prepared."

"Chef muttered something about nice fat ducks this morning." He laughed and tossed his handful of crumbs onto the water. "When I am in residence, I cannot bear to think of not bringing them something in the morning."

"Why don't you instruct the staff to make sure they get something?"

He hesitated, then said, "I do." His features returned to hard nonchalance, while she took her turn tossing bits of bread. "I believe you're wrong about my brother."

"What do you mean?"

"He is fond of you."

"As I am fond of him."

"More than he is of any other."

"You've no cause for worry." She put a hand on his upper arm, and he glanced at her, one eyebrow arched. "It's very odd to me, but nevertheless true, that though Lord William is handsome, unfairly so, I should say, I feel no spark of…" How frank should she be? Enough, she understood, to put his fears to rest. "There is no attraction between us. I believe I ought to feel something in that nature, for what woman would not find in him much to admire?" She lifted her hands in a gesture of her helplessness in the face of such facts. "Yet…"

"Why aren't you in love with him?" His question was sharp and too fast.

She looked down her nose at him, after a fashion, given he was so much taller than she. "Two days ago you were terrified I might lead your brother into an unsuitable marriage. Today you demand to know why I haven't? Do make up your mind."

"Is there no one for you besides Mr. Lark?"

Goodness, but he'd echoed her own half-hearted explanation to Lord William. Or his brother had told him that was her excuse. She scraped more bread from the crusts to which she was now reduced and threw the last of it to the ducks. "People remarry all the time, and happily too."

"That is no answer to my question."

"No." She sighed. "I do not know the answer. I loved my husband with all my heart, that's true. I still mourn him, but does that mean I will never fall in love again? Does it mean others who remarry did not love the first time, or that they love less the second? I think not."

He went still again, proof against the ducks calling for more food. "I've no notion."

"We agree then. I do not know if I will love a second time." There. Now she wasn't lying to him. "Perhaps I will. I know it won't be Lord William. Much to your relief, I'm sure."

"You've no idea."

She shot him a sideways look. Lord, she might yet lose her head over him. She toed a pebble by the rock-lined border of the pond, and they took turns tossing the remains of his bread onto the water, comfortable in the silence. At last, though, she showed her empty hands to the swans and the ducks. "No more, my greedy, beautiful beggars."

Stoke Teversault tossed the last of what was in his hand, and she, anticipating that he would walk back to the path collided with him because instead he faced her.

"Oof."

He grabbed her by the upper arms, and she tilted her chin up and found his gaze fixed on her mouth, and she had been married, so she knew. She knew. Her entire body clenched. She understood men and what they did with women in private, and she was stunned to see that his thoughts had turned there.

She ought to move. Say something. Her stomach was a mass of butterflies, because her thoughts had turned there too, to darkened rooms and whispered endearments, and all the lovely things one could do with hands and mouths and private parts.

Time stopped. Stretched out. She was convinced he meant to kiss her, but that was impossible. He couldn't. He wouldn't. The Duke of Stoke Teversault would never.

He did, though. With a finesse that unmoored her.

Chapter Nine

STOKE CAUGHT UP with the riders less than a mile east of the house. How many days had he endured the memory of kissing George? Too many. For those brief moments when she'd relaxed into his arms and had surrendered herself to him, he'd been finished. Kissing her had been a mistake. He'd lost his head and handled her as if she were a courtesan. She'd been the one to come to her senses and end the embrace. Thank God. Thank God. He would otherwise have laid her down on the path and taken her right there. He'd even worked out the logistics of doing so.

Off the path and onto the soft ground. His coat as protection from the leaves and soil, skirts up, his hands where they should not be. Unbutton and thrust in. Jesus. What he'd wanted to do felt so real that he sometimes thought he had.

The slower riders were in sight. George and Miss Hunter had borrowed mounts from his stable, and much to his consternation, William had put George on Pluto, a spirited gelding who required a firm hand. So far, Pluto was behaving, but he doubted those good manners would last. He did not, in point of fact, have any idea how well the two women rode. He hoped to God William had known what he was doing, giving George a horse like that. His brother often failed to think things through.

They emerged from the narrower path onto a field and spread out. William urged his horse into a canter, and George did the same. Miss Hunter stayed behind. Lord Revers, engaged in conversation with her, paced himself beside her.

George rode with confidence, but in the open field, Pluto's nature would soon become an issue. If her confidence was misplaced, she might be badly hurt. Pluto was sixteen and a half hands, and strong enough that when he wanted his way, he got it. All but the best riders had difficulty with him at some point.

The group spread out according to skill, mounts, and, one imagined, one's preferences about flirting versus the exertion of riding faster than a walk. William returned to ride with Kitty and Lord Revers, leaving George at the head of the field. The distance between George and the others increased. Stoke joined his brother. He nodded at Kitty, who turned pink and looked away. He gestured for William to accompany him out of the young lady's earshot, for what he had to say was not fit for innocent young ears. "What were you thinking, giving her Pluto?"

William's eyes widened. He'd got his brother's back up, but pride be damned. He glanced over his shoulder at Revers. "She'd be bored otherwise. Insulted too."

"Bored." He lowered his voice because Revers and Kitty were so near. "Better bored than thrown off. Are you mad?" George was now several yards ahead of the field, easy to do with Pluto, with his long, easy gait. "Pluto is not an appropriate mount for a woman. If he takes it into his head to misbehave, she could be hurt."

"Best horsewoman I've ever met." William spoke with uncharacteristic sharpness. "You'd know that if you'd ever come down from the clouds to breathe the same air as the rest of us."

He looked ahead to where George rode. To his horror, and yes, anger, she set Pluto to just short of a full out gallop. True, she sat Pluto with no sign—yet—that she could not keep her seat. "She's too small to control him."

"She's not." William's lack of concern was small comfort. He gave a smile, part amusement, part smug pride. "Watch her ride. Just watch."

He had to allow she rode beautifully. She and William were alike in their confidence in all things physical. Pluto was under control and covering ground quickly. "Pray God she'll not be killed if she falls."

"Go after her, if you're worried."

He gave his brother a look that would have incinerated anyone else. William knew him too well and had too much experience with his moods to be afraid of him now.

"Go on, Stoke. See if I'm not right."

"I'll have your head if you're not." He spurred his horse and cantered after George. The reckless woman set Pluto to a gallop. Stoke gave Neptune his head and the stallion responded with a bound that settled into a gallop. He made up the distance quickly, and he would have caught her up except she aimed Pluto at a stone fence. Three and a half feet high, that fence. Pluto could take it easily, but that didn't mean George could, or that she'd stay on the horse when he landed on the other side. If he landed.

Stoke shouted, and Neptune responded with a burst of speed. For a while, he thought he'd come even with her in time to head her off, but no. Pluto wanted the fence, the damned evil beast. She had no choice now but to make the jump.

George adjusted, leaning forward. Pluto gathered himself and went up and up and stretched out in the air. Stoke's heart banged away at his chest for that eternity. Then he, too, had to make the jump. Neptune cleared the fence effortlessly, there could never be any question of him failing a jump like that. Ahead of him, Pluto had already landed without a break in stride. George kept her seat and urged the gelding onward. Stoke followed. Since she slowed, as indeed she ought to, this time he caught up easily.

"Oh, it's you," she said, as coolly as if she'd not been at risk of breaking her neck.

"You little fool."

Her eyes opened wide. "I beg your pardon?"

"You could have killed yourself and injured a valuable horse."

She blanched so thoroughly the freckles scattered across her nose and cheeks became more noticeable. "Lord William said I could jump him. Was that wrong?" She put a hand to her chest. Pluto danced sideways, and Stoke reached for her bridle, but she wasn't the least perturbed. Nor unbalanced either. "Oh, no." She was appalled at the possibility that Pluto should not have been jumped. "I'd never do anything I oughtn't to have with him. He's grand. Just grand. I'm sorry, if I oughtn't have."

"William had no business putting you on Pluto."

"But why?" She patted Pluto's shoulder and clicked her tongue so that Stoke was obliged to follow. At least she was moving at a sedate pace. "He's wonderful. I adore him. Unless I'm much mistaken, he loves to jump."

"You might have been injured." In his mind's eye, he saw her taking the fence. A perfectly timed jump.

"So might you, when you jumped. So might anyone who ever rides." Her eyebrows drew together. "At home, Your Grace, I'm counted an excellent rider."

"I have no knowledge of that."

She tipped her head to one side. "Are you to be informed of all my talents?"

"When they involve dangerous pursuits, yes." She would do anything for him. Make any sacrifice. If he asked it of her, she would refuse an offer of marriage were one made to her. He did not care for knowing what he would do with that information.

"I'll need a list from you of what you consider dangerous."

"So, I'm to be excoriated for fearing you would injure yourself?"

She closed her eyes, and he would have bet anything she was counting to herself. When she opened her eyes again, she was serene. "I believed Lord William had authority to tell me I could jump Pluto. I must have misunderstood him, for I know he would not otherwise have told me so."

"He does. Of course he does." He should not have kissed her. What a dunderheaded mistake that had been, treating her as if there were no question of her sexual availability to him.

"So...you are blaming me for Lord William's failure to inform you he'd told me Pluto was an excellent jumper. I see."

"I have spoken to him." The burgundy of her riding habit went well with her skin and eyes. Her hat, of the same shade as her habit and with a black plume in the band, sat jauntily atop her head, and that too was in complement to her pale orange hair.

"I understand."

"You do not."

"You were concerned for my safety. That is commendable of you." She nodded. "I apologize for any upset I caused you."

"I would have been concerned for the safety of any woman riding Pluto. As I told William, you are too small to count on controlling him if he decides he'll pay no attention to you."

Her mouth tightened. "Am I to understand, sir, that despite the evidence of my competence, you refuse to accept it?"

Such forthright speech was but one of the reasons they did not suit. There were dozens more, but this one would do. "I'll thank you not to be impertinent."

Her expression smoothed out, and two pink spots blossomed on her cheeks. He felt a thorough beast for that, but he was in the right, and she was not. With one graceful motion, she dismounted. "Again, my apologies, Your Grace."

She didn't mean it. That was beyond obvious. She turned her back to him and stroked Pluto's nose. "Lovely animal. Thank you for the magnificent ride." She lowered her voice and whispered, not softly enough to prevent him from hearing her, "I'm sorry your master is unpleasant." She face him with a look of such innocence he could have believed she did not know that his hearing was unnaturally acute. Though, of course, she did know. She extended Pluto's reins to him, giving him no choice but to take them.

"What the devil are you about, Mrs. Lark?" He'd held her in his arms once, twice, now. He'd driven from London to Hampstead Heath after William, detained at Scylfe on business Stoke himself had sent him on, had written to tell him Edward Lark had died and would he please, please render her all possible assistance. He'd arrived to find she'd been coping, valiantly. Her husband's relations were not kind, he'd soon learned, and at one point not long after his arrival, she'd simply broken down. He'd come far too close to offending all decency with her. He'd not held her again until that day by the pond.

With one hand, she scooped up her habit and slipped the loop around her wrist to keep the voluminous skirts from tripping her. Her smile was pleasant, perfectly bland, with a hint of smugness that infuriated him. "I shall walk back to Teversault," she said in clipped tones. "That must allay your fears for my safety." She extended her hand. "I'm happy to walk him back. That is, if you trust Pluto not to trample me out of spite for my inept horsewomanship."

He gave her the sort of look that made grown men quail. To no apparent effect on her. "We're at least five miles from the house. You'll be more than an hour getting back." He pointed at the fence. "How do you think you'll get over that dressed as you are?"

She huffed out a breath. "Five miles is a pleasant stroll. As for the fence, I'm sure I'll manage. If there's not a stile somewhere, I'll go around."

He looked over his shoulder and saw the main group had gone to the left rather than to the right as he and George had done. "I will accompany you back to Teversault."

"I had rather you didn't."

He dismounted and gave her a tight smile. "That is unfortunate for you, ma'am."

She took a deep breath, and a part of him that was not gentlemanly was fascinated by the way her habit tightened across her bosom. "Your Grace. This is absurd. You don't want to be in my company any more than I wish to be in yours. There's no harm in my walking back."

"I will not allow you to return to the house alone."

She frowned hard. "Fetch one of the grooms. I shall wait here. On my honor."

"They've gone that way." He pointed to his right.

"Then allow me to ride back."

He gave her a glower that William had once described as the devil looking back from the mirror. "You'd hare off at a gallop to spite me."

She burst into laughter, and as before, she was transformed from tolerable to beguiling, without him having the faintest idea why or how. "I would," she said. "I would indeed. Unless you'd made me promise not to, and I can't think how you'd succeed at that."

He closed the distance between them and put a hand on her cheek. He wished like hell he'd taken off his gloves and thanked God he had not. She turned her head away, but he pressed lightly on her cheek until she looked at him. This was a dangerous business, staying so close to her. Touching her. "Will you laugh at me again, Mrs. Lark?"

"I don't feel like laughing."

"You may suppose I know a way to make you promise me."

Her eyes snapped to his, and the color on her cheeks spread. "Fiend."

"I am a Machiavelli." He heard the silky tone in his voice and was appalled. He was seducing her, and he had no ability to stop himself. Reckless, unplanned words poured from him. "I think you love me. I think that's why I have the power to bend you to my will."

"I love the idea of you. There's a difference."

He dropped the reins of both horses and put his other hand on her face too. God her mouth was delicious. Not mere speculation this time, but knowledge. "Explain it to me."

"I don't see why I ought."

"I wish to understand."

"I don't know you at all. Not really."

"And?" He'd moved closer, obliterating the former decency of the space between them. She seemed not to notice.

"The man who came to me at Hampstead Heath was everything admirable. I'll be forever grateful to you for that, but I no longer mistake your former kindness for continuing affection."

"A great many people admire me." He did not recognize his voice, his seducer's voice.

"I do admire you." He loved the color of her habit, the contrast of that dark wine color with her pale skin and hair. "Who wouldn't admire the Duke of Stoke Teversault? At the moment, however, I don't admire *you* at all."

"Many more fear me." He smiled at her, and when he did, he imagined asking her to come to bed with him so he could rid himself of this damnable lust. He'd revel in it. Soar through clouds of it.

She went still. Her eyelashes were thick and looked shorter than they were because the tips were ashy blond. Well, then. She'd been married, and he'd let her see too much. Or perhaps not enough.

"Your eyes are lovely."

"What's that to do with anything?"

She betrayed herself with that breathless question, and the next thing he knew, he'd bent his head to her and kissed her again.

Chapter Ten

MORE TIMES THAN she could count since coming to Teversault, George had dreamed of being kissed by Stoke Teversault. In any number of situations vanquished into implausibility, she had imagined, dreamed, daydreamed—it hardly mattered which—that she was alone with the Duke of Stoke Teversault and that her charm, intelligence, and practical, capable nature swept him off his feet. And into bed.

In her imaginings, the duke, being a paragon in all things, would see past her flaws to the beauty of her heart and fall irrevocably in love with her. Under equally implausible facts, she, and she alone of all the women in Britain, drew him from his state of isolation. Awakened at last. She'd kiss him into an exploration of passion.

No such thing had happened the first time they kissed. That was not what was happening this time. Except that he did seem to have pressed his lips to hers with a confidence that turned the backs of her knees to jelly. Lord, but he kissed divinely. She could not fathom why he was doing this again.

Her brain was not functioning, or more to the point, her brain was unable to distinguish the thoughts and reactions that went along with shock, fear, astonishment, confusion, doubt, and joy. A terrible, hungry, starving lust demanding to be sated.

His gloved hand cupped the back of her head, and his mouth turned urgent, Which had not happened that day at the pond. He did know his way around the business of kissing—and then—this wasn't kissing. What they were doing was a prelude to intercourse. My God. Him. The Duke of Stoke Teversault was kissing her as if it was only a matter of time before she gave herself to him.

She put a hand on his shoulder and followed his lead, willing, in fact, to follow him to perdition. His lips parted, urging her to do the same, and so she did.

His mouth was soft, firm. He knew what he was doing, he knew how this was done. As he continued to hold her the hard muscle of his arm pressed against her. Her insides hollowed out, and it was an extraordinary response. Overwhelming, and unfamiliar, and disconcerting. Different from Edward. But then, there had never been any doubt of the feelings she and Edward had for each other.

In the back of her head, she was aware this was how women ruined themselves, even experienced ones, but she didn't care. She was swept away by the impossibility of being kissed with such carnality, let alone that she was in Stoke Teversault's arms. His other arm slid around her waist, and she put her free hand on his upper arm. Her existence became a paradox in which she relaxed against him while tension filled her, and then, mercy, something changed. Their mouths fell into a rhythm that dragged her along with him and melted her inside.

His grip on her loosened. His hand moved along her spine and lower, and breathless, she waited to learn if he would touch her below the small of her back. She wished he would. Hoped he would. His tongue moved past her lips, into her mouth, and that was not something she'd ever imagined between them, and it was stunning. The moment she did the same, the world shifted again.

Briefly, very briefly, he pulled back, but she remained in his arms. There was no denying that fact. She gazed up at him and the heat in his eyes transferred to her and coiled in the center of her and between her legs, and one edge of his mouth quirked up in a slow, dream-fed sort of way. He studied her, and she returned his frank interest.

She liked his strong features, the sharp angles, and then that moment of suspended time ended, and when his head dipped toward hers again, she met him halfway. Kissing him was glorious, astonishing. This time, she knew more about what he liked. Not everything, but enough. She knew what she liked about kissing him, the way he kissed her, the way he reacted when she kissed him.

Eventually, he drew back again, but she stayed relaxed, bonelessly aroused, awash with desire, absorbing the languorous tension of his mouth. She was in a precarious situation, she knew that. Ruin came of encounters like this. "Oh," she whispered. "I like you far too well for this to be safe."

He stepped back, and she watched him wrap himself up in silence and reserve. With one deep breath the last of his languor faded, and she was sorry, so very sorry. "This cannot be."

She dropped her hand to her side. "Why did you kiss me again if you don't want more between us?" She adjusted her gloves. "I had resigned myself after the last time and would have been able to continue as if nothing had happened. But now? I don't see how I can."

"I've no idea why. Stupidity." He'd stripped off his gloves at some point, and now he touched her lower lip with the pad of his thumb. "That's not so. I kissed you for the same reason I threw that poisoned apple into the water."

"Because you dislike Edward's father?"

He did not smile. "Because of your mouth. The shape, what happens to your face when you smile."

"The first time or the second?"

"Both."

The quivery sensation in her stomach wasn't gone, and she had to struggle to pull her thoughts together. "Curiosity satisfied?"

"No."

She wished she were certain of what she might presume now. Nothing, she thought. She did not dare presume anything, not with the way he was looking at her.

"Damn that brother of mine."

"I don't believe I follow," she said. "What has Lord William to do with us? Did you kiss me because of him?"

"He brought you here. He's put you in my path again. He gave me that map, and I took the apple because it was yours and I wanted you to know that I'd beaten William and his bloodhound."

She gave him a sideways look, and he stared at her mouth in a way that made her uneasy. He said, after a long silence that dizzied her with the possibilities, "This madness shan't be repeated, I assure you."

"More than twice, you mean."

"Madness."

"Agreed.

"Sheer lunacy."

She stilled herself, and when she was certain she had control of herself, she adjusted her hat. He'd knocked it loose. "I comprehend you. You're mad. I quite agree."

"I kissed you because your mouth is decadent."

"I can't help what my mouth is like."

"It will not happen again."

"I'm sorry to hear that."

She had a long and solitary walk back to Teversault.

Chapter Eleven

G EORGE'S BRIGHT HAIR was instantly recognizable amid the crowd gathering at the far side of the serpentine to watch the contestants compete in the Dukeries Cup. Lord Revers stood beside her, not very discreetly staring at her bosom. Stoke headed toward them. Before he could question the wisdom of his actions, he'd taken her arm and drawn her close enough to him that she was no longer beside the viscount. "Revers."

"Stoke." If anyone was seeing the devil stare back from a mirror, it was Lord Revers just now. The man must have breathed in brimstone, for he straightened and cleared his throat. "Your Grace." He bowed. "Here to see Lord William win a fourth title?"

"Yes. Mrs. Lark, where is your sister?"

"With Miss Paltree and her mother." She pointed. "Lord Ingleforth is with them."

"Why are you not also with them?"

"Lord Revers said this is a better place to see the race." While she peered the opposite direction, he committed murder with his stare at Revers. Revers edged away from George. "I'm not certain we'll see the end from here," she said, oblivious. "The end of the race is the most important part, don't you agree?"

"Yes. Come with me." He was done denying his obsession with her. "You'll have an excellent view with me."

The look she gave him made his heart leap. She bent a knee.

"That's very kind of you," Revers said, foolishly brave. "We've an excellent view from here." Revers reached for George and brought her to his side. He tucked her arm around his, a silent pronouncement that he was prepared to defend her against him.

"My brother expects Mrs. Lark at the finish." A lie. A rank lie, but the words rolled from his tongue.

"Does he?" Revers's attention shifted between George and him. Let the man think what he liked.

"Yes." He extended a hand to her and slipped into his familiar coldness. For Revers's benefit, but for hers too. "Mrs. Lark. Oblige me if you please."

"It seems I must." She spoke without enthusiasm, and then smiled at Lord Revers.

He took her proffered hand and bowed over it. "George. I'll find you afterward, I hope?"

"For the victory celebration, yes." She peered to the right. "Best we hurry, Your Grace. The boats are in the water."

A murmur went through the spectators, and in several spots among them the betting activity heated up. Stoke took her arm and walked her away from Revers. And the crowd.

She glanced over her shoulder. "Perhaps we should stay with Lord Revers."

"No."

"We'll not make it to a better place. There won't be room."

"My valet is holding the ground." He detoured them around a dozen young men who must have come here from one of the other estates, Sedgemere's, or Linton's, or Oxthorpe's, for he did not recognize any of them as having been at Teversault before now. More spectators lined the banks of the serpentine. There was a great deal of late betting going on.

"What do you suppose everyone's talking about?" She was right. A whisper rolled through the crowd, increasing in volume as some news took fire. He didn't much care what it was, but she did, plainly.

"My man will have heard if something's happened."

She had no trouble keeping up with him. As they hurried to the observation point, it occurred to him that this year he'd spent more time among his guests than he had the previous five years combined.

They reached a fork in the groomed path that led to more lawns and gardens to the right and to Teversault to the left. He stopped walking and George took two steps past him before she realized he hadn't kept pace. "Your Grace?"

He swept off his hat, then replaced it. "I can't behave with you, when you deserve my best behavior more than anything. I am disordered, inefficient. Muddyheaded. That is not a state in which I care to exist."

Immediately, her expression went from empty to concerned. "Kitty and I should have left."

"No. No, you've misunderstood me." She wasn't beautiful, but he was damned if he could think why that was so. He understood beauty yet found this woman who did not fit the criteria for beauty unbearably appealing.

"What is the matter?"

"I want..." If he let her in, she would break him. Own him, have power over him that he could not bear giving anyone. He could not live, not without knowing her, and that meant that the man he was would cease to be. "It's as if I've been asleep these thirty years and only dreamed the world until you came here. I never knew anything before you."

"Nonsense."

"I don't know how to be with you. It is beyond me."

She put her hand on his arm, warm, inviting, but not for him. Not for the man he was. "There's no need for that." She looked back the way they'd come. "I'll rejoin Lord Revers."

"Do you wish to?"

"He's charming. Why would I not?"

"If I said no? What then? No, you may not leave me for Revers."

"Your Grace. I am not entirely—" She fell thoughtful. "If you do not wish for me to watch the race with Lord Revers, then I shan't."

"You and I—I don't know what we will do, you and I." These were not words he'd prepared, and he was aware of his peril in speaking without having his goal in sight. But he did have a goal. He did, and it was beyond reprehensible. "Something—something that is not friendship."

She glanced down, then back at him, her mouth tight. "You must know I will do what you wish of me. I won't have you so unhappy in your own home. It's not right that you should be. I'll stay away from your brother and Lord Revers and anyone else you desire me to avoid. I'll be back at Uplyft Hall before you know it. This awkwardness between us will pass. It will."

He said, "What of discretion, Mrs. Lark? What of that?"

"Discretion." A wrinkle appeared in her forehead. "I don't understand you. I don't think either of us has been indiscreet. I hope I haven't been."

"I cannot be discreet when I'm beside myself with lust. It's unthinkable that I should behave as I wish to."

She blinked at him.

"If you stay here, I will have you." He took a step closer and took hold of her shoulders. "I won't have Revers staring at your bosom whilst he devises the means by which he'll have you in his hands and mouth. I won't have him seduce you when I'm mad to have you myself." He released her. "There. I've said it. All is before you now, every disgraceful thought. Nearly all of them."

He expected her to walk away from him, but she didn't. He'd confounded her. Insulted and degraded her.

"I am willing, Mrs. Lark, to negotiate terms with you."

Very softly, she said, "Are you asking me to engage in an affair with you?"

"Yes. When you are married, not to William. That I could not endure. When you are married again, I will assist your husband in any manner within my power." He hadn't said the right things, not yet. He had no experience with such words.

Her mouth opened, then she hesitated, but he waited her out. Shouts rose up from the observation point of the serpentine. "That's generous of you."

"I will take care of you if there are consequences."

She licked her lips. She'd yet to walk away from him, and that made him reckless.

"You're here another week. Is that right?"

"Yes."

"It's unlikely you'll get with child, but if you conceive, I'll see to everything."

She blanched, and her freckles stood out, more than one saw usually. "We're missing the race."

Words poured from him. Not sweet sounding, not seducing. Plain words. Words that solved his dilemma. "Come to me tonight." This was vague. Ambiguous as to time and place. "To my rooms. I am in the north wing, any servant will direct you."

"You cannot mean that."

"Let your sister attend Sedgemere's ball with Mrs. Paltree and her daughter. They would be delighted to take Kitty since it would mean William and Revers are sure to be close by. I am not expected there. Make an excuse and stay behind. Or return early. Come to me any time after eleven o'clock."

Her answer was a breath. Was it possible she would tell him yes? He wanted to touch her, caress her, but he did not—yet—have that right.

"How else could I have asked you this but plainly and without tenderness?" He shrugged one shoulder. A shout rose up from the banks of the serpentine, but she did not look behind her. "I could have given you words designed to seduce you into my bed. Instead, I gave you truth. That is a gift, to know when and where and what, all the circumstances and expectations I shall have of you. No promises I will never keep. Just truth."

"I can't imagine you seducing anyone." She spoke with a certainty beyond her years, and this was yet another facet of her that spurred his desire for her, her unshakable belief in the weight and worth of her words.

"There ought to be two people freely choosing in such matters." He took off his hat again and held it at his waist. "Seduction is contemptible. I have never done that. Not since I was a boy who did not know better. If you agree to my madness, I want your clearheaded decision, not capitulation because I convinced you that I am a different sort of man."

"In other words, you won't pretend to like me or think me attractive?"

"I do not dislike you." He pressed the brim of his hat too hard. "I have said this more than once. It's time you believe me. As to your looks, I find you arousing, beyond any good sense. Why would I kiss you if I did not find you attractive?"

"Are you certain you aren't seducing me? I feel as if you are."

"When you smile, you steal a man's soul. My soul."

"Now you flatter me?" She rolled her eyes, but her cheeks were pink. She plucked at her skirt, then smoothed it.

He held her gaze. He had her. He could see that in her face, the set of her mouth. "Come tonight. We'll fan that spark to flame."

She stared at the ground for a long moment. "I said to you I would do anything you asked."

"You did." His heart thumped.

"If I agree, you'll believe it's because I had no choice. Even if it's not so, you believe it."

He would not accept a denial from her. "You can but agree, Mrs. Lark. Not when it's all that I will ever ask of you."

"You'll believe I corrupted you, and I think that would be true."

"I've made my peace with that."

"You would compromise your honor for me."

"Since I have already done so, what difference does it make what your answer is?"

"All the difference in the world." Her eyes, her fine and beautiful eyes, filled with determination. "I will not allow you to believe I had no choice but to become your lover. I fear I must make a liar of myself."

"Don't."

"No, Your Grace. I cannot. I will not."

Chapter Twelve

"I EXPECTED YOU'D still be toasting the winner," Daniels said when Stoke returned to his room later that afternoon. The servant had already set out the light meal his chef had sent him tonight, bouillabaisse, bread, a half bottle of Malbec.

"I left congratulations and consolations to those better suited to give them. From what I saw, all the contestants, winner and losers, were well cheered." He slipped out of his coat and handed it to Daniels. He had several hours of work before him while the others prepared for and attended the ball at Sedgemere's.

"Shall I fetch a fresh suit, Your Grace?"

"No. I'll have a bath after I've dined, though."

With Stoke's coat folded over one arm, Daniels headed for the wardrobe. "Your banyan, then?"

"Yes." He sat at the table and addressed himself to the bouillabaisse.

"I'll have the kitchen send up a cold meal later in the evening. Around nine or ten, if you'd like."

"Please." He tore a slice of bread in half and dipped it in his stew. When he'd done eating and was clean and attired in a gold-and-blue striped banyan, he moved to his desk. He brought up the light and concentrated on the contracts his lawyers had sent him for review.

At half past nine, a footman brought a repast of cold meat, fruit, bread, cheese, and a very good bottle of Massoutet. A thoughtful choice. He put away his official papers and fetched himself a glass of the wine. He seated himself on the armchair before the fire with the stack of the personal correspondence that had come in the afternoon post. He had a letter from an acquaintance in Portugal that he set aside to read after he'd looked through the rest. Hugh Hunter had written. He was an excellent and shrewd correspondent, skilled in relaying a great deal of information about his work in France without betraying confidences.

He opened his portable secretary and began a reply to Hunter in which he described the festivities at Teversault in great detail, including George's game of lawn-mall, the treasure hunt, and William's use of a bloodhound. He assured Hunter that his sisters were being well looked after and that both were much admired for their accomplishments. No mention of seduction, attempted or badly failed.

Hunter would go far on his own, but it never hurt a man's career to have a duke behind him. There was much he could do for Hunter and, as well, for the future husbands of George and her sister. Places in the House. Positions with the government. He did not expect George would marry a man who wasn't capable. Whoever he was, he would make a success of his life.

He checked the clock on the mantel and saw the hour had somehow advanced to past midnight. He set aside his letters and got up to refill his Massoutet. The bottle was poised over his glass when there came a tap on his door. His brother most likely, returned from Sedgemere's drunk from the celebrations and looking for a new audience for his stories. He was in no mood, and when he opened the door, he blocked the way to keep William from blundering his way in.

His world both upended and fell into place.

Not William.

George.

She wore an olive green nightdress and felt slippers. The candle she held guttered. He caught her free hand and held it while he drew her inside and closed and locked the door. "Why?" he said in a low voice. "Why, when you gave me such a definitive no?"

"Oh, come now." Her mouth curved ever so slightly. "I refused your improper request and sent my honor to perdition." Her broadening smile made his heart fold over. "Since then, however, I have decided I want you as my lover. I'm sure you'll agree it is a different matter for me to make you an improper proposal."

He set her candle on the table beside the door. Without releasing her hand, he snuffed the flame. "What excuse did you give?"

She laughed softly. "No excuse at all. Lord Ingleforth spilled an entire glass of port down the front of my gown."

"Clumsy oaf."

"One of us, yes."

"Remind me to send him a case of my cellar's best."

Her hair was braided and pinned at the back of her head. He pulled pins from that silky mass of orange. There weren't enough to securely hold the braid. He'd collected no more than a dozen before the coil came loose. He found a few more pins, then unfastened the ribbon at the end and undid the plait. When he was done, he smoothed the strands.

She touched her loosened hair, obviously not at ease, for she could not bring herself to look at him. "It feels wicked," she said. "To be like this."

Her captured a handful of her hair. "Orange?"

"You're teasing me again." She tapped his chest, and he caught her hand.

He smiled. "What brought you here? It couldn't have been my charm."

That elicited a soft, uncertain smile. She caressed his face. "You underestimate yourself."

He was afraid to wait, afraid she'd change her mind, afraid he'd say something to offend her. Most of all, he wanted possession of her, he wanted her to embrace their coupling as she did everything else. He wanted, needed, her to embrace him as she did life. "I want you on your back now."

"On the floor?"

"Yes." He threaded his fingers through her hair and brought it over her shoulder. His heart had grown too big for his chest. "Lovely, lovely George."

She smiled and all for him, for there was no one but him to see. "I didn't think you could say it."

"I saved that name for this moment. I've a few others yet to be consummated." Her eyes stayed on his face, curious. Cautious too. She was here. She'd come, and now he would have her. All her passion for life would be his for at least this night. "Come here by the fire." He tugged on her hand and dropped her hairpins into the pocket of his banyan.

When they stood before the mantel where his half-finished wine sat abandoned, he moved behind her. He settled a hand on her shoulder to let her know he wished her to stay as she was. He rested his other hand on her shoulder too and bent to inhale the scent of her. Her hair fell to her waist, thick with waves from her braid. "Something to eat or drink?"

She shook her head. "I couldn't, I don't think."

"Later, then." He didn't think he'd ever engaged in sexual relations with such a triumphant joy. He swept his first and second fingers along the side of her throat, then under her hair to her nape. His. She would be his tonight. Already, he anticipated the moment when he would thrust into her. Jesus. Yes. Anticipation would drown his ability to see to her pleasure.

"All right." She spoke softly.

"If you change your mind, you've only to tell me." Now. He must make love to her now, before something happened.

"I shan't change my mind."

"I am relieved." He trailed a finger along the top of her shoulder. "What made you reconsider?"

She turned her head toward him, serious. He moved so close there were but inches between his front and her back. "You. The way you kissed me. The way you made me feel as if no other man..." She closed her mouth and bit her lower lip.

Stoke tightened his hands on her shoulders. "No other man?"

"Is you. Anything like you, I mean."

That wasn't what she'd meant at all, but he let it stand. "Yet, here you are."

She faced him, and her grin stopped his breath. "Yet?" she said, eyebrows arched. "I ask you, what is this, *yet*? Do you think yourself a villain? I assure you, my reconsideration was purely selfish on my part. My study of your nuances is incomplete."

"I comprehend." He laughed, delighted, soaring inside. "I am both the object and the beneficiary of your intellectual curiosity."

"Yes, you understand precisely." She set a hand on his stomach, and he watched her smile fade. "No one but you makes my heart take wing."

"You don't know that."

"I do. There are other gentlemen in the world whom I have met. Several in Hopewell-on-Lyft. Your brother. Lord Revers. Lord William's friends. Lord Ingelforth. Even if they were the only men I'd met, you aren't the judge of the matter, I am. And I say it's so."

"How long has it been, that you've compared such effects? A week? A month?"

"A year at least."

"No." He threw back his head, but managed not to laugh. "No. That is not possible. I have been too cold to you for that to be true."

"Since I came out of mourning. You came to Uplyft Hall that spring, early because there was still frost, and we sat down to tea with you and Lord William. You complimented our Colwick cheese."

"You wore green. Silk with bows and lace."

"Did I? I don't recall. You've described most dresses we ladies wear. I remember I looked at you, and you were so quiet. So somber and noble and terrifying, and I thought–I thought there isn't any man more compelling than you."

He pulled her into his arms. "George."

"I miss this." She stroked him from shoulder to mid-belly. "I want to know what it's like with you. If that makes me a sinner, and I suppose it does, then I will have to face God and explain to him that I was weak."

He bent his head and kissed the side of her throat bared when he'd moved her hair over the other shoulder. She smelled of violets, and her skin, God, her skin was so soft. His fingers went to the fastening of her night-robe, the first, the second, the rest too quickly, except he wanted her out of this robe, even while he admired the contrast of her hair against the olive fabric. She took several quick breaths, then a longer, calming one, until he moved forward, his hands underneath the robe to push it off her shoulders.

The fabric fell to the floor, for she'd lowered her arms. In the firelight, he saw the shape of her, and he whispered her name, "George," while his wandering fingers slid over curves and, lightly, lightly for now, over her breasts. Yes, Lord in heaven, yes, lush, delicious curves. Just the tips of his fingers over her nipples, through the lawn of her chemise.

He was in danger of going too fast when what he wanted was to exploit every second of his revelation of her body. He reached for his wine and, one hand still cupping her and, caressing her breast, drank half of what remained.

He offered her the glass. "A premier vintage." She shook her head, and he took back the goblet. "No?" He drained the rest. "There's more here, so later."

She bit her lower lip, holding back a groan, he was sure, because she took a breath, and yes, God, yes, her breast filled his palm. He gathered a handful of her chemise and drew it up, and up, one-handed and then with both when her thighs were exposed, and then until she had no choice but to lift her arms. There was a moment when her hair swung away, then settled over her shoulders. He had his first unguarded view of her naked body.

Stoke stood with her chemise clutched in his hand, his breath gone, thoughts flown, no longer in command of his soul. More bosom than he'd expected, voluptuous, round, a slender waist, strong legs, delicate ankles and wrists. Her skin was pale, too pale. She looked fragile, as if she'd never survive even a second in the sun. Pale freckles were scattered on her skin, nearly invisible, some of them.

He brushed the back of his hand across her upper chest, then swept downward. His mind split in two. Half of him reveled in the knowledge that her body was his to enjoy, that there was no reason in heaven for this perfection except for his pleasure. The other half was a joy so acute his heart was pierced. She'd agreed to this, and it was his duty to give her the pleasure she wanted, to bring her to shuddering climax because anything else would be a betrayal of them both.

He turned his hand and slid the backs of his fingers along her torso. All his brain registered was that she was naked, and he was aroused beyond his ability to survive it. Her nipples were pale, pale brown, as light a brown as her freckles. He swept his hand down, around the side of her, then cupped her. The weight on his palm was more than he could bear.

She arched toward him, a moan coming up from the back of her throat. "More," she whispered. "It's wonderful, the way you make me feel. Touch me more."

In one motion, he pulled her into his arms, swiftly, not half swiftly enough, and carried her to his bedchamber. He joined her on the mattress, his banyan a hindrance to be disposed of as quickly as possible. Hands propped on either side of her, he kissed the top of her shoulder, along her collarbone, the curve of her jaw. Downward to her breasts, as plump as he'd conjured in his crudest imaginings of her. He rested his hips against hers. They were skin to skin. "George. George. I want you now, this minute."

She wrapped her arms around his neck and sighed the words, "Sooner, please."

He didn't yet, though. Instead, he pressed his hand to her mons, slid his fingers down and along her sex and found her wet. Ready for him. He trailed kisses down to her breasts. He licked her nipple once, again, then nipped. He'd been too long between women, too long without seeing his mistress. Too long shutting away the depth of his attraction to her. Those empty months of knowing he'd lost her to Edward Lark and then grappling with the contradictions of his grief for her loss of him.

He closed his mouth over her, and her nipple tightened under his tongue. He drew harder. All the while his hands smoothed her silky skin, and she shifted beneath him, a moan on her breath, arching toward him. A kiss to one, then the other, so soft and round. She sucked in breath when he bit not too gently, enough for them both to react. He moved between her legs and positioned himself to push into her.

"I cannot wait. Impossible to wait," he said.

She opened her eyes and pressed her hands to his torso. Her eyes weren't focused, and her mouth, that decadent, gorgeous mouth smiled at him, so sweet, so wicked. "Your Grace. Don't. Don't wait. I'll go mad."

"Darling George, if it pleases you, call me Stoke." He remained poised above her, watching her face, enjoying her touch, her obvious, undeniable lust for him. He shifted, nudged her thigh, and she responded. He pushed forward into warmth and heat and softness. Home. Yes. Her. Only her. Stunned, he could not think. There was only his cock and her passage.

Her hands tightened on his upper shoulders. "My God, my God."

"Yes?"

"Yes, you beastly, man." Her eyes opened. "Don't deny me now. I'll hate you forever if you do."

"Perish the thought." Stoke reached to stroke her thigh and tug upward on the back of her knee, and when she complied with that unspoken request, he sank deeper into her.

She groaned and pushed her head into the mattress. "Oh, oh, Stoke, yes. This feels so wonderful. You, I mean. I mean you feel wonderful."

He withdrew and moved back, and the pressure on his cock—he wasn't going to last long. Couldn't, and then she met his thrusts, and in a very short while, they'd arrived at a rhythm. He watched her, bemused, besotted, while she worked out what felt good for her, and he came closer and closer to losing his mind.

He slowed their pace, and she matched him. When he circled his hips and angled himself inside her, she bit her lower lip, and her eyes fluttered closed. He leaned down and kissed her, utterly lost, given over to sensation.

His climax approached and for several seconds, he considered finishing. He pulled out and waited, arms holding his weight. Her eyes shot open, questioning. "I don't want to come yet. Forgive me?" He kissed the center of her chest, then down her midline to her stomach, lower to her belly. He adjusted his body and hers, and then, with a grin that felt smug and with words that were, said, "Allow me to make amends."

"How, you fiend?"

"Like so." He proceeded to kiss her sex. She wasn't the least hesitant or ashamed. She pushed toward his mouth and at one point, she pressed on his head. She cried out when he brought her close to climax, and then again as she fell. Nothing held back. She made him feel as if there were no better lover in existence but him.

"My God," she whispered. "My God, what have you done to me?"

He slid back up her body, and she gave him a joyous smile that brought an answering smile from deep within him. He adjusted so that he entered her quickly and smoothly. "My dear. George. I hope I've given you the pleasure you so desperately needed."

"You have." Her breath came in gasps. "I commend you for your diligence." She threw her arms around his shoulders. "You're wonderful. This is wonderful. I adore you like this."

"Like what?"

"Naked." She grinned at him. "Hard."

He never laughed at a time like this. It wasn't seemly, he'd always thought. He'd never had a partner who met him without reserve. George did. She laughed, and if she did, it was because he'd amused her. He laughed too.

She bent both knees and brought his head to hers. She kissed him, took control of that, and he sank into her literally and figuratively. Before long, he was oblivious to anything but the two of them, their bodies and the spark of approaching orgasm.

"Stoke." The way she moaned sent him speeding toward the edge. "Stoke—"

She didn't mind that he thrust hard, for she held him closer, closer yet. Her body was unconscionably soft, and Lord Almighty, she clenched around him, and cried out, a wordless moan, and then a sob. He broke over her, her name on his lips, then incoherent as his climax took him. More than anything, he wanted to come inside her, to finish in her, but he couldn't. He was only just in time.

Chapter Thirteen

⸻

IMAGINATION AND REALITY merged and became a single version of Stoke Teversault and both were now firmly hooked into her being. She would never, ever, forget this encounter, nor regret it, even when she faced the gates of heaven. Heartbreak was the only possible outcome of this, but she did not care.

Stoke would walk away from her, having given her a glimpse of the man behind the hard exterior, and leave her bereft. She'd rather have this now and the pain of his future leaving than never know him like this.

She left her arms draped around Stoke's shoulders. Her palms were on his bare skin, one of his wiry-muscled legs lay half over hers, his right hand covered her breast, his head beside hers on the pillow. She listened to him breathe and missed, with fond sadness, those times when she'd lain awake at night listening to her husband breathe.

With him asleep or very near it, and she hoped, as replete as she felt, she slid from underneath him.

"Stay." His voice was warm and muffled. Sleepy.

George sat on the edge of the bed. She was happy. And afraid. And desolate. "I won't leave yet, if that's what you mean."

He looped an arm around her middle, shifting so that he was on his side and his stomach touched her lower back. She closed her eyes and pushed away the future. She'd allowed Stoke Teversault into her heart, and there he would stay. Let her savor the perfection of this moment. She turned to him, and his hand ended up on her knee. His index finger brushed over her calf.

She touched the bridge of his strong nose, then trailed her fingertip down to his mouth. Lightly, barely touching him. Along his chin, to his shoulder. To the muscles of his chest. His belly. He was magnificent to look at. Here, his quiescent sex.

How would such a reserved man behave now that they had obliterated the distance between them? She'd come here knowing he might shut her out after the act was done. Perhaps he would not want continued intimacy. Though, hadn't he said a week? That they had a week together? "May I touch you?"

Slowly, his eyes opened. Dark-lashed and dark, dark brown. Full of secrets and alive with intelligence. The coldness was gone, melted away in the heat of their joining. She would leave here brokenhearted and without a shred of regret. He curled his fingers around her lower leg.

"I didn't touch you much before," she said. The beauty of him hurt her eyes, her soul, the body he had mastered. Six days. At once an eternity and nowhere near long enough. There wasn't time for them. It wasn't enough. Beneath her fingers, his penis stirred, and she was delighted by that.

The sight of his lazy smile turned the pit of her stomach shivery. "Indulge your every whim."

"All of them?"

"Particularly if they involve your hands and mouth and my person."

She covered his sex, fingers curved over his sac. "Will you show me what you like when I touch you here?" He put his hand over hers and circled her fingers around his member, stirring to enthusiastic life just now. After a few minutes, he released her hand, and she continued the motion. "Like so?"

"Mm."

He was hard now, hard enough for him to put himself inside her, if their bodies had been arranged differently. She bent over him and whispered, "Does that feel wicked, Your Grace?"

His eyes flicked open, fixing on her face. "You cannot doubt it, George."

"I think I do." He was long, and thick, and she did so like to touch him. She looked at his sex and her hand and felt the tension in his body. "I want to worship your cock. May I?"

He lifted his hips when she tightened her grip on him. "Please."

George adjusted herself until she could use her mouth on him. Desire washed over her, flooded her. The taste, the texture, the scent of him was an aphrodisiac. She concentrated on him in her mouth. She swept her fingers down along his bollocks, then followed that with a glide of her tongue.

His put his hands to either side of her head. Pleasuring him like this aroused her even more. She wanted him at heights that wrung him out, to have him shudder with the beauty of completion. He groaned, and sat up, bringing her with him. Their eyes connected, and she went shivery again. He wasn't locking her out. Not yet. Not this time. "I want to finish in you."

"My dear, ferocious, duke, my explorations are not complete."

His eyes brightened, and that made her heart lift. "I deny you nothing."

She ran a hand down his muscled thigh, then back up to his hip. From the pressure of her palm, he understood she wanted him to turn onto his stomach. She brushed her fingers along his back, from his shoulders to the dip at the bottom of his spine. "Here I thought all the magnificent animals were in your stables."

"A common mistake."

She kissed his back, working her way downward. "I've a confession for you."

"Pray continue."

"That day at breakfast, when it was just we two." She followed the curve of his backside. "I hadn't realized until then, when you were in your buckskins, what a virile specimen you are." She whispered to him, smoothing his cheeks. "I adore the *gluteus maximus*. Yours in particular. Your thighs, have you any idea the state you put me in?"

He shifted onto his side. "If I had known, I would have sent the footman away and had your skirts up as far as they might go. I wish I had done. We'd have had more time." With a hand around her waist, he turned to his back, and she stroked his torso, pressed a finger to his nipple. He said her name, more sharp breath than voice. "You've no idea what I've done to you in my dreams."

"I am agog. You've dreamed things. About me?" She grinned and offered him the access to her sex that he wanted. "What's the wickedest of them?"

"I had you on your hands and knees."

"On the floor or on the bed?"

"A bed."

"That's not so very wicked. Your bed or mine?"

"The Archbishop of Canterbury's."

"That *is* wicked."

"Another time, I interrupted you in your bath, dismissed your maid, and fucked you up against a wall." He slid two fingers inside her. "You were wet, and slick, and you begged me, 'Harder, Stoke, harder.'"

"Did you oblige me?"

"I did."

He urged her forward, the two of them moving with only a moment's awkwardness when she did not immediately understand what he was after. Then she did. He leaned against the headboard of his massive bed, one hand extended to clutch the top, the other at her waist. He could see her naked body like this. See her breasts. All her faults. She levered herself up, and he set himself to her entrance and rocked his hips upward at the same time he pulled her downward, and, oh yes, she understood now. He thrust up again, eyes on their joined bodies.

"Do you mind my freckles?"

With a finger, he drew a line from one to the next. "I adore them. I intend to kiss every one of them."

He went deeper into her, and she gasped. Pleasure melted her. In this arrangement, she could see his face, his concentration on her, the flex of his muscles when he pushed into her. He pressed his palms to her stomach, then around her waist and controlled the motion for them both.

She had another of those moments of disbelief. The far too proper Stoke Teversault had his naked cock in her, and that was not possible. Couldn't be at all, and—God, he felt so good inside her. She felt good with him moving in her like this. The angle was more forceful, he went deeper, but she could control that.

"Harder?" Not quite a question of her, was it? More a plea.

"Stoke." She fell forward, bracing her hands on the headboard where his hand had been earlier.

His fingers tightened around her, and he tilted his head to catch her breast in his mouth, but he quickly drew away. "That's not yes."

"Yes. Yes." She couldn't catch a decent breath. "As hard as you like."

They ended with her on her back again and him over her, and her breath caught in her throat, because she was going to shatter again. She would have thought she could never endure something like this, but the harder he thrust into her, the closer she came to annihilation, and when she opened her eyes and saw him there was disbelief that she was here, that Stoke Teversault was naked, moving in her. She wanted to cry at the same time that joy overcame her.

She pressed a hand to his cheek, because she could not say the words building in her. He turned his face toward her hand and nipped at her hand. She met him at every turn, matched him until they were both mindless.

Six days. She had but six days before he broke her heart.

Chapter Fourteen

THE COMMOTION OF the arrival of the Prince Regent was beyond understanding. His retinue descended upon the house and turned the world to chaos. According to Stoke, his chef had been planning the menu for the royal visit since the day the prince agreed to visit. Dinner was an astonishing affair of one sublime dish after another, a different wine with every course. Long before the last course George was at the limit of her capacity to take another bite.

Stoke had hired an orchestra from Nottingham, twelve players in all. The work on chalking the floors had begun the day before. From midafternoon onward, guests had begun arriving. They continued to arrive at a steady pace even now, and before long footmen were obliged to open windows and balcony doors. There were so many people that she wondered if Teversault were big enough for the crush.

The prince made much of Kitty's beauty, and then Lord William escorted her to the ballroom floor. Revers danced the next set with her, and Kitty was a triumph, her beautiful young sister.

She and Stoke danced once. A waltz, but she was awkward from the strain of not betraying the intimacy of their relationship. Stoke did not help when he leaned in and murmured that he'd much rather be upstairs with her than here. What a fool she was, for the edges of her heart whispered that he was willing to have her in his bed, but not in his ballroom, and she knew he did not think any such thing.

Stoke danced with Kitty too, and then Miss Paltree, and a young lady whose name she could not recall who constantly tossed her curls as if no man could resist her. More than once she saw the duke smiling while he led another young lady through a dance. When she and Kitty left tomorrow, her heart would stay here.

The next waltz started, and George slipped away from the ballroom in order to shake off her melancholy. Heartbreak was hours away. That would not come until she and Kitty were in the carriage on their way back to Uplyft Hall. She took refuge in an upstairs parlor far enough away that she could scarcely hear the music. One more night. Just one, and with the party showing no signs of ending, it was possible she and Stoke would not have time to say a proper, private, good-bye.

They would just—end. She would have this week to remember for the rest of her days. She'd been to his room every night and was in his arms whenever they found a moment alone. He was always the lover she needed, tender, vigorous, masterful.

At the parlor window, she stared at the darkness, feeling the break already, the rending of her heart. She didn't want to forget anything that had happened here at Teversault. Not one moment of it. She closed her eyes and summoned an image of Stoke, so handsome in his evening clothes, committing him to memory.

She dug her handkerchief out of her pocket and pressed it to her eyes. No tears, no crying, because she'd had more love and passion than anyone deserved. She stifled them because she'd not be able to go downstairs for half an hour or longer if she succumbed. There was no possible way she could face Stoke, or anyone else, if her eyes were red from crying.

She faced the window, hands gripping the sill, head down, overcome despite her best efforts. What a fool she was to have lost her heart so thoroughly. She reassessed her state and decided she could safely return downstairs, but the parlor door opened before she could move. Her pulse leaped, and she embraced the reaction. She would not miss an instant of these last hours together because she'd let her sorrow push her into tomorrow. They would have their private good-bye here, and she would gather all of him into her. "Is that you, Stoke?"

"Yes."

"I'm glad you're here."

He closed the door and crossed the room. "I've been looking for you."

"Here I am." She patted her head, searching for loose pins, then stopped, struck by the fact that Stoke looked far too serious for a man alone with his lover. "What's happened?"

He joined her at the window. "I have news that will distress you." He lifted a hand. "Not about your brother."

"What, then?" She licked her lower lip puzzled. "You look so very serious, my heart is pounding."

He scrubbed his fingers through his hair. "There's been a scandal. Downstairs. You'll be needed, of course, but first—"

"Good heavens. What?"

He stood close to her and she rested her cheek on his shoulder. "Allow me to explain." He gave her an assessing look. "Before you go downstairs. You're a capable woman, you'll know what to say to her, but best you know the facts."

"Very well." She clutched his sleeve, afraid despite his assurances.

"William was discovered in a compromising situation." He let out a breath. "Revers found them. If it had been anyone else, it might have been possible to keep things quiet until we understand how they feel and learn whether a hasty marriage is necessary. The prince, alas, was with Revers."

Poor Lord William, to have come to such grief and in so public a manner. "Revers and the Prince Regent?" How unlike him, though, to behave so badly when there was so great a chance he'd be caught out.

"Revers, the prince, and ten of Prinny's toadies."

"Oh, dear me." Poor Stoke, to be given this to manage.

"As it is, they came to blows, William and Revers, and that attracted a larger crowd yet." He leaned against the wall, hands in his coat pocket. "Unfortunate words were spoken, I fear, that made matters worse."

George cast about for the most likely woman to have been with Lord William. Revers's sister, Lady Alice, a lovely young woman who had arrived earlier in the afternoon. She ached for Kitty. She would be devastated by this news. Though, from what Stoke had so far told her, Kitty must already have heard. A worse thought occurred to her. "Lord Revers hasn't challenged William, has he?"

"No. Thank God." He took her hand. "I managed to separate them before those words were spoken, though if he does, I would counsel William to apologize and make all possible amends to the injured parties."

"Of course." With her free hand, she straightened his neckcloth.

"To William's credit, when I got him alone he offered no excuses for his behavior."

"He wouldn't. He owns up when he's in the wrong. You know that, Stoke."

"Yes." He lifted her hand and kissed the backs of her knuckles. "Your sister is distraught. I had your maid fetched. She is with Kitty now. In the Grecian parlor. You needn't fly to her straight away. As for my brother—" He drew a breath. "As for William, he was protective of her. As I said, I've spoken with him privately, and he assures me he stands ready and willing to marry her. Indeed, he was adamant about his intention to do so regardless of my feelings in the matter. Or Revers's objections."

"Poor Lady Alice." She put a hand on Stoke's arm. "Is someone with her?"

"Lady Alice?"

"Someone besides Lord Revers, I mean. She'll need a woman's advice until her mother arrives. You were right to come fetch me. This is too awful."

"Your concern for Lady Alice is commendable, but—" He put his hands on her shoulders and stared at her. "George, did I not make it clear? It's Kitty."

She pressed her palm to his cheek. "Of course she's devastated, but it's Lady Alice who must not be left without anyone to see to her."

"Darling." He drew her close. "It's your sister, Kitty. William compromised your sister."

She could not make proper sense of this. Could he mean some other Kitty? "My sister, Kitty Hunter?"

"Yes."

"And Lord William? Are you quite sure?"

"Yes."

"Oh." She clutched his arm. "Oh my. When you say compromised...?"

"Yes. All that."

"My God." Disaster. This was nothing short of disaster.

"You understand now."

"Lord William and Lord Revers came to blows over Kitty? And the prince saw all this?" She sank onto the window sill. Social and political ruin was made of disasters like this. Not just for the woman but for Stoke, whose brother was involved in so public a scandal. "Oh, Stoke."

"William will marry her." The finality of his words caught her up short. "There will be no discussion of the matter. I will not have either of them the subject of gossip. The prince saw them." He closed the distance she'd put between them. "I'll write your brother. That is my duty. But trust I will see those two wed before my letter reaches Paris."

"There's nothing else to be done." There could be no recovery from this. For the rest of her life she would have a connection with Stoke, and there would be no end to her heartache.

"Go to your sister, then. Tell her what's been decided."

"Yes. Yes, I must."

She found Kitty dry-eyed on one of the three sofas in the Grecian parlor, as Stoke had said. Molly curtseyed and, after a confirming nod from George, made herself scarce. "Kitty. My dearest. Are you all right?"

"I don't think I know." Her eyes were wide, pupils huge. She crushed a handkerchief in both hands.

"Stoke says you must be married." She sat beside Kitty, uncertain what she ought to say beyond her immediate future. "He will let us know what he intends to happen when, but it will be soon. A few days, I expect."

"The duke says I shall be married, but what does Lord William say?" The defiance in Kitty's voice gave her pause.

"I've not spoken to him yet." She replied firmly. "I do not see that you can refuse without scandal that will attach to you and Lord William both. This is no youthful indiscretion. What you the two of you did has consequences. Dreadful ones."

"I don't care—"

She lifted a hand. "Not just for you and Lord William, but for Stoke Teversault as well. For Hugh as well. Think what will happen to Hugh if you do not marry. Will you be the cause of our brother's ruin too?"

Kitty's defiance eroded. Her mouth trembled. "Are you terribly angry?"

George put an arm around her shoulder. "Not just now, but I think I shall be presently."

She burst into tears, and George held her until she was reduced to sobs. "I didn't mean it to happen. I didn't. But, but..." Kitty slid off the sofa onto the floor where she folded her arms on George's lap and rested her head on her hands. "I'm sorry. So sorry. I love him, I do, I cannot stop myself from loving him."

"I know. Oh, Kitty, I know. You've been in love with him for ages."

"He's never given a pin for me. I never thought he loved me at all. Not until we came here. We shouldn't have come." She sank into the drama, and George wanted to fall with her into that rolling ocean of emotion. "We should never have let Lord

William persuade us to come here. I hate the duke. I can't abide the way he treats you, and I don't care to be related to him at all. I wish he weren't Lord William's brother."

She smoothed Kitty's hair. "My poor darling."

Kitty dropped her head onto her arms then lifted a tear-stained face. "Let us go home, Georgina. Now. Tonight. I've told Molly to pack our things. We can take a wagon into Bunney. From there, we can post to Hopewell-on-Lyft. We'd be home before morning."

"We cannot leave without speaking to the duke."

"I give this for the duke." Kitty snapped her fingers. "He's arrogant and prideful, and I don't know why you'd care for his good opinion. He's never kind to you. I tell you, I do not like him. No one does, you know. I don't care for the way he looks at you, and I don't like that whenever you encounter him, you come away sad and unhappy. Let's go home, Georgina. You'll be happy again when we are home. We'll be happy there. Just us."

"Ahem."

Kitty sat up straight and squeezed George's hand while George looked over her shoulder toward the door. Her heart sank.

There stood Lord William and just behind him the duke, and it was plainly, awkwardly, horribly obvious that they had both heard Kitty's impassioned declaration.

Chapter Fifteen

"Forgive the interruption." Stoke remained near the door. His future sister-in-law's expression was mulish. She knew they'd overheard her, and she plainly stood by those painful words. George kept a protective arm around her sister's shoulder. He bowed to her. "Mrs. Lark, perhaps you will accompany me. My brother wishes to settle matters with your sister."

The sisters exchanged a look.

"I thought matters were already settled," Miss Hunter said.

"You may trust that they are." He'd not set aside his anger at William for this debacle, and that put an edge on his voice. For the better, he decided, if Miss Hunter were more circumspect as a result. "However, William has convinced me of his need to speak with you at once." He did not spare the girl much of anything. To her credit, though she blanched, she did not dissolve into more tears. "There will be no mutiny from you, Miss Hunter."

He extended his arm to George, in no mood to tolerate insurrection from anyone. She hugged her sister before she went to him.

William bowed as she neared him. "I'm sorry, George. You must believe that."

She paused, looked at the floor and then, at last, at William. "I haven't much to say to you just now."

"I swear on my honor, I did not know I was in love with her. Not until tonight. Not until Revers was nothing but smiles and compliments and devious plots to win her affections."

Stoke took George's hand. "You and Mrs. Lark may settle your differences another time. For now, my advice is that you attempt to repair matters with my future sister." Miss Hunter let out a sob edged with terror. George would have returned to her had he not drawn her to him. "As you can see, William, you may have to convince her that a relation to me is not a fate worse than death. Come, George."

William's attention shot to him, though he could not fathom why until William looked at George and then at their clasped hands. He realized his mistake, then. He'd called her George, not Mrs. Lark. George realized it as well, and she sidled away. Or would have if he'd permitted it.

"You two may quarrel or not just as you like," he said as if he'd not blundered. He looked in turn at William and Miss Hunter. "Nothing you say to each other changes the future. I assure you of that."

When he and George exited the parlor, he left the door ajar. Let William think what he would. His worst imaginings would be correct. They did not speak until he'd led her to the nearest room where they might be private. His official office, it happened. This door he closed and locked. A servant had been in to draw the drapes, so he lit an additional lamp before he leaned against the edge of his desk, arms crossed over his chest. George had stopped in the center of the room.

"Is it true?" he asked.

"Is what true?"

"What your sister said about me."

"I don't recall what she said."

"She said I make you unhappy." He was afraid Kitty saw what neither of them wanted to admit, that he was no suitable husband for any woman, but especially not for George. With more effort than he liked, he erased all physicals signs of emotion from his face.

George gripped handfuls of her skirts, and her continued silence extinguished any possibility of a denial from her.

"Stoke," she whispered, miserably. "Of course you do."

Tears would destroy him, but there were none. His heart withered at this sign of her resolve. "I wish that were not so."

She shrugged.

"Forgive me."

"You are the Duke of Stoke Teversault. You've no need of forgiveness from anyone, least of all me."

"That is your opinion. Not mine." He lifted a hand, then returned to his cross-armed posture. "You need not leave Teversault."

"Under the circumstances, we cannot stay." She faced away from him, and he watched her determined walk to the door. She unlocked the door, but stayed with her back to him, one hand on the wall at her shoulder level. Slowly, she bent her neck until her forehead rested against the door.

"Stay, George." He could not imagine her absence. A future without her was nothing but dismal solitude.

Her hand on the wall fisted. "I cannot stay."

"I don't see why not." He willed her to stay. For him. Because she could not bear to leave him. Because he was selfish. "Tomorrow I leave to deal with the special license."

She turned and leaned against the door. "I've a confession to make. When you've heard me out, you'll see why there's no possible way Kitty and I can stay." He pushed off the desk, but she put up a hand. "Don't, Stoke. Don't make this harder for me than it is already."

For now, for these moments, she was here with him and he would do as she did and live with the beauty of now, no matter how bleak the future might be. He leaned against the front of the desk again, but this time turned his hands to grip the edge. "Go on, then."

"I'm sorry. So sorry. About Lord William and Kitty, for I know you don't approve of her. This is my fault."

"What sort of confession is that? I know you are sorry. It's plain enough. I'm sorry as well for my blockhead of a brother."

"I shouldn't have left the ballroom. If I'd been downstairs, I could have prevented this."

He scoffed. "There's no guarantee you would have seen either of them leave. Two young people intent on an assignation? You've no cause to think that is anyone's fault but William's. His behavior was thoroughly improper, and with Kitty, of all women."

"Precisely."

He gave her another hard look. "A young lady, George, who is under my protection while you two are in my house. It's my brother who compromised her. That's no confession at all." He waved one hand. If he did not manage this properly, she would leave him. He did not know how he would manage if she did, except that he must. "I ought to have been keeping a better watch on William. I suspected he'd developed feelings for Kitty, what with Revers giving him competition."

"We'll share the blame, then."

He gave a curt nod. "Enough of this. I can guess what devastation you mean to deliver me, so there's no more to be said on the subject of confessions. Now, as to the matter at hand. It would be convenient for me and for William if no one had to make the journey to Uplyft Hall and back to fetch you and Kitty here for the wedding. You must be present for that. You must."

She rested a hand on her upper chest and stared at the ceiling.

"Do *not* cry. I won't permit it."

"Stoke." She whispered his name, and that sound would haunt him for the rest of his life, for she'd said his name just so when he'd held her in his arms. "My heart is broken. I cannot bear this. Not now. Not when the hurt is so fresh."

He went still. Her heart was broken? Her heart? "I don't expect that your sister's marriage to William will be so great a trial." He gentled his tone, for she would not wish to see her sister unhappily married. "His affection for her appears sincere."

"Stoke." Her sharp breath was a reproach. "No more of this. No more. Let me have my say so you understand why I cannot stay, despite the inconvenience to us all. I'll not speak of it again, I promise you."

"If you must." He must reacquaint himself with the coldness she'd melted away.

She swallowed once, then again and stared at his feet. "I love you, Stoke. I'm sorry. I'm so very sorry. I promised myself, told myself it would not happen, but it did and I did not know until it was too late to change the shape you'd made of my heart. You understand now, don't you? Everything here will remind me of you. Of us. We'll return for the wedding. I would not miss my own sister's wedding. Not for any reason."

Stoke did not know what to think or feel or say, and that was not a familiar situation for him to be in. He gathered what wits he could. "You love me, yet you plan to leave me? Why?"

"Please, please, don't say anything more."

He crossed to her and took her by the shoulders. "I refuse. Categorically and absolutely. Why should I say nothing in response to so extraordinary a declaration?"

"You needn't. You needn't say anything. I don't regret falling in love with you Not at all. If given another chance, I'd do the same, even knowing you'd break my heart." She swallowed again. "In fact, I knew you would. I knew."

The last of the ice around his heart vanished, and he saw what he had refused to accept. That she *did* love him, that she'd never have agreed to be his lover if she didn't. "You think you can throw me over with sweet words to make your leaving me easier?" He brushed his fingers over the side of her head. "I won't allow it. I won't permit you that."

She put her hands on his wrists and looked into his eyes. "You cannot stop my loving you."

"If you love me, then do not leave me." His voice slid low and urgent. "Don't leave me, George. Stay with me until I am old and gray and feeble. I'm selfish, and cruel and cold. I confess it all to you—"

"That's not so. None of that. I won't hear you say that."

"Then hear this. Stay and warm me with your smile when we are naked and when we are not. Look at me, George. At me."

She did, and she was somber and grave.

"You've brought me out of the deepest sleep, awakened me to life. I will not give you up so easily this time."

"This time?" She tipped her head to one side. "What do you mean?"

"You say you love me, but I say I loved you first. I watched you fall in love with Edward Lark and stayed silent."

She stepped back. "What?"

"I meant to propose to you at Scylfe, though I imagine I would have done it badly enough that you might have refused me."

"No. No, that can't be. You did not say two words to me."

"I did not care for the state of my feelings. Would you have told me yes?"

"What does that signify? If you wish to speculate then I will say if we'd married, we would have found our way. Not without trouble, since you know how difficult you are."

He laughed.

"Lark arrived, and within a day my case was hopeless."

"I did not know. I'd no idea."

"I sat silent at your wedding. When William told me what had happened, I flew to you and kept my peace. I have and I must put duty before most everything else. I am not a kind man. I am not pleasant to be around. No Besett hawk has ever been handsome. Why would I think you, of all women, would love me despite that?"

"Shh." She put a hand across his lips. "Don't say such things."

"I cannot image it being anything but impossible to love me. What remains is that I love you and have loved you, and I will not let you walk away from me merely because I can't believe you care for me."

Her hand on his cheek was unsteady. "I do. I do love you. Foolish man. Ridiculous man."

"Stay with me. Guard my heart, for it belongs to you." He touched her chest over her heart. "In return, I promise I will keep your heart safe, too. We of the hawk line are fierce and faithful lovers." He took her hand in his before he went down on one knee. "Marry me, George. My love. My heart. Marry me the moment I can get a license in hand. Will you?"

"Yes," she whispered.

He trembled at the answer, in disbelief and with a joy that swept away the world and left him with all he'd ever dreamed of for himself.

"Yes. Yes. A thousand times yes."

He stood and drew her to him, and she was in his arms when William threw open the door and strode in. "Stoke, have you any idea where George has gone, her sister wants her and I can't—the devil! Unhand her!"

"Close the door, and take care to put yourself on the other side of it."

"By God, I will not."

"You had best not try my patience any longer." He tightened his arms around her.

"You. You, Stoke! I go looking for George, and I find you in the act of seducing her."

"Seducing her?"

William gestured at the two of them. "What else do you call that?"

"I call it holding her safe in my arms." He drew her closer. "Safe in my heart, where she will forever remain."

William put his hands on his hips and stared at the two of them, eyes narrowed. He looked at George and then at him, and the same several more times. "You had better mean she's to be your duchess. If you mean anything else, I'll thrash you."

"The very best duchess a hawk of a man could want."

"George." William lifted his hands. "Are you sure you want to tie yourself to this old man?"

She leaned against Stoke's chest. "I am."

"Well." William burst into laughter. "I'm damned if I know which of us is luckier, Stoke."

"I am," he said, and he wanted to laugh and cry at the same time. She was his. His. And she was more than he deserved.

George looked into his face. "I warn you, I will make you a most unsuitable duchess."

He tightened his arms around her and kissed her forehead. "To which I reply, my darling, there is no luckier duke in existence."

From the Authors

If any readers are wondering about the origin of the Dukeries, it's a real place. A section of Nottinghamshire containing several ducal estates was nicknamed the Dukeries during the nineteenth century. If anyone doubts so many dukes would live near each other, remember that truth is stranger than fiction. We do, however, doubt that the real Dukeries were ever inhabited by such a collection of young and attractive noblemen.

The four of us previously collaborated in *Christmas in the Duke's Arms*, a quartet of stories set in the same part of England. And because we have such fun working together, we're doing it again this Christmas. Look for *Christmas in Duke Street* in October 2015.

Grace, Shana, Miranda, and Carolyn

About the Authors

ABOUT GRACE BURROWES

To my dear Readers,

I hope you enjoyed Gerard and Ellen's story, because I certainly had fun writing it! I have more Regency romance releasing shortly, including **Tremaine's True Love** (August 2015), the first in my **True Gentlemen** series. This summer also saw the launch of the **Jaded Gentlemen** trilogy with **Thomas** (June 2015), whose story is set in the Lonely Lords world. **Matthew**'s story, the sequel to **Thomas** will follow in September.

If you'd like to stay current with all my latest news and upcoming releases, you can **sign up for my newsletter here (www.graceburrowes.com/contact.php)**.

Now back to the Dukeries, for more happy reading!

Grace Burrowes

ABOUT SHANA GALEN

Shana Galen is the bestselling author of passionate Regency romps, including the RT Reviewers' Choice The Making of a Gentleman. Kirkus says of her books, "The road to happily-ever-after is intense, conflicted, suspenseful and fun," and RT Bookreviews calls her books "lighthearted yet poignant, humorous yet touching." She taught English at the middle and high school level off and on for eleven years. Most of those years were spent working in Houston's inner city. Now she writes full time. She's happily married and has a daughter who is most definitely a romance heroine in the making.

ABOUT MIRANDA NEVILLE

Miranda Neville grew up in England, loving the books of Georgette Heyer and other Regency romances. Her historical romances include the Burgundy Club series, about Regency book collectors, and The Wild Quartet. She lives in Vermont with her daughter, her cat, and a ridiculously large collection of Christmas tree ornaments. She is thrilled to collaborate with Grace, Carolyn and Shana for a second time and looks forward to their next anthology, Christmas in Duke Street coming in October 2015.

Sign up for Miranda's **newsletter** for notification of new books.

www.mirandaneville.com/contact-miranda.php

Visit Miranda on the web at:

www.mirandaneville.com | twitter (@Miranda_Neville) |
facebook.com/MirandaNevilleAuthor | pinterest.com/mirneville

ABOUT CAROLYN JEWEL

Carolyn Jewel was born on a moonless night. That darkness was seared into her soul and she became an award-winning and USA Today bestselling author of historical and paranormal romance. She has a very dusty car and a Master's degree in English that proves useful at the oddest times. An avid fan of fine chocolate, finer heroines, Bollywood films, and heroism in all forms, she has two cats and two dogs. Also a son. One of the cats is his.

Newsletter

Sign up for Carolyn's newsletter (http://cjewel.me/nlWS) so you never miss a new book and get exclusive, subscriber-only content.

Visit Carolyn on the web at:

carolynjewel.com | twitter.com/cjewel |

facebook.com/carolynjewelauthor | goodreads.com/cjewel

Printed in Great Britain
by Amazon.co.uk, Ltd.,
Marston Gate.